Drinker of Ink

A ROMANCE

SHANNON CASTLETON

For Steve—

keeper

of my best poems and love stories

CONTENTS

BUVEUR D'ENCRE

Monday, January 7, 1991
7:37 a.m., library, third floor, poetry aisles
St. Brigid's College, California

I only ever talk to this journal. I confess this to my non-existent posterity: Your mother is not cool. She shuffles around her college campus with a notebook tucked under her arm and a backpack full of Norton anthologies and cookbooks. Her spine is likely degenerating by the second.

It's the first day of winter semester, and I am waiting for my 9 a.m. class—Advanced Poetry Workshop. I've been twenty years old for one month, and already I'm a college senior. I resent my parents for insisting I do everything early, as if early is better.

I am tired.

And why am I at this library desk so early? I should drop my 9 a.m. poetry workshop. I didn't even want to enroll in this section. I wanted to take Poetry from our department chair, but her section filled up within the first five minutes of course registration. The latest word among English majors is that a graduate student from a different department—history, maybe?—is teaching the section I'm stuck in, and I cannot imagine why this would be. What qualifies a grad student in history to teach poetry?

At least Hillary is still my roommate. She's the one lucky thing my early college life got me. From the day we met in our dorm and she said, "You look like a wild little deer caught in headlights," she has pointed me away from pending mishaps, treated my figurative wounds with candy, bad jokes, and music.

She says I should hang out with her and her friends at The Garage— they host a live band three nights a week, and according to Hillary, the guys act broody and reserved but are "cutting-edge" kissers, who would go crazy if I spoke French to them. I could drop my 9 a.m. and start class after lunch. "What's your rush, Vivi?" Hillary keeps asking. "Aren't you like a post-doc wizard of universal knowledge by now?"

No is the correct answer to that question, though I still have the two majors—English and culinary arts, with an emphasis in baking and pastry. I dropped the French minor because I am actually French. So now, I'll graduate with two degrees in December.

If I joined Hillary at The Garage this semester, I wouldn't know what to wear, or how to kiss. "Cutting edge" makes me think of cancer research, which makes me think of Maman, who is trying harder than usual to avoid talk of health these days—that is, when she sees fit to answer the telephone.

But are there truly levels of kissing? If so, just stick me with a badge labeled "primitive."

Kissing aside, The Garage crowd looks so casual and effortless. I tuck in all my shirts and keep a small drawer full of belts. Also, I have so much hair. It's too big for my head, and the waves aren't luxurious, just mutinous and dark, hanging in a jagged V down my back—like I might be the lovechild of Jon Bon Jovi and a princess who was locked in a tower.

I wish I held a remote-control to my life and could fast-forward as though I were watching a video tape. The next three or four years could just squiggle by—these final months at a school three thousand miles away from my family in New York, all the impossible decisions—*What to do? Where next?* More writing for school or for work. Baking only occasionally. Plus my parents' relentless input, and the question of Maman's lifespan.

I want to skip to the day I can write actual books and bake in New York and help care for Maman when she is tired or ill or aching.

By then, a grown man might watch from a distance, maybe sitting on the steps of the Met, as I tie my hair, miraculously smooth, in a knot. He might approach me and ask, "What's your name?" in English or French or possibly in Russian. We could wander the museum and talk about paintings, artists and books, sculpture and pastry, economies and planets and after-lifes.

Later, we could lie side by side on a Central Park lawn and make up our own constellations. He'd touch his fingers to my chin before brushing them down my neck, the whole time watching my face as if even the stars weren't so luminous.

Leaning toward my lips, he'd hover a minute before kissing me like he invented it.

———————

January 7, cont.
10:08 a.m., library, third floor

Just finished Advanced Poetry Workshop.

I walked into class and thought of nothing but kissing until the moment Peter Breznik, the graduate instructor, dismissed us. I have never been kissed—hence, my "primitive" ranking; I have always gravitated toward activities and subjects that might be clearly evaluated, like baking or modern American poetry or statistics. How does one even rate a kiss? If kissing were a class, I'd take it.

Anyhow, boys are a drain on time until a woman is gainfully employed and settled and buying expensive shoes and/or bakeware. At least this is what Maman, when she is available and willing to converse, tells me.

Peter Breznik isn't a boy, though.

He isn't a too-grown man, either. He has sharp adult angles and serious blue eyes that you can tell have read volumes and seen remote places; but his hair spikes up at odd angles at the crown of his head, like a boy who has been wrestling over a soccer ball at recess. And the scruff on his cheeks doesn't seem too robust yet.

"Vivienne Lebrun?" He called my name with a perfect French accent, though he is not French. Apparently, he could tell my name is.

"Right here," I said, to which he nodded, and I swear to heaven he stopped a smile. He moved the fingers of one hand to just below his bottom lip, as if he were brushing some crumbs away. *Here,* I imagined saying, *allow me.*

"Vivienne Lebrun," he repeated quietly. He was only trying to memorize names, but there is still a thump in my chest, like wings or a hammer.

He is a PhD candidate in History, soon to complete his dissertation on something to do with Eastern Europe and World War II, but he publishes poems and holds an MFA in creative writing from UC Irvine.

As for how he became our instructor: Our tiny tribe of an English Department did not have a second professor available for all the interest in poetry this semester, and Alene Bautista, our chair, likes the idea of interdisciplinary writing instruction. After hearing Peter Breznik read at a Humanities faculty event, she offered him a section of Advanced Poetry.

Outside the history department, however, I can't tell where Peter Breznik comes from. Not from France, I am certain, though he does have the barest hint of an accent—German or Austrian. He holds long vowels in the roof of his mouth, and his lips sometimes jut out with consonants. Though occasionally, he hits the end of a phrase and sounds faintly English.

Perhaps he is Danish. Danish and sandy-colored, with the bluest-green eyes that startle and arrest you. He is tall and strong-fingered and casual, in jeans and a short-sleeve, knit collared shirt.

He explained that each week, we will write three poems, three journal entries, and one craft essay, in which we will identify one compelling element in a published poem we admire and explain its effect on a reader. He said he will write us copious notes.

I am not dropping my 9 a.m. class.

———

Tuesday, January 8, 1991
1:17 p.m., on the dust-bunnied wood floor of the Oppen Humanities Building hallway

For two-and-a-half years, I have asked myself: Why did I choose to attend a Catholic liberal-arts college in northern California when my whole life is still in Manhattan? My whole life. As in: my parents and Luc, sweet Hugo the Golden, Fern's Flowers on the corner of 76th and 2nd Ave, Michel's tiny Chocolate Box tucked away on 78th, with the lime and lemon truffles that taste like summer woke up in your mouth.

Which is not even to mention bookshops and the Met and all the people westerners insist are so ornery, but really they're not, if you order food quickly and smile *How are you?* at bus stops.

I keep feeling that if I were in New York, where my life is, nothing could change or ever go wrong, because I'd be aware of everything and everyone I love, and you can only be surprised to the same degree as your ignorance.

I am woefully unaware of day-to-day happenings here at St. Brigid's— oblivious to friendship outside my dorm, and some days I feel so alone. My worry for home looms like a thundercloud. I know Maman has detected a lump, or has even been diagnosed again. Both she and Papa swear she has not, but trust—or the lack of it—always festers between us, a fat, unextractable thorn.

I try to ignore the sting. Sandra-my-New-York-therapist said that to dwell on the origin of pain is to become trapped in a loop—to circle the trauma as if in a semi-truck, until the tire grooves grow so deep, you can't turn out to drive forward.

Wishing to avoid a loop yesterday as I walked to my dorm from the library, I tried reporting past events to myself in clinical third-person sentences, like: *When Vivienne Lebrun was 15 years old, her parents delayed telling her that her mother had cancer. Not because they manipulatively or stupidly planned for her ignorance, but because the timing of events made withholding information seem kinder and more convenient than sharing it.*

Not a paragraph had gone by in my head, however, before I remembered Papa collecting Luc and me from JFK at the end of the summer we spent with Mémère, Papi, and Tante Evelyn in Paris.

I can still feel in my chest the sharp breaths Papa kept inhaling at the wheel of his Volvo, as Luc and I regaled him with tales of Mémère's home-crafted French school, our visits to museums, gardens, and aged great aunts, and my honorary apprenticeship at Tante Evelyn's just-opened *pâtisserie.*

"As-tu un rhume, Papa?" Luc finally asked in his sweet buoyant voice. *Did Papa have a cold?* I want to weep out loud right here on the floor at just the echo through time of that question.

I watched Papa from the Volvo's front passenger seat as he drove up the parkway toward home at no more than 45 miles per hour. Bent forward, he narrowed his eyes at the windshield as if steering us through a blizzard. His inhaling had ceased; he was holding his breath.

I clasped my own fingertips to keep the throb of my heartbeat from burning them.

"*Non, mon fils*"—I have written and re-lived this so many times—Papa answered Luc before blinking down at me.

I knew he had something to tell us. I could feel the words accumulating inside him as though I were sitting beside a pressure cooker.

I should shut my journal right now. I should have shut it eight paragraphs ago.

But my mind has already skipped to Papa opening the door of our apartment that Saturday afternoon and nodding Luc and me inside.

I didn't feel as much as smell an absence: the familiar alchemy that was Maman—yeast, flour, sugar, salt. The warm, promising mix of them—of the woman who had been my mother—gone. A sharp antiseptic had claimed our air.

In the sitting room, Maman sat propped up on the sofa, wearing a lavender snow cap. Not a curl of her chestnut hair showed through.

It was August 23. She was shivering under blankets.

I waited for her smile, but her lips made a tight blank line.

This is where I remind myself that no one meant to deceive me. Mémère, Papi, Tante Evelyn—Maman's family—all of them knew, yet none of them set out to deceive me. Everyone simply wished to delay.

Kissing us goodbye at our JFK gate marked for Paris, Maman had no clue of the tiny cluster of cells burgeoning like a currant-berry in the upper-left quadrant of her right breast. She would discover it within days, but Luc and I would already be spinning in the whirlwind that was summer in France.

How can we bring them home now? Maman asked Papa once she'd discovered the tumor. *How can we fly them back to New York when Vivienne finally had courage to leave us? When she is not even calling us every day? When a lump in the breast is possibly nothing?*

I still feel like I should have known, like I should have been able to hear it—in Maman's voice or her silences; in Papa's brevity with us on the phone. In our grandmother's trembly breath when she whispered *bon nuit* and kissed Luc and me goodnight.

But for the first time in my fifteen years, Maman and I hadn't talked every day. I hadn't been asking myself if she missed or needed me. I hadn't thought about missing or needing her, or wondered if the six kisses she bestowed on my cheeks at the airport would be the last she ever gave me. I think I must have been born asking these kinds of questions.

But I didn't ask them that summer—I spent three months baking palmiers and croissants with Tantie, reading French poetry, and talking to a boy named Gabriel who came to the *pâtisserie* every day at *15h* for coffee. He had eyes precisely the same dark-chocolate-brown as mine. I knew this because he had touched a curl of my hair at the shop counter and told me.

The point is: I wasn't at home, where I could have known things. I was ignorant. While Maman underwent biopsies, scans, surgeries, two rounds of chemotherapy, and retreated to a quiet, rigid place inside herself.

I was completely surprised and am currently terrified—despite time and counseling and healing and the assurance of mostly good, honest people, i.e., my parents—that I will be taken off guard again. That life as I've known it and people as I've loved them will change.

But we did not lie to you, Maman kept repeating that Saturday we returned from Paris. No more than five minutes after seeing her, I lay curled in a silent ball between her and Papa on their bed, while Luc marched about the apartment opening window shades and gathering soccer gear for his evening practice.

I know that Maman believed she hadn't lied to me. She had planned every day to tell me, she said, but then she'd proceed with the next scan or treatment, and I would remain happy in Paris, not knowing.

In the end, she insisted, she and Papa chose to give me the gift they'd always wanted to give me—time to grow in our home country, to make my own map of their city inside my head. If they hadn't given me the time and peace of mind in which to stay, I might never have gone anywhere again.

Vivienne, Maman said, sitting straight against pillows as I shook on her bed, *I do not plan on dying.*

We've lived for five years beyond that now, but I know the rate of breast-cancer recurrence, and I know I don't trust Maman. She was lethargic and withdrawn at Christmas, and she had appointments, and now she's not answering the telephone.

And it is a fact, though I cannot cite statistics, that most people who die did not actually plan on it.

Wednesday, January 9, 1991
7:16 p.m., one of four social misfits sitting alone at new cafeteria tables

The cafeteria's new tabletops are printed with maps. Presumably, all the tables together would comprise the whole world. The whole world in St. Brigid's renowned cafeteria. This evening, I am sitting at Europe. Each time I look up from writing, my eyes trace a route through what used to be a block of communist countries: Poland, Czechoslovakia, Hungary, etc. Places, until only two years ago, no one could leave or enter.

The thought loops me back to Maman—to my inability to leave where I am to see her. I keep wondering if it's strange that she hasn't called this week.

Past semesters, we have talked on the phone, even if briefly, almost every day, but since I left home six days ago, we have spoken only once—the night after I arrived at St. Brigid's. "Where have you been?" I asked her after ringing with my calling card every ten minutes for two hours.

I could tell she was wracking her brain for believable places. "*Euhhhhh*—" Even when she delays, she is French. "Let's see . . . Today I stopped by a new *pâtisserie* in the Village."

"Greenwich? How did you get there? Isn't it freezing out?" It's 11 degrees Fahrenheit in New York, according to the newspaper, and Maman feels boxy in parkas.

"*Oui.* I called a car." Something like a demitasse clattered against what was probably a saucer.

She is such a terrible liar.

But I also lie to myself every time I try to insist in my head that moving away was best for me—the ideal path to independence and freedom from all our mistrust and grief.

I have tried to believe that I came to St. Brigid's for me, but I can see now that I am here for my parents. Because in their minds, if I trusted them enough to leave them, we were not damaged permanently—we were strong and brave and healing.

I wanted to convince my parents of that. I wanted Maman to emerge from her quiet. Though she mostly hasn't. And I am still hurting, and I may never not doubt them. And living away from them and the one city I know as well as the map of lines on my palms is possibly the worst place to be.

But my parents set their sights on St. Brigid's. We visited campus three years ago, at the suggestion of that Pulitzer winner Papa treats for Multiple Sclerosis—Guillaume someone-or-other. From the beginning, Maman was entranced by the super-nuclear charge of exclusivity in the breeze, not to mention the aged sycamores and Spanish architecture. St. Brigid's appeared a means by which we Lebruns might advance our Americanness but preserve what Maman views as our elevated French manners and taste. She and Papa never wished to send Luc and me back to the old country to be educated—they always preferred the new and almost unattainable.

And then somehow, I managed to earn the Kildare Scholarship for entrance to St. Brigid's one semester early, even when my heart always felt a few beats removed from the application essays. When Maman and Papa and I ceremoniously addressed the envelope that contained my acceptance letter, I licked the stamp as if it bore the salve for our aching. I would fly like a once-wounded finch into the unknown West of America and return to them a blazing falcon.

But now I don't know if I can do that. No doubt my parents will sanction Luc's education five blocks away from home in New York. Their sweet, trusting, milk-chocolate-eyed baby. He gets all the uncomplicated options.

My parents know that if Maman is ill again, I will catch the first airplane or Greyhound back to them. I could even hitchhike my way to Manhattan. It's not as if they live behind an Iron Curtain. Even the real one collapsed two years ago.

I would not even have to pack a suitcase for home. There is nothing here that I can't find there.

Thank God for the invention of prepaid calling cards. I'm going to try Maman on the cafeteria payphone as soon as I finish this entry. Or right after I stop to give a girl at the table just behind mine a tissue. She is hunched over a half-map of Asia, crying, and I know I could be like her any day, choking on soup, my shoulders almost imperceptibly shaking. Except I hope I'd be sitting at the United States table, watching my tears splash down on New York.

I don't usually carry tissue, but Maman tucked a small flat package in my backpack as I left our apartment one week ago. Until my plane left the ground in New York, I thought she might have given me a palmier she had baked or a letter.

And so I return to the loop.

Friday, January 11, 1991
5:27 p.m., on a stool in the culinary arts building, hidden behind
an ornamental fig tree

I am out of the loop—in a good way.

I did not catch Maman on the phone last night, but I know where Peter Breznik is from now. A student named Julie asked him at the beginning of class today. She sits to my left and has blond hair that cascades past her shoulders like a bolt of gold silk, and she never has to fidget with it. She never fidgets, period. She sits like a chiropractor's dream in her chair, straight but at ease, looking directly at Peter Breznik when she talks to him.

I have to stare at my desk when she speaks at all—her beauty and poise alarm me. She alerts me to the spinning black hole that exists between the woman I am and the woman I wish I could be.

But Peter Breznik doesn't even seem fazed by her.

After she asked where he was from, he barely looked up from the international poetry anthology he was thumbing through. "You detected the accent. Where would you guess I'm from, Julie?"

"Hmmmm . . ." Julie's voice behind her pursed lips sounded both thoughtful and alluring. Arms folded, she leaned back in her chair. "Switzerland?"

The class, minus me, burst out laughing.

"What?" Julie shrugged, her brow creased in perfectly charming bewilderment. "Does anyone know what Swiss people sound like?"

A few students called out other possible countries, but Peter Breznik (he says we can call him Peter, but even saying his name in my head renders the roof of my mouth numb) had returned to perusing his anthology. "Yugoslavia," he said, and conversation halted, as though he had just said "Saturn." Clearly, no one had expected the easygoing poet-historian to be from a country known mainly, if at all, for being wedged within a hotbed of communist and post-communist countries.

As the class held a collective breath, I allowed myself at least three seconds longer than usual to gaze at Peter-Breznik-the-Yugoslavian. He appeared just as handsome and good-humored as Peter-Breznik-the-man-from-anywhere, except that Yugoslavian Peter Breznik seemed to grow the tiniest bit weary at the prospect of discussing his country.

My three-second gaze came to an end as his eyes caught mine, a barrage of questions sailing past me.

"Wasn't Yugoslavia part of the Eastern Bloc?"

"Is Yugoslavia communist?"

"Did you have to escape?"

And then Julie asked, "Are you a communist, Peter?"

"Oh, wow." Peter Breznik bit his bottom lip as though he were afraid for us. "You guys are obviously English majors."

"I'm not." Julie touched a hand to her chest, as though deeply affronted.

I am, I despaired to myself, *but I could bake macarons or snickerdoodles for you.*

"To answer simply"—Peter Breznik lowered his book—"no. Yugoslavia has never been part of the unraveling Soviet Union, or the Eastern Bloc of communist countries that existed, until recently, behind the Iron Curtain. Yugoslavia is made up of six of its own republics: Bosnia and Herzegovina—one republic"—he held up the forefinger of his free hand—"Croatia, Macedonia, Montenegro, Serbia, and Slovenia.

"It is a communist country, but like all European communist countries these past few years, Yugoslavia is facing division and demand within its republics for independence and democracy. Just this past December, the people of Slovenia—my home republic—voted for independence from Yugoslavia, and our government is working toward that end. Or, I should say, that beginning. Likely this summer." He almost smiled as his shoulders eased down, his eyes glancing over Julie before landing for one second on me, probably because my lips and the tip of my nose had turned blue while I'd been holding my breath, listening.

He lifted his book again. "And I am not a communist. Nor did I have to escape. But"—his gaze came to rest on my desk; I wanted to apologize for apparently sitting directly in his natural line of vision—"out of curiosity, does anyone know where the Republic of Slovenia is?"

I assumed that guesses would start filling airspace and that no one would hear me answering; but in a lingering beat of suspenseful pause, my voice reverberated. "At the northeast border of Italy."

"Vivienne—" Peter Breznik held onto the end of my name in his mouth. "You could be a cartographer."

I could look at your eyes all day, I am relieved to report I did not actually say.

But truly, I have never seen anything so blue-green before. His eyes are like encyclopedia pictures I've seen of Tahiti's Pacific—so clear you can see things swimming: sharks, swordfish, manta rays.

I thought, *You remember my name.* His voice made it light, a quick sweep of breeze, like the voice of a boy who wished to talk poems with me.

But he was an instructor, a PhD candidate, standing in front of my desk, holding a book of poems I'd never heard of, written by poets whose names I couldn't even pronounce. He was a cutting-edge academic, and I was—I am—only primitive.

"Enough about Yugoslavia," he laughed. "For more of that, enroll in my Communism in Modern Europe course. In here, we're talking poems. Vivienne—"

My head snapped up to him.

"A poet is a sort of cartographer, wouldn't you say?"

Hoping he didn't actually expect me to speak words while he was looking so attentively down at me, I merely nodded, opening my notebook as slowly, possibly, as planet Earth revolves around the sun.

He so faintly inhaled before addressing the class. "A cartographer of emotional landscapes. What do you all think about that?"

I would have liked to have had thoughts, but my brain had conjured a map of various places I wished I could inhabit with Peter Breznik—my third-floor corner of the library, Baklava in Queens, the sleepy ocean shore just west of campus.

When he called on me later, he watched me as intently as he had before—Papa always says one listens with one's eyes, and I thought of that as I looked at Peter Breznik: I pictured my words sinking through the pools of his irises to his brain, and I felt like I was going to drown.

He had been talking about "resonance" (a French word first, I wanted to say)—the way a single poem reverberates with feelings and ideas beyond the writer's own—across communities, cultures, generations. He says that a poem must serve as a map to a world outside itself—it cannot be just a cute story or lovely images. It must guide readers to what feels like a shared experience. He says a poem can bind both strangers and enemies, like capitalists and communists. It can resist and revolutionize.

"But how?" he asked.

That's when I risked raising my hand, watched his eyes watching mine as he called on me, and I offered what would be the second answer I regretted in one class period, "Through metaphor."

Peter Breznik tossed his head back like Luc does when an opponent kicks a goal past him. "Are you serious, Vivienne?" Making a fist, he jabbed at the air. "You're a cartographer and a poetry theorist."

When I'm challenged or embarrassed, my fingers shake. I tucked them under the outsides of my thighs, hunching over my desk as if I could curl into a dust mote and disappear.

Peter Breznik reached out to touch the edge of my desk. "Oh. Vivienne—I think I might have frightened you. I tend to be exuberant about poetry. Can you breathe?"

I hadn't been breathing, but I took a slow breath.

He backed away from my desk a little. "'Metaphor' is my favorite answer. I just didn't expect to reach it so fast."

"I'm so sorry!" I frowned at my desk.

Students chuckled. Especially a guy named A.J., who always sits to my left on the front row and isn't even an English major (he must be studying something to do with photography, because a glossed-leather Leica camera bag always rests at his feet like a shrine to the German camera brand). Anyhow, A.J. turned toward me to say, "If only the poet-girl didn't know so much," in a kind of erudite New England accent that echoes old England in the vowels and is saturated with pretentiousness.

Peter squinted at him. "You don't apologize when you have a good answer"—he shifted his eyes, kind and amiable, to me—"or a bad answer. You can just say, 'Keep up, Peter.'"

I felt my head nod as a girl in the back of the classroom sighed like she'd just been blown a kiss by Pierce Brosnan. Actually, Pierce Brosnan has nothing on Peter Breznik, which is probably why the universe saw to it that both men were christened with the same initials.

The girl sighed as if she'd been blown a kiss by Peter Breznik.

And then Peter Breznik started talking about metaphor—how by comparing the abstract to the tangible, like happiness to honey, omitting "like" or "as," a writer could give a reader immediate access to taste, smell, sight, texture—even memory—and convey personal ideas and feelings in ways that resonate among varied audiences—people who might be separated by cultures and continents.

"Time's out." He set his anthology, which he hadn't even had time to use, on an empty desk at the front of the classroom. "We'll end class with a metaphor you probably all know. 'Hope is the thing with feathers.' Emily Dickinson, right? What do you understand about the human experience of hope from that simple comparison?"

Two and three-syllable answers proliferated. *It's a bird. It's soft. It's light. And sweet. It transcends. It's hardy.*

The bell would ring any second. Though I had already exceeded my class-response quota, I threw my habitual reserve to the wind like a bird called hope launching itself from a cliff. "Hope is fragile, no matter what Dickinson says."

"You know the whole poem." Peter Breznik did his almost-smile right at me, no doubt because I had once again distinguished myself as the primmest of all know-it-alls in a class. I never mean to do it. I don't even know that many things—it's just that the things I say are sometimes not the things other people have thought to say yet. Next class period, I'll be the student Peter Breznik is wary of calling on, the one whose hand he pretends not to see.

C'est la vie.

I won't raise my hand again.

Besides, any day I'll toss my hope to the ocean—hope that Maman will stay well, that she and Papa will let me choose to come home, that I can be happy and unafraid, and maybe, one day, love and be loved by a poem-writing European genius.

I wish I could send a letter to Emily—

Dear Miss Dickinson,
Your life was sadder than mine. But hope only flies so far.

Monday, January 14, 1991
8:03 p.m., my bedroom desk, wearing only an oversized Big Apple t-shirt

Just to satisfy my own curiosity after classes today—and because there was no one in the known universe thinking, "Oh! It would bring me such joy to see Vivienne"—I walked to the library and found the number for the Philbrick Program for Writers in Brooklyn. Its integrated Bachelor and Master of Fine Arts in Creative Writing has been astronomically ranked for five years now and boasts exclusivity that even Maman might condescend to nod her pointy chin to. So I called the admissions office and asked about transferring from St. Brigid's.

The woman I spoke to, whose cynical gruff voice made me feel like I was standing in an NYC bodega buying a lottery ticket, said that a transfer was possible, as long as my application blew the writing faculty's minds. "And since you're obviously a type-A personality who is going to ask this"—I could imagine her balancing the phone on her shoulder, slashing names off an applicant list—"I'll just tell you. Yes. You can apply for student funding."

And thus it was that I requested a transfer-student application packet.

If Philbrick would accept the bulk of my writing and literature credits from St. Brigid's, I would abandon my culinary arts degree here, find a job at a Brooklyn bakery, and complete the integrated Master of Fine Arts in Creative Writing at Philbrick.

Would my parents sanction this decision? Probably not. But I am going to apply, and if accepted, ask my parents for forgiveness when I return home in May. Unfortunately, I doubt that I possess sufficient avenging spirit to say that I never meant to deceive them by withdrawing from St. Brigid's and transferring to Philbrick—I was simply withholding information that might have upset them.

Even if I did transfer schools, I would still be on track to graduate from a first-class institution, with a master's degree, before I turned 23. Maman and Papa could sustain hope that I will apply for a job in publishing, work for a few years, and then earn a PhD in something like Writers for World Reformation whole years before I turn 30.

Personally, I would like to learn everything ever known about writing and baking. I would like to write poems, of course, and perhaps teach a little, but I would also like to write essays about all variety of baked goods and pastry in New York. And Maman and I could bake—if she felt well enough—and then possibly Tante Evelyn would box up her flat and *pâtisserie* in Paris, relocate to New York, and help us open our own French *pâtisserie* or American bakery, or maybe some blend of both.

Since I was four and we began checking Paris *pâtisseries* off a list by *arrondissement,* Tante Evelyn promised to teach me how to bake everything Maman hadn't taught me yet, and then one day, Tante Evelyn pinky-swore, we would open a shop. *With your papa's money from all the brain surgeries,* she likes to say when she visits, laughing her trademark aristocratic trill of syllables. I hope her commitment isn't waning. Filling skeptical New Yorkers with expert French pastry and American baked goods is probably as close as I'll ever come to reforming the world.

But poetry can change a life, too. If I ever did teach a poetry class, I would point out that poetry isn't too difficult; it is simply a vast and overlooked country. If you want to understand it, you need to stay a while, explore, and visit regularly. I guess I would like to be what Peter Breznik might call a poetry cartographer. Not on a very large scale—just often enough to point a handful of students to words that might guide them through a day. Or a lifetime.

Oh, and also, I would like to be a mother.

I would like everything, Dear God. Plus a brief conversation with Peter Breznik about poems or Europe. Or his current romantic plans for the future.

Please, God. And thank you.

In the short term, however, I would like to fly home to Maman and New York. To quote characters in Star Trek, which I have never watched too attentively, but which plays in continuous re-runs every night in our commons area: Beam me up, Scottie.

Tuesday, January 15, 1991
5:53 p.m., on the velvet-green sofa in my dorm commons with a lavender-infused sugar cookie I baked in class

Conferenced with Peter Breznik today. Or Peter, as I reluctantly agreed to call him. Though I don't anticipate further opportunity to call him anything.

Everyone in class was required to propose the topic of their first craft essay in his history department office. I arrived two or three minutes early at his cracked-open office door and could overhear him chatting with that would-be spokesman of the literati, A.J., whose strident voice I would recognize even if my head were submerged under water.

As far as I could hear, he and Peter were not talking about poetry. Peter was merely answering personal questions that A.J. kept posing in his pretentious accent, probably clothed in a black turtleneck and a tweed jacket too stiff to bend his arms in.

I leaned against the wall across from Peter's office door, listening to his soft foreign lilt and thinking how perceptions of instructor-student interaction are sexist. For example, no one would spare a single skeptical thought for a male student propped back in a chair, playing twenty questions with a handsome male instructor, while everyone on earth, including other females, would roll their eyes and whisper, "She has a raging crush on him," if a female student were to do the same. And in my particular case, they would be right.

Obviously, I'm a miserable feminist.

Still. The injustice: I will never be able to spend half a conference session peppering my attractive poetry instructor with far-too-personal questions.

Peter Breznik, however, talks as though he is friends with all his students, even A.J., who is as irritating in class as a cheese grater brushed over your knuckles. I imagine that Peter Breznik would answer female students as magnanimously as he would answer males, though, and would likely never guess that any one of them envisioned hanging curtains in a Brooklyn studio apartment with him.

As for A.J., he was getting down to the threads and needles of Peter Breznik's existence. "So how did you get to the U.S.?"

From where I stood in the hall, I could see only a thin wedge of Peter's office—some tight-knotted carpet, one leg of a desk, a sunny-blue corner of window. I could not glimpse even a shadow of his person, but he sounded as easygoing as ever, probably tipping back in a rolling swivel-chair, unworried that A.J. had approximately one minute of conference time left.

"I was born here in California," Peter said, "while my dad was a visiting professor of poetry at Stanford. My parents never planned to conceive a U.S. citizen."

I felt a childish zing at hearing him speak the word "conceive." He had said it so casually, as though it did not connote two bodies wanting and needing and whispering in the dark.

"My family lived between Slovenia and California, as my dad taught here for most of my growing up years."

"Wow," A.J. said like a regular guy from Iowa, which makes you wonder about his lofty accent. Though he found it again in an instant. "I had no idea that citizens of a communist country could travel like that. I thought border-patrol shot you if you attempted to leave."

"No," Peter's voice tightened. A metal creak made me think that if he had been tilted back in his swivel-chair earlier, he was sitting upright now. "Yugoslavia's borders have always been more porous than those of other communist countries, because after World War II, the Yugoslavian government refused to enter into agreements with the Soviet Union that would have restricted travel. Instead, our government thought to create the illusion that communism allows for movement—for social and economic exchange and growth." He breathed his lungs full of air. "It does not. Though I suppose some Yugos might disagree."

"Lucky you were born here," A.J. huffed in a way that tagged an unvoiced, *Instead of being born in the same land as all those other doomed fools,* to the end of his sentence.

I imagined Peter squinting A.J. down to the size of deer tick, but in his characteristic good-natured fashion, he continued with kindness and honesty. "Yes. That stroke of luck has enabled me to earn almost three degrees here. I've lived in the U.S. for so long now, I'm not sure anymore where home is."

An invested third party in the conversation by then, I blinked my eyes closed, wondering how that might be—not knowing where home is, not feeling pulled by it, like a kite unspooled too far on its string.

"Nothing wrong with the nomad's life." Merely the soundwaves of A.J.'s haughty voice shattered the quiet pool of my thoughts. "You can extract what you want from a place and move on."

Peter cleared his throat. "Yes, well, as I mentioned in class, some good is happening in Slovenia, even as tensions rise among other republics. In Spring, I could return to an independent nation."

"That is truly . . . astounding," A.J. declared in un-astounded monotone. "Is your family in Yugoslavia now?"

My feet moved my body slowly along the wall, as though determined to grant my eyes a view of Peter.

"Yes," Peter answered A.J. The thought occurred to me that the reason Peter kept talking might be that he didn't know I had arrived. "My dad—Andrej Breznik—mainly writes essays and articles on political issues now, though his poems were often political, too. A few of his books—both poems and essays—have been published here in the States, and my mom's a hell of a writer herself. My journalist brother, Tilen, is currently gathering personal histories throughout the republics to document life and attitude in what will soon likely be the former Yugoslavia. He and my parents would love for me to move to Ljubljana and teach." Something like a hand brushed over his desktop. "And I have an offer at the University of Ljubljana."

You're leaving for Ljubljana? I wanted to interject. *But you and I haven't even talked poems yet.*

A.J. replied, "Fantastic. How soon would that be?"

"In May. But a lot could happen before then." Peter sighed quietly. "St. Brigid's could convince me to stay, or even an East Coast school—"

Like a New York school? I almost whispered.

Peter continued, "My brother could move here, my parents. Hey, Vivienne."

That's really how his sentences went: *my brother, my parents. Hey, Vivienne.* It felt sort of intimate, as though I were connected to his people, a thread in his fabric. I went rigid against the hallway wall as my backpack dropped to my elbow. But in two seconds, Peter stood at his office door, clapping A.J.—who was indeed wearing a tweed jacket—on the shoulder. "Good luck with your topic. Let me know if you need further direction."

And then Peter looked at me, almost smiling as he often is. I suspect he finds it humorous that I am slightly over-eager in all things related to writing and literature. He waved me into his office.

But A.J. paused in the doorway to scan my being from my hair to my cardigan buttons to my clogs. "All hail the tortured poet," he smirked, and then he bumped past me with his camera bag. He literally turns my saliva acidic.

Meanwhile, only mere feet away from where I stood clutching my backpack to my chest, Peter kicked his rubber door-stop tight, triggering lightning-flash thoughts in my head like, *What if he hadn't?* What if the door had snicked shut, and he'd clasped my elbow with his broad olive hand and said hoarsely, because he was choked with emotion, *Vivienne, I've been waiting all day for you?*

As it happened, he managed to kick the door open a few more inches before turning for his desk and motioning to a chair placed in front of it. "Sit down, Vivienne. I've been making bets with myself on what poem you'll want to write about."

Some females might inspire a self-bet on what they will wear dancing, or how long it will take to kiss her; I rouse men to bet themselves on what poem I'll write about in essays.

I could summon no words to respond to Peter Breznik. I only sat in his student-chair, dropping my backpack beside my feet on the floor.

Peter sat down in his swivel-chair, but instead of asking me which poem I'd selected, he smiled and said, "*Bonjour,* Vivienne Lebrun," in his perfect French accent.

I forced out the question I've been wondering since the first day of class. "*Parlez-vous français?*" I meant to address him formally, as *vous*—because he is my instructor—but once I heard the question outside my head, I thought I probably sounded like a twelve-year-old.

Threading his fingers together, Peter Breznik dug his elbows into his armrests. "*Un peu.* I speak *un petit peu français.* But I can tell you speak it fluently. You're French, I'm gathering."

I leaned down to extract a pen from my backpack, because honestly, I think a spell is attached to his eyes—if you look for too long, you'll start unbuttoning things in slow motion. "Yes." I sat back up. "My parents moved to Manhattan when I was six." I leaned down again for my notebook.

"We're both European then." He nudged the corner of a poetry collection by the Swedish poet Tomas Tranströmer sitting in a corner of his desk. "And a long way from family. I mean, is your family still in New York?"

I wrote today's date on my notepad, nodding slowly to seem as nonchalant as he did, but still academically focused. "Yes," I said, and even as I sat three feet from Peter Breznik, the pull was right there, a tug in my chest, toward home.

Peter stacked a Lisel Mueller collection on top of the one by Tranströmer, and for one of the very few times in my life, I felt thoroughly American. My lifetime reading was mainly comprised of writers from this continent—Jane Kenyon, Robert Hass, Lucille Clifton—while Peter Breznik seemed to have read the whole world.

He said nothing in response to my family still living in New York, so I asked the logical next question, "And your family is in Yugoslavia—I mean, Slovenia?"

"Yes and yes. They live in the Slovene city of Ljubljana." He peered down at his desk as if it were etched with a map. "I miss my family, but

I'm not attached to their country. It's a hard place to live, and the fact that they stay there when I'm—" He looked up, smiling through tight lips.

I think he felt awkward, unaware as he was that I would have listened to the woes of Yugoslavian family life till the end of next semester and beyond. I would have offered to write his memoir.

My brain lurched to fill up the silence. I wanted to return to the topic of where he'd be interviewing to teach in the fall, but that was a topic he had discussed with A.J., and I didn't want to reveal my eavesdropping. Besides, what would I do if Peter Breznik did plan to interview in New York? Suggest bakeries?

Finally, I thought to ask, "You said in class that you're teaching history courses this semester?"

He reached a hand to a book resting on another corner of his desk, this one entitled something about the Balkan Peninsula. "Yes." When he smiled again, I realized that his lips were just as dangerous as his eyes—the pale pink of a crayon box, with the faintest bow along the upper lip. "I'm teaching Communism in Modern Europe, along with World War II and the Eastern Front." He extracted a pencil from a green glass vase. "Were you disappointed not to be in Alene's poetry class?"

"No!" I said so emphatically that my pen jerked forward and scrawled a long line in my notebook. I had wanted to take the English department chair's section of Poetry, but that was before I'd walked into Peter Breznik's classroom three weeks ago and wished his section was scheduled to meet daily into the next millennium.

I turned to a clean page in my notebook. "I mean, I like learning from different perspectives. And—" I glanced up to find Peter's eyes wide and earnest, as though he wanted to hear what I thought, and hoped I would think something encouraging.

But suddenly, I didn't know what to say, or what I could say that wouldn't translate to *I heart you forever.* I wanted to tell him, *You're such a good teacher,* but I went with the slightly less personal, "I like the poets we've read so far. They're from everywhere and span all time periods."

Peter returned his pencil to the vase. "I guess that's the historian in me."

And how old are you? I thought next, the words light as snow on my tongue—they would have floated right off, and he probably would have answered, and then I could have known with greater certainty if my crush on him is galactically delusional, or only delusional by earth standards. Knowing he is 27 might suck a bit of the wind from the sails of my fantasies. But if I were betting with myself, I'd guess he is 25 or 26, and if that were the case, we could have attended St. Matthew's Prep together for one year. We could have passed by one another in the hallway.

Sitting in his student chair, I tried to spy out any framed photographs of him with his arm wrapped around the kind of svelte woman I imagined had already claimed him—a woman almost his same height, wearing something like a breezy white button-up with jeans, hair knotted in a silky chignon—the two of them standing in front of the Louvre or Trevi Fountain, looking like a young Paul Newman and Joanne Woodward on holiday.

The only photograph I saw, though, was one 5 x 7 on a bookshelf, of a beautiful, even sunnier, backpack-toting Peter Breznik in a field of wildflowers, flanked by two equally beautiful and sunny, also pack-toting, though older, people—a man and a woman, who must be his parents. Snow-capped, gravelly mountain peaks carved the blue sky in jagged angles behind them.

When I looked back to him, I saw that he was just waiting, watching my eyes devour his personal space.

I peered down to write CRAFT ESSAY at the top of my notebook page and announced, "I'm thinking I'd like to write about John Donne's use of Latinate and Germanic diction in 'A Valediction: Forbidding Mourning.'"

Peter Breznik straightened up in his chair, pressed his hands in a prayer gesture, touched his fingers to his lips. "Okay, right. Um, that was totally not the poem I had bet on, or the topic. I'd imagined you going more contemporary."

My mind tangled into a knot of questions: He had been thinking of me thinking about poetry? He had imagined my brain and what might be inside it? He had imagined himself inside my brain?

He would totally not say "totally" if he were older than 26.

"More contemporary?" I asked.

He does have a somewhat mature, though faint, "V" of lines that span from the outer corners of his eyes to his temples when he smiles, which he was doing right then. It was making me want to live my life with the sole purpose of seeing him smile, especially first thing in the morning, lying beside him, our three children asleep in bright-curtained rooms, the sharp peaks of snow-capped mountains outside our window.

He pressed his hand to another short stack of poetry collections on his desk, running his index finger along their spines, making my skin tingle. "Like one of these poets." He pushed the little stack of books, spine-first, toward me. I didn't recognize a single name in the bunch.

As he leaned farther over his desk, his quick-tendoned hands fanned the books out in front of me. "Choose one." His eyes narrowed on my face in a way that made me think of a fortune teller. As if I'd telepathed the thought, he said, "Just think, Vivienne: The fate of your essay lies with the genius of one of these poets."

I tugged at a book, unable to tear my eyes from his hands. I didn't even see the book's cover.

"That one," Peter nodded at the collection I'd chosen, "might very well change your life."

I tensed my shoulders to keep from shivering, and then set the book on his desk to look at it: *Anna Swir*, translated from Polish by two other writers. I'd never heard of her, or even read very much of anything in translation. Her collection's title, *Happy As a Dog's Tail*, was printed in slender all-caps beside a nude Eve in the Garden, lifting her hand to a snake coiled around a tree branch.

Words seemed to short-circuit between my brain and my mouth, but Peter smiled good-naturedly. "You know, I was betting on Anna Swir for you. She's a Polish poet I admire, and I wondered if you'd read her as I read your poems this week. You're plainspoken, but vibrant"—I touched the book's cover, as if doing that would steady my heartbeat—"and you're deep, in a light-handed, un-self-conscious way."

He'd read the three poems I'd submitted closely enough to describe them that way, without them being right there, printed out in front of him? I lifted the book from his desk.

"And you're razor-sharp specific—"

"Okay . . ." I felt slightly off-balance.

"You can write about 'Valediction,'" he said. "You can write about anything you like, but if you have time to read Anna Swir this week, you might decide to write about one of her poems. I think you'd learn a lot."

Despite the violent star shower going off in my body, I managed to say, "Thanks, Professor Breznik," but then I caught myself, "I mean—"

"I'm not a professor yet."

"Right . . ." I was sitting so straight, my lower back started quivering. I think maybe my voice quivered, too.

"It's really okay to call me Peter," he said as though he'd picked up on my hesitation. "Or *Pet-er,* short *e,* soft *r,* if you like how it sounds in Slovene." I did like how it sounded in Slovene, but *Pet-er's* head was tilted, his eyebrows arched in an ironic way that said, *Don't really call me that.* Even if I'd said his name in Tagalog, however, my tone would have given my heart away. In any language, I would say *Peter* like a classic film star to her lover, like Juliet calling Romeo from her balcony.

"Right," I said again, without saying *Peter.* "Okay." I bounced to my feet with my notebook, pen, and backpack—I felt like a wild human coat-rack—and suddenly he was stepping toward me, taking my backpack and holding it out for me so that I could tuck away my pen and my notebook before reaching an arm through a strap.

"Thank you," I said, "for the meeting. And for the book."

"No problem." He followed me a few steps outside his office.

Turning to say goodbye, I noticed his chest lift with a breath and saw the quick up-down of his Adam's apple. The image as a whole made me think the word *wistful.* Probably because that's how I felt.

"I'll be at the library next Thursday evening at 7 p.m.," he said, "if students want to stop by for help finding articles to use in future craft essays."

I only nodded, but what's the expression?

Wild horses couldn't keep me away.

Before falling asleep last night, I opened Anna Swir's book to an introduction that began: "Question: What is the central theme of these poems? Answer: Flesh." I smacked the cover shut, wondering if Peter Breznik would expect me to take up that subject, too.

The introduction went on to describe the many varied events a woman might experience in her flesh—love, sleep, fear, childbirth. These are not really subjects I write about—unless one counts love of my family and fear of them dying—so I'm not sure why Peter Breznik thought of Anna Swir when he read my work. I've read nine of her poems so far, and he was right about one thing: I like her. So I guess now I'll determine what he thinks I might learn from her.

Here is the first poem of Swir's collection:

I Am Filled with Love

> *I am filled with love*
> *as a great tree with the wind,*
> *as a sponge with the ocean,*
> *as a great life with suffering,*
> *as time with death.*

I'm not sure Swir's poem is immediately vibrant and specific, as Peter Breznik said he thinks my poems are. Swir is contemplating love, as I often do in my poems, but she is examining love on a large scale, as a weighty abstract entity, in order to convey how love feels to her personally. I don't often make large claims in my poems or refer to big feelings by name. So I could make a point of working on that. I could open a poem with something like: *I am filled with the fear / of losing my mother.*

I struggle to detach from the personal.

Case in point: all these sentences.

It occurred to me last night that I have begun this particular journal because of Maman. Because I believe she is ill again, and just like the last time, she is not speaking to me about it, and I must have someone or something to speak to. And the first time she was ill, five years ago now, I was conditioned to speak to paper.

Upon waking this morning, I was thinking of Sandra the therapist, of our first Wednesday meeting, how she sat in a sunken, red-cushioned chair beside me and set a journal, pressed flowers on the cover, in my lap. "I want you to fill this." She leaned toward me. "I want you to say everything that wild brain of yours thinks to say, right here, on paper."

When I brought the journal back to Sandra the next Wednesday, three-quarters full—every musing, fear, happening, and conversation I'd experienced recorded in painstaking detail—her rosacea-veined cheeks paled a little. "No wonder you implode when your parents don't talk to you. We're going to need another journal."

I feel that way now—as though I will need more pages soon. The more I write, the more I think of to say, and the more space I need to say it.

Unlike my past journals, however, I imagine an audience outside myself for this one: my children and their children and their children, etc. Though at the current rate of romance in my life, I might find it necessary to donate my journals to a university study on personal narrative; I don't know if I will ever be close enough to a man to create another human. I want that more than anything, but—

Peter Breznik walked into class a few minutes ago, where I am still the only student present. Setting some books on a table, he said, "Good Morning, Vivienne. Nice journal," and then, when he saw *Happy as a Dog's Tail* on my desk, "I'm guessing you like Anna Swir."

How do you read my soul like a book?

If only I had the flirting prowess to have said that.

In real life, I could only laugh breathlessly at his observation, because I was literally breathless, and now he is off making copies, and I am ending this entry.

Friday, January 18, 1991
6:30 p.m., my favorite tiny round table beside the front window at Café des Palmiers

A letter arrived from Robert Carson today.

I haven't given Robert space in this journal yet. He's the son of a respected neurologist with whom Papa has published a good deal of research. Until college, Robert lived with his mother in New Jersey but would visit his father on East 83rd whenever he could extract himself from high-school football.

We met him for the first time four years ago, during the intermission of a piano concerto benefit at Lincoln Center. Having recently finished her last round of chemotherapy, Maman was lethargic and gaunt and wanting to return home at the intermission. But then we bumped into Robert's father and met Robert, all dark eyes, chiseled jaw, and boredom, who announced within two minutes of our introduction that he planned to be a doctor. Immediately the color sprung to Maman's cheeks, and she invited Dr. Carson and Son to dinner the following Sunday.

Despite my protests, Maman began inviting Robert and his father to Sunday dinner regularly, seating Robert and me side by side and dotting conversation with news of my brilliance, which never failed to give Robert license to fake-punch my arm and pronounce sentences inspired by Wheaties commercials, such as "This girl's got the brain of champions."

Robert has played quarterback at Penn State for four years now, and according to the letter I just received, his life at that school has been "UH-MAZING" (he truly spelled it that way, in all capitals). Football season has ended, of course—the last of his college career—and I suspect he cries a little every night into his pillow.

Please don't think me too cruel. I allow myself a sharper-than-typical tongue with Robert, because a girl I workshopped with at a New York Young Writers conference three years ago attended his high school in New Jersey, and she said that Robert plays girls the way he plays football, tossing them as soon as he's gone far enough. I am basically the reincarnation of my Catholic French grandmother in regard to relationships: One should proceed slowly, and when two people make contact, they should walk a long way together.

I don't know what Robert sees in me. Or what Maman sees in him, besides his face and his muscles and his supposed interest in medicine. I mean, he is nice and handsome enough, and possibly smarter than many other men who bash their brains around inside helmets. Certainly, he'll catch the eye of some articulate well-read mega-model, just as I assume that I myself might hold appeal for a man who prefers meandering strolls through museums (goodness—Degas! I saw five of his sculptures in a campus exhibit yesterday) over cheering oneself hoarse on aluminum bleachers, arguing yards or downs or what have you, while shoving one's face full of hotdogs.

Besides being smitten with Robert himself, Maman loves that our fathers are colleagues, and that the Carsons are Catholic, and wealthy, and as American as the Super Bowl, though Dr. and Mrs. Carson are married and live apart and expect for everyone to think that is normal. Which it is not.

When Dr. Carson and Robert joined us for brunch over Christmas break, they ended up staying all day and convinced Papa and Luc to watch football on television. After an hour, all four of them had turned Neanderthal, exclaiming, grunting, smacking each other's backs and the furniture. Only Papa still vaguely resembled Homo sapiens, raising his crystal wine glass to cheer on a team whose name his tongue had never before shaped.

I had curled up in one of the rose-colored wingback chairs near the sitting-room windows, with Hugo's giant retriever head in my lap. At half-time, Robert left the television to sit on the windowsill nearest me. I remember Hugo's big brown eyes tracking up and down between us.

"Do you want to play cards or something?" Robert asked. "Or we could just walk to Central Park and make-out . . ."

When I didn't laugh or leap from the chair to fetch my wool coat, he pressed a hand to my shoulder. "Kidding, Vivienne"—which he pronounced like *Viviun*—"I'm kidding." I nearly told him he should dress in a loin cloth and carry a club, but then Maman appeared and set a game of Monopoly and a plate of *mille feuille* on the little round table between us, yanking Hugo away by his collar.

A little round table like the one I am presently sitting at.

How do details of home needle their way into everything?

Anyhow, Robert pulled the other pink wingback to the table and was actually quite skilled at Monopoly, when he was focused and not asking about California and who my friends were and how many were guys, and did I like one guy in particular.

And then I guess there was one sort of bright moment right after he said guys must line up after class for my phone number. When I rolled my eyes, he said, "Believe me, Viviun—they want to."

I still think that was a kind thing of Robert to say. He also complimented Maman on her pastry and completely ignored the television while we played, even when his father would call, "Bob, you should see this." And when Robert asked if we had playing cards, which Maman promptly and joyfully delivered, he taught me half a dozen games, both of us whooping and hollering by the end, not unlike the Neanderthals watching football.

When I beat him at a tight round of Speed, he said, "You kick ass, Lebrun," which did sort of make my heart flutter. And when he asked if he could send a letter to me at St. Brigid's, I thought that sounded like something James Stewart might say to Jean Arnold if she'd been flying across the country after a card game, so I penned my address around the white border of a Joker card, which he tucked inside his wallet.

Besides those encounters, I don't even know Robert that well, as he grew up in New Jersey. Plus . . . *Bob?!* I'm not sure I could ever be with a man from New Jersey, let alone a quarterback named Bob. But he writes that he'll be visiting Stanford's medical school in March, and he hopes that we might spend some time together.

I suppose I might possibly agree to see him. I could take him to Palmiers for lunch or to Arugula for dinner, and perhaps we could walk along the coast, but I don't know if I would kiss Robert Carson.

Or maybe I would. Or maybe I wish I already had, just so that I could know how to kiss the next person—the *real* person—a boy (or would he be a man?) for whom I would actually fetch my coat and trudge through the snow to hold hands with two days after Christmas. I don't know where exactly this real person and I would go—to Central Park, under Glade Arch, perhaps, if there weren't any muggers—and though we'd be standing up, I imagine us like Paolo and Francesca in Rodin's sculpture *The Kiss,* sitting down.

The thought makes me blush right here over my tea, and picture Peter Breznik, who was impossibly handsome in class this morning. Some men have a way of making jeans look so effortless—or maybe it's not that their jeans look effortless, but that their bodies look effortless at looking perfect in their jeans.

Peter Breznik says my name as it is meant to be said—"Viv-iENNE"—the "viv" quick, the long *e*-sound a flicker, blending into the softly-nasalized "enne." As he was talking about feminist literary theory today, I envisioned pulling him close for a kiss by the belt-loop of his effortless jeans, and I gasped at my desk—quietly, but truly; and though I focused my eyes on my pen—which was, in some detached way, writing words on my notepad—I felt him pause in a sentence and look at me.

My hormones make me a miserable feminist.

After class, as students were clearing their desks, Peter Breznik reminded us of the library-research meeting this coming Thursday. "Will we see you there, Vivienne?" he asked as I zipped my backpack.

"Maybe," I said, so as not to appear eager.

Students had exited the room. He was gathering his books and papers as I headed toward the door, but when he glanced up, I was watching him and our eyes held. I don't know how to tell if a man is looking at me and thinking the same things that I am. Was Peter Breznik simply thinking of finding time for a sandwich or a stop at a urinal? Or was he wondering how it might be to kiss the smooth shadowed skin beneath one of my earlobes?

What do I know beyond the fact that a Milky-Way-sized experience-gap lies between us?

After a few seconds in the empty classroom, he smiled—not softly, as he usually does, but bright, exposing his broad white arc of straight teeth. I could only blink my eyes shut and keep walking.

But I could hear him behind me, slinging his worn bag over his shoulder. "You can tell me what you think about Anna Swir," he said, in a wide-sounding way that made me think he was still smiling.

Every time I remember it, I'm jittery.

———

Sunday, January 20, 1991
11:30 p.m., on my bed with a tiny box of madeleines from class this week—still not in New York as I want to be

My entries grow longer. Sandra's eyes would pop out of her head. Papa would say I'm too deep inside myself.

I've opened our dorm-room window, and the gauzy white curtain keeps lifting. On the one hand, it's enchanting—I can imagine Italy outside, an azure coast, the scent of lemons; but on the other hand, it reminds me of death—of a soul lingering, wishing it didn't have to leave yet.

Hillary is at The Garage again. She said I should come and meet her friend Simon, who looks like Tom Cruise and would be happy to "kiss my face off," but somehow that does not sound appealing. Plus, I'm on my period and I'm tired.

I pray Maman will confess soon. Like any good Catholic, she must know she'll feel better once she offers up the truth. It is not that I want to hear she is sick again, but I do want her to tell me what's happening. When she doesn't, I feel myself circling and suffocating in a dark room, floundering for a beam to hold onto.

If she could just look at me as a person who loves her—if she could just see and be seen and speak openly—I feel like I might find surer footing. The wounds on our insides might heal the way divots in sand disappear beneath waves. I am tired of my family pretending we could survive another season in hell, with me 3,000 miles away this time, and Maman, Papa, and Luc avoiding all phone conversation.

Yes, even Luc is avoiding me. He knows that the moment I decide to ask him if Maman is sick, he will succumb to tears and tell me everything he's noticed—her fatigue and malaise, the medications and long appointments. He lived through the first time, too, even if he pulled through stably enough not to miss one soccer practice. And who do you think, Posterity, walked with that twelve-year-old boy to practice and games and hid her surprise whenever he held her hand along the way? Who promised not to tell their parents when, late at night, that boy would creep to the side of his sister's bed and cry that he was afraid?

Do I even need to answer those questions?

It just now occurs to me that maybe Luc knows the whole of things. I would never assume that he and my parents could be so deceiving, but the fact is, Maman might be in the deep woods of chemotherapy right now and I wouldn't know heads or tails of it. The woman who gave birth to me would watch every last hair detach from each follicle of her body and wait to be told that her treatment had failed before she would induce anxiety upon my life or jeopardize my studies.

Talking to Papa this evening (yes, Dr. Étienne Lebrun answered the phone after I called three times) went approximately like this—

"How are you, Papa?"

"Bien, bien, ma petite. Ça va?"

"Ça va bien, Papa. I miss you. Is Maman doing well?"

"Bien sûr, Vivienne! Maman is always doing well! She is at her best when you and Luc are conquering the world, her prized ambassadors of intelligence, virtue, and French good taste."

"Papa, please—be serious! I could tell at Christmas. She's tired! And I'm worried. Has she seen Dr. Greenfield?"

"Ah, Vivienne. Only when you are a parent will you understand the exhaustion of devoting one's every effort and thought to one's children."

"Papa. Maman's first child is on the other side of a very wide country, and the second only needs an adult to stock the refrigerator, which you should hire an adult to do. Motherhood for Maman is no longer exhausting. If I could just be there—I've been thinking—if I applied to the Philbrick Program—"

"Vivienne, listen to me. You will finish both your degrees in California, and you will thank us for opening the doors of the world to you. Once you complete your studies, the earth will be like a globe on your desk—you will spin it and pick any place to go, pursue anything your heart—"

"But Maman is my heart, and you, Papa, and Luc, and New York, and Hugo—"

"Vivienne—"

"Even Mr.-Phillips-the-Doorman. I'm not like you, Papa. I don't need to go anywhere. I could live within a four-block radius my whole life if only the people I loved—"

"Cela suffit! Vivienne! You long for that radius because you worry

that something will go wrong inside it. You wish to control it, but you cannot, and could not, even if you resided within it. Maman and I have made significant investment in both your well-being and your education. We love you with a ferocity and responsibility you do not understand—"

"But even fierce love can listen, Papa. Love is kind, as it says in the Bible. Love does not have to force. Please hear me. I could earn both a bachelor's and a master's at Philbrick."

UTTER, ABSOLUTE, TOTAL SILENCE.

"Papa?"

"Vivienne, do you know, I'm beginning to agree with your mother—you should attempt to meet someone, a motivated young man. Ask him to coffee. Bake him some expert *chouquette* in that class you take. Form an attachment. You need—"

"I need our family! I need to see you and Maman and Luc—"

Maman whisper-coughed somewhere in the background.

Papa corrected himself. "I don't mean to suggest you forget Dr. Carson's boy—"

"Okay, Papa. May I speak to Maman now?"

"*Désolé,* Vivienne. She and Luc are departing for a film he convinced her to see—*What About Bill.*"

"*What About Bob?*"

"Are you referring to the Carson boy?"

"What? No. That's the name of the movie. *What About Bob?* Does Maman prefer not to talk to me?"

"Vivienne. Parents sometimes reside at the center of a child's world well into early adulthood. It is normal that you think to talk to Maman so often and regularly, and that you assume that you are also the center of her world. But your mother has other people and responsibilities to attend to each day. Just because Maman has not been as free as usual for phone conversation with you does not mean—"

"Okay, Papa. I need to go now."

"Come now, Vivienne. You needn't go in a huff. Maman will be home—"

"No, no—I'm just tired, and a little homesick. I'll feel better tomorrow. Will you kiss Maman for me? And Luc? I love you, Papa."

"There's our strong girl. We love you, Vivienne. Spring will come soon. *En avant!* Study!"

I might have exaggerated Papa a little. Just his words, not his lack of empathy.

An hour has passed now, and I keep hearing Luc in my head, saying what he always says when I fail to bring my parents around to my view of things: "You just had to go and tug at their heartstrings, didn't you?"

I wonder where that expression comes from: *heartstrings.* A heart with strings. A puppet heart. I don't think French has an expression for this. Which may suggest that my French parents' hearts don't have strings. Which would explain why I can never tug at them.

My own heart seems hardly to beat tonight. Once, when we were small, Luc stepped on a cricket in the washroom, and it chirped a slow pulse that grew slower and slower for what felt like an eternity. That's what my heartbeat feels like.

In an alternate universe, where I were at least 24 and no longer a student, and had formed dozens of attachments and had kissed many men, both standing up and sitting down, I would ask Peter Breznik to coffee.

_____

Tuesday, January 22, 1991
9:30 p.m., empty main-floor library reference

I've been trying to think of fresh topics to write about. Reading this journal, my posterity might assume that both my interior and exterior lives consist solely of worrying for Maman, attending a poetry workshop, and fantasizing about its graduate instructor. But really, I do many other interesting things. For example, I am enrolled in four courses besides Advanced Poetry: one senior seminar on metaphysical poetry, another on Romanticism, along with two culinary arts courses—Macronutrients and The Science of Baking, for which I bake two batches of cookies and two loaves of bread each week.

Sandra the therapist hoped that journaling during Maman's illness might help me realize that much more happened in my life outside the subjects—or SUBJECT, all caps: Maman's Illness—that consumed me, and that I would then be more eager and better equipped to spread my interest and attention to other subjects, and hence be less debilitated by the possibility of losing my mother.

Of course, Sandra's goals depended upon me writing about varied topics and deeming many things worth documenting. The entries of my actual journal might have comprised an award-winning collection of flash-essays on the terror a girl feels when her parents attempt to conceal her mother's cancer.

As for fresh topics: After Romantic Poetry today, I convinced Hillary to come with me to the kitchen lab to bake chocolate chip cookies. I have been sprinkling the just-browning tops with flaky salt I found in a shop near Palmiers, but I can't decide if semi-sweet or milk-chocolate chips are best. I adore baking American cookies, even though Maman might fear she birthed a simpleton if I told her. She is skeptical of this culinary arts degree, anyway. It is relatively new at St. Brigid's, and I am not sure Administration originally intended to produce degree-toting bakers—I think they envisioned students dispersing throughout the world to feed seven course meals to diplomats and celebrities and put in a good word for St. Brigid's. But two years ago, Admin approved construction of a world-class baking lab right here on campus, and the culinary arts faculty pioneered a baking and pastry concentration within the major. I was the first to enlist.

As for another fresh topic, or possibly a sub-topic of an established major topic: Yesterday evening, I took a short break from reading John Donne (for metaphysical poetry, another fresh topic) in the library Humanities reference area and researched two tertiary topics.

First, Yugoslavia. After reading three articles, I sense that Yugoslavia is a volatile family of six sibling-republics, who all speak different languages, adhere to different faiths, and dislike each other's customs. They seem to have maintained familial ties only by the force of parental dictators, the longest-running of them a Josep Broz Tito, who served as President for Life from 1953 until his death in 1980. He is credited with improving quality of life in Yugoslavia after World War II, but at present, eleven years after his demise, a few of Yugoslavia's six siblings insist on independence and autonomy. Expert opinion is that, for the most part, this will not happen peacefully.

Of course, this propels me back to my loop—my family, Maman, and our lack of proximity: If we Lebruns were a country, our nation would be the opposite of the fragmenting Yugoslavia. We are four generally-like-minded republics, but right now, it feels as if the most authoritative two want me out. I don't wish for separation or warfare; I just want to stay close and love everyone.

Second, I typed the name of Peter Breznik's father—*Andrej Breznik*—into the library computer database, and *voilà!*: He is reasonably famous. And by reasonably, I mean that he has won a Striding Edge Award in journalism, for a series of articles he published about the futility of maintaining a unified Yugoslavia. Naturally, this appears to have made him some enemies, but he is exceptionally respected among international journalists and revolutionaries. And, in the author photo of his books, he is handsome. Not as handsome as his son Peter—his wife's DNA must have amped up the gene pool in that regard—but I checked out the second of his four books, all published in English, and here is his bio:

Andrej Breznik was born in Celje, Slovenia, in the Socialist Federal Republic of Yugoslavia, in 1931. He married the Yugoslavian essayist, Zara Kovač, in 1958, whereupon they spent the next decade writing and teaching in Ljubljana. In addition to his distinguished professorship at the University of Ljubljana, Breznik has fulfilled three appointments in the United States as a visiting professor. Since 1980, Breznik has focused his research and writing on the fraught and complex history of his homeland, regularly publishing work in international news and political outlets. He and his wife currently reside in Ljubljana and are the parents of two grown sons, Tilen and Peter.

I think that reads like a love story. When I write a book, I want my bio to hint at love between each line like that. I want readers to know that I loved someone and that someone loved me, and that we made a loving life together.

Please, God, someday. Send someone.

I might as well accept it: I will probably not think of fresh topics to write about.

Thursday, January 24, 1991
11:42 p.m., my bed again, but under the covers, writing with purple ink

And who would you guess, Posterity, attended Peter Breznik's library-instruction gathering tonight?

That's right: A.J. and me.

I mean, A.J. attended. I attended.

I do not like my pronoun sharing sentence space with his name.

But truly: two students. Which does not seem proportional to the passionate manifestations of devotion on regular display in our classroom—to both poetry and our instructor. Only more evidence, I suppose, that no matter the degree of ardor some people profess to feel in their souls for poetry, most of them would stay home to watch *Seinfeld* before they'd lose an hour looking up published articles on metaphor.

In my experience, it is typically the underlings of academic and even earth life—with wild hair and ink-stains and shadows beneath their eyes—who turn out for library instruction. I legitimize this observation, and I would say that A.J. does, too, with dark hollows below his cheekbones, and glossy-black, shoulder-blade-length hair—which I might covet if it didn't contribute so heartily to his imperious academic image.

As I approached the table that A.J., his camera bag, and Peter Breznik shared in the third-floor reference area, A.J. exhaled. "Well, you knew she'd come."

But then he sat in a chair one inch from mine at the long mahogany table, touching my indexes (which felt as violating as it sounds) and attempting to direct me when Peter Breznik would suggest that one of us look up specific periodicals. Peter had given us a thorough handout printed with craft topics, such as metaphor, simile, meter, and repetition, as well as prominent and lesser-known poets to consider. Mainly, he sat across from us at the table, ready to answer our questions.

But even after I managed to slide my chair a few inches away from A.J.'s, he still succeeded in lifting a reference book from my hands and showing me where citations for *Poetry Magazine* began. And when he noticed me scribbling a periodical title beside the words "figurative language" on our handout, he began explaining the "vehicle" and "tenor" of metaphor to me, poetry terms I can't remember not ever knowing.

"For example," A.J. rested his forearms on the table, dipping his head toward mine, "I could say 'the girl's lips are wet rose petals,' and 'lips' would be the *tenor,* while—"

"A.J."—Peter rose to his feet—"why don't you go make a copy of the essay you asked me for in class the other day. I happen to have it with me."

A.J. slowly redirected his gaze from my face to Peter's. "Sure." He reached a finger to the ring of my notebook. "I can do that as soon as we're done with this." He turned to watch me scoot myself and my notebook another six inches away from him.

"Actually, I have to leave here in twenty minutes." Peter extracted a thin stack of papers from a folder he had set on the table. "You should head down to the main-floor copy machines now."

A.J. accepted the papers, whispering, "Save my place, Poetgirl," before slinging his camera bag over his shoulder and making his glistening-haired way to the copy center.

"That guy is . . ." Peter Breznik lowered himself to the chair across from me. ". . . relentless."

I slouched in my seat, trying to appear as though I wasn't itching to shower after sitting beside A.J., or aware of how rugged and tanned Peter's fingers looked as he folded them together on the tabletop, or of how wide his palms were, or that, for one second, I imagined one of his hands at my hip, like Poalo's on Francesca's, in Rodin's sculpture.

With a meek voice that I might have used with a teacher in eighth grade, I told Peter that I was glad for a research review this semester, to which he nodded with easy-going self-deprecation. "Yes. I could see that by how quickly you located every article on my handout." He peered off in the direction A.J. had sauntered for copies.

My heart dropped at his looking away. Suddenly, I saw us exactly as we were, as if my eyes had flown from my body and stared down from the ceiling. On one side of the table, a primly-dressed, would-be-adult girl—wearing a Hello-Kitty bra, for heaven's sake—beneath her white lace blouse and pink cardigan, staring at the daisy chains and rainbows she'd doodled in the margins of her notebook. Thank God she hadn't drawn puckered lips and heart balloons.

But then there was him, sitting kindly and assuredly across from her, all lean muscles and angles and calm beneath a pale green Yosemite t-shirt, a scattering of honey-colored scruff on his face, his eyes bright— not wide and soaking in the whole world as the would-be-adult girl's were, but intentional and direct, assessing how to act, how to take charge of loose ends and move forward.

A Slavic prince and a perpetually distraught French schoolgirl.

I was staring wide-eyed at his jaw when he looked at me. "So, tell me about Anna Swir."

"I like her"—I started scribbling out a rainbow—"but I'm not sure . . . my poems are like hers."

Peter leaned forward against the table so that his strong, blunt-tipped fingers almost skimmed the top edge of my notebook. Maybe if he could just face the opposite direction when he speaks to me, I could better access words in my brain. But no. He had to give me his narrow-eyed listening face. "Well, you're both trying to say big things in plainspoken ways."

"My poems are mainly personal stories." Glancing up, I noticed a whisper of a hook in his nose, a slight twist from center. For one second, I could imagine that I was simply chatting poems with a like-minded student, but then the certainty in the next words he spoke made me feel like I was 14 again, though I don't think he intended that. "You tell personal stories in your poems, while Swir is more abstract. But like you, in quiet moments and brevity, she packs a big punch."

Doodling another daisy-chain in the middle of a notebook page, I could feel my heart slow a little, until Peter asked, "What do you like about her poems? Answering that might be a way to figure out what you could learn from her." I think it was right then that I looked up and noticed a lovely branched vein on his throat that I wanted to touch, or kiss, if I am honest.

"I love that she makes big claims." I tried not to look at his throat again. "She ends one poem with 'How large this bed is / if it has room enough / for such happiness,' which sums up the whole poem, but not in a deflating or predictable way—"

Yes. I quoted lines about a large happy bed to him, and unintentionally called to my mind the image of him lying in one, smiling, beside me.

My face was an inferno. His seemed impossibly lit up with interest in what I was saying.

I inked a leafy vine beneath a hole-punched flower. "Sometimes I feel like I don't claim anything. I shape memories as poems and trust that a reader will take larger ideas from them."

I think he was craning his head toward my notebook, curious about my doodling. "I like that." When we both looked up from my notebook, he said, "I like what you're saying about your poems, I mean. Maybe in your craft essay, you'll examine how Swir gets away with making abstract statements. You're a hell of a writer. What do you plan to do with your English degree?"

I was caught off guard by his compliment—the same one he had paid his mother in his office—and couldn't think just then what one does with an English degree, so I told him I am also a culinary arts major, even though, I didn't tell him, I might forgo that degree and complete two others in Brooklyn.

"Wow. Those fields of study do not seem directly related." His face was half smile, half concern.

Not that I wished A.J. back, but under Peter Breznik's scrutiny, I wondered, *Where is that jerk?*

A student worker was probably reporting him to library authorities for being an ass in the copy center.

"I don't mean that critically," Peter said. "I have no doubt those majors could work together. My guess is your plan is brilliant." Some fissure in my brain's deep matter vaguely registered that he was suggesting nice things about me, but his delivery was so straightforward, so . . . matter of fact—he may as well have said, "My guess is the sun will shine tomorrow," for all his tone changed with the compliment.

I glanced around the reference area to see if A.J. was approaching yet. When it was clear that he wasn't, I told Peter that at first, I couldn't see how writing and food went together, either, but I liked both subjects, and after a semester of classes, I decided I might like writing food books.

"As in recipe books?" he asked, his spell-casting eyes so blue I wanted to pick up my pen and describe them. Cerulean, robin's-egg, sapphire—I'd have to consult a color wheel.

I said, "Well, there would be recipes, but also essays, maybe even some poems—a sort of collage—about the experience of eating. Eating baked goods and pastry, mainly. In one particular city—like my city."

Dipping his chin so slightly, he asked, "And your city is New York?" And because I had extended my leg beneath the table, our ankles bumped, setting whole forests of dendrites in my legs on fire.

"Yes," I managed to say, "the Upper East Side. Manhattan."

Without even knowing that I wonder about his future plans during every class period of Poetry, and sometimes—or several times—between class periods, he said, "I think I might interview in Manhattan. For a teaching job."

"Which school?" I asked. My heart had taken up residence in my throat. I sat there, unable to breathe. As if Peter Breznik teaching history in Manhattan could have any bearing on my existence. As if he would move there and meet me, of all humans, at Tallulah's for pastry and coffee.

And reach across our table for my hand.

But what if I were living in Manhattan in the fall? Wouldn't I tell him at some point this semester that I was transferring to Philbrick for fall semester? Couldn't I offer to show him around? Couldn't we plan to at least eat one lunch together?

He sat back in his library chair, as though he were fatigued by his job search. Or maybe he was fatigued by my conversation. Either way, he answered, "Hadley College. On the Upper West Side. My father's old friend is chair of the history department. If I interview, you'll have to tell me where to find some good coffee."

Yes, I thought, *I'll draw a tiny map on the back of a poem draft, with arrows guiding you to my favorite tree-shaded bench in Central Park, where I'd be waiting for you with croissants and excellent coffee.*

"Tallulah's," I said. "Try Tallulah's for pastry and coffee on the Upper West Side. Most anyone at Hadley could tell you where to find it."

"Tallulah's . . ." Peter sat up to write the name down in his notebook, doing that smiling-not-smiling thing my heart constricts for. Looking up, he asked, "Do you make pastry?"

"Yes." I braved leaning toward the table—and him—an inch. "My mother began teaching me when I was little. But right now, I like baking American cookies. Which might seem less glamorous than French pastry, but . . ." I looked away, allowing the sentence to trail off, thinking that Peter was probably tuned out, mentally drafting a dissertation chapter, but he leaned in himself and said, "But?"

"Well"—I pressed my index finger to a small knot in the wood table, trying to escape his gaze—"a cookie can be . . . sophisticated."

"Like a plainspoken poem."

I gasped before I could stop myself. I'd never connected baking and writing in exactly that way. I closed my mouth and swallowed. "Yes."

"Do you miss New York?" Clearly, my wonder-struck face scared him into changing the subject.

But his question didn't relieve my emotions. I thought of my park bench and Tallulah's and how even Maman always seemed cheerful there.

I tipped my head to *blink, blink, blink* at my notes, just as a short stack of papers whooshed down on the table beside Peter.

A snide voice fractured the silence that followed. "Oh, Breznik. You made Poetgirl cry. You must have told her she has no future in poetry."

"What?" Eyes burning or no, I looked up to find A.J. peering down at me from across the table, one eyebrow arched, as if waiting for me to share in a joke.

Peter stood up. "Actually, that is not at all what I would say to Vivienne about the future and her poetry. I wonder if you might excuse us a moment, A.J." And then, "Vivienne?" He walked toward the nearest row of bookshelves.

Wobbling up from my chair, I slung my unzipped backpack on my shoulder and carried my notebook, handouts, and pen toward him, a lone tear—I could feel it—streaking my cheek. With an awkward lift of one arm, I tried dabbing the tear away before Peter could see, but when he squinted at my face, I knew he had noticed.

"After that guy over there"—he glanced toward A.J.—"homesickness is the absolute worst. I don't so much miss any one place, but sometimes, my family—" He looked down at my armload of school materials. "Here, let me help you load up."

I squeezed my eyes shut as though that might enable me to evaporate. "I'm good," I said, but he reached for my things, anyway, unintentionally skimming his fingers over the back of my hand as I pulled my notebook to my chest. My skin tingled as if showered by Independence-Day sparklers.

Even as I tried not to allow my eyes to meet his, I saw that he smiled as if comforting a friend. "I'll catch you on Wednesday, Vivienne. Take care of yourself, okay?"

I turned for the stairwell, shoving items into my backpack as I walked.

Hillary was alone in our dorm for once when I returned. I kicked off my shoes, flopped onto my bed, curling up like one of those blue-black roly-poly bugs Luc and I used to collect from our rooftop flowerpots.

I was wiping my face and nose on my sheets when Hillary asked if I wanted to talk. I choked out that I had my period and a crush on my graduate instructor, and I was worried that my mother is dying.

"Damn. That's a lot." She lay down beside me, circling her palm on my back. After a few minutes, she broke out a stash of Kit Kats she had saved from her Christmas stocking, and we lay there eating all of them together, Hillary biting the chocolate off the crisp, saying I should try it as practice for kissing.

I might note here that Hillary and I have little in common, except that our binary lifestyles intrigue one another. Deep down, we wish we could swap existences for some discrete block of time, like three hours. I could get a tiny bird-flipping hand tattooed on my breast, earn B's and C+'s without studying or crying, and make-out with cutting-edge kissers, immune to feelings of remorse or anxiety. And I would never care to call home or be called by anyone who resided there.

Conversely, Hillary could entertain herself by wearing plaid skirts and pink cardigans and baking palatable cookies. She could have thick hair long enough to twist up like Princess Leah's (which I would never do, but my hair would allow for Hillary to do that). And, though she confessed it to me only once, she would like to experience homesickness, to have me wake her from a dream during which she is smiling, and I could ask, "What was your dream about?" so that she could sigh and whisper, "Iowa." Or Manhattan, I guess, if she had switched lives with me. And she would like to experience just once what it's like to have a parent call almost every day.

Essentially, we are adoring opposites.

When I told her what had happened at the library meeting, she pretty much laughed her head off. Tossing my Golden-Retriever plush toy in the air, she said, "Vivi, you hare-brain. The graduate instructor for sure doesn't hate you," which filled me for five seconds with euphoric nausea. I wanted to float back to the library and vomit at the same time. Why is attraction a mix of elation and sickness for me?

Once we finished eating a bag of cinnamon bears Hillary had taken from a guy's backpack, she left to listen to a new local band with friends, and I stayed up to write—first a letter to Maman, to tell her I love her and miss talking and have been remembering my seventeenth birthday. She frosted a six-inch round chocolate cake with ganache and piped red poppies, my favorite, around the circumference and the phrase *mon coeur* in the center, and we ate it after dinner at that 76th Street Turkish restaurant. Maman is not particularly nostalgic, especially since the cancer, but I wanted her to know I would always remember that night. Her cake was like a poem she had made for me.

I thought I would fall asleep after writing her, but the library meeting kept playing in my head, so I opened my journal to write this entry. When I write, my whole mind goes quiet. I can hear a slow heartbeat in my ears.

But right now, I can't turn Peter Breznik's words off—

Like a plainspoken poem.

I think I might interview in Manhattan.

I probably should have studied at home tonight. I could teach my own class on library research.

Luc called at 5:07 this morning and asked if he woke me up. I told him *no* in the kind of voice my child self would have said had a frog in it and asked what was wrong with Maman. Hillary hadn't even stirred through the phone's two piercing rings, but once I began whispering, her shadowy bedhead lifted from her pillow to whisper-shout, "Are you kidding me?!"

"Keep your pajamas on," Luc said to me on the phone. Maman had an early appointment—a *check-up,* he stressed—so he thought he would call while she and Papa were out.

I jumped out of bed—tripping over the phone cord, textbooks, stray shoes, and possibly Hillary's Japanese takeout—until I reached my little box of a closet, stretched the phone cord in, banged my knee on my suitcase, and yanked the door shut.

"Do you think the cancer's back?" I asked Luc, inhaling slowly and deep in the closet's pitch dark. I was so happy that Luc had called and so nervous about Maman.

"You should stop worrying," Luc said. "Maman and Papa would never lie to you."

"Vivi?" Hillary's gravelly morning voice called from outside my closet. "Where the hell are you?"

Closing my eyes to tune her out, I said to Luc, "I don't think they'd tell me things they believed to be lies, but they might try to control a situation to protect me. They could keep certain facts from me, like they did the first time Maman had cancer."

"Vivienne!" I could hear Hillary rustling out of her sheets. My head spun in my closet's darkness.

"Maman and Papa want me to finish my studies here, on my own," I told Luc. "They'd do or say anything they could to ensure that."

"And how sad is that for you, Vivi?" The sharp switch of Luc's voice made my face burn. Is he 16 or 17? He has never taken a superior tone with me. "How sad that you *have* to graduate from St. Brigid's College on scholarship. How unjustified for your parents to want that."

Squashed in with my clothes, shoes, suitcase, and even a stack of old textbooks, I tried to avoid smacking my head against a little shelf on the back of my closet door. But with Luc's angry, almost-man voice in my ear, along with the muffled thuds of Hillary stepping on things in the dark, I could barely remain upright. Shuffling my feet backward so that I tipped against the closet's back panel, I asked Luc the most obvious question I could reach in my mind, "Why did you call while they're out?"

"What would you guess?" he asked as Hillary tapped on my closet door. I felt for the latch to crack the door open, but then paused as Luc resumed speaking.

"I called now because I didn't want them to hear me berate you. Stop pestering them, Vivienne. You tire Maman and make Papa frustrated with both her and you. You act like you need an IV stuck into Maman just to keep your blood pumping. She even said that to Papa—she feels like she's your IV. Well, guess what, Vivi? She's not an IV bag! You're exhausting."

His words strangled my breath. I nearly choked on the question— *Maman feels like she's my IV bag?*

With my free arm flailing for the closet-door latch, I lost balance and slammed face-first—well, right-cheek-first—into the little shelf. The door burst open, ejecting me right into Hillary. The phone dropped as my face hit her chest, my whole head ringing.

Hillary is four inches taller than me, as well as mentally and physically sturdier. Without so much as a backward step, she lifted me upright, leaning down in the gray morning light. "What the—" Her fingers tapped the skin below my right eye.

"It's my brother." I bent to pick up the phone as a drumbeat started up high on my cheek.

"Luc?" I said as calmly as possible into the phone. I did not want him to hear me panicking.

Hillary pulled me to her bed, where I sat with the phone to my ear as she stood looking down at me. I still feel terrible for waking her, and I still can't believe how my cheek hurt—how it still hurts, right now, as I'm writing—like the sun pulsing its maximum heat from inside a shoebox.

Luc did not miss a beat of his scolding. "Vivienne." He began like that—I could see the period after my name, blunt and official—as if he were prefacing a treatise between nations. "I hate to tell you this, but life is better here when you're in California. You're just so damn into everyone's business here, and so *needy*—" I was only processing individual words at this point, not larger meaning. All I could think, besides *There are giant exploding stars in my cheek,* was *Luc curses in casual dialogue now?*

Luc kept on filling the silence. "You're always on everyone's back, wanting to talk, making sure everyone's thriving so that you can find courage to exist. You're constantly worried and tense. Wherever you are feels like standing beneath fire-spewing electrical wires in a windstorm. Maman and Papa keep saying that it's good to have quiet—it's good to breathe air without you—and then you have to call from California to check on them every day, spewing your worry into the quiet." He paused as if allowing me space to respond.

But my body had turned cold as ice. I was rocking a little, back and forth with the phone, as Hillary lowered herself to her bed beside me. Face throbbing, I squeezed her hand. I felt warm splashes on my bare thighs and realized that I was crying.

I could not voice any words for Luc.

Which didn't slow him down for a second.

"Can't you ease up and give them some quiet, Vivienne? They've given you everything." How did he sound so adult, so confident? "All they want is some silence. Let their lives be simpler now. Grow up. They've raised you."

I know my parents would never cut me loose in the world for the sake of my absolute autonomy. I know the love between us is true and deep—it is as tangible within my frame as bread and honey are on my tongue. But I also know that my emotional dependence tires them. I am always fretting. A few times at home, when I have relayed my worries to Maman, she has taken her hair in her fists and begged, "Please, Vivienne. Stop talking now." I try her and Papa's patience with my constant monitoring—with my ravening need to make sure we aren't changing any more than we did when Maman had cancer. I know that much of what Luc said must be true—they must want my absence; their lives must be better without me—and that knowledge made my room seem to tilt this morning, when really my head was falling into Hillary's lap.

I felt the same tilting five years ago when Papa finally explained, *Oui. Désolé, Vivienne. Maman a un cancer.* I lay curled on their bed between them in the white eyelet sundress Mémère had helped me pick out at *le marché aux puces* only 48 hours earlier, when the greatest weight in my mind was the question of whether I would see Gabriel at Tante Evelyn's *pâtisserie* before I flew home to New York.

My hand inside Hillary's was trembling. On the phone, I could hear Luc's impatient breath, "Are you there, Vivienne? Are you listening?"

I thought of hissing that he was still our parents' sniveling baby, who knew nothing about me or my relationship with them. I could have shouted that my parents made Maman into my IV bag when they decided to wait to inform me that she had cancer.

I could have asked how my love for our mother justified Luc's unkindness or our father's—a reputedly empathetic physician's—frustration, or his and my mother's relief to be rid of me. But I did what we Lebruns are truly gifted at in conflict, what our forebears have passed down through generations of meticulously coded deoxyribonucleic acid: I refrained. I sat up on the edge of Hillary's bed, took an audible cleansing breath, and said, "Thank you for helping me see things so clearly, Luc. I have been hoping you would call soon."

And of all the sounds he could have made, of all the words he might have arranged into sentences, my little brother only chuckled.

He said, "Awww! Don't turn all chilly now, Viv."

To which I said, "I would prefer that no one on planet earth ever call me that."

And then I placed the telephone on the receiver.

I think I really hurt my cheekbone.

———

Jan. 30, cont.
Noon, a tucked-away bench in the science building

I was broody in Poetry. Yes, that's another thing we Lebruns excel at—we can brood as miserably as E. Brontë's Heathcliff.

Usually, I walk into class wide-eyed, and when Peter Breznik chances to look at me, I smile and blush, as sweetly and shy as an apple blossom. But today—and here I might note that I was wearing Hillary's frayed stonewashed jeans, rolled up four times at the ankle, and a t-shirt printed with a bikini-clad woman sprawled out beneath the words: *She who dies with the best tan wins.* My hair may as well have been threaded strand by strand into an electrical outlet.

Oh, and my cheek was not just bruised, but burgeoning below my right eye like a fist-to-the-face shiner.

Willing my hair to curtain my face, I beelined to my desk and plopped down like I didn't give a shit. I felt like I'd had a knock-down, drag-out fight with my brother, and my appearance and language reflected it.

All through class, I kept my eyes on my notebook, even when Peter Breznik said in a tentative voice that suggested he sensed something was up, "Vivienne, didn't you write a journal entry on Louise Glück's authoritative tone?"

I glared at my pen. "I can't remember." I couldn't summon much interest in a poem's tone—authoritative or otherwise—when just then, my mother could have possibly been disrobing for a breast exam, feeling like my IV bag, and sighing in relief that I am almost not on the same continent as she is.

"Since when does front-row chick forget anything?" a guy on the other side of the room asked. Harrison, I think. Not related to Ford.

And then, from my left, A.J. said, "Bad day for Poetgirl." Which is now a name that a few students besides him have been calling me.

Ignoring the comments, Peter planted his effortless jeans right in front of my desk. "I remember that it was a very good entry, but we'll come back to it."

My eyes shot up without my consent, and there he was, his brow pinched in a suppressed version of alarm as he stared unabashedly at my cheek. I snapped my eyes back to my notepad.

As soon as the bell rang, I grabbed all my things from my desk and planned to essentially dematerialize from the classroom until a gentle but strong hand grabbed my elbow. "Hang on, Vivienne." Peter Breznik hadn't even set down the poetry collection he'd been holding in class. Students trickled from the room with saucer eyes that assured me their ears were pricked for whatever Peter planned to say to me.

He dropped my arm and waited for the classroom to empty. Nodding at my cheek, he asked, "What happened?"

I tapped my fingers along my right cheekbone. It felt tighter than it had when I'd left my room, and now as I write, it feels even tighter. It's throbbing and hot, like a boule not long out of the oven.

The empty classroom thrummed with disquiet.

I spoke to Peter's chest. "I ran into a shelf in my room this morning." *Inside my closet,* I added silently.

Damn my brother.

When I braved looking up, Peter's eyes narrowed in a cautiously-concerned, deep-thinking way. He was clearly assessing my honesty, as new students appeared in the room for their 10 a.m. class, their craned-forward faces instantly curious.

Hefting his bag over his shoulder, Peter touched my elbow again, pointing to the door. "Can we talk in the hall a minute?"

My elbow burned as intensely as my cheek hurt. I followed Peter from the room like a guilty-yet-devoted puppy.

Apparently opting to trust my injury explanation, Peter paused in the hall. "You should get some ice on your eye to help ease the swelling. No one likes wondering if a woman's been hit."

The directness of his statement made me flinch like ice had actually been applied to my face. I stepped back. "As in, hit by a man?"

His face grew incredulous. "Yes, by a man. Why would I tiptoe around that?"

I'm not sure he tiptoes around anything. I think he likes to say what he means. I think I like him to say what he means. You could say, *Peter, are you feeling unwell today?* and however he answered, you'd believe him.

But returning to the sentence about wondering if a woman's been hit. Besides revealing his sound moral character, was he saying that *I* was a woman? Like, from his perspective? And had he really wondered if a man had hurt me? It would be only logical if he had, but still, my mind had to tingle at the thought of him wondering about my well-being, particularly when the people I loved most were supposedly so happy that my being was elsewhere.

His shifting feet interrupted my tingling. "I've been hoping to catch you for a moment after class. I wanted to say I'm sorry about the library meeting last week. I should not have asked personal questions about your family or New York. Or did I offend you in some other way? Push

Anna Swir too hard? You don't have to read her. The last thing I want to be is a clueless academic, or to act like that"—he lifted a hand to tug at his hair, clearly in search of a word—"that . . . guy—that . . . A.J.!" His hand fell. "But sometimes, unwittingly, I say or do things—" He stopped as I heard myself take in a sharp breath. "I shouldn't disparage another student," he said.

I would have helped him write a book called *Disparaging A.J.,* but I had to ask, "Unwittingly?"

"Unintentionally—"

"I know what it means." I didn't need synonyms. I just needed to make sure he had used that word in a sentence. *Unwittingly?* Who ever said that, besides English-gentleman grandfathers, Shakespearean scholars, and courtly love poets? "It's not a word you hear every day."

"Well, there you go," he said. "Sometimes I say things." Yes. Wittingly or unwittingly. And now I had a crush on his vocabulary.

I knew I should be saying he hadn't offended me, or excusing myself to go find a quiet spot where I could think through the breaking news that my parents basically wished for me to establish residency in California— to yank the line from my so-called IV drip—but Peter Breznik's canvas bag strap had fallen diagonally between his pectorals, alerting me to the trim muscular breadth of his chest. I could see the ropy blue veins of his forearms as he shoved his hands into his jean pockets, and I wanted him to hug me.

He drew a tight breath, shrugging. "But . . . you're okay?" The hallway had emptied. I noticed that his shoulders relaxed a little.

The restrained Lebrun in me wanted to say, "Yes, thanks for asking, I'm fine," and mince quietly away, but he was looking at my cheek again with a wary expression, and then at my hair, and then at the woman and the words printed on my t-shirt. Few sentient beings would believe I was fine; and even in my self-pity and despair, I sort of wanted to say more than six words to him. Plus, I looked kind of like a bad-ass, not a schoolgirl, so I said without thinking too hard, "I was just tired last week at the library, but this morning, my brother called to discuss an issue that devolved into family drama."

Right away, I wished I'd said something edgier—like, *My brother pissed me off on the phone earlier.* In retrospect, I realize what I actually said might have sounded slightly more adult. *Très bien, Vivienne,* Maman would have praised—well, she might have praised, in the old days, when she spoke more—*you're developing.*

"Are you heading out?" Peter pointed down the hall. "We could walk for a minute."

I have my feet to thank for falling in step beside him, because my brain, despite its new sadness, was blocked by a storm of endorphins. Peter's hands were still in his jeans pockets, but—curse my endocrine system—I wondered how it might feel for my hand to be held inside one of his.

"Your brother called kind of early, didn't he?" We were approaching the main doors of the building, as students chatted on mauve vinyl benches or in clumps on the floor. From anyone's periphery, Peter Breznik might blend in with us undergrads, but when you face him head-on—or turn your head up like I have to do—the angles of his face are just sharper, grown up, his eyes observant and thoughtful, as though they've seen more, and *see* more, in a given moment.

"He called at 5:07," I said. "The numbers are emblazoned on my retinas."

Peter's head tilted back with a laugh. He held a glass door open for me as I rushed through saying, "Thanks," in a barely audible whisper.

He led the way to the library steps. "I would have been in active REM sleep at 5:07 and threatening to send explosives through the mail if my brother called that early. Was everything all right?"

You have a brother named Tilen, I thought, *a father named Andrej, and a mother named Zara.* I wondered if their second child, Peter, had ever been needy, and if his parents had ever grown tired of him.

But his question surprised me because I'm unaccustomed to directness.

Not wanting to dwell on my family drama, I reverted to Vivienne the Restrained. I said, "Yes, things are good now," though after Luc's phone call, things felt sadder and harder than they had beforehand.

Along the walkway to the steps, leaves shook in the breeze. I wrapped my arms around myself thinking, *That's evolutionary grace—that human beings have two arms long enough to hug themselves.* But even as I thought the words, I knew that a person's own arms aren't enough. A body wants another person's arms to hold it. It does not long to hold as badly as it longs to be held. *Here,* it wants another body to say, *rest here a while.*

Walking up the library steps beside Peter Breznik, I wanted to reach for his arms and wrap them around me. They looked strong and warm and protective. One of his hands could have pressed my hip.

And then, probably because I was lost in my thoughts and had been shuffling around, barely lifting my feet since I hung up the phone on my brother—or maybe because my subconscious had hijacked my legs in a pathetic attempt to get Peter to hold me—I tripped on the last step to the library entrance portico.

I braced myself to slam on my knees, when one of Peter's arms shot around my waist and his other hand grabbed hold of my elbow, pulling me up the last step, alongside a giant stone column.

"Seriously?" I said, stamping my foot. As Peter let go, I touched my shirt where his arm had been. For a split-second he'd held me, and it felt exactly how I'd imagined it would: like stepping into a cottage warmed by a fire as lightning flashed out the windows.

"Sorry!" Peter glanced at my waist. "You just looked like you'd go down if I didn't help." His face had turned to mild alarm and regret.

"No, no!" Could he tell I was trying to catch my breath? "I just feel like the universe is orchestrating my fall today—literally, figuratively, allegorically . . ."

He smiled. Not as if at an overwrought child, but as if he understood me and empathized and thought I was funny.

I only stood there, mortified and shivering, a cold mist beginning to fall outside the library's marble portico.

As I was thinking that Peter would say goodbye, he did something instead that I might have memorialized in a few blazing sentences, which would have sufficed for the whole of this journal entry. But Posterity: By now you must know how I prefer rising action and detail.

At the top of the library steps, Peter opened his romantically-worn canvas satchel and pulled out a heathered-blue sweatshirt. "Right now, at this moment, I'm your friend, Vivienne, not your instructor. You've had a tough morning, and you say you're fine, but I can tell you might be unsteady. It's chilly and you're shivering. Please take this. Just leave it on the back of your chair after class on Friday."

When he tucked his blue sweatshirt over my folded arms, I simply looked down, debating. I could A) politely refuse his clothing and risk suggesting that I didn't want him, even in that moment, to be something more—or different—than my graduate instructor.

But another option—B—was for me to take his sweatshirt and warm myself in it, be held by the sleeves his arms had worn. I could wear it all day and sleep in it and try with all my might to infuse my scent into it, and then leave it for him with a gift of thanks tucked inside and see if he'd catch-hold me again sometime later.

Strike my brother from creation if I didn't suppress what felt like a smile coming on for the first time today and choose option B.

Peter's sweatshirt smells like Dove soap and peppermint.

It might be easier to give my parents space if I had regular access to a caring man's sweatshirt.

Friday, February 1, 1991
9:08 pm., on my bedroom floor, leaning back against my bed

The Philbrick transfer-application arrived today.

I haven't attended class since Wednesday. I look like an abused teen bride. I knew my cheek hit my closet shelf hard, but I never thought for one moment that it would purple and swell like a gorgeous ripe plum on my face.

Anyhow, I'm tired, and I've finished all my assignments for the week. I missed Poetry today and Baking on Thursday, but at least I have Peter Breznik's sweatshirt to console me.

After my shower, I wore my damp hair loose down the back of his sweatshirt, and now it smells like Dove soap and peppermint mixed with apple cider vinegar. I was almost brave enough to wear it to bed, but somehow that seemed too intimate, and wrong, in that it felt like I'd be taking advantage. When at last I lie down with a handsome man's sweatshirt, I want the man to willingly be there, wearing it.

I have not called home since speaking to Luc on Wednesday, and no one, of course, has called me. For Luc to say things to me that he knows would enter my heart as a trowel stabbed in soil suggests that something is not as it should be. True, he might be sister-kind's most sarcastic, most tormenting brother, but he is not cruel; he has never truly wounded me. He has never not wanted me in our home. He is proud of me for summoning courage enough to set off for St. Brigid's, but he has said before, in quiet moments when we've been alone, that he would be proud of me anywhere and would help me do anything, including persuade Maman and Papa to let me transfer to a college in New York. The change in his intent and behavior feels like an alert that life in our apartment might be unraveling, that Luc might feel helpless and believe the one agitation he can help manage is me.

Or maybe this is the man he is growing up to be—fierce, biting, intolerant of another's need. Perhaps he has simply acted on what he hears and observes at home: Maman and Papa are weary; I try their patience; I must be quieted.

I am embarrassed to say that I have often felt like the hub of my family's figurative wheel. I was the one who leapt from my bed to ready Luc and myself for school the entire year that Maman was ill, and I kept doing it, because she was tired in the mornings, until I left for college. While she was sick, I sent Papa's Oxford shirts out for laundering, soaked the dirt stains from Luc's soccer clothes, made Tante Evelyn's *Coq au Vin* and our other favorite meals for dinner.

I held cool cloths to Maman's neck when Papa was at work and she vomited; I steeped her chamomile tea, baked a crusty peasant bread she could always keep down.

Blushingly, I admit that I've wondered how my family manages without me now, but the even more absurd question I ask myself is, *How can I survive without them?* Why do I not feel more autonomous, when all I required during our last major crisis was one therapist and six journals?

But all along, in their minds, my help was unnecessary. I worried needlessly and depleted their energy. I was a dent in our wheel's rim. I was never the hub I supposed myself to be.

I am nonetheless applying to Philbrick.

The Pennsylvania groundhog did not see its shadow today. I'm too gloomy for Spring to come soon.

But I am trying to see myself more clearly, to understand my own fears, and gauge how I might do better, be braver. I keep browsing the leather-bound photo album I filled when I first left for St. Brigid's.

I wish I had more photographs of Maman and me. I have the typical ones—her holding my noodly body against her bare chest a few days after giving birth. Her cheeks are flushed pink, and she appears tired, but so happy and relieved. She is kissing my black curls and raising her sleepy eyes at Papa, who watches behind the camera. Even though I am naked as a jay, every detail looks warm: Maman's breast and her face, her hands on my back, her chestnut hair in a loose heavy braid.

What does a mother think in a moment like that? Certainly not that her days are numbered.

In another rare picture of us together, Maman sits cross-legged in front of a Christmas tree, with toddler me in the nest of her legs. I once told her I vaguely remember that night—the shimmering lights and metallic-red gift wrap, the shiny gold trays filled with sweets. "Vivienne," Maman laughed, "you were too little to remember. You have entered the picture and created a memory." But I don't think so. I also remember the soft warmth of her arms and *"Douce Nuit"* playing scratchily, and you can't see those things in the picture.

I wonder what Maman might see in that image that I can't—what she herself feared, what she hoped for.

Before she had cancer, she would sometimes tell Luc and me how she had wanted more children—a brood of chortling French Catholics passing a deep pot of cassoulet around her table. "But then we would have been *trop gros* for Manhattan," she'd inevitably say, reaching her arms out. *Too big.* "And God knew the Lebruns would be sad not to live in New York." Luc and I would giggle, basking in the undivided sunlight of her attention, oblivious to the loss she might have felt every day.

But if she did feel a loss, few could have guessed it. Back then, she wasn't so reserved. She would cuddle Luc and me in our beds and sing, help our little hands shape pastry. On walks, she would drill us in English and French. She made motherhood a purpose-driven, tender endeavor that I revered as the highest vocation.

For instance, when I was ten, Maman and I babysat our friend Genevieve's baby, who at one point required a bath. I stripped right down and hopped into the water, smoothed the baby girl's bald head with a cloth, rubbed the baby soap on her legs and belly. Maman said, "Vivienne! You are so good with infants. You could grow up to be a cardiologist for children—you could save lives."

To which I said, "Or I could be a mother like you, who loves giving baths to my babies."

Maman smiled at me, blinking, a long time.

But after the cancer, her tenderness abated—not because she didn't feel it, I think, but because she couldn't bear its ache. She had to detach in palpable ways to believe the rest of us could survive if we lost her.

During my first semester at St Brigid's, Maman sent me a small framed print of Mary Cassatt's *Summertime,* in which, presumably, a mother and daughter sit on a skiff on a pond, looking down at something the viewer can't see in the water. The mother is reclined on her elbow, the girl sitting up. They seem close enough to each other, the girl's legs disappearing into the mother's peach skirts. But there is also a distance—a "formal feeling," Emily Dickinson might say—between them. You can sense it in the different angles at which they view the water, in the studious looks on their faces. This mother and daughter do not wax sentimental. If later they discuss what they saw in the water, they do not chit-chat or giggle; they converse. They reflect and expound, pose hypotheses, reach conclusions.

I think my mother sees me and herself that way. At least since she survived cancer.

As I grow older, our pictures become more like Cassatt's painting— no captured embraces or delirious smiles. We are braced for something in the distance.

Maman quietly steers the little boat of my life. Even 3,000 miles away, I feel her directing me over the water. I want to take the oars, to detach to an extent, as Luc says she wishes, but I don't want her to leave the boat—not by distancing herself further, and definitely not by dying.

I can't keep afloat without her.

In a picture I considered leaving safely in my desk drawer at home, Maman and I are standing outside a flower shop in Brooklyn.

I am 15. It is May.

We had taken the train together from Manhattan to visit a seamstress friend of Maman's—Esmée—who lived in a Park Slope Brownstone. I remember brushing my hand through ornamental-pear blossoms in a curb strip before entering Esmée's place to try on two dresses Maman had asked her to make for me—one pale blue, the other just-barely pink. I would leave in five days for Paris.

Walking back to the train, Maman and I passed the flower shop in my picture. Peonies exploded from the storefront—blush, rose, coral, white—in baskets and buckets and even old work boots.

I had brought my little Olympus camera and wanted pictures of the peonies. "Here," the florist opened her shop door, "I'll take a picture of you two together."

I handed her my camera.

The mother and daughter staring out from the picture are smiling, the mother's arms wrapped around her daughter in a tight sideways hug. Neither knows yet that a pearl-sized lump is growing in the otherwise pink tissue of the mother's right breast. Her body is replicating a small garden party of cancer cells, but when she finds out, she will, as I keep writing, convince her husband not to tell their daughter just yet.

Because finally, the solitary fretting girl will be living a summer without her parents in Paris. She will be baking *croissants au miel* and walking *Jardin des Tuileries* in her spring-blue and almost-pink dresses. The first time she hands a tall dark-eyed boy two palmiers over the counter of her aunt's *pâtisserie*, the boy will smile and tell the girl she's pretty. *Tu es jolie.* As though he had known her since kindergarten.

The girl can still hear him say it.

Of course, the mother can't foresee all these details, but she will sense their shape on the horizon and will refuse to thwart their arrival. Because if she does that, she believes, her daughter may never leave home again. And there is so much in the world to leave home for—education, exploration, employment. A misstep now and a future is lost.

Please don't say anything yet. A last, desperate gift of tenderness.

The eleven-year-old son will be fine, but the girl will return home from Paris and spend ten days crunched up on her side, unspeaking, on cushions that line the wide sill of her parents' bedroom window, because if the girl lies in their bed, her every twitch will pain her mother's body.

A few days after the girl finally returns to school, a Sister will announce on the loudspeaker that another Sister the girl hardly knew died of cancer.

The girl will take a hall pass to Attendance with the poise of a candy-striper delivering aspirin, but on the phone with her mother, she will buckle to her knees. Her principal will accompany her home in a taxi. She will not return to school for three months.

But in the picture I keep, no one can possibly know this. Peonies are bursting like fat happy cells.

The daughter is wrapped in her mother's arms. They are smiling, even if the sun in their eyes shines a little too bright. They have Brooklyn's best *éclairs* in a small white paper sack and two dresses the colors of springtime in a large one. The next day, the whole family will attend a concert of Vivaldi's Four Seasons.

Who was that woman? I wonder as I study Maman in the picture.

And who was that girl? She was solitary and fretful, but she did not expect to find Death, blank as the moon, bearing his scythe beside her mother's bed for a year. She believed life went on a long time.

Stay there, I always think at the mother and daughter embracing in front of that flower shop, the peonies puffed out like small cushions.

Stay there and feel the world holding still.

Sunday, February 3, 1991
10:00 p.m., my bedroom desk

In which Maman condescends to call on the telephone.

I wish human beings woke up to announcements like that: *In today's chapter of your life, thus and thus shall transpire. Fini.*

As it is, many things go as I predict, but some things fly up in my face out of nowhere, like bees (or closet ledges) which can sting you or give you honey. Or I guess they can sting you *and* give you honey. So: Painful things can be sweet and sweet things can be painful.

I kind of hate that metaphor.

Nothing sweet can come of my mother's suffering, or of me being here if she is suffering there.

Yesterday evening, Hillary and I pedaled bikes to the coast and set out walking for miles. She kept making me yell as loud as I could into the wind to help me release what she calls my turbulent energy. The coast was practically empty, so we did not get too many condemning stares, although a few passersby looked twice at my cheek.

And then today, miracle of miracles. After Mass, Maman called. I am sure that she meant to appease me, to maintain a semblance of our life as it was last semester, but I can't say she truly succeeded. Her voice was tight, though she laughed once or twice, and she kept trying to end our conversation. We spoke for possibly eight minutes.

I should have accepted her efforts; I should have gag-tied the skeptic in me and been glad for moments to chat while she and I are both still alive and breathing. But self-absorbed mortal that I am, I was sullen. I was fifteen again, hanging my head with my hair in my eyes, grunting *Mm-hm* and *Uh-huh* as fill-ins for *You're not open with me. You don't want me at home. I don't trust you.* The thought did occur to me, as, for possibly fifteen seconds, Maman described visiting The Met Cloisters in last week's snow, that I could decide to act my twenty years and simply tell her what Luc had said to me.

But I think my genes are stacked high against openness and even higher for self-infliction of pain. And also for generalized infliction of pain—on anyone who has hurt me.

I should have been kinder and trusted her words on the phone, even if I couldn't see her face as she said them. She sounded happy to talk to me, and she seemed to have honestly been busy. When I asked for the second or third time what else she'd been doing since I left Manhattan, she was able to supply actual names of friends whose various gatherings she had baked for. She bakes for free, of course, and she's a genius at it. For her, concocting exactly the sweet or savory thing that a dinner, a baby shower, a birthday *fête* needs is like formulating a prescribed medication, and doing it makes her happy.

Just as I began to ask, "What else?", she deflected to me with an uncharacteristic rush of questions. "But how are you, Vivienne? How are your classes? Have you baked something new? Have you been able to spend time with other students?"

I gave her a skeletal report of things, briefly mentioning, to her irrepressible though fleeting delight, that Robert Carson had written me a letter. I did not mention applying to Philbrick or nearly shattering my cheekbone, however, or that I was wearing my graduate instructor's blue sweatshirt for the fifth day in a row.

She and I were Cassatt's mother and daughter on a raft: occupying shared space, keeping lots of important thoughts separate.

"I must go now, Vivienne," Maman said after I told her I liked my poetry class.

I tried one last question. "Would you prefer that I—"

"*J'ai beaucoup à faire,*" she said in a crisp voice that may as well have belonged to a telephone operator.

"You have a lot to do?" I felt like I was calling out to her from behind a closed door. "Maybe you could try to do less—I wish—"

Her oven timer buzzed in the background.

"*Au revoir,* Vivienne. *Ne t'inquiète pas pour moi.*"

Don't worry for me.

My heart began climbing my throat.

But praise Hillary: I imagined yelling into the wind with deep force from my belly, which allowed me to breathe and say un-effusively, "*Je t'aime, Maman,*" before she said, "*Bonne nuit,*" and hung up.

I keep reading that last page.

I want to believe that Maman is well and give her space to enjoy her supposed health, but her increasing avoidance triggers a hitch in my brain, like fingernails on a chalkboard, whenever I almost stop worrying.

Nothing she says feels right to me. Am I obsessing? Papa would say, *Oui, Vivienne. Évidemment.* He'd say I need a neurological evaluation.

But if my obsessing is truly warrantless, why is everyone speaking so little and so harshly? Why don't they all simply laugh at me? Why are they working so obviously to keep me in California?

Luc claims that my distrust frustrates our parents. Well, I arrived at Mass with a toothpaste dribble on my chin and no bra this morning. I'd say they're administering a fair dose of frustration themselves.

Wednesday, February 6, 1991
1:04 p.m., atrium of the science building

Well, Peter Breznik has his sweatshirt back.

I ended up missing classes on Monday. I stayed in my room with my slowly diminishing shiner and completed my transfer application to Philbrick. I even called two of my former writing professors, who, after I explained why I was applying—*my mother's health is uncertain, my heart is set on an integrated master's*—agreed to write my recommendations.

Fortunately, Monday is Hillary's busiest day with classes and work at The Garage, so she wasn't in our room to hear my phone conversations with professors and the St. Brigid's transcript office, or to see me complete forms, write my letter of intent, and assemble my writing sample. The longer I worked, the more certain I felt that I will not say anything to Hillary about Philbrick unless I am accepted—only two percent of all applicants are—and unless I truly decide to transfer.

I do not want Hillary to worry about me or attempt to dissuade me, or to possess information that she might *unwittingly* pass on to others. And selfishly, I do not want her to commit to another roommate for fall semester when I might very well not have sufficient courage to snuff out the light of my parents' vision for my education.

But returning to the clandestine clothing return in Poetry. This morning, I looked like myself again, except for a smattering of violet-blue freckles on my cheek and a slight tender mound of puffiness. I entered the Poetry classroom with Peter Breznik's sweatshirt tied around my waist, which I wondered if he wouldn't appreciate—he might not like the thought of it soaking up pencil marks or crumbs or sticky handprints on chairs, not to mention the idea of my rear-end sitting on top of it. But I didn't want to wad it up in my backpack or transport it to him in a separate bag, so I just walked in with it covering my backside and sat at my desk.

Everyone was joking before class like they always do, guys asking Peter about hiking, and then buxom-blond Julie said, "Oh, Peter! You should take us this summer!" And then a girl with ratted bangs and sea-foam-colored eyeshadow, whose name might be Tiffany, said, "We could go over a weekend," and I thought about saying, "I'm wearing his sweat-shirt." But that, I'm quite sure, he would not have appreciated.

He was chuckling amid the banter as I leaned down to pull my note-book from my backpack, and when I straightened in my seat, he was talking to me. "You seem mostly recovered, Vivienne."

I looked up in time to see him almost-smile as he glanced at his sweatshirt sleeve dangling from my waist.

"Yes, thanks." I bit my lips together.

He breathed in like he might have said something more, but Julie interrupted with "Ohhhh! Vivienne's back! Now when Peter says things too complicatedly"—*Honestly, Julie, is that even a word?*—"Vivienne can translate."

Peter Breznik laughed. At first, I thought he was laughing at me, but then he said, "I've never been told I'm complicated," in that straight-for-ward way he has.

No one would think he was flirting, except maybe Julie, who said, "Complicated's not necessarily bad . . ."

One would have to be literally deaf not to hear the ellipsis in that.

When we were finally all sitting in our workshop circle, Peter said he wanted to discuss William Carlos Williams' decree, "No ideas but in things," by which Williams meant that we understand abstract ideas by conveying them via tangible objects, which is a lot like Peter Breznik's favorite topic: metaphor. He is always bringing it up in new ways.

He said, "Consider the idea of happiness for a moment. What *things* convey happiness for you? Make a list in your notebooks."

The first thing I wrote down was strawberries, because they are bright and cool and sweet, and every May until Maman had cancer, we would drive to Connecticut to pick them. After that, I wrote down lime truffles at Michel's on my family's street. And then I described our street in June when petunias burst from their flowerpots.

And then I saw, as clear as Peter Breznik's blue eyes, Maman crossing the street to our apartment, carrying warm bread and balsamic.

"What about 'grief'?" Peter asked. Seated at a desk, he was crossing out words on a single sheet of lined paper.

The room fell almost as still as winter as students wrote down their grief-things. Of course, right when I heard the word *grief,* I pictured Maman's pale face above a blue-checked hospital gown, tubes punctured into her chest, but when I picked up my pen to write, I simply envisioned myself and wrote—

> *empty beach,*
> *gray sky, a gull circling.*

"So, go," Peter Breznik said. "Read a thing that speaks grief to you, and then the class and I will tell you what larger ideas or feelings resonate." Most students' things evoked loss, death, or suffering—Peter's thing was a dead Canada goose alongside a road, its question-mark neck slumped forward in grass.

After I read, he said, "So for you, Vivienne, grief is loneliness," which, unsurprisingly, sounded self-absorbed when I heard it out loud, but I realized that, yes, grief is loneliness for me, but not the kind you feel after being alone for a few hours, or just wishing you had friends on a weekend.

I clarified. "The loneliness one feels amid a loss or a death, or after a length of suffering."

"I felt that," he said. "A sense of an empty afterward."

Lately, when he and I exchange comments at all, I notice that a couple students make eye contact with each other and appear either disgusted or amused. I think most students find me too serious. I mean, you'd assume that students in an advanced poetry workshop might be somewhat serious, but even the most committed English majors can still view a poetry course as inconsequential as dryer lint.

Straightening in his chair, Peter looked around our circle of desks. "We're always saying 'show don't tell' when we write, but can you articulate why? Saying 'I feel grief' will most likely not resonate with even one reader in any kind of meaningful or physical way. Not many readers, if any at all, will feel grief in their own skin, or sense it in a way they never have—a way that alerts them to our shared human experience of grief, as if for the first time."

I love when he waxes passionate like that. I feel like he is speaking poetry about poetry. I scribbled notes furiously, fighting the urge to prop my elbow on my desk, rest my chin in my palm, and listen.

He continued. God bless his eloquent heart. "But if a writer says grief is a goose slumped in grass, or a gray sky void of all life but a gull"—my mechanical pencil-tip snapped when he connected my grief image to his—"what do you sense about grief that you might not have sensed before?"

I committed to myself to keep my lips pressed together. A.J. spoke up from the desk he always situates beside Peter in our workshop circle, "In regard to the goose, you feel that grief followed something beautiful."

Truly, Peter Breznik coaxes poetry from even the least poetic among us.

"You feel agitated and helpless," a girl named Renée, whose hair is mostly high bangs, said. "You don't want a graceful creature like that to be dead. You want it to fly again."

"And someone could sense that, even if they had never experienced the same grief or loss themselves, right?" Peter leaned forward in his desk. "They would understand the image—the *thing*—and be flooded with the emotion."

I was glad other people could answer insightfully, but whenever it happens, I want to raise my hand and ask Peter, *But you think everything I say is brilliant, right?*

As if he could hear me asking the question, he looked across the circle at me. "But what if I said 'grief is loneliness'?"

I looked at the paper on his desktop. "That's two ideas—grief and loneliness. They're abstractions."

When I glanced up, A.J.'s eyes were shifting between me and Peter, as if he were mentally framing us for a wide-lensed photograph.

Immersed in giving words to ideas about poetry, Peter pressed his palms to his desk and said that abstractions can resonate, too. "Just because some elements of writing—like 'no ideas but in things!'—might hold true a lot of the time doesn't mean they hold true all the time. Sometimes ideas are best expressed as ideas."

"Can you explain that some more?" Julie pointed her pen at him.

I couldn't help but jump in to explain the potentially complicated. "Sometimes you just have to say what you mean. Forget tangible things and metaphor. Just say 'grief is loneliness,' or 'I am alone in my grief.'"

Peter watched me and nodded—I assume in agreement—as the bell rang, and I still had his sweatshirt tied around my waist. I found myself wishing for one flash that he could just tug it off me, and then that tiny thought devolved into a movie-screen-sized image of him pulling me close by my waist and saying something like, "I have an *idea . . .*"

Today is just full of ellipsis.

Students were putting their desks back in rows and stopping up front to chat some more with Peter. No one was paying attention to me. So I untied his sweatshirt and set it over the back of my chair.

Unzipping my backpack, I discreetly withdrew a small gold-tied cellophane bag full of little bittersweet chocolate chip cookies I made in the cooking lab last night. I realize they're totally American, and Peter might prefer more refined treats like—I don't know—a hazelnut wafer, but he is an American citizen, so I'm thinking he can't detest cookies. Plus, they're one thing that holds the idea of happiness for me. And I guess that more than wanting to leave a token of thanks for Peter, I wanted to reveal a small thing about myself. I suppose the cookies were a kind of metaphor.

I shoved the little bag into one of his sweatshirt sleeves—I'd made sure it was too fat to fall through the wrists, and then I dropped a lined 3x5 notecard in, upon which I'd written:

> *Thanks for the sweatshirt.*
> *I stopped shivering.*

I didn't sign my name because who knows? Unexpected things happen, just like I wrote in yesterday's entry. Someone else could get to his sweatshirt first. You think you're doing something sweet, but you could get stung by a girl named Julie, or a would-be erudite named A.J.

It is 4:53 p.m. now. I licked my Philbrick application envelope closed after Poetry and dropped it at Campus Mail. Now I am sitting at a table in the science-building atrium after dozing off in Macronutrients earlier. I love food, but I don't see the point of reducing it to numbers.

Maman's telephone call yesterday feels like a tiny wind-up box in my head. Even between this entry's paragraphs, her words play again and again.

Ne t'inquiète pas pour moi.

I wonder if, since January, she has worried for even one minute about me.

Friday, February 8, 1991
9:14 p.m., leaning over my bedroom desk, having just returned from brushing my teeth

I am struck by what could be the title of a poem to submit in next week's packet—

If I Am Not Who I Thought I Was

Sunday, February 10, 1991
1:07 a.m., under my sheets with a flashlight

Not even going to lead up to this: Robert Carson called five hours ago. As in, somewhere in Pennsylvania, he dialed numbers that signaled the phone in my St. Brigid's dorm room to ring and interrupt my hard-earned poem-writing concentration. I think there should be currents in the phone lines designed to cancel out superfluous efforts at communication like that.

He said, "Hi, is Viviun there?" and right away—well, right after I heard Rocky Balboa holler, *Yo, Adrian!* in my head—I thought, *Robert.*

And then I glanced at the framed representation of Maman and me on the skiff, and thought, *Carson*.

"This is Vivienne." I accented my name properly, and then asked, so that Robert wouldn't know I could recognize his voice, "Who's calling?"

"Viviun!" He sounded like he had just scored a touchdown. "Your mom gave me your number!"

Of course she did. "Gave it to whom?" I held onto the *m* a second.

"This is Robert! Robert Carson!" He sounded cocky but earnest. Try as I might to see him as a slow-to-evolve ape in a Penn-State jacket, I could only envision a dark-haired, muscle-cut duke in a tailcoat, extending a bouquet of flowers on a doorstep. My lamentably romantic heart would now insist I be nice to him.

"Oh. Hey, Robert. How are you?"

"Uh-mazing," he said, thus granting me leeway to be a teeny bit snooty.

"I would expect nothing less," I said.

To which he actually laughed, as if he sort of detected my sarcasm. Which would be fine. I'd be fine if Robert Carson were slightly more astute than I give him credit for. After all, if loftier plans fail, he could be the guy (the man? Robert is 23, I think) who ends up teaching me certain preliminary things about human intimacy.

"But how are *you*, Viviun?"

I decided to give the shortest possible answers and ask focused questions in return. "I'm fine. What made you think to call me?"

Robert's chuckle was a low happy rumble. "Your mother, actually."

The conversation so far was making me a case study for Papa's personal Theory of Escalation—his idea that without constant and deliberate intent and control, human emotion does not generally intensify slowly; it skyrockets.

In this case, already agitated by hearing that Maman had encouraged Robert to call me, I felt flames flood my cheeks and course down my arms until I wondered if I was going to explode. "My mom told you to call me?" When she herself would prefer to hear from me . . . never?!

How can Maman infuriate me so fiercely, yet be one of the few people on earth I would never agree to let die?

"It's okay, Viviun." I felt like Robert was patting my head. "I was with my dad in New York this past weekend, and your mom said you've been needing a friend. I told her I'd make a great friend. I'm very sensitive." In my mind, his eyebrows were waggling, exactly the way Peter Breznik's would never.

Maman had spoken to me two times in four weeks. How did she know what I needed?

I opened my mouth to tell Robert that I felt nothing short of uh-mazing and goodbye-thank-you-for-calling, when I realized that by so doing, I would forgo an opportunity to hear a semi-objective report on my family. "Oh, Maman! She is so caring."

"How cute is it that you call her *Maman?*"

I bit my bottom lip to avoid addressing that comment. "But how did she seem to you? It's funny"—I nearly said, *It's almost ironic,* but felt that might be slightly too much for Robert. (Forgive me, Posterity: I'm prejudiced against men who play football and girls.) So what I said was, "It's funny that Maman worries for me, because I am always worried for her and hoping she's doing well."

My heart was not prepared to warm even .00000001 of a degree toward Robert Carson, but I think it did warm, possibly, with his answer. Apparently, he does notice people beyond himself and is capable of assessing them.

He sighed like a quarterback might after watching a football sail past his head. "Actually, your mom seems tired since you left—just washed out, I guess, and serious. She's been sick before, hasn't she? I think she really misses you. And your brother does for sure—he's less of a smart ass when you're not around. But your dad—well, he's always kind of somber, isn't he? I always figure it's because he's French."

"We're all French," I said and would have been snippier about it if he hadn't just given me what emerged in my head as a clear little Polaroid of my family.

I could see them as though the image were framed on my desk: the soft waves of Maman's dark hair falling slightly unkempt around her pale face, her chin jutting subtly forward in what I've come to recognize as a defiant-yet-hurting way, her body spent by what was possibly a mass production of cells again.

Please say nothing yet, I imagined her whispering to Papa, his eyes two dark stones, his jaw clenched.

"I think you make people brighter, Viviun." Robert distracted me from the scene in my head with words that sounded almost like poetry.

Emotions escalated inside me: relief to finally hear what seemed an honest observation of my family; anger at them for obviously manipulating the truth they were facing at home; sorrow that once again, my parents would not share actual facts with me and that they did not want me near them.

Additionally, I felt irritated that I could hear Robert Carson's voice in my dorm room at all, though I did feel a hint—I mean, infinitesimal traces—of gratitude that he had, in fact, called me.

For one second, I entertained the thought of disappearing to somewhere like Alaska, just to give my parents the utter extreme of what they evidently want from me.

Robert cleared his throat in the long-distance hum of the telephone. "So, Viviun." I could tell he was taking a drastic turn from the topic of my family.

"Yyyyes?" I sounded like a critically ill patient myself, anticipating a two-months-to-live prognosis.

Robert chuckled as though my trepidation were cute. "Do you remember my letter? I'm visiting Stanford in March. I'm not sure of the exact dates yet, but, you know, I thought you might like to hang out a little. It would be nice to talk again. I'll be there for three days." His voice was as suave as a duke's amid a chat on the weather.

I halted in front of the full-length mirror on my closet door and saw that I was wrapped from my shoulders to my knees in the phone cord. "Talk again?" I couldn't help repeating, high and forced, like a parrot. "In California?"

So many questions as I tried to unwind myself from the phone cord: *Three days? In March? Did he really want to see me, or had Maman asked him to see me? Did I want him to want to see me? How tired had Maman truly looked? Had she looked only tired, or also sad?*

"Are you there, Viviun?"

"Yes, sorry—" I stepped from the last loop of phone cord. "When in March again?"

"I don't have the dates pinned down yet. The medical school only gave me a window—probably the first week—"

"Just call a few days before you leave Newark." I had opened the planner on my desk to a March that looked as bare as the Sahara. I squinted at the dates as though some previous commitment might appear. "I guess . . ." I shook my head in a stupor. "I mean, if I have time. We could possibly meet up for coffee—" I paused for a second, suddenly aware that a coffee date might be a small price to pay to hear a little more about my family. Still, I didn't want Robert to think I was eager. "My schedule is pretty full, but—"

"You're not easy, are you, Lebrun?" Robert interrupted with a voice that didn't sound ironic or rhetorical.

"Not usually," I answered honestly.

"Well, lucky for us, I'm a strategic genius."

"And I'm an everyday genius." I didn't think before voicing the words.

"I know," Robert said. "That's what makes you so challenging."

I thought about laughing. After all, receiving a semi-seductive-though-chauvinistic compliment from an acclaimed college quarterback isn't exactly painful. It sort of felt like a ribbon curling up in my belly.

"I'll be in touch in early March, then, Viviun. Good talk."

And just like that, I was a teammate he'd slapped on the butt.

"Please tell my mother I'm thriving."

I have more to write about, but it's already 2:30 a.m. I'm falling asleep between words.

How will I   avoid seeing   Ro—

———

Monday, February 11, 1991
10:24 p.m., empty main-floor reference of the library

Last night marks a seismic shift from what I used to call normal.

After Robert confirmed what I've suspected about Maman's health, I've decided to give her and Papa what Luc says they want—what Maman, without even voicing a word on the subject, made clear she would prefer when she called me: my total immutable silence.

I have not decided if I will agree to meet up with Robert in March, however. That will have to be a gametime decision.

What if—if we saw each other—he wanted to kiss me? Would I let him? I am not so prejudiced against football players that I can't admit that Robert is obviously kinder and more astute than I give him credit for. And before losing my wits to the bottomless depths of Peter Breznik's blue eyes, I always imagined myself enamored of brown eyes, like Gabriel's in Paris. Like Robert's.

I keep wanting to hold out for Peter, though. After all, odds might be approximately five hundred billion to one that by the time Robert arrives, Peter will have pulled me into shadows between library shelves and kissed my face off.

That is technically still a small chance.

As for my parents, I do not have the courage to disappear to someplace like Alaska, namely because of bears, hunger, cold, and the potential difficulty of finding sound shelter, but I do like the idea of disappearing by silence—as far as my family is concerned, that is.

Walking beneath the breezy sycamores from the cafeteria to our dorm after dinner this evening, I told Hillary I was cutting my heartstrings.

She stamped on a fallen leaf. "Just hearing that makes my left boob hurt."

"My parents hate that I worry so much and pester them about my mom's health," I said. "Which is funny because something is definitely up with her health. But they want me to be less dependent on them. For my . . ." I couldn't decide on the words. *Emotional Health? Emotional maturity?* I went with ". . . my emotional stability."

"If I detach," I clapped my hands together for emphasis, "I'll feel stronger. What they say or don't say—what's happening, what isn't . . . None of it will hurt me so much. I'll just cut the heartstrings. Pull the IV that Luc says I've attached to our mother."

An egg-yolk of sun was inching down a pink horizon. I envisioned my parent-dependent self slipping away.

Hillary slowed down a little, staring into the sunset. "I'm not sure a loving person like you should disconnect from your family like that."

I stopped to look at her. "But you're relatively loving, and you disconnect from your family."

"Not intentionally." She guided me by my elbow along the sidewalk. "No one in my family would even get your IV analogy, and none of us have any heartstrings. And how would you cut yours, anyway? I mean, figuratively."

"I'd stop calling them." Tugging my arm away from Hillary, I folded it over my other arm, around myself. "I'd stop writing them. I'd stop answering their calls for a few weeks. I'd give them what they want— complete silence. A daughter who doesn't need them for her happiness or survival."

We turned from the sunset toward our building.

"And you'd be doing that to lighten everyone's hearts, so to speak. To be more independent. Not to piss off the people you love more than anything? The people who love *you* more than anything?"

What makes Hillary so smart? Is it merely the year between us? Is it that she doesn't have heartstrings? No one she's not really attached to has almost died?

"They view me as a parasite," I said, "a wood tick."

"You inject them with love?"

"And insanity."

As we approached the steps to our building's front door, Hillary stopped as though a hedge had shot up before her. "What if someone from your family calls to tell you something important? What if your mom is sick or gets sick, and she or your dad calls to tell you?"

I marched up one step to our dorm before whirling back to her. "But that's the whole point—something is happening. Shutting me out is *something happening*. If they decide to tell me what that is, they'll leave a message explaining, and I'll call them back. Or they'll wait to tell me in April."

Hillary began digging in her purse. "Cut your heartstrings." She looked up, holding a pack of Neccos. "See how it goes for you. And for them. Maybe you'll feel stronger. Maybe it will calm everyone down." She zipped her purse closed with a flick of her wrist. "If it backfires, you can always come to me for candy."

Inside our room, Hillary found Junior Mints in her sock drawer, which we ate with the Neccos, lying cross-ways on my bed, our legs stretched up the wall so that our heels tapped the cool pane of our window.

When the phone rang, Hillary turned her face to me, her eyebrows a five-second study of disbelief and disappointment. "You're really doing this?"

"Snip," I made scissor-fingers over my heart.

The caller was only a love-starved guitarist looking to meet up with Hillary.

Even as I recount my plan, I know it is childish. I know it will devastate me. It is not an act of independence; it is an act born of hurt, an act of retaliation, because I depend on my family and care for them so much. I should bear up like a good Catholic and endure the remaining eleven weeks of the semester. I should endeavor to grow up and angle my way back into my parents' good graces, so that they won't handcuff me to a seat inside a California-bound airplane the day after I tell them I intend to transfer to Philbrick.

Eleven weeks of the semester isn't even much time, but when I think of it as a potentially large wedge in the imaginary pie chart that I fear might represent the rest of Maman's life, my lungs feel sucked dry of oxygen.

Maman as she is now would never allow herself to grow teary-eyed over eleven lost weeks together, but I might cry myself a small koi pond in which all the fish glow a melancholy blue.

So I guess I'll just punish all of us.

If, by some irrational chance, Robert is right and I do make some people, like my family, feel brighter, I guess those people might start to feel dimmer.

I am losing my sparkle.

———

Wednesday, February 13, 1991
11:38 a.m., sitting on the library steps while the sun is out
10 days since I spoke to Maman, two days since I severed my heartstrings

Another day of Poetry, and I assume Peter Breznik took his sweatshirt back after class last Wednesday. He did not acknowledge my presence today—I don't know if that was deliberate. Most likely, it was simply another day of class for him. In my head, I stick out in the classroom as if I am draped in neon-green duct tape and cow bells, but from his perspective, I am probably another student who will recede into gray in his brain within ten minutes of the semester ending, even if I did almost sleep in his sweatshirt.

Still, when I sort of nearly raised my hand to say something about how a Polish poet named Wisława Szymborska had managed to render a poem called "Reality Demands" both personal and political, he called on a girl next to Tiffany, which seemed somehow deliberate.

I felt slightly morose throughout our discussion, though I still marked up my book and took notes like a dictation secretary on speed. Just before the bell rang, Peter Breznik handed back the most recent batch of poems we'd submitted. In my packet, I'd included my latest, "If I Am Not Who I Thought I Was," in which I set out trying to emulate Anna Swir by crafting absurd but generalized statements, and I don't know—even though it was absurd, it still felt overly personal. Since the poem is resting, along with Peter Breznik's response, next to my journal as I write, I can copy it—

If I Am Not Who I Thought I Was

I would not catch the bus to Manhattan.
I would un-bake the bread, unbraid
my hair. You and I could sail a patched raft
to Alaska. If I fell off, a humpback
would save me. If I slept till tomorrow, you
would lie down beside me. When enough days
had passed, you would pull me to shore
by my wrist, the night so quiet,
we could hear the stars ringing.

As I drafted, I told myself I was writing about me and Maman, but now that I read it again, I wonder. Or maybe I don't wonder—maybe I just pray that Peter Breznik did not wonder if it was about him. But why would he? I am tucking his response to my poem between the pages of this entry as a kind of early Valentine to myself.

It is sort of an intimate exchange—me giving him poems and him writing responses. As I write, I anticipate what he might think—about what I'm writing, i.e. *will he like it?*—but also about what he might think of me, as a writer and as a person. If I write that I have imagined my own soul departing this life through the wire filaments of a lightbulb, will Peter Breznik find that description surprising? Will he think I have a brilliant mind for absurdity? Would he ever whisper against my hair, *Vivienne, promise me you'll never think of departing?* I make poem decisions based on how I wish he could respond.

And when I read his responses, I can't stop myself from wondering if he ever means some feeling or idea beyond the black and white definitions of his words. When he wrote that he hurt inside and out as he read my poem about a dream of my mother rolling me as flat as pastry dough, did he mean that the imagery merely triggered corresponding physical sensations? Or did he mean to suggest that his heart ached for my aching, that if it were permissible, he would hold me?

Typically, he begins his responses to me with *Hello, Vivienne*—or *I was so glad to read these poems, Vivienne,* but in his latest response, he calls me *Dear.* And while I sat immobilized in the library for five minutes after reading that word attached to my name, wondering if he might mean it tenderly, I can only assume he addresses all his students that way. Responses must come to feel cursory—one falls into habit, opening with *Hello* to the first six students, and then shifting to *Dear* simply to shake off the tedium. I know he must feel that—he writes at least a half-page for everyone. Even so, as Peter handed his response to me in class today, A.J. glimpsed the length of it, waited for Peter to pass by, and could not refrain from lowering his thin lips toward my head. "If your poems require that much ink to correct, you should probably settle for an office-assistant job, Poetgirl."

A.J. should move to L.A. and audition for every degenerate-creep role available.

Here is Peter's latest response, folded inside my journal—

Dear Vivienne—

I can tell you are learning from Anna Swir—you are not trying to relay a personal story, but to convey acute personal emotion via enchantingly vivid hypothetical statements. Though your poem is still personal in that tender way that is so unique to you, I do sense that you are working to reach beyond yourself by addressing a question—not just one personal memory—that is common to human experience. As you revise, you might consider the following:

1. *Who is the "you" that the speaker of your poem addresses? Specifying this might enable readers to connect more viscerally to the poem. Is the addressed "you" a friend, a family member, a lover? Right now, I am unsure how to focus the poem's sense of longing. I think the speaker is addressing a lover, but I feel that you have left this unclear, and so I am unsure of how to relate. I believe I simply need greater clarity.*

2. *Who is the poem's speaker in relation to the more spontaneous (reckless? adventurous?) person she says she would be if she is not who she thought she was (this sentence feels like a riddle—I hope it makes sense to you)? I wonder if the speaker's new vision can't effectively resonate with me if I don't understand her old view. The poem's vision is quiet, sensual, magical. I would very much like to know more about the speaker.*

I hope my comments do not overwhelm you. In the end, I think you can address my concerns with just a few lines and simple clarification. As with all your work, I look forward to reading where revision takes you.

Please be in touch with your concerns and/ or questions.

Another vibrant poem—

Peter

Do you see the ambiguity I wrestle with, Posterity?

I wish I could submit a reply. I would write—

Dear Peter Breznik—

Thank you so much for your response to my poem. I think you found the issue and imagery compelling, but I understand that the poem must nevertheless be spliced and reassembled, with greater specificity and context.

As I know without question—and believe you must suspect at some level—I do not have the emotional fortitude to articulate my questions and concerns to you in your office; hence, I will endeavor to capture them here, where your eyes will never catch sight of them:

1. *When you say, "in a tender way that is so unique to you," do you mean to suggest that my tenderness resonates with you, and that you, in return, feel tenderness when you read me? And how would you classify this tenderness? Would you have a moment to specify?*

2. *Yes. The "you" in this poem is problematic. Allow me to explain why this is: I have a mother complex. I am not sure that this is an actual, documented complex, at least in the way I experience it, but nearly everything I write might be about or addressed to my mother in some way. As I drafted this poem, I tried to believe I was speaking to her (I should clarify: She is possibly dying), but I knew in my heart that I was speaking to you. I wonder if you could tell me if that, too, resonates with you, or if it unproductively exceeds the scope of your ability to relate or empathize. Once you've provided that information, I can revise accordingly. And I would be happy (though let's face it, also terrified) to call you my 'lover.'*

3. *In regard to the speaker-of-this-poem's existential crisis, i.e. who she thinks she is vs. who she might be: When you say you would "very much like to know more" about said speaker, are you saying that you, yourself, would like to know more about me, the poem's writer, or simply more about the fictional construct we writers call "the speaker"? Because if you would like to know more about me, the real writer, I would insert different fragmented details, such as: Everything you (as in you, my instructor) say makes me want to be smarter and braver, more worldly and more talented. Or maybe I would say that if I am not the devoted heart of my family that I believed I was for so long, I might persuade myself to leave them and travel the world with you. Or I could stay with you, and you*

could be my axis. But surely you can see: My strongest revision depends on you clarifying.

Oh, and

4. *Have you decided to interview in Manhattan yet? No doubt your father's friend the department chair would be happy to show you the city, but does he know enough about bookshops and bakeries? Would he have time to sit in Central Park's East Meadow with you, sharing a basket of little cakes he had made, while the two of you read and/or drafted poems together? Would he allow you to bend to kiss him as evening's cool light breathed out through the city? Just know that I would, if you moved there.*

Like you, I hope my response is not overwhelming. If you have questions and/or concerns, I would prefer you write them down, as I am convinced a certain spell was cast upon your eyes at birth, and I do not trust myself to keep a coherent thought in my head, beyond Should we kiss?*, as they look at me.*

Mes amitiés—

Your student of poetry—

Vivienne

Happy Valentine's Day to him.
Must run. Already three minutes late to Romantic Poetry.
But last thing—while his response gives rise to great stirring swells of desire and inquiry in my soul, I still have to ask: How could he not have mentioned his sweatshirt?

———

Friday, February 15, 1991
7:27 p.m., Café des Palmiers, with an éclair
12 days since I spoke to Maman, four days since I cut my heartstrings

Today made up for the fact that I spent Valentine's Day researching descriptive-meditative-poem structure in the library. And also for the fact that my family did not send a card with a box full of pink *petits fours* in the mail as they have since I started school here. Love killers. Why do I feel guilty for not dialing their phone number, when one can only assume that they think of tweezing their eyebrows before they stoop to thinking of me?

Prior to workshopping in Poetry earlier, students turned into journalists firing questions at Peter Breznik as though he were St. Valentine reincarnated.

Though Peter always seems to cringe at personal questions— *Ummmm . . . haven't you asked that already? You really want to know that? No. Not answering that. What???*—he typically relents to answering most inquiries and must feel some zing of pleasure, or at least a gentle wash of gratification, knowing that he is of such spirited interest to one small classroom of humans.

Today's Q & A went approximately like this:

> Q: Did you do anything for Valentine's Day, Peter?
> A: What? No. That's not a day in Yugoslavia.
> Q: But you said you're American. Wouldn't your girlfriend expect you to celebrate the holiday?
> Q: Wouldn't you at least give her flowers?
> A: Who? My Valentine? Possibly. If she were American and expected flowers.
> Q: So she's not American?
> Q: And you're not romantic?
> A: Who's not American? I think I'm romantic. Are you guys ready to workshop?
> Q: Is your girlfriend Yugoslavian?
> A: Let's arrange the desks for workshopping. What time is it, anyway? Look—we're boring Vivienne.

I sat up so fast, a poem I'd been working on flew to the floor. My heart started up with its nervous pumping. "Wait, no. I'm not bored. I'm just listening." *My eardrums throb from listening so hard,* I could have added. *And do you have a girlfriend, Peter Breznik?*

And if he did have a girlfriend, I thought, how would I summon the will to go on, to keep eating and sleeping and not communicating with my family, and keep writing poems about my mother but mostly about Peter? I glanced at Julie and wished she could ask my questions.

"I bet Poetgirl's full of questions," A.J. snidely-but-correctly guessed.

Students began arranging desks in a circle as Peter picked my fallen poem up off the floor. He glanced at it before setting it on my desk. "Anything you'd like to ask, Vivienne?"

A host of questions scrolled through my mind in fast motion: *Girlfriend or no, could you ever envision your hand on my hip? Is 20 years old too young for you? Any news on the position in New York?*

Peter never talks much about his job search in class, but he has mentioned Ljubljana and St. Brigid's, so I felt okay about asking the question that looms like a distant mushroom cloud in my mind, "Do you think you'll decide to teach in Ljubljana?"

His fingers brushed over my desktop as he turned to an empty desk next to mine in the circle. Sitting beside me (yes. I wrote that, Posterity: Peter Breznik SAT BESIDE ME), he spoke loud enough for only those listening to hear, "I don't know yet. But I think teaching in Ljubljana could be a good thing." He looked suddenly pensive, perhaps studying a map of his life inside himself. "I'm still interviewing for positions here at St. Brigid's, and"—he knocked a fist on a corner of my desk, which felt like he was knocking on a door to my heart—"I still might interview at Hadley."

I looked down at my desk, noticing that the workshop circle had quieted. *Why only 'might'?* I wanted to ask, wishing I were beguiling and assertive enough to convince him to consider New York. The way Julie, sitting across from me, would have.

"But in the meantime," Peter resumed his more teacherly volume, "I like your poem title, Vivienne."

I glanced at the poem he had placed on my desk—"What Can I Blame Her for? Even My Body—". I was trying out a fragmented title that connected to the first line of the poem—not Anna Swir-ish at all.

"It makes me feel like you intend to say something." Peter lifted his hand as if he might drop it on my poem for emphasis, but then he pulled it back and addressed the class. "Let's examine titles today."

Ah, Peter Breznik. Sometimes you feel like the title of everything.

I can imagine typing "Peter" as a poem title in my current life's Table of Contents. It would appear right below the essay, "Maman, Have You Thought to Call Me?" and a few titles above the very short story, "He Sat Beside Her the Day after Valentines' Day."

I could barely feel my extremities with Peter's hands one foot away from mine during workshop, or hear anything except a question in my head that could serve as the first few lines of the poem entitled "Peter"—

> *Imagine you got to know me*
> *and even like me a little. Could you choose New York*
> *over California and Yugoslavia?*

———

Wednesday, February 20, 1991
11:36 p.m., almost dozing over my bed pillow, but not. The telephone has not even rung tonight

I have not found a minute to journal this week, but I wanted to record a few things before the day ends—

1.

Before class this morning, Peter Breznik stood at the front table pulling things from his canvas satchel, as if in preparation for discussion: a few poetry collections—one by Jorie Graham, whom I consistently cite in responses; a romantically-worn (like his satchel) leather-bound notebook; one pen and two pencils; a stack of marked up drafts and responses; and then—when I saw it, I jammed the tip of my pen beneath my thumbnail—an empty gold-tied cellophane bag. "What was in that?" Julie asked, as he smoothed the bag flat and pressed it between pages of Jorie Graham's collection.

He glanced up, but not quite at me. Usually, I would purposefully not be looking at him, but right then, I could not look at anything else. He started pushing the classroom's front table out of the way for our workshop. "It was full of sophisticated little chocolate chip cookies."

My whole life, I've thought a man's face was his greatest attracting quality, but when I dared look at Peter Breznik, as I did for about ten seconds today, I realized there's more to attraction. For example, the way a man can so obviously communicate a private message, such as, "I got my sweatshirt and liked your cookies," to an introvert, while at the same time speaking so nonchalantly and directly with an extrovert like Julie, made me want to privately kiss Peter Breznik speechless. That is, at a later date, perhaps when I have had more practice kissing.

2.

After that, workshop was awkward and anticlimactic. A.J. had written about an intimate encounter he'd presumably had, and students were trying to act expert about it, telling A.J. the descriptions were accurate, so that everyone would know they had seen similar things, in similarly sexual contexts.

Peter was tipping back in his chair, uncharacteristically quiet, but occasionally making unusually critical comments like, "I don't even get that description," in a perplexed yet confident voice that made the just-barely women blush and a few of the so-called men snicker.

I sat in the circle feeling sparkle-less (despite lingering embers from the sophisticated chocolate chip cookie affair), praying no one would remember me, because if anyone was unqualified to comment on the poem's context or description, it was me. But of course, Peter Breznik insisted on hearing from everyone. "What about you, Vivienne? You're quiet today."

I hunched over my copy of the poem as though I were addressing it. "I'm just not getting its purpose. Rhetorically, I mean. Is the speaker of this poem praising the woman or the moment, or just love—or, um . . . intimacy—in general, like maybe John Donne would have? Or is the speaker elegizing the woman he's describing? Or is he simply making her a sexual object?" I could hear the wall-clock ticking and feel my face burn, because I'd been put on the spot, but also because I had noticed the graceful arc of Peter's collarbone disappearing beneath the neck of his golf shirt.

I went on as if it were my scholarly duty to fill up the silence. "If there's no sure rhetorical purpose, it just kind of reads like . . . pornography."

A few chairs to my left, A.J. scoffed. He lowered his voice for whomever was next to him, but anyone could have heard him. "As if she'd even know what I'm writing about."

Peter tipped forward in his chair and stood up, consulting his watch. "That's a sound reading—" He glanced at me; I glanced at his collarbone. "Right now, A.J., these descriptions do little beyond titillate readers who claim to understand them, and they objectify the woman whom the speaker of the poem claims to"—his suntanned fingers made air-quotes— "'caress in his heart.' I'd say you have some revision to do."

3.

Following that, we took the last 15 minutes of class to write odes to *actual*—Peter stressed the words—*everyday objects*. The hopeless but inexperienced romantic in me blushingly wondered if he was scribbling away in his journal an ode to bittersweet chocolate chip cookies, but when he shared what he had written, it was a brief piece about his grandmother's knitting needles, and not at all sentimental. He seamlessly (my pun) connected to the "rough weave" of her birth country, and how he wished he could help unpick it, "stitch by flawed stitch."

When he reads his own work, his face goes tight and a single sharp crease appears between his eyebrows. I feel like he is having a conversation with himself—*Is that the right word? Have I conveyed that idea?*—and I am torn between wanting to press the crease smooth with my thumb or enter his head to listen.

I shared a haiku praising chocolate.

4.

Just before the bell, Peter returned his responses to our craft essays. In addition to squeezing thoughtful questions and ideas about Anna Swir's poem "I Knocked My Head Against the Wall" between my paragraphs and into the page margins, he printed clearly in lines, like a poem, at the top of the page:

> *Dear Vivienne—Thanks*
> *for the cookies. I'm glad*
> *you stopped shivering.*
> *Keep steady.*
>
> *- P*

Once seated in the library, I folded the whole page so that it fit in my skirt pocket, and I just kept it there at my hip, like a kiss, all day.

5.

Maman left a message on our answering machine last night. "*Bonsoir,* Vivienne. Call me this evening, please. *Merci.*"

It has been 17 days since I spoke to my mother.

———

Thursday, February 21, 1991
3:42 p.m., on a blanket under a sycamore outside our dorm, sun again
Another day since I spoke to Maman

March is approaching, and just now I remembered that Robert is coming. I told him to call before leaving New Jersey, but what if he doesn't? Or what if he calls but doesn't leave a message?

What if he appears unannounced on this campus? He has my address on a Joker card. I didn't think of it at the time, but that card presented a perfect opportunity for me to be an actual joker—a quicker thinker would have scribbled a false address.

But now the joke is on me. Robert can bypass the phone we never answer and show up outside our dorm.

Maybe—please God—he's decided against Stanford and isn't coming at all.

Or maybe he's perceived that I'd be a primitive kisser.

If only.

———

Friday, February 22, 1991
10:53 a.m., a desk wedged in a corner of the library basement
Another day

Twenty minutes ago, raven hair aglow in the Oppen Building's fluorescent light, A.J. approached where I was drafting an essay on a bench near a window and asked if we were cool after Wednesday.

"Wednesday?" I shut my notebook.

He set his camera bag on the floor before sitting down on my bench. I tilted as far away as possible.

"Yeah, you know—in Poetry? Peter was pissed at me."

Posterity: I'm not always too quick on the uptake. Case in point: I asked, "Peter?"

"Okay . . ." A.J. said. "Clearly, you're mostly book smart. You know? Peter, dashing grad student—"

"The instructor?" I felt a skin-prickling need to speak as generically as possible.

A.J. peered at the flush I could feel on my cheeks. "Please. The one you wish would seduce you inside a custodial closet?"

"What?" I scooted down the bench till half my rear-end slid off.

"*Riiiight.*" His eyes rolled. "You remember the 'objectifying'"—air quotes—"poem I wrote?"

"And that completely dissolute thing you said—" I teetered on the edge of the bench.

"Yeah, that. You were commenting on my poem—"

"As a sound-minded reader—"

"And I was commenting on you. Because I was offended, and you're a hot-ass smarty-pants, obviously begging for a guy to unbutton that—"

"Keep your apology—" I jolted to my feet. "You asshole!"

I think that last bit had to do with my acute lack of sparkle.

Hauling my backpack off the floor, unzipped and overflowing, I bear-hugged it to my chest as I marched toward the building's glass doors, regrettably not fast enough to miss hearing A.J. "Everyone can tell how bad you want Peter."

So now I am hiding in the library basement. I can't cry; I can't even laugh hysterically. I want to scream into the air vent to the right of this desk to release my mortified energy.

I want a man like Peter Breznik to hold me. In a tree swing, at the coast, on a blanket over grass. I anticipate the heat and tingling.

But I also want to be held without sparks—that is, quietly, like the marble woman in Rodin's *Hand of God*, the way she is curled in the rough-sculpted hand, obviously unfinished, resting.

Wanting. That word. The dark way A.J. said it. I would want Peter Breznik in the dark and in the light.

Can everyone tell that I want him?

———

Sunday, February 24, 1991
5:52 p.m., waiting on my bed for Hillary to arrive home and drive us
far away for dinner
Not counting days since I spoke to Maman

Even though the main things my brain wanted to do today were—

1. wonder what my family was thinking at any moment I thought of them—if my parents were feeling worried, enraged, sad, remorseful, penitent, relieved, etc., in regard to my not calling them, and if they would ever forgive me;

2. think of friends and/or doctors I could try to call in New York this week to tease out information about Maman;

3. telephone Philbrick Admissions and leave a message asking if any minds have been blown by my application yet;

4. vicariously experience, via imagination, the bittersweet jolt in Peter Breznik's mouth as he ate the chocolate chip cookies I made for him;

5. report A.J. to Campus Security

—I have managed to think about one other thing.

All the faces I see in a day are caught in some subtle emotion— cheerfulness, perplexity, hangover, stress—made visible by the constellation of feelings and ideas inside them.

Maybe one person was kissed under a streetlight last night and another was handed a speeding ticket. Maybe a girl found out she was pregnant.

So much happens to and inside every human being on this planet— it's as if we are all small infinite worlds. And how do we connect? How do we come to see each other's constellations?

Peter Breznik (many thoughts lead to him) says poems are one way to connect.

I say food is another. I think every baked good and poem is a world. When you create one, you hand a person a view of the stars within you. When you eat someone's bread or read someone's poem, you walk the roads inside them—their memories, their joys, their sadnesses.

In thinking about the space between people and the ways we connect, I began another poem about Maman—

> *First, there is the question of distance—*
> *the millimeters through the breast to the tumor, the diameter*
> *of the tumor in the breast.*
> *Measurement, incision, stitch.*
> *How many steps to the softest chair, to the daughter's desk—*

I don't know what comes next—maybe mention of a poem Maman read me, or a cake she baked. The poem doesn't sound like Anna Swir. I wonder if the scope is too personal, though "distance" obviously serves as a metaphor. Peter is always saying to expand, to think larger, to resist what comes easy.

I just look at him while he talks and think, *Close the distance already.*

Monday, February 25, 1991
So late. Almost asleep in my bed
Why pretend I'm not counting? 22 days since I spoke to her

Papa left two messages tonight, both the same, word for word, on our machine: *Vivienne. C'est Papa. Et-tu vivante? Rappelle-moi, s'il te plaît. Tout suite.*

He asks if I'm merely alive? Clearly, his expectations of me are diminishing. Whatever happened to *How are your classes, Vivienne? What are you writing?,* and his inevitable joke, *Are you sure you don't want to be a neurologist?* Apparently, Papa's main concern now is that I'm taking in enough nutrients to survive.

I guess he'll see for himself in April.

In the meantime, I intend to perfect the art of the blank face in my poetry class, so that everyone can forget I want Peter.

Before entering the classroom today, I thought consciously through all the features I could name on my face—forehead, brows, eyelids, cheeks, nose, lips, chin, etc. I tried to mentally isolate each one and relax.

It must somewhat be working, because Peter did not say hello to me today, although the aquamarine-eyeshadow girl who sits beside me, whose name is actually not Tiffany, but Stephanie, leaned into my ear to ask, "Are you sad, Vivienne?", after which Peter's honey-gold head inclined toward us for three seconds as if he had possibly heard, but I said in a voice as flat as the American prairie, "I'm great, Stephanie. Thanks for asking."

I don't want Peter to feel like I hate him, but I want to change public perception. It is one thing for a female student to objectively think that her beautiful male instructor is . . . well, beautiful, but it is entirely another for her to publicly reveal in her face what she's thinking—to be, as a poet might say, "easy to read." If we are all walking the planet as discrete and variously shaped poems, the most obvious poem would be the least interesting, as well as the easiest to laugh at, judge, or discard.

I would like to be known as unreadable.

That being said, there is nonetheless a poem in my head that I'm drafting for Peter—

Love, I have never been loved
the way I want you
to love me—

As for other things I'm perfecting: For my Science of Baking project, I have committed to perfecting the chocolate chip cookie.

I wonder if Robert will call soon or ambush me on campus with a visit.

Tuesday, February 26, 1991
9:14 p.m., third floor, library Humanities reference area

Each day I wake up and cross myself: *Forgive me, Father, for I have sinned.*

It's been 23 days since I stonewalled my parents.

I heard Hillary speaking gently into the phone as I entered our room two nights ago—*Maybe just give her a week or two*, or something, but she insisted that she was advising a Garage regular named Jake, who had been caught cutting-edge-kissing a girl who was not the girl he now needed to give space to.

In other news, I have been rewarding myself after two hours of library study with twenty minutes of research on Yugoslavia, because of my burgeoning interest in my Yugoslavian/Slovene instructor's affairs. I mean, *world affairs.* Seriously.

Information is not easy to find—in newspapers or journals—but one journalist said that President Bush will not support declarations of independence from any individual Yugoslavian republic, because he feels that could destabilize Yugoslavia as a whole, along with the countries surrounding it. Bush also insists that the U.S. will remain uninvolved in any Yugoslavian conflict. But in another article, a correspondent argued that such a stance may lead to fiercer conflict between Yugoslavia's historically combative republics, namely Croatia and Serbia, whose people seem generally to wish to graffiti each other's doors, pillage each other's gardens, and light the tails of each other's dogs on fire.

I wonder how Peter Breznik feels about the escalating conflict. I wonder if he will return to his family.

Thursday, February 28, 1991
7:04 a.m., library basement, not studying for Macronutrients
25 days . . .

I want to draw ladybugs and stars and a tornado of Japanese blossoms.

So . . . it turns out that Julie is nice. And highly intelligent. She caught up with me in the hall after Poetry yesterday. "Vivienne, you have to help me with essays," she said.

I felt that cavernous gap inside, spanning the distance between who I am and who I wish to be, i.e., who Julie is. I paused, looked down the hall and asked, "Me?"

Julie laughed—not in a nervous, flatter-you sort of way, but in a musical, sincere way that alerts you to the fact that her teeth are nice.

"Yes, you! The craft-essay queen . . ." She is fluent at speaking ellipsis. "I'm helpless at writing them." She did seem kind of nervous at that point, but not shady-nervous, not like she was intending to mock me. To be honest, I felt like I was making her nervous.

Can you imagine, Posterity? Julie is the same kind of effortless as Peter Breznik. Her glossy hair holds loose curls all day, and she strolls around in jeans as if her *derrière* was sculpted from her mother's womb for them. Oh, and she can wear scoop-neck t-shirts that dip to the shadowed V of her breasts as though she doesn't notice or give a damn. Also, she has breasts, like most women do. I'd never stumble and call her a girl. Julie is distinctly a woman. And, as I've now learned, she is kind and smart, too.

I hate to imagine other people in agony over writing—it really is one of the most painful endeavors that language-wielding creatures can undertake to do.

Standing in the hall, I said, "We could meet at Palmiers tonight at 7," as though we were two women planning to meet along the Seine.

Which made Julie's Cinderella-blue eyes stretch practically as wide as tea saucers, as if she believed a commoner like me possessed nerve enough to deny her. "Really?" she said. "Okay!"

She was already sitting with a notebook at a table beside the shop's front picture-window when I jingled through the door. "Vivienne"—her pointer finger stabbed through the air—"over here."

"Hi," I said, and we ordered tea, hers with three cubes of sugar, mine with honey and a splash of cream. I took the first sip. "You'd like to talk about craft essays?"

"Well, yes." She clicked her pen as she lay her notebook open on the table. "I read a poem and think, 'Wow, that's nice,' but I can't write three pages about how an image is helping a poem resonate." Her head dropped till it touched the cover of her notebook. Even her glossy curls looked distressed. "Or whatever Peter says a poem does."

I forbad my face muscles to react to the sound *Peter*, breathing coffee-laced air into my lungs instead. "A poem's images often come in clusters."

Julie began writing my words down.

"No, wait—I'm not an authority—"

"To me you are." Julie stabbed a period to the end of her—well, to the end of my—sentence. "And to Peter."

"Wha—" I leaned forward for clarification, but Julie was deep into imagery.

"As in . . . a cluster of grapes? Or . . . clovers?"

"Actually, yes." I tugged at the string of my teabag, too timid to ask why she thought Peter considered me authoritative. Holding to the topic of imagery, I explained how a poem's images often come from a similar realm—like from the same vine, the same home, the same basket. Or, a small cluster of images might seem related, but then those images could evolve into a different cluster, all the while creating a tone and a world— emotions and ideas—for a reader to inhabit and relate to, or even to see completely anew.

"From . . . a . . . similar . . . realm . . ." Julie's note-taking penmanship is elegant.

"Exactly," I said. And then we spent the next 1.5 hours drafting Julie's essay on imagery.

Once we'd finished, Julie ordered me a box of a dozen pink macarons as thanks, but I opened the box right away at our table, and we ate six cookies together, talking until the shop closed at 10. She is an art history major and wanted to hear my thoughts on Rodin and Degas. As it turns out, she was one of three St. Brigid students invited to help with the Degas exhibit on campus. "Can you imagine how totally awesome that was?" she asked with raspberry-macaron crumbs flying childishly from her mouth, but also maturely, in the way that she didn't care.

"Yes!" I laughed.

"You know . . ." She grew serious, sipping from her second cup of tea. "I honestly believe you can."

All through the evening, my arms kept lighting up with tiny sparks of connection, the way they did the day I met Hillary. I felt brave enough to say, "Um, Julie? Can I ask you a question that will probably reveal how hopeless . . . and hapless . . . I am?"

She dropped the other half of her raspberry macaron into the box. "Please . . . your image is kind of un-tarnishable to me . . . Get it?" she laughed. "Your IMAGE?! Ask anything."

So I very quietly related to her what had transpired between A.J. and me in the Oppen Building and what A.J. had said about me wanting Peter. "Do you think that, too?" I asked.

She tapped the back of my hand on the table. "First—"

I waited for her to tell me that everyone was meeting after class to blow darts at a giant sketch someone had made of Vivienne the instructor-wanter, but Julie said, "A.J. is an asshat."

I exhaled carbon dioxide that might have been embedded as deep as the tips of my pinkie toes.

"And that camera bag!" Julie's eyes rolled so far back, I wasn't sure they'd roll down again. "He hauls that bag around like he's St. Brigid's paid photographer."

"I called him an asshole." I could feel my face wince.

"Good girl." The café lights outside the shop's picture window gave her face a trustworthy glow. "The thing is . . . and I'm not sure this answer will provide any comfort, but . . . I've wondered lately if it could be the other way around. That is . . . I wonder if Peter might have a tiny crush on . . . on you."

The chamomile in my stomach seemed to swirl and expand.

I wonder if Peter might have a tiny crush on you?

I'm leaving that space on the page to visually convey the white noise of disbelief I felt in my brain.

I wanted to run from the café and turn cartwheels in the street, but also lie down and brace for a truck to run over me.

Did Julie think I was fishing for her to share an observation like that? She was biting her bottom lip, fine lines around her eyes crinkling.

I inhaled deeply, hoping my stomach might possibly un-clench a little. "No, no. That's not even possible, no matter how tiny. I just don't want for everyone to think—"

"Think what?" Julie closed up our cookie box. "You might be a little younger than him, Vivienne, but it's totally possible. You're both writers, for crying out loud. And he's not that old . . . I mean . . . he can't even be 28—and you're the picture, like seriously, a painting—of a French poem goddess. No . . ." She glanced out the darkened window beside us, pausing for a second to think. "You know what you're like?" She smacked her forehead. "The resemblance just hit me!"

"Resemblance?" I think I was rocking a little.

Julie swiped up her pen to point at me. "You're a baby-doll Sophia Loren, Vivienne! But French!"

Sophia Loren was an exuberant comparison. I looked down at my padded A-cups: The baby-doll part was right.

Julie was still air-stabbing her pen. "A mini Sophia Loren, spouting humble insights that anyone can see light our hot graduate instructor's brain on fire." She slapped a palm to her notebook. "I should write that down."

My rocking was not even subtle now. "I really want to stop spouting humble insights."

"Impossible." Julie pointed to the coffee-shop door. "Shall we?"

I couldn't exactly move yet.

I asked, "What does he do that makes you think he might have a tiny crush on me?" If my wanting him showed up like neon-green stars on my face, what did his wanting me—or liking me, possibly just a tiny bit—look like?

Julie folded her arms on the table, leaning in thoughtfully. "Well . . . he might not be as readable as you—you get nervous and splotchy when you talk in class . . ."

Even now I am thinking, *Please, pleeeeeeeeeeeease say I don't do that.*

"But he . . . when you talk . . . he just goes . . . quiet. Observant. With everyone else, you can see him thinking of what he'll say next. He'll glance at the clock or turn to the next poem he wants us to study. But with you, he just . . . he just listens. And sometimes, I swear, he tries not to smile."

The bliss-fear turned to a mallet inside my rib cage. I knew the look she was talking about—Peter Breznik's listening face.

I thought he gave his listening face to everyone. I thought it simply meant he was listening.

Willing my body to cease rocking, I sat with my eyes locked on Julie, but all I could see was a fast-motion slideshow in my head that one might entitle *The Beautiful Faces Peter Breznik Makes in One Class Period*: his Agreeable Face with wide eyes and nodding; his Skeptical-but-Respectful Face with pursed lips, tilted head, and eyes squinting off in the distance; his Good-Point! Face with lips pressed together, smiling; his You've-Lost-Your-Mind Face with furrowed brow and a slight grimace.

In three seconds, I realized that his Listening Face—eyes softly narrowed, a whisper of a smile on his lips and forehead—was a face he might give only me. For one moment, everything inside me went still. And then my brain started churning out questions: *What have you done, Vivienne? Did your face cause his face? Your wanting his wanting? What will you do if he really wants you? And what do you think he actually wants?* I felt the back of my chair for a sweater to button up in forever, but of course I'd left my room without one.

I folded my arms around myself, as I tend to do more and more often now. "I need to be more aware."

Julie stood up with a laugh. "The unawareness is probably part of the appeal."

I am tired of feeling unaware, though—unaware of the lives of loved ones I can't see, unaware of how others perceive me, of looks on the faces right in front of me.

I collected the macaron box and my backpack and stood to follow Julie from the shop.

Slowly, we walked toward campus. "Vivienne"—she stepped beside me in a meandering way, one leg crossing lazily in front of the other—"going back to the humble-insights thing . . . Someone would have to cut out your tongue if you wanted to stop sharing insights. Poetry flows out of you . . . Why should you silence that just to escape notice of four rows of twitterpated would-be academics, who take themselves way too seriously? Anyone can tell that Peter thinks you are . . ."

I kind of like how her ellipsis fuel anticipation—you find yourself leaning in, wondering what words will come next.

I didn't want to rush her . . .

While Peter thinks I am . . .

"Brilliant," she said.

As I write, I am picturing his wood-chopping, bird-cradling hands in my hair, his just-barely-bent Slavic nose at my cheek, his lips feather-soft at my jaw.

I am imagining him whispering poetry.

Something by Keats—

Bright star—

Julie pushed the "cross" button at the last intersection before campus. I peered up at the stars, more radiant than they are in Manhattan, where most nights, you can't even see them. The Big Dipper stretched out like a basket for warm bread I could share with Peter Breznik.

Julie said, "Whatever he thinks of you, he thinks it in a sweet, quiet way . . . and honestly—word in the history department is that he would never cross a line with a student. He'd never embarrass you or give students or faculty any reason to talk. Especially right now, when he's interviewing at St. Brigid's. But I still hope he says something to you when the semester's over."

"Like what?" I wondered out loud.

Julie did a little twirl on the sidewalk. "Oh, I don't know—something like, 'Vivienne, come to my place to read love poems this weekend!'"

I paused beside the bench where Julie and I would part ways, thinking that if Peter did have even a farthest-star-in-the-sky-sized crush on me, we would not have to read love poems together to convey how we feel. Just exchanging poems we both love would be like gifting our hearts to each other.

Standing with Julie in the glittering dark, I felt almost entirely happy.

"You know why *he* probably doesn't have a clue that you want him?" Julie faced me with a fist at her hip.

"Why?" I heard hope turn bright in my voice.

Julie giggled. Maybe giggling survives childhood. Like self-absorption. "Because we're all looking at him like we want him. Even one or two of the guys."

We giggled together.

"I'm just the most obvious." My skin prickled in a whispery breeze.

"Noooo . . ." Julie shook her head. "I think you might be the only one he'd want back."

I walked the rest of the way home alone under St. Brigid's dark-branching sycamores, wondering if anything Julie said could be possible.

I suppose that I, too, have a wanting face—wide-eyed and splotchy, my breath running out. It's a face I've only ever made for Peter Breznik.

As I opened the door to my room after leaving Julie, the telephone stopped ringing. I was relieved to find that Hillary wasn't home to hear it again, and further relieved that nobody left a message.

When Hillary finally arrived back at our room, I pretended I was asleep, but my brain was a basket of images—Peter's eyes and his hands and the scruff on his face. His worn, easy jeans, the taut breadth of his chest, the hidden fluted edge of his collarbone. His lips.

Bright star, I kept thinking.

What if he did have a tiny crush on me?

What if my parents are glad I haven't called?

What if I move to Manhattan and Peter decides to teach at St. Brigid's?

I am going to be late for Poetry.

And really: What is the point of macronutrients?

Friday, March 1, 1991
11:41 p.m.—I am honestly writing this on the toilet, but will say no more of it, at
risk of conjuring an image
26 days . . .

It is truly a testament to the tightrope I walk between child and adulthood that the major themes of this journal are fear of my mother dying and a crush on my instructor; or, speaking broadly, in more adult terms, death and sex.

Clearly I have written enough this week, but I wanted to document that—

1. On the subject of death, or in regard to Maman, i.e. the possibility of her dying, I will never, no matter how childishly I'm behaving, be settled. I do not understand: How did humankind arrive at this planet and learn so much, only to always have the incomprehensible gaping sorrow and shadow of death looming over them? How has the human heart evolved to love so sharply and fiercely—to crave intertwining its strings with another's—when our species would be much better off if we could love less or not at all? Animals do not love, science claims, and they continue to propagate their species.

And—

2. On the subject of crushes, which tend for some people to lead to sex, I looked at Peter Breznik in class today—not blankly, not wide-eyed. I just looked at him while he was talking about Tomaž Šalumun, a Slovene poet he admires, and when he read Šalumun's line, "I have a body. With a body I do the most beautiful things that I do," I looked up from the text, and Peter happened to look up from his book at the same time, his eyes meeting mine. He said, "That is one of my favorite lines of poetry," as if he were telling just me. Julie coughed from somewhere behind me as I nodded my head a few times up and down, not blushing.

Also, Peter has a faint crescent-moon scar curving down to his lip from his right nostril, and his smile, like his nose, is a teeny-bit crooked. It makes me want to bake for him.

Evolution can't be the sole force at work in us.

I hope Hillary doesn't wake when I flush the toilet.

Saturday, March 2, 1991
Under my sheets with a booklight I picked up at the campus bookstore
27 days . . .

I have tried for three hours to sleep.

Speaking of three, Maman left that many messages with Hillary this afternoon, while I was studying at the library. I don't want Hillary to have to fabricate my whereabouts, so I study or bake day and night and never say where I am.

Hillary reported that the third time Maman called, she said "Hillary" as she usually does, like her tongue's been paralyzed, because saying "Hillary" is like swallowing glue for French people. "Hillary, I would like you to write down my words exactly," which Hillary did, and Maman's words were: "Vivienne, you are behaving as a child with this silence. Call me tonight, no matter how late. - Your Mother."

God, forgive me: I read Hillary's note and burst out laughing.

Also, Dear God, please help me to sleep.

And please let Maman not actually be sick.

And if she is sick, please let her not be suffering.

Monday, March 4, 1991
7:09 p.m., library, third floor, poetry shelves
Days, days, more days

I called home earlier this evening when I knew my family would not be at home. On Monday evenings, the Lebruns dine at *Maison Lili*. That they maintain the tradition assures me they haven't dispatched a search and rescue team to California.

When the answering machine picked up after five rings, I left a message I had composed in my head while taking notes during Macronutrients:

> Bonsoir, ma famille! C'est Vivienne. *I hope you're at Lili's, ordering* crème brûlée *for dessert. I'm sorry I haven't found a moment to call. I've been keeping busy, as you encouraged, Papa, and I believe I was frustrating you all with my dependence and worry. I hope everyone is doing well. Kisses for Hugo and Mr. Phillips our doorman. And Maman—I hope you're not letting Luc get away with leaving his boxer shorts on the washroom floor. I love you all* avec tout mon couer. *Maybe we could talk next weekend.* Ciao.

Maman was kind not to say in the message she left with Hillary last night that I *am* a child, even though she said I was behaving as one. I know that I am, but my childish anger feels like an avalanche—one little crack, and no one can stop it.

I'm not even sure I know what I want—for them to welcome me home and bless my transfer to Philbrick? Or simply for them to be honest about Maman's health? I think I can't settle for less than everything.

As I was marking the period of that previous sentence, Peter Breznik walked by the Humanities reference desk in the heathered-blue sweatshirt we've shared, and he saw me. I did not have time to perfect my blank face—every large and small muscle engaged as if the sun were about to explode from my temples.

"Vivienne!" Peter said—well, energetically whispered (was it energetically? It was louder than a whisper, and he did his wide smile). He came to stand next to my desk.

"Are you writing something you like?"

I clapped my journal shut. "Just tracking my thoughts." I tucked my journal into the depths of my backpack.

"I've noticed you do that," Peter smiled.

I thought of the things that Julie had said—how Peter's listening face might possibly be his wanting face.

He was looking right at me, eyes narrowed a little. "Journaling takes a lot of discipline."

"Or neurosis," I said, because lately, I can't curb my sarcasm.

I wanted to loop my pinkie finger around his.

He took a step back. "Good writers seem to have plenty of that."

Can we just talk like this? I wondered. *Me and the Slavic historian-poet instructor? Are we crossing a professional line?*

He cannot be more than 26 years-old—27 tops. Younger than even Julie estimates. I could almost naturally be friends with someone of that age.

"I blame the neurosis on my French ancestors."

He laughed a good-humored breath.

I typically glance away when Peter looks at me in class, but I watched him watch me as we conversed right here in the library. He looked at my eyes and at the dark freckle on my left cheek. He quick-followed my hair from where I'd pointlessly tucked it behind my ear, to where a curl wisped over my elbow. I tried to look even longer at him, but it was like my eyelids and lungs were battling a timer-system. After ten seconds, I had to blink and breathe again.

"So how did your French family end up in New York?" he asked.

Gazing up at him from my library desk, I was torn between a sense of student humility that pressured me to say, *I know you have so much to do; you can get to it if you want to,* and an I-can't-believe-my-luck impulse to yank him by his hand into the wide-bottomed chair I was sitting in and whisper, *Now we can hear each other better!*

But he simply stood there, looking down, listening or wanting. I couldn't tell if it was one or the other. Or neither. Just my wondering is probably crossing a professional line.

Look at what Julie has done to me.

"My father was invited to work at a specialized neurology practice in Manhattan."

Was that answer too elitist? As soon as I finished the sentence, I imagined Peter's family enduring the iron fist of communism, managing to break free for brief teaching appointments in the U.S., while my family flew over the Atlantic almost as effortlessly as summer breezes.

Peter nodded, unoffended. "And how did you come to major in English? I'm guessing you read and write just as easily in French."

"Oh, I love writing in English," I said. "And reading. Especially reading. So many sounds and cadences." I figured that was probably answer enough, but Peter really does do a good interested face, so I added, "But sometimes I feel like I'm swimming between languages—for instance, one thing might exist as two for me—*maison* and *home*. Or another thing, like *vanille*, might always be French. While *chocolate chip* can only be English." I could feel even the tip of my nose flush.

Peter glanced over my head, but not with his eyes raised as if growing bored, but lowered, as if searching for a chair, which would have been, without question, like leaping over a professional line.

"I relate to that," Peter said. "It's almost the same for me with Slovene. But I always wanted to cast Slovene aside when I was younger, relegate it to a second language." He ran a hand through his honey-gold hair. "But also, I don't think I'm as nimble as you. I mean, at living between two languages."

Hearing that, I realized I rarely devoted much thought to the idea that living between dual histories and languages might be difficult—that a person might feel more at home with one heritage, and more tentative about the other, or even resentful. My physical attraction to Peter seemed always to be amplifying, but in thinking about what he'd just said, my interest in what he knew and what he thought and how he'd lived intensified, the way New England leaves deepen and burn through the fall to new color.

Peter tugged at the neck of his sweatshirt. "By the way, I can tell you didn't wash this." He lifted the collar to his nose and sniffed.

The schoolgirl in me wanted to dive beneath my desk, crunch my knees to my chest and chant, *No-no-no-no!* until Peter turned for a library exit, but the girl—the woman, I guess—that Julie had seen in me—the "brilliant" young woman Peter might sort of almost have a tiny crush on—*she* leaned back in her chair, eyeing the blue-heathered fabric she'd spent five days lounging around her dorm in. "You could have washed it yourself."

Peter's head tipped back like he was going to laugh, but then he sniffed the neck of his sweatshirt again. "I might have guessed you'd leave behind the scent of apples." Then he sniffed at an arm. "And so-phisticated chocolate chip cookies." He sniffed again. "At least in one sleeve."

Brilliant-woman Vivienne disappeared in one gasp, while Peter-the-Poetry-421-instructor's eyes glowed the blue of dusk before fireflies. I'm pretty sure my mouth was stuck open.

Stepping away, he adjusted his satchel-strap. "Good to see you, Vivienne. Good luck with your journaling."

And then I guess he walked off to find books.

"Maman," I want to say to her on the phone tonight, "I flirted with a handsome man in the library, and I don't think he minded."

But even if Peter does like apples and cookies, he still must wonder if I'm some sort of gutter rat for not washing his sweatshirt.

Thursday, March 7, 1991
6:07 p.m., on the floor of the Oppen Building, waiting an hour
for a poetry reading to begin
Seriously done counting days

Besides re-living every eight minutes or so my two-minute library flirt with Peter Breznik and fearing that Robert Carson might step out from behind a bookshelf or a tree or the dim television alcove in my very own dormitory, I am dreading Spring Break. It is not for three weeks, but I can't help thinking that until this semester, I have always flown home to New York. Since this Spring Break would be my last at St. Brigid's, however, I agreed with my parents that I could save them the airfare and myself the upheaval by celebrating this one Easter here, with Hillary.

That seemed like a bearable idea in December, but in December, I was with the people I would miss seeing at Easter. I was talking to them; we were dunking croissants in *chocolat au lait* and watching classic American films till midnight. Except that Maman would skip *chocolat* and retire by 9 p.m.

But we were conversing with each other in December, unfazed by any upcoming wide stretch of time or distance. And Luc kept sneaking into my room in the wee hours to hide tiny fluorescent-haired troll dolls in perilous locations, such as on the edge of my pillow, or smack-dab on my chest, or at the brink of a toilet seat. By the time I left for St. Brigid's, I thought that maybe I wouldn't miss him so terribly.

I shouldn't even miss him now. But I do. I miss where he is and whom he is with and everything he can see that I can't.

I didn't call home this past weekend as I said I might, and Maman left a voice message first thing this morning: *Bonjour, Vivienne. C'est Maman.*

Though I've tried at least twenty times to hear it otherwise, I think that her voice was trembly. But almost as soon as it turned that way, she snapped like a rubber-band back to herself. I can write her every word by heart—

You know we are humoring you, n'est-ce pas, *Vivienne?*

Yes, I was aware of that, and at her first skip from English to French, I also knew that I was unnerving her—possibly even hurting her, as I've intended to. The knowledge sent a nauseous thrill up my spine, the kind of rush evil despots must feel upon destroying the innocent.

We are humoring you just like when you were une petite fille—*no more than six*—*and you insisted on walking yourself to Michel's for* des truffes au citron, et *Papa and I walked the whole way behind you, at a distance. This feels* comme la même chose *to me*—*Papa and I allowing you to feel autonomous. Except that it is not cute, Vivienne, and we are not ten feet behind you and cannot save you when you go too far.*

Clearly, and uncharacteristically, she was determined to use all our voice-message tape. She hasn't spoken so many consecutive words to me in years.

I remember that day, though, when I walked to Michel's, wearing a pale-yellow dress that I loved. It had white smocking on the chest that made me feel like a jaunty milkmaid. When I handed Michel the smooth dollar bill Papa had given me for polishing our old parquet floors on my knees right beside him, I believed I could walk anywhere in Manhattan and be safe. But the only thing I wanted was to walk home, to cuddle against Papa's chest for stories, and eat Maman's bread with olive oil and salt.

I ate my *truffe au citron* and skipped the whole way back to my parents. So little about me has changed.

I understand the comparison Maman is making—that back then and now, she and Papa have tried to help me assert independence. But in their minds—and in mine, too, when I'm thinking clearly—my current behavior makes a mockery of independence. My silence risks damaging our connection, our necessary dependence on each other for strength and understanding and love. Maman doesn't want me to push that far.

But how can she feel that her own behavior is still parently and benevolent? Does she truly not see that she and Papa have added sad twists to our story since that day at Michel's? Darker intentions, half-truths, not to mention their own deliberate silence? I don't think Maman's comparison holds up entirely, which makes me think she is floundering to help me see reason. I have caused her to flounder.

The rest of the message transpired as—

Do you know, Vivienne, je pourrais téléphoner *the counseling office at St. Brigid's at any time and request that they find you and suspend your enrollment until* tu m'appelle—*you call me.*

—as if I needed translation—

But I am waiting for you to return to yourself. You are an adult, pour l'amour de Dieu, *Vivienne. And I am your mother. What if I truly were ill again—which as far as we can tell, I am not—but what if I were? You are wasting time and demeaning yourself.*

She said, "as far as we can tell." She knows something is off inside her. She's trying to find out what it is.

And then she went full *Français* on me: *Et Vivienne, je voudrais discuter de ton manque total de confiance en nous.*

She would like to discuss my complete lack of trust in her and Papa.

I could write a whole journal explaining solely that. Or maybe every journal I've ever written explains that.

A bientôt, Vivienne. *Papa and I will not call again but will wait for you to assume your adulthood and call us.*

Each time I listened to her message this morning, I felt caught between anger that she couldn't see how her own silence hurts me and devastates my trust in her, and a fluttery disbelief that she was not currently keeping silent.

Students are lining up outside the auditorium doors for the poetry reading now. A.J. is sauntering around snapping pictures of students and flyers on the wall announcing tonight's poet. I've heard that A.J. actually is some kind of campus photographer, just as Julie had joked about. He'll probably sign a few of his prints from tonight and frame them to bestow upon the English department.

I don't remember poetry readings in images like photographs, but in sounds—the timbre of the poet's voice, the speed at which he or she reads, how or if they cue listeners to the shape of each line. Every writing professor makes poetry-reading attendance worth the points of a significant essay, but I would be here even if no one ever knew but myself and the mites burrowing into the carpet.

This semester, I come for the poems, of course, but also for the even one-in-two-hundred chance of catching a half-inch glimpse of Peter Breznik's shoulder, or his knee, or the heel of his soft leather hiking boots that were probably stitched from the hide of a bell-collared cow that roamed meadows in Switzerland.

Last Friday, however, Peter canceled class for all this week ("For a job interview and a longtime Slovene friend who is visiting." "A woman?" that nice girl named Stephanie asked, while Peter thumbed through the book in his hands nonchalantly, and I pressed my fingers to my throat to keep from asking, *Just how friendly is she?* and *Are you interviewing in Manhattan?*), so I do not have much hope of seeing him tonight. Unless he has returned from his interview and is required to attend the reading. In all likelihood, he is probably at this moment engaged in passionate conversation in a museum or a restaurant or a gallery (he would never watch or attend a sports event, would he?) with a Slovene bosom buddy or, given his avoidance of the issue in class, with a perfectly bosomed Slovene lover. There are only so many possibilities.

But maybe, right now, he is sitting down at a wood table at Tallulah's, having finished his interview at Hadley. Maybe he is ordering *un croissant au miel* with coffee and making a note to himself to tell me he remembered my recommendation.

Maybe he's thinking, *I could meet up with Vivienne here in August,* or *I wonder if Vivienne ever thinks of moving back to New York.*

Just please God, don't let him forget that we've shared a sweatshirt.

And please God, as well: In her talkative state, do not let Maman find the counseling-office number.

I am not prepared to talk yet.

———————

Saturday, March 9, 1991
11:39 a.m., on a rose-printed towel at the coast with a yellow notepad

Not feeling like building up to things:

Robert appeared yesterday afternoon, and I can't find my journal.

And Peter is possibly interviewing in New York or is engaged in stirring conversation, or worse, with the longtime Slovene love of his life.

All those facts/possibilities are tiny fuses in my heart that spark escalating degrees of agitation.

Actually, the journal issue is not sparking. It's firing.

I am so enflamed and palpitating that all I can do is write these sentences on yellow notepad paper that I hope to insert in my journal when I find it—if I find it—while Hillary and her Garage friends and Robert Carson, of all people, play some sort of Robert-led football game here on the beach.

Oui, Papa, I am this deep inside myself.

And oh, Sandra-my-therapist, yes. I have finally entered the loop that descends straight to hell.

The last time I wrote in my tangible journal was right before the poetry reading two nights ago. I swear I zipped it in my backpack before I even entered the Oppen auditorium. Though after the reading, I did stop at the library to draft an essay on the chemical reactions between amino acids and sugars in baking. The point being that when I opened my backpack twenty minutes ago at the beach, my journal was not inside it.

I printed my name on its inside cover. On the one hand, that gives me hope that an honest St. Brigider might pick it up, obtain my number and address from Campus Info, and then return it to me without reading too much; but on the other hand, I realize now that I have enabled anyone who finds it to match my name to my person and know exactly whose deranged life they are reading. And even a St. Brigider who would not accept a billion dollars to cheat on a test or plagiarize in a paper might still be tempted beyond their strength to Xerox-copy the contents of a journal with *Love is an ever-fixed mark* fingernail-scratched on the cover, and distribute, for a fee, my journal among the student-body.

Right now, I can only go for about three minutes without wondering where it is and what could go wrong if I never found it; hence, here I sit at the coast at lunchtime with intelligent, fun-loving people— even Robert fits easily in with them, hurling a football into a flock of sweat-suited girls (the guys tired quickly in Robert's macho-man glow and ran for the water)—and all I can do is document my concern for a journal I would probably be better off losing.

One potentially good thing is that Peter, as I guessed, was not at the reading, so if I somehow dropped my journal in the auditorium, he would not have been the one to retrieve it, though something tells me he is the one person on this elitist campus who would not feel a dried dandelion petal of temptation to sneak a peek, which means maybe he would be the ideal person to find it if it is lost.

At least half my poetry class was at the reading, A.J. and his camera among them, so that means approximately ten people exist right now who could without question change the course of my life at St. Brigid's. I would need to transfer to Philbrick tomorrow.

Honestly, though? The best thing that could happen with my journal is that some merciful, unbeknownst-to-me being finds it and reads it and then marches it straight to the counseling center, where it would be read and evaluated, precipitating I myself being called in and evaluated, and unfortunately, but probably rightly, being placed in a different poetry class, or sent home to Manhattan and Philbrick, God willing.

As a brief sidenote: I found out this past week where I can pick up brochures for coach busses that transport people the 3,000 miles from here to Penn Station.

Right now, however, I am sitting on a windy beach thirty miles south of San Francisco with a notebook in my lap, looking up every minute or so to find that Robert Carson is truly and alarmingly within a beach rock's throw and is not some svelte-muscled apparition that I have conjured in overthinking about home.

He's real, no question, the squealing girls in their pastel rainbow of sweatshirts leaping up from the sand to capture his tangible football, his about-to-pull-a-prank-on-you eyes finding mine every time I glance up at him.

He is the perfect torment, isn't he? One of the only human beings I don't miss from home, appearing languorous and lean on my dormitory steps yesterday, as if to flaunt in my face his own ease in leaving home, and to summon to my mind the three New Yorkers I wished could be sitting where he was.

I had been trudging up the sidewalk to my dorm before I saw him yesterday. I was grieving Peter's absence in Poetry and whispering a line that I had tried to fit in a poem all week: *All we remember is the last time we remembered—*

And then I looked up, saw Robert lounging on the cement steps leading up to my dorm, and remembered the last time I saw him—sitting above a Monopoly board, his confident hand reaching out for my Joker card.

On my dorm building's steps, that very Robert's eyes nearly popped out of his head in surprise. He said, "I thought I was in New York for a second."

Glancing around me, I thought the same, but saw only St. Brigid's sycamores, its red-tiled roofs and sweeping lawns, its backpack-laden students. I simply stood where my feet had stopped walking.

"I did try calling you," the out-of-place Robert Carson said. "But then your mom had us over for dinner a few nights ago and said not to bother with the telephone." He was leaning into his thighs on the steps, standing up, walking toward me.

I was squinting the way one does at the lens of a microscope. Robert seemed to be growing larger, though in reality, he was only growing closer.

"Our phone is . . ." I shook my head, "complicated."

"Like you." Robert paused a forearm's length away before bending to touch his lips to my cheek, almost like a French *bise*. "Hi, Viviun." He pulled away. He was wearing a red-checked dress-shirt and trim khaki pants that almost glinted with a just-pressed sheen. He smelled like leather and sage, like my memories of nights in the city.

"Hello, Robert," I managed to say, stepping back, remembering how he'd joked about making out at Christmas. He didn't seem to be in that kind of joking mood as he stood in front of my dorm. He was almost reserved, quiet.

"You look different here." His eyes made a down-up sweep.

"Different in what way?" I smoothed a hand over my hair, which, as both a taming and calming effort, was pointless. I thought maybe I looked like I'd gone feral at college. I hadn't conditioned my hair or plucked my eyebrows in weeks, and I wondered almost simultaneously if Peter had noticed and if Robert might feel repulsed by the sight of me.

Folding his arms, Robert bit his bottom lip, smiling. "You look wilder."

I wanted to repeat my last question: *In what way?* "Wild" like a woman who would do wild things, or like a woman who lived in the wild? Did he think I would take his observation as a compliment? And why had he said "wild-*er,*" as if I'd progressed from already wild to more wild? Peter Breznik would never have left a statement like that open to interpretation.

I wished for the calendar to turn to Monday already, but suddenly, Robert's hand wrapped loosely around my bicep.

"Your mother sent a gift with me, but I left it in my hotel room. Do you have a date or big study plans tomorrow? I could give her gift to you then, and you could show me around your campus."

I winced.

"Or I could take you to dinner."

"How are you getting around?" I asked.

"By taxi," he answered. "You're familiar with those, aren't you?"

I peered off toward St. Brigid's perennial green lawns through the trees.

Did I want a gift from Maman? Or would I prefer to send it back, to make clear that I couldn't be bought or appeased with some prize like a child?—though I confess once again that I agree with Maman: I am behaving as a child.

Robert let go my arm. He tucked his hand in his slacks pocket, and with just that action, that subtle retreat, I allowed my eyes to shift back to him. His head dipped almost penitently, the joking half-grin on his face subdued and surprisingly, after four years of knowing him, familiar.

He was not what I wanted from home, but he had come from my home. He knew where I'd lived, and he'd conversed with the people I loved there—he'd perceived their heartache when I'd asked how they seemed back in February.

And Maman had given him a gift for me.

I felt my lips almost curve in a smile. "You forgot to bring the gift with you?"

The half-grin on Robert's face went full throttle. "It might have been more deliberate than forgetting."

I hefted my backpack up higher on my shoulder, stepping past Robert toward my dorm. "And you call yourself a strategic genius?"

Robert huffed behind me in mock offense. "Okay, then"—he didn't move to follow me—"maybe you could say I'm a hopeful strategist."

I climbed the first three steps to my dorm before turning back to look down on him. "Forgetting my mother's gift was remedial, at best."

"Then say you don't want it, genius."

That is essentially how Robert and I came to be here today, at the coast with Hillary et al., Robert diving just now, shoulder-first, into the sand to catch the doomed throw of the one girl among us in this coastal gloom who is braving a bikini top. As I scribble away on wind-damp yellow paper.

And Robert still hasn't given Maman's gift to me.

For the sake of fairness and accuracy, I will note that Robert has dark wavy hair that falls seductively into his luxuriously-lashed brown eyes, while the angular cut of his cheeks and jaw is reminiscent of convenience-store romance novels—not the actual text, of which I'd have no clue, but the covers—a raven-haired, devil-eyed duke looming over a swooning lady and thinking, without question, about exactly what he'd like to do with her bodice.

Not that Robert has ever given me personally any reason to believe that he is truly like that. He merely looks like that. I'm sure his face and physique pose daily struggles.

Anyhow—I keep wondering if my journal's absence means that God or His saints or His messenger angels are meting out my punishment for dishonoring and stonewalling my parents. I would try to repent, but my heart would not be invested, and to truly repent, one must cease committing the sin one desires to repent of, and I am not yet ready to cease.

Interestingly, even more than slightly (and sickly) enjoying the torment I inflict on my parents by committing this sin, I think I am feeling some small burst of independence (although, yes, I have memorized the bus route from St. Brigid's to Penn Station). My never-ending angst for all things concerning Maman might be quieting to the tiniest degree, and in place of the angst, I feel a faint twinge of desire to think about my own future. If Philbrick accepts me for admission this fall, I could work twenty-or-so hours a week at a bakery—perhaps at *Geneviève* in Brooklyn; Maman knows the pastry chef. And then, after I graduate in two-and-a-half years with an MFA in creative writing, I could beg Tante Evelyn to finally come to New York and help us open our own bakery.

Assuming my parents will eventually forgive me for somewhat deceptively applying to Philbrick, and will, by some holy miracle, bless my attendance there, they might agree to let me live at home for a year or so—if I promised to leave the apartment by 6 every morning and stay busy with school and work till 11 each night. Or if Maman were sick again, I could help care for her in a temperate way. I could create a balanced life for myself and help make her life easier at the same time. I could be different. I could be strong, for myself and for her.

And once I begin work on my master's credits at Philbrick, I could possibly teach an intro-to-poetry course. I could write articles and essays at night to submit to food journals and collect for my book.

And maybe, at some point, if he were teaching at Hadley, Peter Breznik could meet me for coffee.

****

Well, Robert finally broke from the Baywatch football scene someone should have been filming and walked to the bottom edge of my towel to sit down across from me. "Are you writing about me?" He reached over the towel to pull at one of my ocean-spray-induced ringlets.

"Actually, yes." I tugged my head away. "I'm describing you for my posterity."

"Did you get my abs?" He rose to his knees to beat on his twelve-pack, disbelieving—to his credit—that I would ever condescend to describe anything so mundane.

"Yes—let me give those some words." I marked the four asterisks above these paragraphs, wondering what Peter's abdominals might look like. If I were to see him at the coast or a pool, that is. Peter looks strong, but slightly gaunt, like a man who has worked very hard and been hungry. If I were ever to touch any part of him, I think it would first be as comfort, and then as desire. And then I would want to feed him *pot au feu* with a peasant loaf just out of the oven.

When I looked up at Robert, I almost expected to see Peter. "Do you have my mother's gift?" I asked.

In a quick lift and leap over my beach towel that I can only equate to how a jungle cat might spring from the trees, Robert planted himself beside me. So close, the sharp coastal wind whipped my hair in his face.

"Yes," he said in the quiet between our bent heads. "But the weather would hurt it. How about I take you to dinner tonight?"

"So remedial." I pushed his bare shoulder away. *But why not?* I thought, my heart quieting a little. *Why shouldn't I go?* Robert was there, the side of his knee bouncing warm against mine in the wind, while my family and New York, Peter and my dreams of writing and baking, were always intangible and just out of reach, like bright words I know and long to speak, but remain at the tip of my tongue.

I told Robert I don't eat just anywhere.

"Me neither." He wrapped a pointer finger in a windblown curl of my hair. "But you can choose."

He is playing frisbee with the Garage guys now, and I am obviously writing on this yellow notepad again, wondering if I should cancel our dinner plans and risk forfeiting Maman's gift so that I can do a thorough journal search of Oppen and the library, but I think that might have to wait until Monday. Buildings close at 8 p.m. on Saturday night and remain closed until Monday. At least that means that my journal's fate is decided: Either it's been taken or it hasn't. There is nothing I can do before Monday to change its status. And a glimmer of possibility does still exist that it is wedged between my dorm bed and the wall.

We're packing up in ten minutes, but I keep thinking about how tonight will be my first sort-of-date at St. Brigid's. And it's with a guy from New Jersey, from a city ten miles from my family's apartment.

When I told Hillary earlier that I was going to dinner with Robert, she squealed over the sandcastle we were building and nearly smashed our best turret by hugging me. "I don't know Robert, but he seems pretty funny, and he has killer eyelashes."

I wish I had repented already and could tell Maman I am going on a date with the man of her dreams, but I think I might have to endure her hard feelings the first time I call her, and tonight doesn't seem the best time for that. I mean, it's only a date with Robert—even yesterday I might have faked strep throat at the thought, but I accept that he feels like some aspect of home to me—something like a streetlight that you never knew you noticed until the road went dark. In four-and-a-half months, he and I might swap coasts and rarely see each other again, and for some reason that thought prompts equal parts disappointment and relief in me.

Still, I sort of want to dance a waltz in our room and ask Hillary to French-twist my hair when we get home. My body is growing adept at managing elation and sorrow and guilt at the same time. And wanting. And longing. My body is managing those feelings, too.

And though Peter is probably being tended to by the sophisticated intellectual Slovene I've imagined for him, who has obedient blonde hair and pillowy lips that she touches to his neck as she spoons him in bed (just please God, not in his blue sweatshirt) I feel a bit traitorous for accepting a date with Robert.

Peter has held my heartstrings for so long.

Sunday, March 10, 1991
1:04 a.m. under my bedsheet with my booklight, still writing on this fill-in notepad

Do you know, Posterity, what a normal almost-woman would write in her journal tonight? Besides the fact that she would be writing in her *everyday, TANGIBLE, NOT-LOST JOURNAL???!!!!*

She would be feeling tiny blinking lights in her fingertips and a tingle of wings between her chest and her shoulder blades, and, I don't know—maybe her lips would be warm from kissing, as she wrote something like, "I had a lovely time with Robert Carson tonight. While I have been prone to judge him harshly, he was in reality the kind of gentleman I have always dreamed of dating, with his dark hair combed down, but curls falling one by one over his forehead throughout our dinner at Arugula. He looked like a rogue Mr. Darcy, in his navy-blue slacks and white button-up. We talked about school and New York and movies and even our favorite desserts as we ate the decadent gelato before us, our hands inadvertently touching."

But no: Vivienne Lebrun—dating-less, romance-less, ever-hopelessly seared through the heart by the delusion of love she can't shake for a full-grown, world-traveling, does-he-even-notice-her?-probably-not graduate instructor—*that* Vivenne Lebrun faces the reality of writing, in her makeshift journal, that the very same instructor she is hopeless for was AT THE DAMN RESTAURANT.

Once I embrace all-capitals, Posterity, you can know I am teetering.

So yeah.

Can you imagine if I could actually say, "So yeah," like that? As in, "So yeah. Peter Breznik was at the restaurant. We said hi, and then I made out in a phone booth with Robert Carson and gave Peter Breznik a thumbs-up as he walked by."

But no. Oh, no. I do not say, or do, things like that. What I have to say on this page is

What.

The.

Hell.

Peter had a date. Her skirt was too short. She was beautiful. Beyond Julie beautiful. Beyond earth beautiful. Beyond, I would go so far as to say, this galaxy's very concept of beautiful.

She was like the Blue Fairy in Walt Disney's *Pinocchio,* blond hair spun from gold, a halo of light encircling her at-least-six-foot being.

She was exactly the woman I had pictured for Peter—this longtime friend in town for the weekend—except that by some merciless smirking trick of the universe, she was even more perfect than I had imagined.

And I thought Peter and I had been making connections. In class. In the library. Between the lines of my poems and his notes on them. In the soft blue threads of his sweatshirt.

What on God's asteroid-pocked earth is happening to me?! How can I be heartless enough to reject the two people (three, if I can summon forgiveness enough to count Luc) in creation who love me, and then be delusional enough to believe that the one person who would never even notice my existence might slowly be losing his heart to me???

Allow me to set the scene.

I was seated across from Robert at a small, white-linen-topped table right in the center of Arugula, awaiting our salads. Robert had asked me why Italians wouldn't have named gnocchi "little footballs," when I saw Peter standing just inside the restaurant entrance.

Before I could even think to avert my eyes, Peter and his longtime friend were following the restaurant host through a short maze of round tables toward me and Robert, the friend one step ahead of Peter, who lightly pressed the fingertips of one hand to the silk-covered small of her back—the softest, sweetest, most subtly-possessive male gesture.

I pretended to search through my purse in my lap as they grew nearer our table, but just as I was about to say, "Robert, I forgot something back at my dorm," and insist that we leave, I heard my properly accented name spoken as a question in Peter's voice.

"Vivienne?" He stopped beside our table, his friend's hand curled around the crook of his elbow.

I sat paralyzed, looking up at him. A pen dropped from my purse to the floor, and Peter's gaze followed it.

He bent to pick it up, handed it to me, and then turned to Robert. "Hello," he said in a tone that Papa might have used if he'd ever had the chance to address a boy who planned to go out with me—authoritative, amused, and the slightest bit skeptical. Because obviously Peter views himself and me that way—not as father and daughter, of course, but possibly as, I don't know . . . fond cousins.

When I only bit my top lip and straightened in my chair, Peter extended a hand to Robert. "I'm a friend of Vivienne's—Peter." He was narrowing his eyes, but not precisely in his listening way.

A friend of Vivienne's. I suppose I should have felt a zing up my spine when he didn't say, *I'm her instructor.* But *friend?* It sounded like the equivalent of "my barber."

Robert smiled at me, oblivious, clearly expecting me to introduce him, while I'm pretty sure at least 75% of the blood in my body had deposited itself in my face.

Robert looked back to Peter. "Great to meet you, man. I'm Robert. Visiting Viviun from New Jersey. I'm also interviewing for med school at Stanford." His eyes locked on me. "But that's second to seeing Viviun."

"Viviun," Peter said, nodding. "Of course." He touched the elegant hand at his elbow. "This is an old friend of mine. Sonja, meet Vivienne and Robert."

An old friend—I could hear an unspoken romantic history: hand-holding, kiss-stealing, midnight strolls through Europe's most storybook cities.

The Blue-Fairy friend smiled benevolently, as if about to ask how she might grant all our wishes. "So nice to meet you." She spoke with a faint Slavic accent. "Robert. Vivienne." She pronounced my name correctly. I watched her hand tighten around Peter's elbow.

"Right this way," the restaurant host interrupted what was sure to have been a lively conversation, what with the four of us shifting our eyes from one to the other, wondering, *Just who the hell are you?* Or maybe I was the only one wondering.

"A pleasure to meet you, Robert," Peter said. "Enjoy your night, Vivienne." He nodded again, following his longtime friend and the restaurant host to a table approximately five feet from mine and Robert's before I'd spoken even one word to Peter himself.

So many words sat clenched in my throat—*you I love see please me us talk my heart*—not in strict grammatical order, just words that held what

I felt for him. Only a week ago, I was terrified by the thought that Peter might have noticed me, but tonight, I am terrified by the thought that he probably hasn't.

Having helped seat Sonja, Peter eased into his own chair, facing her, and me, if he had just tilted his head to one side or the other of Sonja's apparently mesmerizing face.

"He seems nice." Robert eyed me from over the fluted rim of a wine glass. "Do you want some?" He extended the wine to me, as though aware that I needed mild sedation. He knew from our family gatherings that my parents occasionally allowed me a sip. Had he noticed that Peter had tumbled my thoughts like linens in a dryer?

I swallowed as I leaned into the table, imagining how the wine would run down my throat, numbing all the sparks in my body. "No, thank you." I reached for my fork as our server set salads before us.

"Oh, wait," Robert said. "Your mom's gift. I should have given it to you before we left your place. It'll go nice with your dress."

I looked down at the shallow V of my neckline. I was wearing the simple black wrap-dress Maman gave me at Christmas—the one that ties at my waist so that what I do have of curves is suggested to the greatest, though still saddest, extent possible. I had felt almost womanly leaving my dorm with Robert before dinner, but after seeing the longtime friend beside Peter, I felt like Barbie's kid sister—Kipper or Skipper—the one that girls never put on their Christmas lists.

"Here." Robert pulled a small gold box from his jacket pocket. "She said you'd be surprised enough to call her."

I set down my water glass, stunned by the glittering box. My thoughts flew to Peter. Had he seen Robert hand me the gift?

But Peter, I could see by leaning barely to my right, was wondering absolutely nothing. He appeared to be lost in the comfort and vision that was his longtime friend named Sonja. She reached across the table to run a thumb over what must have been a spot or lint on his shirt collar, as he sat ramrod straight in his chair, clearly hypnotized.

I couldn't decide if I wanted to A) march over to their table, yank the longtime friend from her chair and tell her to go back to the motherland; or B) grab Robert's free hand and press it to my lips just to see if Peter might pry his eyes from his friend; or C) dissolve into tears in my chair.

But no. There would be no marching, yanking, grabbing, or dissolving. "Open it." Robert set the box on the table, just in front of my plate.

I wasn't sure I wanted to accept a gift from Maman yet, but I most surely did not want Peter to think I was entranced by a gift from Robert. So I lifted the lid as casually as possible, nearly dropping the little box on my salad.

Peter, Sonja, Robert—the entire restaurant—faded in my head until I was a single consciousness in the dimly-lit dining room, an imaginary spotlight flicking on above me. "Her ladybug necklace?" I set the open box to the side of my salad plate, staring. *Her ladybug necklace?*

"Is that good?"

I raised my head to find Robert sipping again from his wine glass.

"It was her mother's." I touched the six tiny ladybug charms on a gold chain in the box, each of their bodies a glittering red crystal. "My grandmother gave it to her before she passed away."

I could have been a statue entitled *Girl with Her Mother's Mother's Necklace*—my body felt paused outside the spinning world. Why would Maman give her necklace to me? Was she trying to let me know in what she perceived as the gentlest way possible that I was right—she was sick—and the necklace belonged to me now? Or was she simply trying to offer me a gift that was precious to her, that would say without words, *I love you this much, Vivienne. Please call me.*

"I don't know—" I folded my arms tight against my ribs, still peering down at the necklace. "I don't know what she means—"

"She probably means she loves you." I barely noticed Robert rising from his chair to stand behind mine. "I bet it's pretty easy to love you." Taking Maman's necklace from the box, he unclasped it. He fastened it around my neck, his fingers warm on my skin.

Returned to his seat, he watched me. "Your grandma had pretty good taste." He stabbed his fork at his salad.

I touched the little gems that hung sharp and cool below the hollow of my neck.

The rest of the night played out in disjointed slow motion. Robert and I ate. He tried to teach me about football, using a cherry tomato as a ball and marking scaled-down yards on the tablecloth with our silverware. Every minute or so, I would finger Maman's necklace and notice that Peter's longtime-friend's hands were invading what I would have deemed his personal space. She liked touching his arms, his hands, his shirt collar. A few times, she touched the food on her fork to his mouth.

I felt like my face filled up a movie screen, with Peter Breznik as the sole audience member, sitting on the front row watching me. But every time my eyes beat the force of my will and glanced at him, he was staring at his own private super model, likely blinded by the white-hot glow of her sex appeal.

Between analyzing Maman's gift and stealing glances of Peter, I could barely speak a coherent sentence for Robert.

When our petite crystal bowls of gelato arrived, he was waxing almost poetic about the virtues of practicing orthopedic medicine, but after taking a first bite of chocolate gelato, he set his spoon down in his bowl. "You're distracted."

"Wait, what?" I asked. Though Robert was correct. I had been interrogating the friendly Sonja in my head. *Do you write or read poems? Have you ever almost slept in Peter's blue sweatshirt?* I know I've sometimes speculated on the cultured, intelligent woman Peter must love, but I think that woman is a vision of who I want to be when I'm thirty.

Willing my eyes to focus on Robert, I reached my hand a few inches toward him on the tablecloth. "My dad sounds like you when he talks about brain surgery. You'll be a good doctor, Robert."

I really love that restaurant—Arugula—and I can't even remember right now what I ordered.

The only infinitesimally good thing regarding Peter happened when I stood to visit the washroom. I passed him so closely that his strong-tendoned hand resting at the edge of his table grazed the outside of my thigh. He looked up and said, "I enjoyed reading your work this week, Vivienne."

I halted a moment beside his and Sonja's table, touching my necklace again, saying that I had worked hard on those poems, because truly I had. They were specific but attempting to reach out to the world, to be resonant, to resist mere cleverness and anecdote. They were trying to make Anna Swir proud, not to mention Peter Breznik.

"Not just the poems," Peter said, "but a few other things." He has my craft essay on Tomaž Šalumun and Czesław Miłosz as well, which are basically tributes to the way Peter has taught me to read those poets.

And then he said kindly, in a completely magnanimous, unresentful way that practically seared my heart with its lack of jealousy, "That's a lovely necklace."

I inhaled what felt like a wrenching sob, but then swallowed when I realized he'd given me a chance to say, "It's a gift from my mother." I was even quick enough to add, "Robert's not my—he's a family—" But then a waiter interrupted us to ask Sonja if her swordfish was prepared to her liking.

Who even pretends to like swordfish?

Anyhow, little difference my twelve words to Peter will make.

Now I remember—I ordered bruschetta. With fresh Romas and garlic, and basil snipped right out of a pot, along with parmesan and olive oil and a hearty sprinkling of the kind of flaky salt I like to dust on my cookies. I ordered it as a main course and kept wishing Peter could taste it.

In the real world, my journal is probably being Xerox-copied for campus distribution as I write.

At least I might live in New York next semester.

I wish Hillary would get home from wherever she is tonight.

Robert walked me to my dorm from Arugula. I did not feel pinballs catapulting inside me—well, actually I did, but they were in my thigh, where it had been grazed by the side of Peter's hand. I did not feel pinballs for Robert, though after the beach, I had been open to the sensation—he is handsome and kind and a good-humored conversationalist. Shouldn't that be enough for attraction?

Walking beneath the moonlit branches of sycamores, I wanted it to be enough. I wanted warm arms to enfold me. I wanted the breath of my name to be kissed to my ear. But the arms and breath I wanted weren't Robert's.

Just before I unlocked the door to my building, he touched my arm. "Viviun?"

When I looked up at his eyes, which might be darker than mine—I could not even see the irises in the moonlight—he said, "Do you think we could try this again in New York? Going out, I mean? I know you think I'm a football-chucking dolt, but I like talking to you."

Right then—*right then*—I wonder now. If I had stepped closer to him, reached my hand to his wrist, would he have kissed me? Would I be writing now that his lips were soft, that he was gentler or fiercer than I had imagined? That for five seconds he made me forget about Peter?

He had said that he liked talking to me.

Still looking up at him, I envisioned Peter listening to me in the library, tilting his head down, watching so intently, as though he were collecting my words in a jar in his head that he'd empty later, just so that he could hear them again.

I couldn't imagine baking Robert one cookie.

Just to defy my own disinterested body, I said, "Yes, we could talk in New York this summer." Because why not? The man whose face I saw in my head was probably sharing his body with his longtime friend named Sonja at that moment.

Maman likes Robert. She likes him enough to entrust him with a necklace that holds a good part of her own maternal history.

Perhaps one day soon, I will call and describe last night to her. If Peter Breznik—ha!—doesn't profess his love to me first.

When I try to lie down, Maman's necklace digs at my skin, but I can't take it off, even if it was Robert who clasped it. Wearing it makes me feel like she's here, like even if she is sick and even if one day she is gone, I can keep her this close, lifting and falling with my breath.

———

Sunday, March 10, cont.
11:33 a.m., at my desk while Hillary is still sleeping
Almost six weeks since I spoke to my family

My journal is not in my room. I parted with all reason after writing last night—tore off my mattress cover, emptied my dresser drawers. No journal.

I remade my bed, sharply folding each sheet corner. I reorganized the clothes in my dresser.

When, in the dark, I sat on my bed covering my mouth with both hands, I thought I would cry, but I didn't. Instead, I lay back on my comforter and slept in my dress.

Of course Peter Breznik will not profess love to me. I woke up this morning knowing that, just as I know I must speak to my parents soon. A little light had switched on in my brain in the night, as must happen to babies when, for the first time, they wake clapping, *Sunshine!*

The light in my brain was shining on a tiny sign that read, "Grow up, Vivienne." All day I've felt a bit older.

And my leg still burns where Peter Breznik's hand brushed it.

And, as I should have been seeking the Lord at Mass on His day, I wrote a letter of apology to my parents that I will drop in the mail tomorrow.

I will copy it out here, so that I can read it whenever I need to remember how I sound when I am rational and penitent:

Dear Maman, Papa, and Luc,

Please forgive my silence these past weeks. I hope you are all healthy and enjoying early spring in Manhattan. I am sure Central Park is sprouting in green and Maman is looking forward to strawberries.

The truth is, I went silent because a beloved confidant, who shall remain unnamed, informed me that my far-away worry and need are a burden and agitation to you, and that you have all been more at ease these past two years in my absence. I was not very rational or mature after hearing this—I decided the best course of action would be to give you what you wanted, which as far as I knew, and still know, is silence. Even though I told myself I was trying to be more independent and was doing you a service, I knew I would hurt you, and I pray for your forgiveness.

I pray every day that Maman is well. God has blessed us these five years, and I am grateful. When I pester to know how Maman is doing, it is not always because I feel worried or weak or believe that the return of her cancer is imminent. It is because I love her and want to be near her if she is hurting. I want to be near all of you, though I know I can be stronger, more trusting, and more adult.

All of you are all my happiness. Please call soon. And Maman, thank you for sending your ladybug necklace. I do not believe I deserve such a gift, but I will wear it every day until I see you.

Vivienne

I wanted to write, *I have applied to Philbrick*—but I decided to start small and ask them to forgive my silence, knowing that I might have to ask them to forgive me for other infractions later.

As for my literary endeavors, I have been reading a book of Chinese poems in translation for Poetry. They are plainspoken, with simple sentences arranged gently on lines, and full of nature and wanting. Here is one by someone anonymous, written during the Six Dynasties, which means almost nothing to me, except that love hasn't changed in a very long time.

What Is the Matter with Me?

What is the matter with me?
With all the men in the world,
Why can I think of only you?

I think I will write a poem like that. I will alter the title and the rest of the poem just a little and submit it (not really) on Wednesday—

What Is the Matter with You?

What is the matter with you?
With the alarming shortage of poets in the world,
is it really so hard to pick me?

I can see Peter's typed response already: *Vivienne, I am confused by the "you" in this poem. I wonder if you might specify.*

I am tired of this yellow notebook. I rarely feel as cheerful as yellow. It undermines the bleakness within me.

What if I never find my journal?

———

So much to say, and so much of it hopeless.

I want to shape the day just as it happened, though.

I fell asleep beside my bed on my knees last night, praying the rosary, eventually deviating to say my own prayer along the lines of, *Our Father, Who art in heaven, if my journal could burst into flames wherever it is right now and be struck from the earth, I will call my parents tomorrow and honor their every desire, even if they desire for me to learn autonomy at a school someplace like Singapore, since California might not be doing the trick. Just please protect my life's record from devious and/or loose-lipped mortals like A.J., and preferably also from Peter Breznik. Glory be, etc. Amen.*

Also I prayed that if last night seemed a good night for God to take me, He could, with my blessing, as I felt that the multiple social and emotional fractures I'd caused might have become irreparable.

I woke at 5:12 a.m., ravenous and jittery.

Leaping out of bed, I kept dropping things in the dark—my alarm clock, my brush, my earrings.

"Vivi, calm down." Hillary rolled onto her back in her bed, her voice airy and high, as if traveling through the depths of a cave. "St. Brigid's isn't the Death Star. If a student finds your journal, they'll probably try to return it." She covered her eyes in the crook of her elbow, looking tired and spent in the pre-dawn dark. I wanted to kneel beside her bed and thank her for enduring my figurative spewing electrical wires, as Luc has so kindly described my existence. And then I wanted to ask her to hug me.

"You have such a merciful view of humanity." I clipped my bra-strap. "Any stranger would read a lost journal." I pushed my head through a t-shirt that had been wadded up on top of my bed for three days. "St. Brigid's isn't big enough for this kind of scandal."

Hillary pulled her Millennium Falcon comforter over her head. "But the people are kind enough, Vivi."

I shoved my stamped letter to my parents into the front pocket of my backpack, heart punching my chest as if shot from a canon.

I tromped to the library in time to be granted entrance between two librarians and proceeded to search for my journal in every restroom on all four library floors, past every desk I have ever studied at, even though I had searched my usual study areas on Friday. I kept wondering if someone could have stashed my journal in a wastebasket or a return-bin, or between psychology books on insanity as a joke.

Student library workers had begun wheeling their carts around like groggy proletariats, as a few puffy-eyed students dropped into chairs at computer databases and desks. I had just exited the fourth-floor restroom and was turning down a world history reference-book aisle so that I could cut over to Humanities, when (a person would have to be as blind as a baseball bat not to see this coming) I bumped into Peter Breznik.

As in: literally. My breast rammed his elbow as he stood scanning a ten-pound reference book.

"*Oh Vivienne!*" He clapped the book shut and leapt back.

On reflex, I pressed my hand to my breast like I was pledging allegiance. "Good morning," I said, still too shy to address him as "Peter." My tongue felt caught between blurting, *Sorry my breast touched your elbow!* and *I can't believe your elbow touched my breast!* I was despairing and exhilarated and in throbbing pain.

Peter glanced at my hand on my chest and blinked in a prolonged way that made me think he was trying not to look there. "Are you okay?" he said, because I guess a grown man can do that. He can ask an almost-woman if she crushed any tissue when her breast was nearly impaled by his elbow.

I lowered my hand. "I'm great," I said in a pitchy voice that made me think of teenage girls in sit-coms. "How was—"

I'd never lie about this: I almost said "The Blue Fairy." Was his long-time-friend Sonja heating coffee in his apartment right then?

I finally thought of a more general question: "How was your weekend?"

Peter looked tired—more yeoman farmer than Slavic prince—wearing an impossibly soft-looking, nubby gray sweater that his Yugoslavian grandmother had probably knitted. His honey-gold hair was more disheveled than usual, so that he looked closer to age 18 than 30, and I felt like his eyelids had extra folds in them. I wondered if Sonja had dropped him off at a curb somewhere along campus this morning, or if he had sprinted to the library from her arms.

Turning his profile to me, he slid the reference book he was holding back onto the shelf. When his head swiveled back to me, he made that editing-inside-himself face he can't hide when students read poems out loud in class, his cheeks and eyes squinching, brow creased. "It was . . ." he rested a forearm on the bookshelf beside us and sighed. "The weekend was just . . ." Clenching the fist of his arm on the bookshelf, he made a perplexed sound like, "Meh."

When I only stood there thinking, *BUT WEREN'T YOU SHARING YOUR PILLOW WITH YOUR LONGTIME GIRL-PAL SONJA?!!,* he tilted his head. "But it was cool seeing you at Arugula." He raked a hand through his hair as if suddenly remembering his bedhead. "And cool to see you before class in the library. I like bumping into you—" He glanced at my breast again. "I mean, I like when we run into each other." His hand shot up to wrap around his offending elbow, when it could have easily reached for my arm, or my hand, if only he'd have wanted it to. "Why is it so hard to find the right way to say that?" His glint of a smile felt like a match lighting up in my belly. I hadn't thought him capable of fumbling. Not ever in front of me.

He took a deep breath. "I mean that it's good to see you, Vivienne." He bent to lift his satchel from the library floor. "Your date seemed nice."

"My date?" I wanted to explain who Robert was, but I don't think I could have drawn enough air for that.

"Yeah—you know—the future medical student who accompanied you to Arugula, bearing a gift from your mother?" He slung his satchel strap across his body and opened the front pocket as though he had suddenly seen enough of me. But instead of dashing off, he pressed his satchel pocket closed without extracting anything.

Maybe, the thought wisped through my mind, he was trying to assess something—about me, or the weekend, or Robert—just as I wanted to find out about Sonja.

But why would he? Sonja could order wine and tap crumbs from his chin with her elegant manicured index finger. And she was probably quite confident about sleepovers.

But still, part of me thought—the part that hopes lightning bugs are fairy-sprites and mice take tea in shoeboxes—*she might not have read Anna Swir.*

Be rational, another part of me countered. *His eyes never left Sonja's face at Arugula.*

I was pretending to study reference book spines—*Europe 1924-1926, Europe 1926-1928*—and was suddenly and randomly entranced by numbers. If Peter were 28, I told myself, I should exit this aisle and resume my search for my journal. But if he were even just one year younger—27—the number seven is lucky and youthful, and 27 is not so terribly far from 20—I could maybe/sort-of/almost imagine us meeting up to bike along the coast after finals. I could less ridiculously envision his blue eyes caressing me over coffee. Or dinner. Or after he ran his finger along my collarbone.

(I don't really mean "his blue eyes caressing me." Or maybe I do. The language center of my brain has been malfunctioning since my breast opposite-of-caressed Peter's elbow.)

He twisted his satchel around so that it rested behind him. He was still peering down.

Why shouldn't I ask his age? I wondered. My life had been flashing before my eyes since before sunrise. I had no pride to lose, and even if I had, I would lose it as soon as Peter picked up a copy of my journal, or as soon as A.J. handed him one and said, "I'll dial and you can speak to the asylum."

I was unsure of the appropriate tone to assume just then with Peter, so my breathless voice came out sounding skeptical, "How old are you?"

His head snapped up, much like the pulse in my throat, but he didn't look like he felt violated or irritated. He closed his eyes and sighed apologetically. "You're right. I'm acting like I'm twelve. Commenting on your date? Who does that?"

"What?" I whispered.

Peter had been almost unnoticeably shifting his weight from one foot to the other but stopped. He was probably growing antsy to leave,

Sonja's shimmering form occupying most of his conscious, and unconscious, brain space.

"I've just wondered how old you are." The words rushed out of me. "Since it seems like you've accomplished so much already."

He glanced at his watch, as if looking for the answer to how old he was, but also as if I had kept him too long.

"You don't have to tell me your age—or stay!" I shook my head. "I'm so sorry I ran into you—I mean, your elbow!" As I pivoted on my left foot to turn from him, I felt a tug on the top loop of my backpack. When I turned back, he let go the loop and pressed his hand to the strap of his satchel.

I lifted my eyes from Peter's hand on his chest to his eyes that were narrowed in their listening gaze.

"Vivienne, you don't have to be sorry. I'm 26. But here's a question for you. Have you ever spoken my name?"

He's 26? I was thinking. *So when he turns 56, I'll be 50? We're practically Irish twins.*

I had expected that if I ever learned that he was younger than 28, my brain would explode like fireworks over the Hudson. But instead, I pictured the small bright wooden house that Mémère sent Luc and me many years ago for Christmas—the one covered with elaborate doors that we had to unlock with tiny gold keys hidden inside the little house's walls.

In my mind, as I stood watching Peter Breznik watch me with his listening face (or was it his wanting face?), a hundred little doors in my mind began opening.

I pushed my fingers under my backpack straps. "I can say your name—I just choose not to. You're my instructor."

His eyes narrowed further. "And how old are you, Vivienne?" Was he implying that my choice not to say his name was juvenile, or was he sincerely wanting to know my age?

Everything was hushed, as if we were in . . . a library.

"I'm twenty, but you know"—I tried to make breathing in sound less like gasping—"the wisdom of my poems probably ups me to at least 27."

He pressed his lips tight, looked off in the distance, nodding thoughtfully. I could practically hear the bright-polished cogs of his brain engage, no doubt churning out thoughts like, *Your age explains everything!—why you're so timid and awkward and have carob-colored hearts in your eyes when you see me.*

He looked at me. "A green finch scissored by like a pulse on a heart monitor."

That was a line from a poem I'd turned in last week. He was looking at me and quoting my poem from memory.

"I wrote that," I said.

"I'd have thought a person would have to be at least 29 to write a line like that." He wasn't shifting his feet anymore. He was standing up tall, looking down at me, his fists in his pockets, his lips curving into a crooked smile. "You must have done quite a few things early."

I reached a hand to a bookshelf to keep myself balanced. To hear my own words spoken by his voice so easily, as if they had a home in his brain—as if he'd cleared room for them there, kept them close and set them apart. It made me want to tell him everything: that the poem was about my mother when we weren't sure if she was living or dying, that I am terrified right now that she is dying, that I have jumped from the skiff I have sailed with her and am floating away and am not sure she will take me back.

I wanted to tell him that I'd lost my journal and if I didn't find it today, I might catch a Greyhound to New York, because I have a hard time existing amid uncertainty and loss and the possibility of emotional exposure. And also, I wanted to let go the breath I felt like I'd been holding since I was 15 and say, *Could you wrap your arms around me?*

Even more irrational, he looked at me as though he would say yes—he would pull me against him and press my cheek to his sweater that looked so worn—it was probably knitted during WWII—and he'd let me just breathe and count his heartbeats.

The *click* of my swallowing burst the quiet enveloping us. I thought briefly of saying that he had likely done a few things early himself to be earning a doctorate and teaching at St. Brigid's at age 26—in two departments—but I worried suddenly that I was taking our moment in the stacks more seriously than he was. I tried to shrug as though people recite my poems all the time. "My teachers always say I'm advanced."

I don't trust that I read his body language so objectively, but his chin turned up and his eyes slightly widened when I said that, as though he, too, had been inside the quiet settling like a conduit between us. "I think I wrote something like that on your last batch of poems—*Vivienne, these are—all caps—ADVANCED.*"

I bounced my backpack up on my shoulders again in a way that signaled I intended to go, but as I pulled my fingers from one backpack strap to wave a nonchalant goodbye, he touched the tip of one of his hiking boots to the toe of one of my Keds. I froze, staring at our shoes in a half-turned-away, half-wishing-I-could-rest-in-his-arms position.

"Say it," he whispered.

I pulled my foot back, my eyes darting to his and then back to our shoes, separated now by so much tight-weave burgundy carpet. "Say what?" I asked.

Fists still in his pockets, he shrugged his shoulders, his lips spreading into a wider, crookeder smile. He looked like a boy who had just handed a girl a note asking if she'd want to go steady. I glanced at the titles on book spines again to make sure they were still etched in English and not in the chicken-scratch language of an alternate dimension.

"My *name,*" Peter whispered.

A warmth filled my chest like tea poured into a cup. I let go a breath. He wanted me to acknowledge him beyond his role as my teacher. He wanted me to say that I noticed him, which he has said to me, in a sense, many times, in his responses to my work and when he tries to talk to me.

Julie appeared in my mind, sitting across from me at Palmiers: *Word in the History Department is that he'd never cross a line.*

Yet he had just tapped my shoe and asked me to say his first name in a dimly lit aisle of the library. It was innocent enough that I could still see a line in my mind between us, but it was pastel-blue watercolor, not thick-tip black Sharpie.

I was just looking at him, not blinking.

"I say your name every day, Vivienne"—he quick-shook his head, taking one step toward me—"I mean every other day. I'm sure you can say my name one time in the library." He nudged my shoe again. Twice. He had touched my shoe twice. "I'm defending my dissertation next month and visiting my family in Ljubljana for the summer, and who knows where I'll go after that. You don't have much time to call me by my name."

"Excuse me—" A student librarian shoved her book-crammed cart down our aisle, squeezing between us.

I blinked my own eyes closed. When I opened them, Peter was stepping backward to exit our aisle.

I wanted to cry, "Wait! Wait! Peter!" And actually, I wanted to cry. He was leaving.

He was leaving the library and possibly The United States of America. Forever.

And possibly, I would be leaving St. Brigid's.

All I could order my body to do was turn in the opposite direction as he whisper-called, "See you in class, Vivienne! You have impeccable taste in t-shirts!"

I looked down to see, for the first time since leaving my room, that I was wearing a black kid-sized t-shirt that I had dropped on my bed last week. It was the one Luc gave me at Christmas, in memory of the three or four times Maman had allowed us to watch after-school television as children. Emblazoned on the front are a semi-naked, although-armed, He-Man, Teela, and Man-at-Arms, a lightning bolt charging into He-Man's raised sword, "I have the POWER!" printed in a slanted white font over everything.

No one could believe I was 27 in that t-shirt.

One hour later, I walked into Poetry eight minutes early and found my journal on top of my desk.

My journal.

On my desk.

In Poetry.

A fluorescent ceiling light flickered over the leather-bound notebook so that it flashed like a gift from heaven, or a missive sent straight from hell. Even as panic began needling my brain, I thought clearly of two possibilities: Someone had found it, kept it shut, and returned it, or someone had found it, read it, and planned to humiliate and/or wreck me.

Finding my breath, I stepped to the front of my desk, bracing to hear a choir of angels or shrieks of the damned.

"Isn't that shirt a little sexy for you?"

I looked up to see A.J. sitting at a desk in the back corner of the classroom.

He appeared as demon-like as humanly possible, blowing wisps of black hair from his eyes, his camera bag like a guard dog slumped at his feet.

Had he arrived at class early to set my journal on my desk? Was asking about my t-shirt meant to distract me from that possibility?

His tone was menacing and superior, and I could have sworn my journal buzzed in the ceiling light. I felt edgy and charged and not in a mood to be bullied. All my frustration over every word he'd ever uttered to disparage me built up as pressure in my mouth. When I spoke, my voice shook with anger. "I bet you look at your little-boy He-Man books with a flashlight under your covers at night."

Watching me, A.J. rose from his chair, his green eyes so flat, I wondered how light gets into them. One wet-glinting side of his mouth curled up. "Actually, under my covers, I study pictures of you, Poetgirl."

My heart beat like a game of whack-a-mole. "As if you have any."

My legs, on their own, stepped back as A.J. walked calmly down his aisle and turned toward me. "Aw, Poetgirl." He stopped at the side of my desk.

I nearly tripped over my feet to the other side, intent on keeping solid matter between us.

"You think I give two shits about poetry?" His fingertips skimmed the cover of my journal. "The bleeding-heart erudite prigs like you can have it." He pointed to his camera bag at the back of the room. Obviously, it wasn't a guard dog, but I could imagine a sleeping rabid Pitbull inside it. "My art is pictures, hot-ass, which speak more than your whiney twelve-line zingers ever could." Leaning over my desk, he kept watching me.

I clenched my hands into fists.

"I see you sometimes—marching to class, or scribbling in that"—he smirked at my journal—"cliché of a diary, and sometimes I take a picture. You have no idea the images that get passed around on this campus.

And lots of guys get off on that prim sexy look you're flaunting." He sounded so composed, like he spent his free time illuminating Bible text. But he rounded to the front of my desk like a wolf as he spoke, and I side-stepped behind my chair like a trapped thing.

I wanted to ask where he had found my journal, but all I could do was try to breathe through the pounding inside me. I could force nothing, not even CO_2, from my mouth. What had I thought I'd accomplish by goading him? What was the point of his desk-stalking?

His glowering eyes dropped to my journal. I envisioned my brisk walks to campus, the innumerable places I've written.

As if tracking my thoughts, A.J. squinted and pressed his palms on my desk, framing my journal between his hands. His head lifted to my face. "I see you everywhere. I left a couple photos on that table once for Peter." He pointed to the table that Peter always set books on.

The pure crystalline stupidity of the idea enabled me to activate my vocal cords. "You're a lying ass." My face felt like an eruption of those bang-snaps kids toss on the Fourth of July. I backed into the desk behind me.

Bodies had begun shuffling in the hall outside the doorway, voices carrying into the classroom. I swear I heard Julie exclaim, "Hello, Prince Charming!" to someone—probably Peter. I wanted to reach for my journal, but I didn't want to touch A.J.'s hands.

Abruptly, he stepped to the right of my desk, looming over me, speaking faster. "The way you keep noticing my ass makes me think you want it." He glanced at the doorway. "We could get it on in the hall, Poetgirl." Another quick glance, his voice lower, "But we all know you're saving it for the"—he tapped my journal and mouthed the word—"*INSTRUCTOR.*"

A thick heat poured out in my chest.

I looked down at my journal and then up at A.J., picturing his stroll into the classroom before me, the lazy way he would have dropped my journal to my desk.

He'd read it. My journal had been in his hands.

My words had been in his head.

Those facts felt more violating than even his claim that he secretly watched me and took pictures. I thought I'd imagined every possible humiliation that might follow the loss of my journal, but my imagination had failed. I had thought of someone making copies or handing my journal to Peter, but I hadn't come close to foreseeing this actual hell: An empty, combative, misogynist boy had been in possession of the rawest, most exposing desires of my heart, and could, from now on, appear at the quietest, least-expected moments to torment or tease or manipulate me. I stood glaring at his neck, unable to imagine drawing breath in my suddenly altered universe.

Yet there I remained, a foot away from the most wretched human being I knew, fists clenched like they meant to pummel his ribs in. I wondered if I was having an aneurysm. I wondered how people like A.J. existed—people who didn't love people; who didn't seem to care if other people loved them.

A.J.'s eyes locked on my journal again. "I bet Peter would love to know you write *allll* about him." He reached down to lift the cover. I lunged forward on instinct, only to be stopped by A.J.'s hand on my shoulder.

"What's going on here?" Peter stood just inside the classroom door, eyes wide and scanning me, a handful of students craning their necks behind him.

"Ask her." Letting go my journal, A.J. stepped away and nodded. "Or should I tell him, Poetgirl?"

Please God, even now as I'm writing in the library, I want to be vaporized. *Is* there an alternate universe? Another planet? Please could You beam me up, Holy Father?

The whole class had assembled behind Peter Breznik.

I was standing, but my legs had been cut off from blood-flow somehow. My skin was on fire. Tears scalded my corneas.

I did not want to be weak; I did not want to explain or say I was sorry. I did not want to cower behind my desk anymore. I hefted my backpack up higher on my shoulders, looking at Peter, who was looking at me like—I don't know—like he wanted to save or banish me.

"Peter—" I paused at his name, even in my distress, for emphasis. "I think I've reached a limit."

Peter stood very still, inhaling so that his chest puffed even broader than normal. As I stepped around my desk toward the door, students cleared away. Julie stood alarm-eyed and flushed, pressing her manicured hands to her mouth.

"A.J. You and me—outside a minute." Peter held my arm as I passed him. "Vivienne. Don't forget your journal."

His hand on my arm didn't drop right away. Students were approaching their desks, everyone too uncomfortable to look at each other, let alone at me and our graduate instructor. As I met Peter's eyes, his palm moved to my elbow.

"Peter—" I said his name again.

His hand fell. "I'll call you."

I retrieved my journal from my desk and left for this basement corner in the library.

Walking here, I somehow thought to drop my letter to my parents into the blue box outside the Admin building. It's strange how even in new distress, old distress doesn't leave you.

It's 11:15 a.m. now, and I am writing in my actual journal. I feel like it's already next Wednesday. Peter touched my breast, my shoe, and my arm in one morning, and now A.J. has possibly ended my life as I've known it.

By the time I arrive at next Wednesday, a thousand new heartaches will have found me.

I had to pause my writing after that last sentence to think for a while. A question keeps scrolling through my brain like a movie credit: *Who do you want to be, in the next week, and after?*

I have *The Norton Anthology of Poetry, A Guide to the Romantic Poets,* four poetry collections, three college-ruled notebooks, eight recipes for chocolate chip cookies, a Philbrick course-description booklet, and a bus timetable in my backpack. I have parents from whom I've estranged myself for over a month, a brother whom I allowed to shut me out of the life I thought I was central to, a mortal enemy who holds power to expose me in ways I would without question struggle to recover from, and a graduate instructor I have undoubtedly lost to my own careless documenting.

Where can I even go from this moment?

I want a body to hold me now. I want a body to be my home.

I can still feel Peter Breznik's palm at my elbow, the way I always feel him after he's touched me.

I have to be my own home now.

A.J. has read my journal. He will tell Peter the worst of it. It is possible that A.J. copied portions, by machine or by hand, or that he took pictures of specific pages—he could show anyone he wanted.

I keep looking up for a camera.

Papa used to say: "What is the worst that could happen, Vivienne?"

Well, Papa, I answer now, *beaucoup des choses:* Students could mock me, professors grow skeptical of my presence; Peter could be ashamed and feel I've too publicly crossed a professional line—he could ask me to transfer Poetry sections. He could ask me that anyway, since I engaged in an altercation in his classroom.

He probably would not lose his chance to teach at St. Brigid's because of my journal, but would he bear censure from authority for interactions I recorded?

Fortunately for us both—though the thought blinds my brain—he will probably leave the U.S. in May, and I will say goodbye to St. Brigid's. Everything I've written will whisper away until even beetle antennas on walls twitch louder.

Which leaves me to devise an independent course and mantra:

Manhattan, Philbrick, teaching. Writing, bakery, books.

I imagine the pads of A.J.'s fingertips touching my words.

I don't know if I'll write in this journal again.

Monday, March 11, cont.
8:36 p.m., lying on my bedroom floor even though that's disgusting

The fact is, I should never write in this journal again.

Do you understand that, Vivienne? Your rarely present wiser self is addressing you: Wrap this journal in a scarf and hide it at the back of your sock drawer.

Or at the very least, live by a rule: This journal does not leave your bedroom.

Or revise that rule: This journal does not leave the three-foot circumference surrounding your bed and your desk.

Or—Papa would agree—*stop writing about yourself altogether.*

But I must write (this is the usually present, unwise Vivienne again), and there are pages left. Wasn't it Charlotte Bronte who said, "I am just going to write because I cannot help it"? Words are like that for me—relentless and choking. When I give in to writing one word, a Niagara follows. Words white-cap out of me. Should I give A.J. power to stop them?

Hillary is busy with a theater project this week. She'll be gone around the clock, and I'll miss her, especially now that I am anxious about going out. I need her to walk across campus with me, to knee A.J. in the crotch against a wall and tell him he'll get something sharper than her knee if he ever mentions my journal again or lurks nearby with his Leica.

Heaven knows St. Brigid's won't investigate malicious photography. At the beginning of every semester, Admin and student-body convene for an opening address, in which our male president, a supposed staunch Catholic, waxes eloquent on topics such as human dignity, integrity, honor, and respect, and spends the meet-and-greet afterward touching and flirting with any female student or professor ignorant enough to pass by within five feet of his hands.

But would an angry woman's knee to the crotch send an accurate message to A.J.? The most effective response to him might be apathy. If I were to see him again, I think I would say—

Nothing.

I would keep walking. I would not lower myself to glance at his camera lens.

The telephone keeps interrupting my sentences. Although she won't be home much this week, I asked Hillary not to answer the phone until my parents leave a message saying they received my letter. Until then, we'll let all calls go to our answering machine. Peter said he would call me, but after he spoke to A.J. in the hall, I firmly—as in the immovable stance of Mt. Everest—doubt he'll have more words to say to me, unless he would like to suggest I transfer into the other section of Poetry 421. Or visit a therapist. At some point this week, he will probably advise both.

Anyhow, if he were to call, he would leave a message.

But hang on—

That was Peter ringing our phone, sounding as passionate as 911 dispatch.

It's over.

I can hardly summon the will to transcribe what we said, which conversation I've listened to precisely 24 times, because the machine didn't stop recording when I answered.

This is exactly what we sounded like:

He started to leave a message. *Yes. Vivienne. This is Peter Breznik. I'm calling because—*

> *Hello? This is Vivienne.*
>
> *Vivienne. How are you?*
>
> *Ça va, I mean—I'm okay. How are you?*
>
> *I'm guessing you might be worse off than I am.*

Because I'm the one who—even if I didn't outright profess love to him—described in a journal, in furious detail, (which has no doubt been gleefully re-capped for him, courtesy of A.J.) the zeal of my attraction to him and implied without question that I would not be sad to devote the rest of my life to his care. Also, I probably wrongly conveyed that he might return my affection.

> *I suppose I've seen better days. I'm so sorry—*
>
> *Vivienne—*

No, really, I can't even tell you—

I think we should talk in person. Could you meet in my office tomorrow at 2 p.m.? We can discuss options for moving forward with the class, and talk about—

Options? As in, your current class is no longer a given? Because of everything that's happened with A.J. and my—

I think I've come up with a better situation.

-

-

-

-

-   (The dashes are seconds. I timed them.)

-

Vivienne?

-

-

Okay.

Is tomorrow at 2 p.m. convenient?

Yes, it's convenient. I'll see you then.

Thank you, Vivienne. I'll be waiting.

The line clanked off like a steel bolt between us.

I know I've determined my independent course and mantra. I'm prepared to move forward. But I keep thinking about the line Peter blurred yesterday. In my head, it transformed to a route we could have traveled together, toward an apartment in Brooklyn, in which there would have been two desks at two windows, perhaps with a view of magnolia trees and my bakery. Peter could have held me at night in our narrow bed that maybe the subway would have rattled as we slept, and then further down the route would be children, two blue-eyed, one brown, and though Peter would love them all equally, he would call the brown-eyed girl *mon petit rêve,* or however one says *my little dream* in Slovene.

And there would be books we had written, and bios—

Even living on my own, Brooklyn would be lovely. I'm sure I could write and bake there.

But what on earth will I wear to my 2 p.m. meeting with Peter tomorrow?

Wednesday, March 13, 1:12 a.m.

I don't know where to begin.

After missing today's—or now it is yesterday's—classes and changing my outfit six times, I made what felt like a military-themed march to Peter's office.

I debated wearing a red mock turtleneck, but I can never detach red from the Chris de Burgh song, and I was definitely not wanting to connote music or cheek-to-cheek dancing; so I went with a long-sleeved, black silky button-up with shoulder-pads. I pushed tiny gold square studs in my ears, and then shifted Maman's ladybug necklace so that the tiny black and red crystals glinted like flecks of hot coal at my collarbone.

I wore liquid-black eyeliner, and my shoes were black, too—slender pumps with a thin-buckled strap around my sheer-black, pantyhose-covered ankles.

Finally, I switched out my backpack for an envelope-shaped black clutch that dangled from my shoulder on a beaded gold chain. I had wanted to look like a woman prepared to receive a verdict, but I looked like I was enlisting for duty.

Standing at Peter's office door, I debated a two, three, or four-beat knock. Two would have been too timid, and four would have echoed Beethoven's Fifth. So with three firm beats, I summoned Peter Breznik to his door in a seal-gray suit and an ice-blue tie. His eyes were luminescing. They dropped to my shoes and flew up to my face.

"Are you going somewhere after this?"

I pressed my palm to my purse at my hip as if it held answers to the mysteries of life and creation. And then I lied. "I have another meeting."

He tugged at the knot of his tie, which, I noticed, jutted out to one side a little. An image of Maman straightening Papa's tie before work lit up like a projected slide in my mind. Strange how I have been so angry at her but want so much to do every last thing she's ever done in her life. For a millisecond in Peter's office doorway, I wondered what day she'd receive my letter.

Kicking a wedge beneath the door to keep it wide open, Peter raised a hand to rub the back of his neck. "I had a meeting with the history department this morning—"

About the delusional and volatile female student in your poetry class? I nearly interrupted but stopped myself, knowing that Peter would come to that.

"Which is why I'm wearing a suit."

I'm sorry, I wanted to say. *I'm sorry that you had to dress your gorgeous self up because of my poor behavior.*

"But if you have a minute after we talk, I wondered—" Peter stopped when our eyes met. My eyeliner probably rendered him speechless. His arm fell from his tie to his side. "Have a seat, Vivienne."

I sat in the same chair I'd occupied when he'd given me Anna Swir— when for the very first time, he'd described my own poems to me. The roof of my mouth turned prickly and hot. I silent-chanted my independent route and mantra: *Manhattan, Philbrick, teaching. Writing, bakery, books.*

He sat down in his chair, leaned into his forearms over a snow-white sheet of paper set precisely in the center of his desk. He smiled. "How are you?"

I could tell he was trying to be careful—like a doctor bearing both good news and bad.

"Fine," I said.

I was thinking, *This is such a small moment, housed in such a small space, but it will spin like a planet in my memory.* Peter's body and mine had hardly ever touched. He'd never held my hand or my waist; we'd never occupied the same material space for longer than a class period. Yet I had given him my words.

From the first tentative ink stroke I put down on paper, I knew I was writing to him. The weight of each word and the shape of each line, the vibrance and surprise of each image—everything I wrote was for him, intangible gifts I imagined him opening and taking inside his mind for safekeeping.

I had envisioned him holding my poems to a window's clear light, turning them in his hands to various angles before sitting down to respond. The words he wrote to me would accumulate in my chest, imprint their rhythms on my pulse. In this way, he would feed my next poem. He was an energy inside me.

Sitting across from him, waiting to hear my options and working to store the image of the faint crinkly V's at the corners of his eyes, I felt like our meeting would be some kind of event—a quiet one, yes, yet it would resonate over days and months and years of one life: *Here was an ending.*

I pictured him suddenly in the library, sniffing his sweatshirt that I'd infused with my cider shampoo, telling me it smelled like apples.

"Would you like some tea?" He glanced over his shoulder at an electric kettle on a bookshelf. "I have chamomile."

I gripped the student chair's armrests, wondering why he was prolonging the inevitable.

Was he planning to mention my journal? Certainly A.J. had given him highlights in the hall when they'd spoken yesterday.

I wasn't sure whether I should lead out with apologies: for embarrassing him both personally and professionally by detailing my fantasies concerning him on pages that I had failed to guard with my life, or for making a scene in his classroom by egging on an angry, devious, camera-wielding ass. How had I planned to end that discussion with A.J.? By punching his nose with my kitten strength?

I decided to stick to the business of my termination as a student in Poetry 421, as it seemed a more straight-forward topic.

"I'm ready to hear my options."

"You know what? I'm taking this off." He stood from his chair to remove his suit jacket, my eyes no doubt stretching as wide as if he were spur-of-the-moment undressing. Stepping to a skinny metallic coat tree near the open door, he hung up his jacket. "When I was a kid, I refused to even wear shirts. So you can imagine how stifling that thing is."

Thank you, I thought to say but didn't. *Thank you for giving me here at the end an image of you taking your shirt off.*

I fingered Maman's necklace. Words—I have never written this sentiment—failed me.

Re-situated at his desk, Peter lifted the crisp white paper, his neat golden eyebrows nearly touching in the middle. "You look like you think I'm about to crush all your hopes and dreams."

I found myself instinctually and perfectly channeling Maman. "By all means, present the options, so that I can know if they'll crush me." Of course, Maman is not one to fanny-slap or high-five, but I think she would have given me a few quick *bises* on the cheek for saying that.

Maman, I thought, would never cross a line. Pursing my lips as she does when she's sticking to a plan, I vowed that I would be her, no matter how attractively Peter leaned forward in his desk—like the south-pole to my north-pole magnet. There was only one way this meeting would go—in a straight course toward my re-assignment to Poetry 421, section one, which was already too packed with aspiring poets.

"So here's the thing"—Peter leaned farther forward to lift a pencil from the green-glass vase on his desk. "We both know Admin wouldn't get around to addressing A.J.'s behavior till three semesters from now, if ever, and A.J. thinks he's graduating in May. So I talked to Alene Bautista last night—she teaches the other section of Poetry 421—and we think we can handle this ourselves. Are you comfortable with that?"

I could feel myself squinting as I'm prone to do. He had an interview this morning and stayed up last night sorting through my fate with the English Department Chair and Haworth-Award-winning Alene Bautista?

The intensifying effect of his blue tie below his eyes was making me seasick.

I looked at my watch. It's silver, and it clashed with the theme of my outfit, so I'd kept it under my shirtsleeve, but at that moment, I needed to appear less crushable, less invested. "I think I'm comfortable with that. I agree that Admin won't do much to help." And though I risked exposing my heart, "You really think we need to do something?"

Pulling back a little, Peter appeared to be examining the tooth-gouges in his pencil. "Yes. I think we need to do something. I mean, I don't think A.J. is dangerous. He said he told you that he takes pictures of you, but then he swore on his vintage Leica that he doesn't. But I'd still prefer for him not to breathe the same air as you."

He didn't give me a second to process that.

"Like I said, he's finished with St. Brigid's at the end of the semester, and he needs this poetry elective to graduate. I've agreed to let him stay in my class, with the understanding that if he so much as accidentally looks away from my face at a female student, he will fail and lose his opportunity to graduate."

"You've talked to him already?"

He straightened in his chair. "Last night. It was a short conversation."

The ladybugs of Maman's necklace thumped just below my collarbone. "And what are you thinking for me?"

"Well, I feel like you should have one option, but Alene says you need three."

I'd been right. My words and actions had been too disruptive.

End of poetry. One option.

I squeezed two beaded ladybugs together. "So tell me."

He scooted his chair closer to his desk, presumably so that he could push his paper closer to me and thereby ensure that I could read every 12-pt. Times-New-Roman-font word. He touched the first bulleted item with his pencil tip.

"Okay, first we think you should have the option to drop the course altogether. As you know, Alene's the department chair—she'll sign off on it."

I just have to ask: Shouldn't sheer pantyhose be cooler than tights?

"I think I would not prefer that," I said.

He angled his pencil off to the side. "That's what I told Alene. So second, you could remain enrolled in the class, and we'd just finish it off on an independent-study-type basis. You know, I'd give you assignments. You'd finish them on your own and submit them to me."

"Why wouldn't I choose that?" That was really an option? And he hated it?

Because the point was our separation. Not only had I contributed to a public disturbance with a camera-wielding man-boy in Peter's classroom, but I had also romanticized even casual exchanges between myself and him in a journal that would likely go public.

Peter penciled light circles around the third option. "Well, because my preferred option is this—that you simply transfer to Alene's class and finish the semester without me as your instructor."

I leaned down to the side of my chair as if to unzip my backpack, or to just pick it up and go, but then I remembered that it was currently spilling its contents at the foot of my bed in my room, so I sat up. I un-snapped and re-snapped my purse. "You choose that option." I meant it as a question, but it settled between us as an irrefutable statement, a stone wall holding back a deep churning sea. "Isn't Bautista's Poetry section full?"

"No section of any class is ever entirely full. Alene would add you." Though it seemed physically impossible, Peter leaned even farther to-ward me at his desk. I felt like he would have taken my hand in his if I had reached for it. He would have said he was sorry, but he had realized something important yesterday: I was too young, and in writing so care-lessly, I had exposed him to students, and possibly to colleagues, in ways that had destabilized our friendship and potentially his career, and noth-ing could be done to undo that. He could no longer be in a class with me.

His voice was so soft, even as he crushed my hopes and dreams. "In my mind, that's the only option."

My own voice trembled as a last fluttering leaf on a branch. "But I wouldn't be with you. Not ever. If you don't want me to be physically in your class, at least let me choose the second option so that I can finish the chance I had to learn from you as my instructor."

He pressed his pencil again to the side of *Vivienne may choose to transfer into Poetry 421, section one, taught by Professor Alene Bautista.* I tensed for the sharpened pencil-tip to snap.

Peter's eyes held mine, his head inching slowly toward the paper. "But Vivienne, that's the point. I would no longer be your *instructor.*"

Because I would be something else, he implied with his emphasis.

But had he really implied that?

Although the idea contradicted the outcome that I had tamped into every fold of my brain over the last 24 hours, I thought I vaguely un-derstood what he meant, and why he preferred not to spell it out point for point in his wide-open office while he was technically still my line-re-specting instructor.

But too much had happened since yesterday. I'd made too many turns—I'd finally accepted a more rational trajectory without him.

If A.J. had snapped a picture right then, it would have shown up on the negative as a blindfolded girl in a maze. I pressed my fingertips to my eyelids.

A slow beat commenced in my temple, like the ticking of an alarm or an explosive. True, for the past two months, I had been constructing mental images of Peter and me together as if in a sunlit love montage accompanied by Van Morrison, but was Peter Breznik saying that he, too, could imagine us together?

He dropped his pencil into the green glass vase. "I mentioned that I'm traveling to Ljubljana in May—"

"I have to think." I stood up.

"Vivienne." Peter rose to his feet across from me. "I'm not sure what's happening inside your head right now—I'd pay money to see a visual rendering—but I don't think we've been on the same page since you left class yesterday, and I wonder—have you read the response I left for you recently? You weren't there, so I—"

"I wasn't where?" The pulse in my head was quickening.

"You weren't where I was when I left my response for you. I tucked it inside one of your books—if you'd brought your backpack to our meeting instead of that little billfold, you could check it right now."

Was he irritated with me? Impatient? Chin tipping down, he darted a glance at his open office door before looking again at me, his eyes wide and expectant, as if projecting a silent code I was meant to interpret.

Tick, tick, tick, in my head.

"What's wrong with my purse?"

He tugged side-to-side at the knot of his tie. "Nothing! I just like your backpack. I like *you* hauling your backpack. Not that I wouldn't carry it for you—I would—because it looks heavy. I just—"

"No, that's okay—I'm not really a purse girl. But I have to go. I'll look for your response."

The ticking was slowing, like a timer unwinding toward its last second—*Go. Go. Go find what he wrote you.*

"But Vivienne—"

I think I transmogrified from his office.

One good thing about carrying a purse instead of hefting a backpack is that you can run with a purse. Except if you're wearing ankle-strapped pumps—even low pumps. I mean, technically, a person can run in them, and I did, but I lacerated the virgin skin of my ankles, and right now—hours later— my heels feel as though I hammered glowing-red coals into them.

By the time I stood outside my own door, I was paralyzed.

Until Hillary swung it open in a cowgirl hat and chaps, assumedly part of her theater project. She looked down at my shoes like Peter had earlier. "Your ankles are bleeding." She turned her head back to our room. "Robert the Misjudged sent you flowers, and your parents sent you a package."

I slipped—well, limped—past her through the door. I didn't even ask if there was also a letter from Philbrick. I only said, "I need my backpack."

Hillary stayed wedged between the door and its frame. "Robert sent daisies, if you're struggling to turn your head two inches to the left—the Gerbera kind—pink and red and yellow and white. There are like 500 of them."

Already kneeling beside my backpack at the foot of my bed, I glanced to where the daisies burst from a vase on my desk like a flower explosion of Trix cereal.

Hillary stepped into the hallway, as if sensing that I had entered my own soundproof box of a world. "Vivi, I have to work on my theater project till late. Are you going to be okay here?"

"Pretty sure." Backpack unzipped, I held up three fingers of my right hand, as if in a Girl-Scout oath. The ticking in my head started up again.

"Try not to be alone!" Hillary called before the door slammed shut.

In a silence that felt like suction cups on my ears, I began rifling through books in my backpack. Anthologies, collections, recipes, notebooks. No response from Peter tucked anywhere.

"Where would he have put it?" My eyes laser-beamed the ceiling, as if maybe God could tell me.

Receiving no answer, I stood to shake my backpack upside down as though it were a half-split stubborn pinata. Books slammed to the floor, dog-earing and page-crushing in one great heap.

And then, like the plop of a minnow after a blue whale's splash, my journal hit my foot. It opened to three folded sheets of lined paper.

I had only folded one page inside my journal—Peter's response to my poem about who I'd be if I was not who I thought I was. I had never tucked in two more sheets of paper. Had he when I wasn't aware of it?

I bent to pick up my journal, pressing it closed on the three unbound pages as I lowered myself to my mattress.

The journal fell open as I balanced it on my lap, the brisk angles and sharp loops of my words beckoning like inky metaphors. That's what they are, words: all metaphors. Shapes and sounds we imagine as tangible, embodying things, ideas, emotions. I say *raspberry,* and it fills you with sweetness. I say s*hadowed skin beneath your earlobe,* and you can feel his lips touch you there.

I untucked Peter's long-ago response from between the pages I'd written him. Folded inside that response were two more pages.

Only someone who had handled my journal could have inserted pages in that way. When I unfolded them, they were filled with his handwriting.

He found my journal. The words came as a dandelion wisp on a breeze.

He might have only written a poem response, I told myself, and right then, I determined I'd be okay with that. I touched the fingertips of one hand to my breastbone as if vowing, *I'll be content with whatever he's written.* I just wanted his words, addressed to me, no matter their rhetorical purpose.

I will keep them in this journal forever—

My Dear Vivienne,

Before you question my integrity or succumb to arterial fibrillation, allow me to tell you, and please believe, that I have not read a single word of your journal that was not addressed to me. Though I sense that nothing would engage my intellect more fiercely or give me more pleasure than doing so.

I watched your journal—you must be wondering—drop from your back-pack after last Thursday's reading. I had slipped into the auditorium late, having just returned from New York, and sat on the back row, missing every word of the famous poet for watching you. The way you bent in an aisle seat over your notes, writing fast enough to catch every word spoken, plus, no doubt, your own blazing thoughts, which I was left to only imagine.

A male student sat beside you, interrupting your writing every four-or-so minutes, clearly wishing to secure your attention, until you shook your head firmly, and he stopped. I walked in your direction when the reading ended, but you were in a rush to depart.

I did, however, see your journal fall from your open pack, so I picked it up, knowing you would be panicked to find it missing. But when I called your name, you had already disappeared into the halls of the Oppen Building.

I planned to obtain your phone number, Vivienne, but when I stopped by my office, my father called about a matter that required some attention. I walked home after midnight, and then made the mistake—or the lucky decision (you will determine which)—to take your journal from my pack at my apartment. I wanted to see something of yours in a space that was mine, and to be honest, it looked quite at home there. I left it on my desk overnight, and on Friday morning, just before leaving to collect an old—and now former—friend from the airport, I went to move your journal to my pack again but dropped it.

As I believe, Vivienne, that the breadth and vivacity of your imagination warrant academic mapping and study, you will no doubt be able to feel within yourself my own disbelief—and wonder—and happiness—when your journal fell open to a page addressed, "Dear Peter Breznik." Of course, I might have tried harder not to see your words on the page, but I rationalized that since what you'd written was intended for me, I would not be amiss to read it.

And so I did, Vivienne. I read you. Not as an instructor reads a student, or as a critic reads a poet. I read you as a boy reads the girl whose mere presence and voice spark sudden fire in his chest. Afterward, I knew that I could not return your journal until I had written you.

If you find what I have done dishonest, forgive me. Though I am not sorry, and would like to address the questions you posed in your letter.

1. You ask about the tenderness of your poetry. Does it stir a tendresse in me? Do I feel tenderness when I read you? I think of these lines you submitted last week—

Again I remember how the soul leaves the body
like mist rising off the East River.
Again I remember my father crying—

—and Vivienne, I fight an impulse to pull you to my chest and keep
you there.

2. *Does knowing that I am a "you" in your poems resonate with me, or does*
   it exceed the scope of my ability to relate or empathize?

Allow me to begin by relating. I have a father complex. My father, Andrej
Breznik, is not remotely ill, as I am sorry to hear your mother might be.
He is hearty and hale and reporting on imminent war in Yugoslavia. As
is my older brother, Tilen, who is also in good health and is reckless with
his life, and—to my father's great joy—ferociously politically minded.

I, too, as you might have guessed, am politically minded, but I respond to
world events in quieter ways, which disappoints and perplexes my father
and his like-minded firstborn, my brother. I suppose you could say that
I also have a brother complex. But I have addressed poems to both him
and my father before, none of which they have read, and it is cathartic to
write them. I must accept, however, that I lack your skill in addressing
two "you's" at once. I cannot think of a line from my father poems that
might simultaneously address you, Vivienne—not that I haven't thought
of you and your work as I drafted one, but those poems usually unfold
with images of my father's uncut gray hair, his sandpaper stubble, his
cracked-calloused hands that leave my skin scratched whenever he em-
braces me.

Do not misunderstand. He is a good man, and I do not doubt he loves
me, but I will never understand or please him, no matter how many poems
or essays I write.

All that to say—I empathize with your mother-complex. I feel an ache in
my chest when I imagine you grieved or suffering.

I think that perhaps the greatest evidence of resonance is wanting to some-
how write back, to demonstrate that one has felt similarly (as example,
this response to your response). On Sunday, I began a poem for you—

Vivienne, can you imagine me unclasping that necklace?

I'm not certain about it. It's possibly too straightforward. I admire the subtlety of your own efforts with "you." I wonder if you, Vivienne, might teach me.

(And just incidentally, what would be so terrifying about being my lover? Feel free to not read that hypothetically.)

3. *Would I myself like to know more about you, the writer of your poems, or simply more about your poems' constructed narrator, the "speaker"?*

I'll be succinct:

You, Vivienne. Every fragmented detail.

4. *Have I decided to interview in Manhattan?*

Perhaps I could answer you in person.

5. *Full Disclosure: I might have noticed that just prior to your journaled response, you wrote that I likely address all my students as "dear." This is not actually the case. I believe I typically begin responses with "Hi," or "Hey," or sometimes, I dispense with an initial greeting and say, "Thank you for sharing these poems, So-and-So." I suppose that's an opener I use when I feel little connection to a writer and their work, but to you and your poems, I have always felt some degree of attachment. For the record, I have never in my academic or personal life prefaced "dear" with the singular possessive "my," as I have in this letter, and I do not wish to imply that I feel I possess you, as one would possess, say, a Volkswagen. I think "my" in this case is lifted from a kind of metaphor—it is the "my" of "my heart's desire." I leave you to work out how you fit in that metaphor, and then decide if it resonates.*

As always, Vivienne, I hope my response is not over-long or overwhelming. I realize—as you no doubt realize as well—that in reading your personal writing and responding so personally myself, I am violating the professional line between us. What justification can I give for this? I'm a writer. I was written to by the human-equivalent of a meteor shower. I might as well cleave off my left hand than try to resist writing back.

As you cannot be both my student and my lover at present, I trust that these words will, as all our words have, remain between us. Beyond your integrity, I ask only that once you have found this response and read it, you reply to me in person, in my office, when I am no longer your instructor. If at any point before the semester ends, I can devise a way to absolve your current status as my student, I will contact you directly.

And if between the time you wrote to me and are reading this, you have pledged yourself to the debonair future medical student I watched in slow-motion lift your hair from your neck to clasp the necklace he presented you at Arugula, I would be desolate to hear it, but would wish you great happiness and many vivid flashbacks of our brief, extraordinary acquaintance.

All best, etc.—

Peter

p.s. I'm sorry about my eyes. I don't know that they've ever affected anyone in quite the way you describe. I'd close them or look away if I could live with the thought of not seeing you.

A.J. had never read my journal.

A.J. had never touched my journal.

I lay back on my bed, Peter's response in my hand, my world recalibrating like a bowling-alley pin deck.

Peter Breznik had touched my journal—he had set it on his desk at his home, held it in his hands and read a significant but very small portion. He knew enough—I mean, he knew basically everything (who knew I could capture so much in a one-page response?)—but I hadn't endangered his career or his dignity. According to him, I hadn't even made him laugh. I mean, I made him pick up a pen and write back.

Peter Breznik had written me a letter.

Peter Breznik, PhD candidate in History, sometime instructor of poetry, always-poet, son of Andrej and Zara, brother of Tilen. Raised in California and Slovenia, owner of hand-knit vintage sweaters and apple-scented sweatshirts. Lover of Eastern-European poetry in general and Anna Swir in particular. Promoter of metaphor and tenderness.

Maker of searing images. Blessed with blue eyes, unkempt honey hair; effortlessness in denim. Keeper of my poems and my heart.

That Peter Breznik had read a single page of my journal.

He had fought an impulse to hold me.

He, of all breathing lifeforms on this crowded planet, had envisioned my face and called me *my*.

And he had possibly interviewed to teach in Manhattan.

My parents' package sat on my pillow behind me. I kissed the fingers of one hand and reached them past my head to press the smooth cardboard box. I wanted things to be right between us, but their offering would have to wait. For the first time since I was pulled from my mother's womb and dropped onto her breast, bearing her features and streaked with her blood, I was choosing someone before her.

When Peter opened his office door to me, his cursed blue eyes did the same down-up sweep they'd done when he saw me two hours earlier. I froze, mentally tallying my clothes to make sure I was fully dressed— skirt, shoulder pads, belt, eyeliner—and oh, yes: My pointer finger tugged at a crystal ladybug still resting below my collarbone. Next, I noted my tights, run through to threads at the ankles, and anchoring it all, my wool-lined, pink-crocheted slippers. I hooked one foot behind my ankle, revising the scenarios I'd envisioned as I walked/ran the path to Peter's office: I would spend my first non-student moments with him in pink house shoes.

And of course my hair was more electrified than I'd expected. His hair had been mussed in all kinds of direction since I'd light-sped from his office earlier, and his icy-blue tie was hanging from his spindly coatrack.

He said, "I worried you wouldn't come back," quieting some of my heartstrings and stirring some others.

Rumpled and weary, he struck me as an earnest farmer again—a modern-day version of Thomas Hardy's Gabriel Oak, who would look a woman in the eye and say, "Whenever you look up, there I shall be—and whenever I look up, there you shall be."

Looking down at my speechless form in the doorway, Peter's chin dipped closer to his chest. He inhaled and closed his eyes, bringing a broad hand up to rub at them. As soon as his hand dropped away, he leaned past my shoulder and glanced down the history-department hallway, one corner of his lips stretching up in a grin that seemed caught between bashfulness and mischief. "You make me self-conscious." His voice tripped all the hair on my arms up.

After reading his letter, I assumed that my tongue would be loosed by God or Cupid, and that I'd be able to speak eloquent, spur-of-the-moment, heart-piercing sentences, either straight to his face or into his ear, but as is typically the case when I see him, I just stood looking up, afraid of my airways constricting. "I read—"

"Come in here." He loosened my hand from Maman's necklace, pulling me toward him, into his office, the door snicking shut behind us, triggering a flash of image and idea: a splintered door swinging open, light filtering in. On one side, a before; on the other side, an after. Even if a person stepped right back through the door, that action would still be after; the body would be altered in some way for having stepped through—even if the alteration were as simple as growing five seconds older.

"I love that face." Peter and I stood between his desk and his student chair.

I barely heard my own voice say, "What face?"

"The one you're making right now—when your lips part a little and your brow's pinched. You look like you're trying to see something, but it's something in your mind—you're thinking."

I shut my mouth, then opened it. "I was picturing a door."

His closed-lip smile spread slowly across his face, and though it is a loss not to see his teeth when he grins, his closed-lip smile is the rarer gift, I think—the soft one he saves for people he lets into the quiet.

"I opened a door for you," he said, as though he apprehended every glint of my metaphor.

His letter to me: an opening door. I had walked through it.

A ripple of worry blurred over his forehead. "Do you want me to prop my office door open?"

"No," I said, holding his gaze as if our sudden proximity didn't strike enough fear to send me sprinting for my dorm and the comfort of whatever might be in my parents' package.

I thought, *Your eyes are the sky, not the ocean.*

"Is your mother dying?" he asked.

All I could think is, *You remember that?* I swallowed. "I don't know yet. But I think I'll know soon."

He took my hands inside his. "I hope it's good news."

"Thank you." I wished I had brought my journal. I wanted to open it up, jot down the date and time, to write, *Now, at this moment, my hands are in Peter's. I think he is looking as baffled as I am. Well, I must look awestruck. He's baffled. The point is that our skin is deliberately touching. The point is that he touched me deliberately.*

I felt like he was waiting for me to decide—which words to say, how many, how close. I felt full of breath, of insistent momentum, a hushed force along a line etched toward him.

I breathed in as I hadn't breathed for weeks, inhaling the scent of chamomile and pencil shavings. All thought of New York and Ljubljana and job offers vanished.

Something like a bottle stopper popped loose in my brain. "I don't want to be your student anymore."

He nodded. "Okay."

I couldn't make my eyes look away like I used to. "I thought A.J. had taken my journal and read it. I thought that he'd tell you everything and that his description would be lurid and damaging—I thought my behavior was the main reason you were removing me from your class—I thought I had made things inappropriate between us. I was certain I'd mortified you and hurt your career. I was going to catch a Greyhound—"

"Vivienne—" Peter let go one of my hands to pull at his hair, eyes alarmed as though I'd confessed to nearly abandoning my college education and tossing grenades at my future because I thought I'd embarrassed a man. Which, actually, I had just admitted.

"I should have returned your journal immediately," he said, "like an upstanding instructor would have, like a decent human being. I'd never create a reason for you to be tormented by that"—he shook his head—"asshole."

He took back my hand to smooth my palm with his thumb. I thought, *This is a place I have never been. Here, with a man, our skin touching.* It hurt to breathe air. "Shhh . . ." I extracted a hand from his, touching one finger to my lips. "It feeds his ego when we talk about his ass."

He chuckled, tugging me closer, as I did what felt easiest. I unthreaded my fingers from his and leaned in.

Had Maman ever needed anyone to help keep her standing?

Peter's Oxford shirt ran cool under my cheek, and underneath the fabric, the taut warmth of his chest. A hand lifted up to cup the back of my head. "Vivienne."

A sharp breath left my throat as his other hand came to the small of my back, his whole palm pressing in.

I thought of ways I'd been held before—by Mama, Papa, Mémere, even by Gabriel for the five seconds he said goodbye to me in Paris.

I thought, *This is how it feels to be held by Peter Breznik.* I had imagined it, but at the same time, I hadn't really imagined it—not as a real image, like a photograph, in which you would see the knots of the carpet under our feet. The image I had conjured was more of an impression—like Monet's *Sunrise*—shadow and light and reflection. It may or may never have existed.

Being held by Peter in the actual world was a sensation of starlight— that silver hum over the coast when the sky is still illumined, night trembling like water at the brim of a glass. I wrapped my arms around him, my face turned in, my ear at his heart.

"Thank you," I said. I let go my breath till my shoulders fell, his palm circling up my back.

"Thank you?" he asked. "I was about to beg your forgiveness."

I clasped my hands tighter around him. "I forgive you." A corner of my lips touched his shirt. "And thank you for holding me just now, and for finding my journal and giving it back." His chin touched down on my hair. "And for reading me and writing me and for being my instructor." His hand paused at the center of my back.

Peter Breznik's hand was paused at the center of my back.

"And for not being my instructor."

The silent beats of laughter in his chest jostled me until I pulled just barely away to look up at him.

I knew that look—the questioning, narrowing eyes, his chin dipping in.

His wanting face.

My stomach turned to waves in a bottle. Maman would have said, *Think twice, petite.*

But I couldn't think as he smoothed my hair from my face, touched his fingers, like rain, to the quiet skin beneath my earlobes, his thumbs brushing along my cheeks. "In class, you're always looking away." His close-lipped smile made him look almost mournful. "I can never get a clear look at you."

Caught by the wonder in his gaze, I blurted, "My eyes are brown. Like my mother's. And I don't know how to wear eyeliner." When he kept looking, and the silence kept growing, and I was pretty sure my cells were exploding, I closed my eyes. "I mean, I don't know how to wear makeup."

"Me neither." He smoothed his hands down my neck and rested them on my shoulders, effectively harpooning the sun from my universe. I opened my eyes as he took a step back.

He said, "I could never tell, just looking at you."

I pressed my fists together in the shape of a heart and lifted them to my chest. "Tell that I can't wear makeup?"

"No, I like that you can't wear makeup. I couldn't tell what you thought of me. I mean—no offense—you have a crazy genius look, even when you wear pink cardigans and pearls. I always assumed you were thinking big thoughts about poetry, drafting poems for a Pulitzer in your journal. But at least one time, it turns out, you were writing to me. Every time I handed you a response, I imagined you reading it and thinking, 'Poor Peter—*l'idiot.*'" He said the word in his perfect French accent.

"What?" I giggled. His sky-blue eyes were glittering baffled half-moons in his face.

I bounced to my tip-toes and kissed him. Quick on the lips, the way I might smack a kiss to a baby's cheek.

He caught my wrist as I came off my toes, pulled my hand to his chest and smiled—a blissful, adoring, full-toothed smile, his chin angled in the faintest questioning way, as if to ask, *Did that count as a kiss for you?*

I stepped away, my cheeks flushing fire. This was the part I both dreaded and dreamed of—when our lips might touch and I would have to learn how to be kissed, and how to kiss him, and how to take air in my lungs at the same time.

Just then, I thought we could save it all for later; we could go for a walk, stroll through the library, I could take him to Palmiers—but he was too quick. Before I'd stepped farther back, he had hooked me by the waist and set me on his desk as I heard myself chirp like a squeak-toy.

His fingers cradled my head again, tilted my face, and then he was slow again and smiling.

He was bending toward me.

I was more than ever right then a scared little deer caught in headlights.

Peter's kiss started out as a question—a tingling pull at my bottom lip—*Vivienne, do you want me to kiss you?*—to which I found his top lip—*Yes, I think so, kiss me,* and then I could feel his lips smiling, smiling and breathy and catching at mine, making a quiet sentence—*I like you, Vivienne, I like being near you, I like this*—our chins touching and pulling away, sometimes our teeth tapping, his hands cupping my head, angling it to vary the sentence—*I like you a lot right now, Vivienne, kissing you feels like twinkle lights in my face. Do you like this, Vivienne?*

And I lost my fingers in the hair at his neck, remembering to breathe, to keep myself steady. *I like this, I love this, I want to be your koala.*

Without warning, he began a new paragraph, kissing my jaw, at first lightly, as if to say, *Next, we'll see how you tolerate my lips on non-lip areas, like this delicate jawbone*—kiss, kiss, kiss, kiss—*do you like this, Vivienne?*

I sat straighter on his desk, pulling him into me; I tried kissing his eyes, his forehead. I could hear little breaths escaping my throat. *Yes,* my kisses said, *keep going. You're like lemonade and sugar dust and pop rocks!*

We kept kissing a little bit faster. He kept whispering, *Vivienne.* I kept growing more adept at being kissed and kissing him and breathing.

And then his lips touched the shadowed skin beneath my earlobe.

I gasped and lurched back out of his hands that had been cradling my head, and when nothing was behind me, fell flat on my back on his desk, dangling from my shoulders over nothing, head vertical. Tiny blue and white stars filled the expanse beneath my eyelids.

"Vivienne!" Peter grabbed my hands, pulling. "Vivienne, are you hurt? Tell me what I did!"

As soon as my head was upright, I lost consciousness.

I woke like a caterpillar in Peter's lap, in his student chair. I was curled knees to chest, as though planning to spin a cocoon on him. My pink slippers had dropped to the floor.

All the messages I sent to my legs to stand up were refused, muscles burning in total exhaustion. My thoughts kept getting buzzed by a cerebral fly trap.

"I shorted out." I finally arranged words in my head.

Peter smoothed my hair, face tensed in concern.

He was good at smoothing my hair. Much better than Maman. He was good at holding me.

Peter Breznik was holding me.

"Do you short out a lot?" His lips pressed my forehead where my hair starts.

I didn't think so. The words kept slipping down a tunnel. But no, I had never shorted out. "You kissed the shadowed skin beneath my ear-lobe and my heart exploded." I pressed my palm over the silky-cotton fabric of his shirt. "I like your blue sweatshirt better."

"Do you have a heart issue?" His hand covered mine.

Yes. I had a heart issue: It was holding me. "You are my heart issue, and I have never shorted out." I shifted on his legs to loop my arms around his neck and study his face, probably like a drunk. "I want to be your koala. Did I say that already? You know how they cuddle onto things?"

His laughter burst out like a beam of light in his dimming office.

I closed my eyes. "Let's kiss again." I tried pulling his face down to mine.

"Easy, slugger." Peter's smile flashed as bright as his laughter. "I think you need to refuel. What are you dying to eat?"

"Did you not like it?" My muscles woke up and tensed on command. I pulled away to stand, but his arms remained locked around me, his grin—if it was possible, brightening. I tapped a finger at one of his shirt buttons. "I'm not good at it yet, but you know I can learn. I just need feedback and a teacher. Like writing."

"Vivienne," Peter glanced at my lips. "I'm not your instructor anymore, and you don't need anyone to teach you."

He was tugging my head gently away from him—for breathing room, I thought, for a moment of space—until he began leaning in, and in the slowest route a mouth has ever traveled, he pressed his lips to the shadowed skin beneath my earlobe again.

His breath hitched on an inhale. "I want you to be my koala."

Posterity, it is 3:41 a.m. now. When I started writing this entry almost three hours ago, I felt like my heart had morphed into a nuclear energy plant that would power my wakefulness eternally, but now my eyelids feel like sandpaper, and my right shoulder is kinked from propping myself up on my bed to write. I suppose I could imagine my pillow as Peter's chest, burrow into it, and rest.

But I can still feel his lips on my skin, his hands in my hair.

I can still hear every word he spoke to me. Beneath the lamplight at my dorm entrance, he brushed his lips over my ear. "Vivienne, you're better than poetry."

Suffice it to say: I threw my heart into kissing him—

———

Wednesday, March 13, 1991
9:07 a.m., library, third floor

I think my lips are swollen.

And Maman sent me Manhattan in a box—little tokens from places she knows I love—and how I can even part from the first sentence of this entry to write this one is a testament to the fact that my brain is addled. I am one second reliving Peter's kisses—when his fingers dance into my hair, the whole world goes blank—and ten seconds later, I envision him waiting for me along a small patch of grass between buildings at Philbrick. And then I replay a highlights reel from his questions last night: *What's your favorite city/ocean/museum/constellation? What do you think of President Bush? Have you read much Elizabeth Bishop? What comes to your*

mind when I say "Slovenia"?—and mere seconds after that, I find myself
scripting a poem for Maman made of words I wish I could say to her—

> *Thank you for sending*
> *Manhattan in a box. I love you*
> *so much. I'm so sorry.*

> *I wish you were here and could meet the man*
> *I've prayed might father my children.*

Last night, after Peter telephoned Alene to say I'd be joining her
poetry class, we left his office and ended up parked in his old VW Jetta
in a tiny lot facing the ocean. Reclined in our seats, we gazed out at the
sky through the windshield, just talking. We had picked up grilled cheese,
raspberry shakes, French fries cut-and-fried-on-the spot, and every three
minutes or so, Peter would set down what he was eating, take up my hand
and trace circles on the back with his thumb. Or else he would lean as far
as he could toward me, and I would scoot toward him, and we'd kiss, his
fingers reaching into the hair at my neck.

At one point, we lay back, searching out constellations, his fingers
threaded through mine below the gearshift, when suddenly, he let go
my hand and pointed to a blinking cluster of stars below Ursa Major.
"That," he bent forward, "that little knot of starlight. It must be some
identified thing, but what do you think we should name it?"

I craned my neck to peer into the sky outside the windshield. "Name
it?"

Peter said, "How about 'The Lights in Vivienne's Eyes When She
Talks to Me'?"

Even in starlight, I could see he was smiling.

I swatted at his arm, laughter tingling from my throat like the shimmering stars we were looking at. "It's a ladybug," I said.

"Like the ladybugs on your necklace that another guy clasped around
your neck right in front of me?"

"You weren't even looking!" I touched the beads on my chest. "It's a
necklace my grandmother gave to my mother. I told you! My mom sent
the necklace with our *family friend Robert* to give to me."

Peter pulled me close by my shoulder, kissed the top of my head.

"What about your longtime friend Sonja?" I tilted back to look at him.

He was watching me like I was smart and adorable and maybe even almost beautiful. I was probably looking at him like he was insane.

He laughed. "Sonja grew up two floors down from my family's apartment in Ljubljana. We were friends our whole lives, and then . . . she wanted more."

When his eyes found mine in the near-dark, he was grinning. "But I told her last Saturday that I'd already lost my heart to a poet who never looked at me for longer than three seconds."

I pulled back in my seat, laughing as I shielded my eyes with my hands. "It is so hard to look at you!"

"Oh, that's right . . ." Peter tugged at my wrists. "There's a spell on my eyes!—or my eyes cast a spell? Vivienne!" He tugged harder. "Why won't you look at me?"

"I can't!" I struggled against his grip until suddenly, my hands flew away, and there he was—holding my wrists, eyes wide, smiling.

As he lowered my hands, I forgot about Sonja. Peter's lips touched mine.

Reclining again a few minutes—or maybe a lifetime—later, we gazed up at our Ladybug, my hand curled in his. The sky reminded me of a kaleidoscope—all the shapes and brightnesses of clouds and stars shifting, or the earth imperceptibly shifting beneath them. It struck me that by walking through the door to Peter's office after reading his letter, I had set every last particle of my life in motion.

For the first time—which seems almost as impossible as the fact that I was in the passenger seat of Peter's vehicle, kissed delirious by him—I wondered what Maman would think of him. I wondered how he could fit into the pieces of my life that I could see spinning in the sky just then. *Manhattan, Philbrick, teaching. Writing, bakery, books.* Plus, Maman was most likely ill, or could be at some point in the future. I would never not go home to her. I would never not go home, period. As far as I knew at that moment, Peter had interviewed at St. Brigid's and possibly in Manhattan, but he was also considering a position in Slovenia. In one month, he would leave to see his family in Ljubljana for the summer—a world I had no frame of reference for. Add to that the planetoid-sized fact that I am 20 years old, and one has to wonder: How could I fit into his kaleidoscope?

"Hey, Vivienne Lebrun." Peter had shifted sideways in the reclined driver's seat. "What are you thinking? Are you warm enough?" He reached for my waist, his fingers grazing the skin beneath the hem of my blouse. When I flinched in surprise, he smoothed my blouse over my hip, resting his palm on the silky fabric. "Tell me."

I shifted sideways, too, touching my fingertips to his cheek. "In your letter, you said we could talk about Manhattan. Did you interview at Hadley last week? When do you leave for Ljubljana?" *And will you come back?* a cricket-sized voice in my head asked.

Peter lifted my palm to kiss it. To be honest, we were slightly cramped—at least he was—but the wind had turned chilly outside. I couldn't take him to my dorm, and I'm sure he could tell I wasn't prepared to be invited inside his apartment. His car was a safe, tied-off pocket of the world where we could just be, even if we had to twist at strange angles.

I expected him to sigh, perhaps pull away, explain that I should snuff out all hope for Hadley. Instead, he slid my palm to his cheek and leaned closer.

"I'm flying to Ljubljana in May, to be with my family for the summer, and to visit the University's history department. But I wanted to tell you. Yes. I had coffee at Tallulah's and interviewed in New York last week. Hadley and St. Brigid's both offered me positions this morning."

"What?" I twisted onto my knees in my seat, as if I were about to pronounce an impassioned prayer to him, or to God. I felt like I might shout, *Praise Heaven!*

And though Peter now had three job offers to consider, I could only envision Manhattan—the Hudson, the skyline, the lights of the Empire State Building. And Tallulah's nestled in there, a table waiting for us to link our legs underneath it, discuss poems, sip coffee.

"Why didn't you tell me?" I wanted to dance on the roof of his car with him. "You should have said it first thing—when you opened your office door to me! You should be celebrating somewhere—this is a life-event kind of day!" And then, quiet and fast, as if asking a parenthetical question, "You liked Tallulah's?"

Peter laughed as he pulled my face down to his. He kissed my lips and my eyes and my cheeks. "I loved Tallulah's," he said.

"Peter, wait—Peter." Every time I said his name, I laughed against his lips, trying to pull away.

"*This* is a life event, Vivienne."

"Peter." Though my body wanted to lift over the gear shift and crash into him, I mustered enough strength to seal my lips shut and lean back. "You haven't decided yet?" My heart filled up my trachea.

I was thinking that Hadley or St. Brigid's would be the best choice for him. Teaching at either college promised security in an adopted country, ensured research funds and access to nearly any academic opportunity that Peter could dream of. Choosing either of those schools meant that he and I—if we wanted to—could possibly be together.

But please choose Hadley, I thought. Hadley is every bit as lofty as St. Brigid's, and some years, a few of Hadley's programs rank even higher than the same at St. Brigid's. And Hadley is three thousand miles closer to Ljubljana than St. Brigid's—Peter would only have to hop across the Atlantic to visit his family.

Of course, *I might transfer to a school in New York* was the sentence I wanted to sing like Julie Andrews in *The Sound of Music,* spinning out of Peter's car into the parking lot, arms outstretched, face glowing with love for one man and all God's creations. But I couldn't even whisper the words right then. I didn't want to risk saying them in a way that might sound like I expected Peter and me to be together in New York. Plus, first real job offers are one of life's milestones. I wondered if saying, *I might transfer to a school in New York* might sound childish and lame in the brightness of Peter's achievement.

Peter reached for one of my hands. "All three offers are contingent upon the success of my dissertation, obviously, but Hadley's offer is very strong, Vivienne. St. Brigid's might match it, but Ljubljana does not even come close. I mean, if I were to choose Ljubljana, it wouldn't be for the money."

For at least five seconds, I knelt on my seat with my hand in Peter's, thinking, *Why did he open a door for me when he might be the one who walks out? Why did I let myself enter?* "You still might decide to teach in Ljubljana?"

This is what people do, I thought. *They connect; they kiss. One goes to Europe, the other stays in North America.*

"I don't—I don't know." Peter reached for my other hand. "I'd be a fool not to accept at St. Brigid's or Hadley."

Of course he would, I thought. *Peter is not foolish.* Yet I could feel a qualification, a *but . . .* wavering at the end of his sentence.

"But Yugoslavia is home to you?" I tried to guess at where his words were heading. Ocean waves in the distance conjured images of far-away shorelines.

"It is a home to me and it isn't. I'm not sure Yugoslavia has ever felt like my home. I mean, Yugoslavia as I've known it won't exist for much longer. But Slovenia—" I could hear the low beat of his Slavic accent.

"I do feel a history there," he said, "a sort of allegiance—but I don't see much of a future, or even feel much desire to pursue one. My family has to travel to Trieste, in Italy, for toothpaste and blue jeans, for God's sake. Why would I go back?" In the darkening shadows, I couldn't find the blue of his eyes. He was always so sure of himself in class—so open and to-the-point—but right then, in dim light, he seemed uncertain and guarded.

"Why *would* you go back?" I tried to keep my voice even, as though I were asking, *Why would you choose that supermarket over this one?*, but my hands made fists inside his palms.

"I'm not really sure that I would." Gently, he tugged at my curled fingers, one by one, smoothing open my hand and entwining our fingers. "You smell like almonds," he said in his usual sure voice. I could hear his smile in the darkness. "Where is your home, Vivienne?"

Wherever you are, I startled myself by thinking. "New York," I said out loud, "where my family is." *Where I hope the rest of my education will be, along with the rest of my life.*

Peter nodded. "Slovenia is where my family is. Where we come from. And I want to believe that it can somehow be better—that I could help it be better—even if in the smallest way, like teaching. But when faced with the choice, I think I'd prefer for my family to come here. With a job at St. Brigid's or Hadley—"

Could he not have at least named Hadley first?

"I think I could bring them here. I think they could live a good life."
His words, and my heart, gained momentum by the sentence. "They
could be happy. I could be happy. Though my brother would be the
hardest to convince. I mentioned him to you in the response you found
in your journal today."

"And on the day my brother called early—when I slammed into a
shelf with my eye." *And your dad mentioned him in a bio,* I thought.

Peter laughed as though he'd heard what I'd said and what I'd
thought. "That's right! I wanted to take you to my house for coffee that
day. I wanted to injure whomever had hurt you."

I wanted to move into his house until May and meet him at John F.
Kennedy in August.

I said, "I really liked your blue sweatshirt."

"I'll give it to you." His face almost glowed in a swath of streetlight.
I could see the glint of his eyes before he shut them, breathing in, and I
wondered if that was how lying with him in a bed would be—just quiet:
the two of us curled toward each other, talking.

I mean, we wouldn't always be talking.

And children could be laughing outside our windows in Brooklyn.

"But what about your brother?" I asked.

"Tilen," Peter said. "He's eight years older than me and fearless as
hell. I'd give my life for him."

"But you don't think he'd live here?" I tried to picture Tilen Breznik—
tall like his younger brother, perhaps, but darker, more fiery, maybe—a
man Peter Breznik would die for.

"No." At some point Peter had begun tracing the line of my jaw,
occasionally brushing up to my earlobe. "I mean, not *no*—just not easily.
He's a journalist, like my dad, except Tilen was never a poet first. There's
little quiet in him, or caution. He'd leap into a spray of gunfire to get a
true story, which is pretty much what a journalist is going to have to do
in Croatia soon."

"He's in Croatia?" I remembered what I had read about escalating
violence in that republic.

"Yes," Peter answered. "He's gathering personal histories and following unrest between Croats and Serbs living in Croatia. He and Hana,

his wife, are there, staying with her parents. Hana had a baby six weeks ago."

"You're an uncle." I reached a finger to his forehead as if sticking a star there. "Next thing you know, you'll be a professor."

"I have a ways to go before that, but yes, I'm an uncle, and Hana and the baby and Tilen could be here. But Tilen feels responsibility to watch up-close as Yugoslavia unravels—to give an honest accounting and help build anew whatever is left standing. I respect that—I admire him—but truth-telling is a death-wish over there. What will truth matter when"—Peter shook his head—"if Tilen is harmed, or—worse? That is one reason I'd teach in Slovenia—to keep my brother alive."

"But how would you do that from a neighboring country?"

"I think he'd come back to Ljubljana. If I were there. If I agreed to help publish a political journal, or organize international support for war correspondents. But I think—"

I wanted to reach my mouth to his, to cancel out words and feel like all that mattered was *here*. That *we* took precedence over every other *them* and *there*, though I knew that could never be the case, at least, not for me.

"I think—" I waited for him to say something like, *I think we shouldn't think about this at the moment*. But Peter has rarely said what I expected him to. "I think," he tried again. "I mean, I haven't decided which offer. But I think I might like"—his warm hand moved to my neck—"I might like . . . a life in New York."

Since January, I have heard Peter speak many words that I did not anticipate, and I have typically felt upon hearing them that my soul might launch to the sky. But in the silence following *I might like a life in New York,* I felt perfectly and disbelievingly quiet. I feared that my voice might shatter his sentence, which seemed suspended in tiny glass letters between us.

I wanted to tell him about Philbrick, but he said, "How did you get me talking like this?"

The words I ended up saying came by themselves, without need for arrangement or command from my brain. They just *were*—as any true thing is: sunlight, heartbeat, crocus in April. I said, "I want to know everything."

"It's so easy for me to tell you." His hand combed the ends of my hair. "Have I even said that you're beautiful?"

"It's pretty dark in here." I shivered from cold and from the happiness of his words, and from just being so long near him and knowing I could still be near him in the fall, in New York—if he decided to make a life there, if Philbrick accepted me.

His hand lifted to cradle my head. "You're beautiful the way birds are beautiful—the way they startle you from gray and inertia. The way each bird's song is completely its own. And your words—I've never—"

"Had you ever been to New York before interviewing?" If I had allowed him to finish his sentence, my heart would have burst, and I don't mean figuratively. The organ—it would have exploded.

Peter's smile crept across his face as though someone were slowly drawing it there with a pencil. "You're humble, Vivienne. I'll give you that. But someday, I'll make you listen to me describe how I see you. You can shake your brilliant, unbrushed head all you want, plug your ears even. But yes. My parents took Tilen and me to Manhattan once."

I reached a hand to his heart, hoping that would tell him that I'd heard what he'd said about birds and beauty. About me.

I stuck to our new line of conversation. "Maybe you passed me on a street in Manhattan. I'd have been in a yellow dress, holding my mother's hand, observing you."

"I hope that happened." He closed his eyes for a second. "But maybe, if I end up at Hadley, and when you're done with St. Brigid's in December, we could see—you know—if we like this—being together. In Manhattan. I mean, I'm pretty sure I'd like it, but you have a lot to do—you want to do so many things, and I want you to do them. Your food book—"

I almost choked on the words, "I'd like that. This being together."

"Yeah?"

"Yeah!" I giggled. "I mean, yes." I straightened my face, looking right at him. "I would. But it's Brooklyn."

"What's Brooklyn?" Peter's hand touched the skin at my waist and did not lift away.

Now I was helplessly shivering. "Where I want to live. Eventually. It's Brooklyn." I needed to say something about Philbrick. "And actually—"

"You're freezing." Peter turned in his seat. "I left my jacket in my office. Hold that thought for one moment." He stepped from his Jetta and nearly leapt over its hood. Swinging the passenger door wide, he pulled me from the car and wrapped me in his arms in the nighttime breeze. He felt like a giant one of those hand warmers Maman always slipped into our gloves at the Finger Lakes in winter.

He leaned down to my ear. "I've never been to Brooklyn."

"You'll love it," I said into the heat of his chest. I pictured the flower shop, the peonies, the sun in my eyes. Him and me in a brownstone kitchen, arranging cut cherry branches in a vase. "I've applied to transfer to a college there this fall—"

Stepping back, Peter held me away from him. He looked like I'd just told him I was having his baby. I didn't know if he was about to ask, *How did this happen?* or demand that we spend our lives together. "Which college?" he said, like, *Out with it. Quickly.*

I couldn't stop shivering. He was rubbing his hands up and down my arms. "Philbrick," my teeth chattered. "The integrated master's. I haven't heard back from them. I was probably crazy to apply, but even if I don't get in, I could take you to Brooklyn in August if you were there."

His hands squeezed my elbows. "What about baking and pastry?"

"I'll work at a bakery. I'll keep learning."

As Peter pulled me close again, I extracted my hands from the little hollow they kept between his chest and mine, so that I could wrap my arms around him. "New York just keeps looking better," he whispered. "You know you'll get into Philbrick. You sent samples of your poems and essays?"

"Yes." I pressed my ear to his heart.

"They'll pay you to transfer." He rocked us side to side in the parking lot.

I held him so tight. I held him as if my arms were strong enough to keep him with me forever.

And that's how we stood until a flashlight-wielding officer happened by, blinding us with his beam of white light. "I'll give you two minutes to kiss her, young man," he said, "but after that, this lot is closed for the night."

Words have not been breathed into language that could describe the kaleidoscope—ladybugs, peonies, laughing babies, bright birds—that spun in my mind as Peter Breznik cried, "Brooklyn!" and seized two minutes to kiss me.

Thursday, March 14, 1991
2:36 a.m., at Peter's

Maman cried on the phone yesterday, and tonight/this morning my eyes are swollen. My lips are still swollen, too, but for different reasons.

I meant to list the contents of Maman's package yesterday, but upon finishing the last sentence of my previous entry, I felt a hand on my shoulder and looked up to find Peter standing beside my carrel in the library, his eyes holding mine with an unsure, searching look that I read as unspoken questions: *Have you changed your mind? Is it okay that I'm here?*

No doubt my eyes were asking the same. I took his hand from my shoulder and held it to my cheek, and then one thing led to another—him dropping to his knees beside my carrel, me stroking the flaxen scruff on his cheek, him touching his fingers to the side of my neck, and *voilà!* we were silently kissing like love-starved bookworms in a forgotten corner of the library, adjacent to shelves filled with eighteenth-century English poetry. I could practically feel the souls of poets rising from their books to gawk at us.

When finally we drew back to breathe for a second, Peter said, "You're too young for this," to which I said, "You're too old," and he laughed and pressed his forehead to mine. Fingers at the back of my neck again, he said he had a full day of dissertation defense prep, but could he please pick me up at 7:00 p.m. so that we could eat together and I could tell him all about transferring to Philbrick?

After a circuitous route of more kissing, during which he whispered, "I can't leave you," I managed to extract my lips from his to say that I had class in four minutes.

As soon as Baking ended, I walked home to my dorm and sat on my bed. The quiet in my ears thumped like a clock. Peter would arrive in three hours and forty-five minutes, but the silence in my head didn't lighten at that. My thoughts kept rippling outward, reaching to touch the unnamed thing I could feel approaching: essay deadlines in my literature classes, a rough draft of my own perfect recipe in Baking, my first day in Alene Bautista's class—

When the telephone rang, I knew immediately.

"Maman?"

"You picked up." Her voice sounded tired—a rich satin ribbon fraying. I tried to picture her, serene and all-knowing on our little raft, but all I could see was a choppy current.

"I'm so sorry, Maman—" I had scripted a thousand ways to begin a first conversation, but all I could remember was that single line. "I'm so sorry. I'm so sorry."

I could have kept going, as if making a poem, altering words at the line endings—

I'm so sorry, I'm so
sorry. I'm so sorry. I'm
    so

      sorry—

I couldn't picture her face. I couldn't picture her hands. I wanted them to brush up and down my arms as they had when I was little. "Your necklace," I choked on the first image in my head. "I'm wearing it—it's beautiful. But why—"

"Your brother confessed what he said to you. After we read your letter last night."

I slid from my bed to the floor, stretching my shirt to my face. "I'm so sorry."

"He was hurtful, and you were afraid." That was the first time her voice seemed to catch—the first time on the call, and maybe the first time in recent years of conversation. She drew a sharp breath. "Papa and I push you to be strong without us, but we haven't secured your trust. When we leave you to yourself, you feel abandoned."

"It's my own—"

"Vivienne." I could feel her voice in my head, blanketing my attempt to appease her.

"I should trust you, I want to, I—"

"Oh, my love."

I lifted my dripping nose from my shirt, sure that my ears must be equally filled with mucous. "What?" I asked. I couldn't remember when Maman had last used a term of endearment.

She inhaled a stuttering breath. I could tell she was pressing her whole mind into English, as if the formality it required of her might allow distance from what I felt as a jagged wound between us. "It is terrifying to be a parent. To choose to behave one way with your child, and then watch what comes of it. It is like planting a garden with aster and dynamite, but you never know which, and either sprouts up at the oddest times to remind you of what you did well or poorly."

My face was so hot. Tugging at the phone cord, I stood and stepped up on my bed, pressing my forehead against the cool window that spans the length of my mattress. "You have always been well-intentioned, Maman," I said in a pleading voice, as though I weren't crying for me, but for her, and wished to persuade her that she had never made a choice that had hurt me.

"*Peut-être.*" She slipped into French. I could picture her for a second, tracing her fingertip around the rim of a demitasse. "We thought we withheld truth from you when I was ill to protect you. We didn't want you to be hurt or have fear." The French in her wording—*avoir peur,* "to have fear"—as if fear is a disease one contracts, like cancer. I have had fear for so long now—I think no amount of surgery or therapy could root it out of me.

Resting my head against the cool windowpane, Maman's quivery breath at my ear, I felt so weary of having fear. I wished a doctor could treat it on a cellular level, poison it with an intravenous drip.

"Maman." I silently tapped at the window as though she were on the other side of it. Wet with my tears, my fingertips left damp spots on the pane, my own little cloud on an almost-spring day. "I need you to talk. Please tell me the truth now."

"Yes." I could feel a straightening as she said it, as if she had nodded and sat taller. I crouched to my bed to steady myself for whatever she was preparing to say.

"Go on," Papa's voice emerged, soft in the background. He must have been sitting next to her. Maybe he was squeezing her hand. The strange thing was that he didn't sound sad. "Catherine—" He almost sounded baffled that she was struggling. I folded my knees to my chest, waiting.

"Vivienne—" Maman's voice went sharp on the last syllable. "I have not lied to you. I have been coming to terms with a possibility I never expected. It is both difficult and joyous to me."

I can accept that, I thought. *The cancer is back, but it's treatable.* The treatment would be difficult, but the outcome would be joyous: We could still be a family on this planet. And Maman was talking. Maybe she would be able to keep talking this time.

"In January," Maman said, "I learned I was six weeks pregnant."

I remember that in an earlier entry, after writing that Julie thought Peter might have a tiny crush on me, I left inches of white space to represent the thought-obliterating shock of that information, and that shock felt like the greatest I could feel in my life.

But this shock—the lightning-flash image of a baby curled up inside Maman like a question mark. This shock and its resultant speechlessness would take entire blank pages—every page left in this journal, at least— to barely adequately represent. Maybe there is no metaphor, no image to capture it—

A vast, empty, snow-swirling planet?

My hand shot to my belly. "*Hhhhhhh*" was all that exited my mouth.

"Vivienne, stay with us," Papa said, this time closer to the receiver.

"Papa and I were shocked as well, Vivienne," Maman said.

But they couldn't have been as shocked as I was because they were at least aware that pregnancy was still possible after Maman's cancer, and that the two of them continued to engage in potential pregnancy-inducing activity. Whereas, if the thought had ever even occurred to me, I might have guessed they engage in such activity a few times a year—maybe on Christmas and their birthdays? And I guess I assumed Maman's body had lost interest in that particular activity after cancer.

"I—" I couldn't think of a verb to follow. A simple auxiliary phrase, followed by simple description? *I am feeling like I may need mouth-to-mouth resuscitation in about fifteen seconds, as I now have a history of fainting.*

I didn't have to think long, however, because Maman spoke with a trembly voice. "Forty-one is not too old, of course, but with all that has happened, I never considered—that is, I never meant to be careless, but

Papa and I were only able to have you and Luc. I thought the days of my *maternité* were over. But God knows I would never medically disrupt my fertility, not even after illness, and so now—" She stopped, no doubt mortified that she had hinted at any aspect of her life as a sexual being. When I started my period, she gave me a box of tampons and instructed me to read the enclosed pamphlet. When I left for St. Brigid's, she kissed my cheeks and snapped, *"Ne couches pas avec les garçons, Vivienne,"* and I've never slept with any boy ever.

We do not delve into matters of sexuality.

But in that brief pause between Maman, sitting as I imagined in our round kitchen nook—maybe with the slightest swell to her belly—and me, falling onto my back on my bed, I envisioned the detached gaze she's always worn on our imaginary skiff warming up a little, her eyes finding mine, hopeful that I might look at her and nod, or cover her hand with my own.

I felt like I could see her—as suddenly as a starling takes flight: a devoutly religious woman with her own autonomous, treacherous body. A woman who loved a man and bore his children and had refused to shut the door—not even in life-threatening illness—on the small possibility of creating life.

But then I sat up. Why hadn't she simply told me she was expecting when I began questioning her health two-and-a-half months ago? Why had she allowed herself and me—and Papa, too, I assume—to wait out the past weeks in such misery? Why did she risk flaring my insecurities by withholding the truth of her health from me?

A month ago, I would have swallowed my questions, but at that moment, I leaned into my bent knees on my bed and asked them. "Why did you not simply tell me, Maman? At the beginning, when I first knew something was happening with you? Why did you allow me to have fear and sulk and hurt us all? Why is speaking the truth so hard?"

If I had expected her remorse, I'd been mistaken. She exhaled a little huff. "It may surprise you to hear, Vivienne, that relieving your worry is not every moment my top priority. Or that while you agonize or panic, I might endure even greater struggle."

My forehead fell to my kneecaps. Had she been sitting before me, I could not have looked in her eyes. I returned to the only sentence I could remember. "I'm so sorry—"

"You could not have known, Vivienne." Her voice softened. "You might have behaved as an adult and spoken to us sooner, but I would not have told you this news until today."

Tears flooded my throat. "But what were you enduring? Why would you not tell me?" I pictured myself during our estrangement, lying on my bed, listening to the phone ring till it stopped, preoccupied with thoughts of Peter and poems. Maman had been suffering, and it would not be entirely true to say that I had been in a state of wretchedness.

I didn't even write down the contents of the package Maman took such care in sending. There had been a small square white note bearing Maman's sharp cursive script—*J'ai des choses a te dire*—a tiny pink bow tied through a punched hole in the corner. She had things to tell me, she'd written—she had wanted to talk—and I hadn't even read the sentence twice. I had tucked her card back in the box with Michel's *chocolat* and Maman's palmiers, and various other bright tokens of home.

The pink ribbon, I thought in that moment on the phone. *The baby is a girl.*

But right then, Mama was attempting to supply honest answers. "For weeks, we were sure I would miscarry, Vivienne. I have had to be careful, to rest. And then there was medical pressure"—she hastened her cadence—"to terminate." The words she might have added—*the pregnancy*—hung blaring and silent, at the same time, between us.

And I knew without asking her to elaborate: She might have been walking around these past five years with death's shadow flickering in and out of her periphery, but she was still an unfaltering Catholic. She would never terminate a pregnancy. She was committed to what she had taught me to see as the exacting, unmatchable work of giving life and shaping it.

"I could not tell you, Vivienne, because I could not manage other emotions than my own."

Other emotions such as *figurative spewing electrical wires.*

"I did not want to burden you with another *possibilité* of loss. I want you to feel strong—"

And so she chose silence. Because she loves me. Because she wants me to be okay without her. Still, I wondered if she truly couldn't see a connection between her guardedness and my anxiety for her well-being.

I spoke quickly so that I couldn't second-guess myself. "But not talking to me hasn't worked so well."

The soft breath she expelled reached my ear as both defeat and compassion. "You are right, Vivienne. But some things I must keep and settle within myself. When I learned I was pregnant, I did not want to hear questions or concern or comfort—from you or anyone. I needed my head to be quiet, so that I could hear deep inside, to where my own voice speaks clearly. I depend on that voice now, since—"

Since the cancer, I almost finished for her, but a voice in my own head was speaking to me. *She never meant to hurt you.* She has told me that herself so many times, but I was hurting too much—too loud—to hear her. Meanwhile, for all this time, she has been listening for an inner voice to guide her, and probably to calm her. Because she is hurting. She has fear for herself. And now she has fear for a baby.

Which does not ease my fear but does ease my hurt a little.

"It's a girl, isn't it?" I forced the words through my throat. "I mean, she is—the baby. You sent the pink bow."

"*Oui,*" Maman whispered, her voice wavering. But then, slightly louder, "We have had many sonograms. But the pink bow—*c'était l'idée de Papa.*"

Yes. Of course Papa would have thought of that. Maman is not often prone to sentimentality.

I could have asked so many questions—*Will you be safe? Could the cancer come back? What will we do if it does? Can doctors tell if the baby is healthy?* But anticipating the clamor of those questions was a good part of why Maman didn't tell me about the baby in the first place.

I pictured her sitting, her hand maybe resting on her belly. "Have you felt her kicking yet?"

Maman laughed little breaths that made me think of my own giggling. *Was she happy, then?* I wondered. *More happy than afraid? Would she still be happy if I were there?*

She waited a few seconds before answering. "Yes, Vivienne. She wiggles around. Papa calls her his *petit poisson.*" His little fish.

"And you were my *petit oiseau,* Vivienne," Papa said from beside her. "Much crazier."

He was right—I was his little bird. Sometimes he still calls me that. His pigeon, actually. Because I always fly home.

But my sister—maybe she will swim a wide ocean.

Loving God, I prayed, *let us all be together.* Out loud, I said, "Do you think I could feel her when I come home in May?"

Maman sniffled.

"I've never felt a baby kick inside its mother."

"They do more than kick, Vivienne." Papa's face must have been hovering right next to the phone.

"You felt Luc," Maman said, "but you were little."

I loved that detail—the picture of it. Maman reading little poems to me in my bed, perhaps—pressing my palm to her belly when she felt a flutter. I would have watched her in wonder.

Maman's voice on the phone remained tender. "When you are home, you can feel her and talk to her. I'll be six months. Perhaps we could find linens for a nursery."

Six months at the start of May. I tallied the rest of the months on my fingers. Maman could have a baby by the middle of August. I might be preparing for Philbrick. Peter might be working in Manhattan. I could call him to say that the baby had arrived, or I could tell him on a street outside Hadley.

After a few weeks, I could invite him to meet my new sister. To meet my family. If I were home. If he were there. If I had transferred to Philbrick.

I couldn't broach that idea on the telephone. I will bring it up in May, perhaps when Maman and I go shopping for the nursery.

I could feel a drumming in my ear as I asked a kernel of a larger question. "Could I be there—at home—when she's born?"

Papa's voice filled my ear. "No matter what, Vivienne, you will be here."

"And if not—" Maman spoke from the side.

"She will be here." I could picture Papa nodding firmly.

I shut my eyes and breathed, tried to douse my typical worry with oxygen.

Maman will be well.

She will have a baby girl.

I will be there.

And if I asked at the right time, conveyed the right reasons, I would, God willing, live there.

I kept swallowing my fretful questions. We did not mention cancer.

Maman and Papa asked about me, how my classes were, how Hillary was, what we were up to, if I'd made any new friends. I gave affirming vague answers.

I did not describe much of my weekend with Robert, but I thanked Maman for her necklace.

I had imagined that when we finally talked, I would tell my parents about Peter and maybe even about Philbrick, but I guess I had not grown up entirely in one phone call. They had kept another secret from me. So I held onto mine. I could feel them like razor-edged jewels in my fist.

When Hillary stepped through our bedroom door a few minutes after 7, I was curled up on my bed like my new fetus sister was curled inside our mother, except I was weeping. For everything. For living in California; for the words Luc had said to me; for punishing my mother with silence while she had had fear and worry; for wanting to be held by my former poetry instructor more than wanting to make amends with my parents; for my parents' forgiveness; for the beautiful, miraculous, devastating news that Maman was having a baby.

When Hillary opened our door, she took one look at me and the telephone, separated from the receiver in my hand, and she stepped back into the hall, allowing the door to shut behind her. Three minutes later, a lanky man in inky jeans ducked in, head shrouded by the hood of a black sweatshirt. I smacked my pillow over my face, assuming Hillary had invited one of her friends over.

But then I heard her. "You said he's the hottest man on campus. When I saw this guy waiting on a bench behind a sycamore, I assumed he was yours."

A large, warm form knelt beside my bed. A hand tugged my pillow away.

I could barely see through my tears.

It was Peter.

My throat had gone dry. "You'll be arrested for coming in here."

"I'm not a professor, Vivienne, or your instructor anymore. And you couldn't even tell it was me." He smoothed my hair away from my face, his own face apprehensive and serious. "Is it your mother?" His lips pressed my temple.

When I nodded, his eyes did a sweep of my room. "Gather up whatever you'll need at my place. I'm taking you there to rest a while."

Hillary froze behind Peter, her eyes locked on mine, as if telepathing, *Is that what you want? Will you be okay?*

I looked at Peter, already standing, scanning my room for essentials. "I'm sure you'll want your backpack." He hefted it up on his shoulder. "And maybe you'll want to see a chiropractor? What the hell is in this thing, Vivienne?"

I propped myself up on an elbow. "I need all of it."

He lifted my arm to help me up from my bed.

"And maybe I'll take some sweats—" I glanced at Hillary, and then back at Peter. Maybe it was because he was grown-up and experienced and not quick to turn giddy that he could appear as though nothing unprecedented was happening for me. His face looked only focused and concerned in the shadow of his sweatshirt hood, as though all he could imagine doing in the next four-to-twelve-or-so hours was helping me. I knew that if I asked him, he would not even touch me at his place. He would listen and talk and take care of me.

But just in case I were to stay a long time, I stopped in the bathroom for my toothbrush.

And now I have been all night at Peter's.

It is 6:08 a.m., and he is asleep in his recliner, while I have been writing at his desk. His place is a rented 1950's red-brick cottage that is open and spotless, with wide picture windows and narrow-planked dark hardwoods. His writing desk is so old, I think Emerson could have originally owned it. And there's a skinny hidden drawer in the side where a writer could keep secret letters.

After feeding me honey-toast and broccoli and a not unimpressive omelet with Swiss cheese and tomato, I told Peter about Maman, my silence, and the baby. And then I told him about applying to Philbrick.

He sat with his arms folded atop his small square kitchen table, sometimes leaning back and stretching his legs, and at just the right moments, asking the quiet kind of perceptive questions he always asked in Poetry. Sometimes he'd reach over the table to take my hand, but mainly, he listened.

As I felt our discussion wind down, he stood to extract European chocolate from a cupboard above his kitchen sink. "I was hiking in your homeland last summer—" He selected a bar wrapped in ruby-red paper. "I meant to give these to friends in the history department, but I found I liked them myself. You write haiku praising chocolate, so—"

"You remember that?" I thought of the day he'd set aside A.J.'s poems and instructed our class to write odes to actual objects.

Fast-forward ten weeks and there I was—sitting at Peter's kitchen table, having revealed all my familial heartbreak, allowing him to take my hand, pull me to my feet and into his arms. "That class was—still is—mostly about you for me," he said with my cheek over his heart again. "I wish I could have known you were hurting. I mean, I did know, a little—your poems made a sort of collage. But"—his palm between my shoulder blades pressed me closer—"I'm glad to see a more complete picture now."

When we moved to the sofa, I nestled into his side.

Which, I might add: My instincts with him make me feel like a small doting animal. I have never been the object of romantic *tendresse* or affection, but my body seems to know what it wants when it's near Peter Breznik. I lap up his nearness like a kitten laps milk.

But I don't think it's in a dependent way. It feels grown-up and equal, like maybe he drinks up my nearness, too.

Breaking his chocolate, Peter placed little squares in my palm, and we sat there, composing haiku in its honor. He claimed his attempt was superior:

> *Chocolate on the edge*
> *of Vivienne's lip. Hold still, sweet—*
> *right there—I'll kiss it.*

When the chocolate was gone, Peter set the wrapper on a small coffee table in front of us.

"Unlike you, I don't know if I've ever felt so much concern for my family. My dad was struck by a truck once, reporting in Macedonia, while I was at UC Irvine. I remember that I actually prayed for him, and I grew sincerely tearful on the phone with my mom, but five days later, I heard he'd be well, and I didn't spare much more thought for him. But you"— he rested his chin on my head—"you suffer when you're away from your family. You're in agony when they are suffering."

"No." I wiped at my eyes with the hand that wasn't wedged between us. "I haven't been in agony lately. And maybe I should feel stronger, but mostly I feel so guilty. You should tell me I'm selfish. And now I've applied to Philbrick. I'm not even honest with them—"

His chin lifted away from my head. "You'll find the right time to tell your parents about Philbrick, and you'll navigate from there. But why would I tell you you're selfish? You heard what I said about a truck and my father and my level of concern for him?"

"I'm selfish because while my parents have been agonizing over the question of carrying a baby, I've been punishing them and falling in—" Yes, you can fill in the blank, Posterity: I'm a child. *Love* is the word I was headed for. "I mean—I've been so happy for any second just to see you. I've worried over my family, but I've been distracted, I—"

Peter's fingers slowly brushed back and forth on the skin at my hip. I felt a thousand tiny heartbeats pumping there.

"You call this—this falling"—his lips pressed my head again—"distraction?"

I held my hand to his on my skin, to calm the sensation of a dwarf sun exploding to life in my abdomen. "Yes—" I looked down at our hands. "*This*—I mean—you—are distracting. I am distracted."

"Vivienne."

Straightening himself so that I had to sit up beside him on the sofa, he shifted toward me, turning me by my shoulders to face him. "I'm glad you talked to your parents today. But Vivienne, your family is *there,*" he nodded in a direction I assumed might be east, "and you're *here.*" He leaned down to kiss my forehead. "You should never stop caring for your family. They're a source of air and art for you. But *this,*" his hands tightened on my shoulders, "this is a thing you can have right here. This is your life right now. It might be both happy and sad, but where there's happiness—like, good, bright happiness—you take it."

I stared at his April-blue eyes and coppery hair, at the pale hook of a scar from his nose to his lip. I couldn't think of anything I wanted but him.

"I sound like your teacher." His hands began slipping from my shoulders.

Turning my whole body toward him on the sofa, I folded my knees underneath myself and kissed him. As if I had been born to kiss him, just as surely as I had been born to love and live within the little sphere that is my family; as if kissing him were an ability stamped on my DNA. His fingers skittered up my neck, past my hairline. "I take you." I was breathless. "You're happiness."

Laughter erupted from Peter's mouth against my lips, but still we kept kissing until I lay beneath him on the sofa, the taut weight of his legs on mine.

I thought, *If this is what he wants, he can take it. I'll be his happiness.*

When my fingers touched the sharp knots of his spine just beneath his sweatshirt, he lifted his head and gasped. "Vivienne. You have school tomorrow." By which he really meant "today"—it was after midnight.

But his reminder had me turning my head away from him into the sofa cushions, flushed like a schoolgirl.

He tilted to the side of the sofa and dropped his knees. Keeping a hand on my arm, he bent to kiss the shadowed skin just below my earlobe.

"Hey," he said softly. He tugged at my chin so that I might decide to look at him. I inhaled, turning, meeting his eyes. "There's a lot going on inside, and outside, your head right now. I'm not sure you need to add this"—his hand motioned between us—"to everything you're sorting through. We have time. I want you to be sure about what you want."

I closed my eyes again, nodding. *Graduation, Philbrick, teaching. Writing, bakery, books.*

Maman, Papa, Luc, a new baby.

Peter, Peter, Peter.

He pressed his palm to my stomach. "When we decide to be together in that way, we won't be making time for school the next day."

Not if, but *when*. The word multiplied in my head, as if reflected between two mirrors. "Or the next day." I reached a pointer finger to the crinkles at the corner of one of his eyes.

He kissed me.

"Or the next," I started giggling.

"Hell, no," he grinned, pulling me up by the hand.

He insisted I sleep in his bed, but I insisted I sleep on his couch. "Fine," he said, "I'll sleep in the recliner." He spread a sheet over the sofa cushions for me and fluffed up a pillow from his bedroom. When I lay down, spent and in sweats, teeth thoroughly brushed, he snapped out a softly-worn quilt so that it fell gently over me. "*Lahko noč*," he said. "'Easy night.' Zara Breznik says it."

Bless your womb, Zara Breznik.

Peter switched off the lights, but in the silvery glow nosing in through the blinds at the front picture window, I watched him sit with a blanket in an exquisitely distressed leather armchair on the other side of the coffee table, recline it with a handle, and lay his head back to sleep.

At 2:30 a.m., I woke to a dream of a swaddled baby girl flying out of a Ferris wheel. I was in the seat beside her when she fell, and I was the one who caught her.

There was nothing to do after that but flick the switch of the green lamp on Peter's desk in the corner, open my journal, and write.

Posterity, if you dislike reading about me kissing a man who may or may not turn out to be your many-great grandfather, please, be my guest: You can skip those parts.

––––––

Tuesday, March 19, 1991
5:18 p.m., an empty tasting table in the baking lab

In 40 days, Peter will defend his dissertation. Four days after that, I will leave for New York, and Peter will fly to Vienna, where his parents will meet him and drive him to Ljubljana. Peter and I haven't spoken of much beyond that. Not because I don't want to. I want to ask him every hour which school he's thinking of teaching at. I want to beg him to please dial Hadley right now and accept their offer. I want to tell him Papa is good friends with a realtor who could find Peter a respectable Upper West Side studio. But then I would be the person I've been with my parents—the fretting, short-circuiting girl who needs reassurance to exist. And anyway, Peter doesn't make me feel fretful. He looks me in the eye and makes me hope that things can work out.

Even after almost two weeks, I can't imagine a day without him.

Yesterday evening, he and I wandered toward the coast holding hands, his pant leg brushing mine, the scent of warm bread and cinnamon in the air, a few windchimes on shopfronts jangling. A woman in pink-suede heels strolled toward us, walking a Golden Retriever on a braided pink leash. On instinct, I crouched down with my arms out. "I have one of these at home!" I cried, as if I were waking to that pink-leashed retriever on Christmas.

The woman came to a halt as Peter knelt beside me on the asphalt, running his fingers with mine through the dog's yellow coat, listening to the woman—who kept eyeing Peter, as beautiful worldly women faced with handsome men do—tell me her dog's name (Coco), age (4), and Coco's general retriever tendencies toward goodness (too many).

When, after a few minutes, the woman snapped her dog's leash to go, Peter pulled me up by my hand and just stared at me there on the sidewalk. "You're so full of love for things." He shook his head. "For living things."

He peered into the distance, almost indiscernibly shaking his head again. I could tell he was thinking. He encircled my waist with his arm as we walked. "My whole life, wherever I've been, I've only felt like I was pausing before heading somewhere next. But right here, with you—" He stopped beside a wood-slatted bench along the sidewalk, smiling down at me. "I just want to stay a while, be still. *Tranquille.*" He paused on the French word. "That's probably more accurate."

"Moi aussi." I switched to French, jolting a little at the truth in my words. *Me, too.*

I could feel our separate energies—his an easy, forward momentum, mine a pensive, backward pull; and there we stood, at rest together. Yugoslavia in turmoil, Maman's life in the balance, but between Peter and me, a thrumming in the air like happiness.

As evening foot-traffic slowed, we talked on the wooden bench and kissed like Rodin's Paolo and Francesca. With Peter's hand on my hip and his breath in my mouth, I opened my eyes and found his lightly shut. I don't know what I expected—just, I guess, that he would look less hungry or awestruck or entranced than I felt. But even with his eyes closed, he had a disbelieving, aching, blissful look on his face that I wanted to belong to just me forever.

Wednesday, March 20, 1991
11:35 a.m., my bedroom desk

Maman called this morning as I was opening my eyes to an image of Peter and me last night studying at his kitchen table, his fingers occasionally threading into mine or lifting one of my hands to his lips, while his eyes remained locked on a book or his notes, as if the proximity of our skin was not remotely distracting.

After a brief, "*Bonjour*, did I wake you?", Maman cleared her throat. "I found a poem you wrote me. When you were eleven. It was in my closet, in a shoebox."

Straining to suppress the first question I thought of—*Do we just reflect honestly on our memories now?*—I tried to remain focused on the practical. "A poem? Really? What does it say?"

I could hear the un-crinkling of what I saw in my mind as a tiny worn scrap of gray paper.

Maman held her breath at each line-ending and read the poem twice so that I could transcribe it. I envisioned the baby inside her—my sister—listening.

MAMAN
Maman is French, like pastry and ballet.
She teaches me to bake crackly bread—

"Soft with your fingers! Softly," she says.
At night, she sings "Une chanson douce."
Je veux la chanter pour toi. *Her fingers*
tickle my arms. She is so soft. She likes
the park in April, swans and walks
to museums and libraries. Sometimes
she takes my hand. Sometimes she says,
"You know the way," and she follows me.
She makes sure I arrive there safely.

Maman paused a long time after the second reading, in a quiet that felt warm and tight, like not just I, but both of us, were clenching our jaws and trying not to sniffle. I wondered if the baby had fluttered at her voice—at my words being read by our mother.

"Do you remember writing that?" Maman asked.

"I think so." I sat up in my bed to find that Hillary had left for the morning.

I could see in my mind my yellow sixth-grade desk under a brown composition book, but that image quickly morphed into Peter's kitchen table and his broad olive hand jotting notes on lined paper.

I felt myself caught in a slingshot—held to this spot, St. Brigid's, by the force of my ardor for Peter, and my hope that his ardor for me might be as anchoring. But I also felt myself about to shoot eastward with speed and relief, back to Maman, Papa, Luc (though we haven't yet spoken), and home. And to Peter, if only he could decide to teach there.

Maman and I spent the next 96 minutes discussing unprecedented subject matter (including seven tense minutes about Robert). That is a longer span than we have spoken in months, maybe since she was ill— about my classes and what I've been writing and baking, about how it feels when a small body tumbles inside you, about when I'd be home and what I was hoping to eat first.

Pregnancy hormones must have overtaken Maman's mind.

I couldn't make my tongue shape the name *Peter* or form any question about leaving St. Brigid's.

And though I kept squeezing my eyes shut to stop myself, I could not overcome the way I have been conditioned by her illness to picture her—ashen, in a pale blue-checked gown, talking from a hospital bed.

At the end of our call, I asked if she felt sick anymore.

"Vivienne," her voice turned quiet and small, as though she were scared, but at the same time, about to reveal a secret. "Do you know the story in the Bible of the woman with an issue of blood? She reaches for the hem of Christ's robe and is healed of her plague."

I felt a palpable weight—made of time and love and fear and hope—descend from my scalp to my foot soles. I don't think I could have moved my limbs.

"Yes," I barely whispered.

"For what I think will be long enough, I feel like that."

On the phone, I said, "God is good," but all day I have wondered what she meant by that sentence.

What, I ask all saints in heaven, *what could possibly ever be long enough?*

Delivering a baby? Is that living long enough? Delivering two babies? Three?

Is seeing one daughter reach twenty long enough?

Or finding one body, among all the bodies in cities and villages, in vehicles and trains, amid wars and rush-hour traffic—one body that knows precisely how to hold you. Whose heart, when you're held, fits just beneath your ear, whose mouth speaks your name with just the right intonation—is finding that body long enough?

What if we lived for 900 years? Then, if your mother fell sick, could you kiss her goodbye?

Could you let go the hand that had touched you everywhere?

What is she thinking?

No time is long enough.

Thursday, March 21, 1991
8:03 p.m., at Peter's

At 7:42 this morning, Peter called to say he would be standing outside my dorm in ten minutes.

"What's happened?" I cracked open two slats of my bedroom

window's cheap metal blinds, as if to search for some portent: a lingering red moon, six crows on the sidewalk.

"Nothing!" Peter laughed, but when I kept holding my breath, he could tell I was worrying. "Nothing bad, Vivienne! I promise!"

Twenty minutes later, we sat at a tiny round table at Palmiers, sharing coffee and croissants.

One of his kneecaps bounced between both of mine underneath the table.

"Something good happened?" I felt like I was sitting in his office, waiting to receive a verdict again, except that he was stroking his fingers up and down the back of my hand this time.

"Even the tendons of your hands are beautiful—like sandpiper talons." He lowered his head to study the back of my hands more closely.

"Okay, you're crazy." I covered his hands with mine. He had returned me to my dorm at 2 a.m. this morning. My eyelids felt inflated, and my heart kept stuttering. I had to be at Baking in three hours.

"By the way," Peter bit off half a *pain au chocolat* from the plate set between us, "I need to know . . ." His words became incomprehensible. I choked on a laugh with coffee in my mouth as he extracted a wrinkled sticky note from his hoodie pocket. "Do you know where this is?"

I took the note from him, lint dulling the sticky tab.

305 W 89ᵗʰ St.

I answered on New Yorker autopilot. "It's on the Upper West Side, kind of high up, pretty close to Had—" My hand came down on his like a claw in one of those arcade machines.

"Ouch!"

"You're accepting at Hadley." I could feel his warm skin, the sturdy bones of his fingers.

"I've accepted. Past tense. This morning. Contingent on the dissertation." He lifted my free hand to kiss the back of it.

All I could do was watch him, thinking that I'd probably landed in another woman's life. I felt dizzy and miraculous for being alive and sitting across from a man, who only one month ago, I would have picked from a line-up of all the earth's men as the one who was too beautiful, too smart, too grown up to ever think twice about me. I felt like a woman born with summer-bright eyes to a world where nobody leaves or dies, who knows that the day, the month, her whole brilliant life will turn out exactly as she's dreamed it.

In my real life—which is blessed enough—I am always braced for illness to strike, for reservation, uncertainty, silence.

I didn't know how to proceed in the life I had landed in.

"And you're living at this address?" I smoothed out the sticky note.

"Yes. It's a studio. Kieran O'Connor—my father's friend, Hadley's history department chair—owns it. The rent is a pittance. He says I can have the keys in August."

I pictured us sitting as we were right then, in August, at a miniature kitchen table in a New York studio. I could almost hear Peter say, *Vivienne, don't go yet.*

"That's really good news." A tear blinked from my eyelashes.

I didn't know exactly what we were to each other at that moment— boyfriend and girlfriend, soulmates, future lovers? I still don't know as I write this entry. We have never named what we are together. Him and me, two people who give words to everything.

But I think it was love I felt in our hands. It was new and fluttery, but sure and safe.

Leaving the rest of our breakfast untouched, I walked beside him to his car with my head pressed below his shoulder, my lips smiling drunkenly. We drove to the coast, where we sat in the sand, his arm around me, pulling me close, shielding me from wind, while I told him all the things we would do in New York.

———————

Sunday, March 24, 1991
9:10 a.m., a bench beneath the sycamores, with a box of chocolate chip cookies I baked for Peter

I just have to write the sentence:
Peter is working in New York.
I mean, PETER IS WORKING IN NEW YORK!
ALL-CAPS!!! EXCLAMATION MARKS!!!!
PETER!!!!! ME—*VIVIENNE!!!!*

IN NEW YORK!!!!!!!!!!!!!!!!!

But—strangest thing—I received a letter from Philbrick yesterday. It was waiting on my pillow last night when I returned home from spending all day searching out bookshops along the coast with Peter.

I'll tape it here—

Dear Vivienne Lebrun:

Thank you for your interest in transferring to Philbrick. We have very much enjoyed reading your application and would like to inform you that it has made the final round of our selection process. This year's selection has taken considerably longer than usual, as we received 324 applications and are able to accept only fourteen new writers and one transfer student. Of those 15, we are able to offer funding to four. The fact that your application remains in our final pool of candidates speaks to the high quality of your work.

Thank you for your continued patience with our admittance process. You may expect to receive a final word from us by April 30th.

Sincerely,

Elin Rhys
Faculty Chair, The Philbrick Program for Writers

p.s. Dear Miss Lebrun, you dazzled them. –S.B., Dept. Administrator
(we spoke on the phone in January)

When I called to read the letter to Peter last night, I had basically accepted the fact of my rejection—all my plans for New York in the fall spiraling from my mind like dead leaves. But Peter said no way—no person on earth could reject what I write, unless maybe his or her heart was cinderblock (his words), and S.B.-the-Department-Administrator would not risk her job writing a postscript like that if Philbrick faculty had not already chosen me as their surefire transfer student.

"But would you like me to sing you to sleep on the phone?" he asked.

I'm sure he expected me to laugh, but I've loved his voice since the first time I heard it say, "Welcome to Poetry."

"Would you?" I asked.

A few seconds passed. He said, "How about I read you a poem."

Which he did—"True Love," by Wisława Szymborska. I read it weeks ago for his class and remembered the first stanza as he read it tonight on the phone—

> *True love. Is it normal,*
> *is it serious, is it practical?*
> *What does the world get from two people*
> *who exist in a world of their own?*

Does reading me a poem about love mean that he loves me?

That question distracted me from thinking about Philbrick all night.

Thursday, March 28, 1991, Spring Break
6:32 p.m., at Peter's kitchen table, while he makes something with cabbage for our dinner

I am almost not worrying about Philbrick.

I am trying to think instead about how I can't capture everything. In any given moment, I am trying to remember *now*, even as my brain lurches forward, planning the days ahead.

Here are six things I've loved from Spring Break—

1.

I keep asking Peter to teach me Slovene, but he says that is like asking him to stab a bouquet of sharpened pencils into my skull—it is that cruel to teach and even more painful to learn. On Tuesday, however, I sat on his sofa asking potential dissertation-defense questions that he answered from his kitchen table, and when finally, after three hours, he stood and collapsed to his sofa, he pulled me onto his lap and whispered something in Slovene. *Najlepša hvala.* Every time I tried to say it, he kissed a different spot on my face before repeating it.

Najlepša hvala.

Which is to say, *Most beautiful thank you.*

2.

On the topic of Slovene: Yesterday, Peter placed his Anna Swir collection of poems in my hands for keeps and called me his *miška,* his little mouse, which should probably feel sexist and demeaning, but really, it only made me think of kissing him in the rain, in a fedora—if it would stay on my hair—in a place with fat-spired buildings, like Moscow.

3.

Peter sings (his voice is scratchy but on key and—big surprise!—attractive) U2 and Sinead O'Connor's "Nothing Compares 2U" in his Jetta. At particularly passionate measures, he has taken hold of my wrist and used my fist as a microphone. This is one thing I might miss in New York. I'm not sure we'll ever drive a car there.

4.

Peter's ears are beautiful. Da Vinci would have paid good money to sketch them. They are perfect human ears, inner curves like the delicate whorls of a shell, soft slender lobes connecting seamlessly to his face.

Yesterday afternoon—not long after he first called me *miška*—he fell asleep on his sofa, so I just squished up beside him, studying his profile and tracing his ear with my finger.

Not even stirring, he startled me when he said, "Vivienne, are you seducing me?" I think he's decided that neither of us will be seducing the other before we part ways for the summer.

Still, I kissed his perfect ear and said, "Only a little."

5.

Peter said I should perfect my chocolate chip cookies in his kitchen. After each batch I bake, he writes one sentence that he insists is a poem. Today's was—

I feel like you mixed these in the bowl of my heart.

6.

I removed my watch from my wrist on Monday. Each day, I pretend that hours aren't quantified, that any minute I spend with Peter is somewhere in the universe an infinitely expanding forever. A raindrop in earth time, but from a far-away planet, a clear sea that has never been measured.

Though by the end of each day, I can't fool myself: At present, we have 34 more days before he leaves for his family in Slovenia.

Eight-hundred-and-sixteen hours.

One-million, four-hundred-sixty-nine-thousand seconds, though I took at least twenty seconds to write that number.

The present we live in vanishes before we blink, let alone write it down in ink.

I'm not sure that I want to remember that sentence, and not solely because it rhymes.

Saturday, March 30, 1991
1:18 a.m., kneeling beside my bed

I have been thinking about my sister, beyond wondering if Maman will remain healthy and if the baby will survive until she is pushed or cut from our mother.

At the oddest moments—between Peter's kisses, between sentences I write about bread or Wordsworth, or even as I step from the shower—I find myself trying to envision my sister. In newborn photos, Luc and I look almost exactly alike—pudgy red cheeks, whorls of black hair, dark eyes so large we could barely open them. I imagine our sister looking like us, but one never knows—she could be bald, or flaxen-blond like Papa's brother. And Maman's Papa has green-blue eyes—our sister could possibly inherit them.

I can see myself bathing her the same way I bathed Maman's friend's baby when I was small—bare-legged and kneeling right in the tub, wringing out a soft cloth on my new sister's head, bending down to kiss her slick tummy.

How is she becoming so real when she is not even viable outside Maman's womb yet? She hasn't breathed air, and still I would grieve to lose her. Already I love her. Already I imagine braiding her hair, singing her songs, reading her poems at bedtime.

Already I imagine reading my own babies poems, with an ache so deep, right in the space I imagine my womb to be.

I think I want nothing more than that—to be a mother, I mean. And right after that, to be the mother of Peter's babies. I know that kind of maternal yearning makes me a miserable feminist, but maternity is what I want—the same way I want nourishment and shelter. Every other thing I wish for radiates from that desire. Except for Peter. He is the wish that encompasses all wishes.

Earlier this week, he received an envelope from his mother containing five photographs of David, his new nephew, whose eyes were sealed shut in that just-barely-unwrapped newborn way. Maman always says that newborns resemble no one but newborns, yet even with his eyes closed in his pinched newborn face, Peter's nephew looked like a baby Peter.

"That is very weird." Peter might as well have been holding up a magnifying glass, he so closely studied each picture.

I spoke the words I have been thinking for days now. "I can't wait to hold my little sister."

"Me neither." Peter's words struck me as more surprising than my own. "It will be like holding a baby Vivienne. How could one not adore her?" He didn't even look up from his photographs to see my face, mouth open, brow tensed, one-hundred-percent astonished.

He had imagined my sister, too. He had thought of New York, and us, together.

———

Sunday, March 31, 1991
2:16 p.m., the park across the street from Peter's house

Easter has turned out to be lovelier than I expected. My family called at 8 this morning, singing out "Happy Easter!" all together at their handset. We shared our plans for the day, mine absent any mention of Peter or my intent to withdraw from St. Brigid's, theirs absent all talk of illness or pregnancy.

Luc sounded pleasant but reserved, as if he knew he had tipped my already-teetering sense of personhood off the ledge of a ten-story building nine weeks ago. But at the end of the call, he said, "I'm glad you'll be home soon. I miss you, Vivi."

It is hard not to feel like a hypocrite when I talk to them. I have communicated by a month-long silence that my mother's silence is abhorrent to me and that I would like for her to no longer be silent—that is, not to withhold potentially life-altering information. Meanwhile, I am choosing to withhold potentially life-altering information.

Peter says I should simply call my parents and explain what I plan to do, but I am certain that they would never agree to Philbrick over the phone. It is too easy for them to say no, to shut down the whole venture, just as Papa did in January after I simply said the word *Philbrick*. On the telephone, my parents are gifted at ending a conversation as soon as they are done listening. I could try saying *Philbrick* again, but either one of them would cut in with, "We have invested too much in your success at St. Brigid's. You have one semester left. Grow up."

If I am in New York, in my parents' apartment, standing before them, they would have to eventually hear my reasons for wanting to transfer. I could detail a solid, efficient plan that included a master's degree, and I think they could better envision me living an adult life in New York.

Peter asked yesterday if I truly needed my parents' permission to transfer to Philbrick, and I said that I felt like I did. Even though my St. Brigid's education hasn't cost my parents much money, they have made selfless contributions, both tangible and intangible, to my success, and I would still want and need their support at Philbrick. I agreed three years ago to attend St. Brigid's for them, but we still, the three of us, made that decision together, and I would want us to be aligned if I transferred to Philbrick.

All these worries are pointless, however, if I don't receive an actual acceptance to Philbrick. Who takes this long to decide if they like someone's writing? What are they doing with my submission until April 30th? Cutting it into its individual words to see if they can arrange them with more dazzle than I did? If Philbrick faculty loved what I wrote, wouldn't someone have mailed confirmation by now?

Even as I've worried, though, Easter has turned out to be lovely. After my family called, Hillary and I attended Easter Mass on campus, while Peter attended off-campus with St. Brigid's history department chair, Fletcher Ahlstrom, who is nothing short of disconsolate over Peter leaving St. Brigid's.

I feel Professor Ahlstrom's pain. One of us was bound to be heartbroken.

Now it is afternoon, and Peter and I are lying belly-down on a blanket at a park across the street from his house, as children dressed in pastels squeal across a wide lawn swinging straw baskets.

Peter is regaling me with tales of Slovenia but keeps nuzzling my cheek with his just-bent Slavic nose, trying to interfere with my writing.

He is stealing my pen—

> *Let it be written in Vivienne's journal that Peter was here, propped on his elbows beside her, thinking unreservedly filthy thoughts inspired entirely by her. And let it be known that she is lovelier than springtime, her hair like a knot of bellflowers. And though she is endeavoring to wrangle her pen from my hand just now, I shall persist in writing that one day soon she might like visiting Slovenia. We would walk through Ljubljana and pass the old music school, where arias still float from the windows. And though my father will suggest she sleep on a cot, Vivienne, in truth, would be sleeping with me. But should that fact fail to convince her*

I have commandeered my pen at last.

PETER BREZNIK KNOWS (and if he has forgotten, he is reading these words as I write them) that I cannot visit Slovenia at present. I have degrees to earn and people to care for, and PETER HIMSELF has committed to innumerable plans we have made for New York. And what on earth would I, not to mention the academic study of history in the United States of America, do if Peter Breznik stayed too long in Slovenia?

With a long blade of grass, he is stroking my jawline—

———

Peter's parents called just as we returned from the park yesterday afternoon. An armed clash had broken out earlier in the day in Croatia, at what is called The Pitivice National Park. Serbians have long occupied specific regions in Croatia—they're called *Croat Serbs,* or *ethnic Serbs,* even though everyone is supposedly Yugoslavian. Evidently dismissive of that fact, Croat/ethnic Serbs went so far as to declare an autonomous territory for themselves within Croatia last year.

According to Peter's parents, Croat Serbs overtook the Petivice Lakes park yesterday morning and then ambushed a convoy of Croatian police. The Croatian police force ultimately recaptured the area, but suffered casualties—six men wounded and a 21-year-old police officer killed in machine-gun fire. Tilen Breznik was supposedly present.

Neither his parents, nor his wife, nor his many close friends throughout Yugoslavia had heard from him since the skirmish broke out, and all parties were skeptical that Croatian officials had accurately reported injuries and fatalities.

By the time Peter hung up the telephone and explained the situation to me, he looked like a ghost newly detached from its body. His face appeared drained of blood. He stepped to his desk with a halting gait.

"I can take you home," he said in a voice that reminded me of automated phone messages.

I thought of Maman when she was ill—how, once, when she was hurting the worst, I convinced her to allow me to lie beside her in case she needed anything. I climbed onto her bed as quietly as a snow leopard, lying as still as possible, imagining that I didn't have to breathe and that all the breaths I saved would go to her.

I was pretty sure I could store breaths for Peter.

"Please let me stay." I stood near the sofa, knowing how his kind of fear felt—like anyone who touches you will shatter the glass shell of your equilibrium.

"I think I'll study. And write a little." He dropped rigidly to his desk chair. "Tilen's not dead. He just hasn't found a phone yet. I mean, I'd kill him the minute he returned to Zagreb. If I were there. But he's not dead. He can't be."

I retrieved my backpack from where I'd dropped it near the front door that morning. "Do you want me to make you something to eat?" I asked. "Soup? Or pasta?"

"No—" He lifted a stack of books from the floor beside his desk. "Unless you want some. Are you hungry?"

"No," I said, "I'll just be here."

He peered from his desk at me, face still as pale as thin clouds. "I'd like you to be here."

Sitting down in a corner of his couch, I opened a book in my lap, trying to replace a panicked face with a reading one. Before I made sense of two words, however, my eyes returned to Peter. I studied him as his body processed his fear.

Unaware of my gaze, he propped his elbows on his desk, balled his hands into fists and pressed them into his scrunched-shut eyes. He sat like that, breathing in, breathing out, until my own breath matched the rise and fall of his shoulders. Eventually, he alternated between staring down at a book without turning pages and peering up at the ceiling with his hands pulling at his hair.

I wanted to kneel beside his chair and hold him. I wanted to cradle him and his fear in my arms.

Just as I meant to rise from the couch, Peter lowered the heels of his palms from his eyes. "You're so far away over there." He squinted at me as if through a tunnel.

And then the telephone on his kitchen table rang.

Leaping across the sitting room, he seized hold of the phone, practically shouting hello in Slovene before correcting himself with, "I mean, hello? This is Peter." After about ten seconds, his fist pumped the air as he smiled at me with the intensity of daylight breaking over the ocean.

I wrapped my arms around my knees on his sofa, watching his cheeks pink up, relief like a cool sheer cloth settling over his face. *Tilen wasn't dead.*

Too curious and concerned to even pretend I'd returned to studying, I simply listened to Peter speak Slovene. His language is soft, spoken up front in the mouth, tongue trilling on double consonants. Sometimes

I think it almost sounds like Italian, but it is not so staccato, every few words marked by a *jjj* or a *sh* sound.

Hearing Tilen's deep joyful voice on the line, even as I sat one room away, I felt tears well up in my throat. Although Peter's words were as indecipherable to me as sparrow chatter, their tone felt as warm and familiar as my own native tongue.

Somehow, perhaps because of how Peter speaks of the distance between them, I had imagined that he and his family loved one another less fiercely than mine did. I had assumed his heartstrings to be detached from his homeland and stitched firmly to this land. But even if Slovenia did not feel like home to him, Peter still loved people who lived there, who spoke his first language and longed for him to be near them—to share traumas, miracles, tears, embraces.

Although, please God, forgive me—I still wouldn't want Peter to live in Slovenia.

Once he had run out of breath for more sentences, he lowered himself to his kitchen floor, leaned his back on the refrigerator door, laughing until tears splotched his cheeks. Lifting his head, he met my eyes. "Come here!" He did not even pull the phone away from his face as he reached out one of his Michelangelo-sculpted arms to me.

"No, no," he continued in English, drawing me into his conversation. "Not you, Tilen—God knows you won't come here. Although you should humble yourself for Hana and David, and"—he raised my fingers to his lips when I sat down beside him—"so that you could meet this girl." He set our two hands together on my knee, his eyes holding mine, happy crescent moons of light in them. "This woman I met . . . She's nothing short of . . . brilliant." His whole face lifted with a smile.

A wide, I-won-the-Pulitzer kind of smile. Kindled, I think, by . . . me. *This girl . . . This woman he met.*

I feel like maybe I should stop documenting, so that when Peter leaves for the summer and realizes that I am possibly irreversibly emotionally stunted, I won't come back to words that remind me of how his skin smells like soap and is always, without fail, warmer than mine, the perfect temperature to lean into.

Peter held the phone between us.

Far away in Croatia, Tilen Breznik switched to English himself, his words brushed by an accent only slightly more distinct than Peter's. "No!" I could hear his exclamation point like a stapler-punch. "Since I know you would choose brilliant before beautiful, I must assume it has happened, Peter! You finally found a woman smart enough to—"

"She's right here, Tilen. Say *živijo* to Vivienne."

"*Živijo*, Vivienne!"

"Hello, Tilen." I tried to imagine him. In the few photos I've seen, he is darker than Peter, a tiny bit shorter, and often looking as though he's been trapped for a picture. "Peter's been waiting to hear from you. I'm so glad you're safe."

"Oh, she is lovely, Peter! I can tell from the quiet in her voice." The tenderness in Tilen's own voice set a butterfly storm aloft in my stomach. "Vivienne, do you know—my brother has a habit of attaching himself to the cruelest women. Granted, most of them have been more beautiful than brilliant."

"Tilen!" Peter grinned as I raised my brow at him. He mumbled, "It might be a little bit true."

"A little bit! Peter Breznik! Master of understatement!" Tilen's laughter was deeper, perhaps easier, than Peter's. I could feel Peter's body relax at the sound of it.

"Cruel women like Sonja?" I lowered my head to the telephone, intent on not looking at Peter.

"Sonja!" Tilen cried. "Princess Grace Kelly of Slovenia!"

"Okay, that's an overstatement." Peter rolled his eyes, his face still flushed with the relief of answering the phone to Tilen.

"A supermodel of the highest order!!" I embraced exclamation marks.

Tilen sighed. "The cruelest."

"Poor Peter," I giggled.

"Ah, Vivienne." Tilen pronounced my name like Peter does, the last syllable elegantly stressed. "I can tell that you would never be cruel."

In the pause following his sentence, Peter pressed a kiss to my forehead.

"So please." Tilen's voice called my spine to attention. I straightened against the refrigerator. "Tell my brother that he must teach history in his own country—"

"Tilen, no teasing," Peter said. "Vivienne's a committed New Yorker, and I'm—"

"You are a Slovene, Peter! A fact that has never been more important than it is at this moment. Vivienne, could you not join Peter in Ljubljana?" Tilen sounded like he had just glimpsed a table piled high with every last gift he'd ever wished for at Christmas. "Say you will come! You don't have to marry—"

"Enough!" Peter sat straighter, too, his free hand at my elbow.

But I do want to marry Peter, I thought, my face no doubt stricken.

Peter covered his eyes, speaking into the phone. "I've accepted a job—remember? A good one, Tilen, so your pleading is useless. Why don't you just tell Vivienne about the time I drove Ati's car through a shopfront window? You know—vivid endearing tales of my youth?"

"Ah, yes." The words were like a firm head-nod. "I shall do that when you come to Slovenia to see Peter, Vivienne. Our Ati would love you. He would assemble a little cot and set our mother to scavenging pink bed linens. Tell me that would not feel like home to you!"

"You're so kind—" I tried filling the tight beats of silence. "I—"

Peter pulled my hand to his chest.

"Peter? Are you there? Have I lost you?" Tilen's voice sounded tinny.

"No, no. Not at all." Holding the phone to his ear again, Peter conversed with Tilen for a few minutes more in Slovene. After saying what seemed like goodbye, he held the phone out for me again.

"Vivienne, I am planning to see you here soon!" Tilen's far-away voice was jovial, but I don't think he was joking. "And don't worry— Peter thinks you are brilliant *and* beautiful. When he describes you in Slovene, the words make a poem."

Glancing up, I found Peter watching me. "Nearly all Peter's words make a poem," I said.

Tilen huffed a soft laugh. "Don't let it go to his head, Vivienne."

Right then, Peter's head descended toward mine. He didn't even glance at the phone as he said, "Come to Manhattan this fall, Tilen."

"Be safe in Zagreb, Tilen!" I touched my fingertips to Peter's lips as they hovered in front of mine.

"God bless you, Vivienne. *Au revoir,* my friend. *Adio,* Peter."

After the line crackled off to a buzz, Peter pulled me in tighter beside him, both of us still on the kitchen floor, our backs against the refriger-ator. His legs looked effortless in his jeans as usual, while my legs stuck out of my knee shorts.

"Tilen and one of his photographer friends followed the Croatian police up to the park's entrance," Peter said. "There was snow on the roads, dense fog—the whole venture was treacherous. Tilen was present for the ambush, of course, documenting it. His friend—Mats, I think—was taking pictures. They weren't able to reach a phone until a few hours ago." Peter squinted into nothing straight ahead. "I think maybe I forgot how crazy he is." He rested a hand on my thigh.

"You mean he loves you like crazy."

"I know he does, but—how did he remain Slovene, while I became—"

"A professor?" I tried to fill in for him.

"No . . ." He kept squinting, running his hand through his hair. "While I became . . . homeless."

I could have asked, "Where do you want your home to be, Peter?" or "Do you want to live near your brother?" But I didn't want him to answer those questions. I didn't want him, let alone myself, to hear what he might privately wish for.

Anyhow, if I had given voice to those questions, I would have only wanted to ask them again later, and then probably again a short time after that. And then I would be exactly that person I do not want to be—the pesterer, the worrier, the figurative spewing electrical wires.

What I couldn't keep from saying was not void of worry, or at least a vague sense of electrical wires. "I'm so sorry, Peter. I'm sorry I can't go to Slovenia. Not right now, and maybe not—"

"Shhhhh." Peter pulled me into him until my head rested under his chin. "I know, Vivienne. I know that. I wouldn't ask it of you."

Closing my eyes, I tried to fill my mind with only the sound of our breathing.

Finally, I said, "You probably feel homeless because you were born in California."

I could tell his lips over my head were grinning. "You really dislike California."

The two of us burst out laughing.

And then we were kissing and not thinking about brothers or ambushes or homelessness at all.

In my mind, I was a phosphorescent nervous system, lighting and flickering, being touched by him.

Monday, April 15, 1991
7:21 p.m., at Peter's

Obviously, I'm avoiding my journal. It reminds me of how many days have passed since I last heard from Philbrick, and worse, that my days with Peter are numbered.

I've attended Alene Bautista's poetry class six times now. To receive an A, I will have to submit a portfolio of ten significantly revised and polished poems, along with a ten-page essay on a craft mechanism of my choice. If Peter were still my instructor, I'd try to write a ground-breaking work on the magical transference of human idea and emotion through metaphor, but as Peter is currently brushing my hair as I write in his recliner, and is not, thank God, my instructor, I would rather keep reclining here and ask if he knows how to braid, and then I could write a craft essay next week about something easy, like stanza-shape.

The buzzer is sounding on the fourth tray of my supposed-to-be perfect cookies. Perfection might be easier if happiness were not so distracting.

Thursday, April 25, 1991
10:46 p.m., library, third floor, not studying for Metaphysical Poetry

I saw Peter for 48 minutes today—he is busy preparing for his dissertation defense next Thursday, and almost equally busy talking on the phone with his parents about Tilen, and with Tilen about Ljubljana and his parents. I've named Peter's apartment The War Rooms, since it's where he prepares material and strategy for his defense, as well as for conversation with his family.

He called last night to ask if I would stop by his office at 4 p.m. today, and when I arrived at his open door, he stood up from his desk, pulled me in by both hands, allowing the door to sigh shut behind us.

"Hello," he smiled, bending happily to kiss me, as though that kiss and that moment existed free of all others, as though every touch before and every touch I imagine after were not pressing in around us.

I held him close as he lifted away. For the countless time now, I rested my cheek on his heartbeat.

"I have something for you." His hand crept up my neck. "Two things."

Pulling just barely away from him, I noticed two brown-paper-wrapped packages on his desk.

"They're gifts," Peter said, tugging me back to him. Circled around me, his arms felt as sound and snug as a bed in the morning. I couldn't believe they'd be gone so soon—his arms and the rest of him. Not gone from existence, and not for forever, but still, his person would be so far away. On a globe, almost half-way around the earth. He keeps reminding me that it's only for three months—he'll call and we'll talk; he says he will write me letters. But I know he can't call or write too often. Calling is expensive, and his hours will be filled up by his family and the unrest just outside their soon-to-be-independent country. Also, it may occur to him as he observes his brother, older and wed to a woman of common nationality and similar background, that an undergraduate New Yorker is not exactly a catch.

"Unwrap the larger one first," he said, chin touching my head before he released me.

I weighed the larger package in my hands—it was soft and light and cushiony. With the first tear of paper, I saw the heathered-blue fabric. "Your sweatshirt—"

"Vivienne, you're shaking." Peter's hand cupped my elbow as I hugged his sweatshirt to my chest.

He was right—my hands were tremoring, and I still don't know why. I think I was feeling time passing—the seconds ticking by in my nerve-endings. Five days more wasn't long enough, even if I'd see him at the end of August. And who could know for how long that reunion would be? I might be sentenced to return to St. Brigid's after Labor Day.

"I don't like leaving people or places." I tried to laugh instead of cry into his sweatshirt. "I'm really bad at goodbyes."

Peter unfolded his sweatshirt from my arms and held it in front of my chest. "Whenever you wear it, pretend that I'm wrapped around you, okay? And don't wash it. I'll wear it once I arrive in New York, and I'll just breathe you in, even after you've left my apartment."

"Okay." I couldn't help but smile at that. At least I'd stay busy over the summer with everything my family would need to do to prepare for the baby. And maybe I'd be working at a bakery and prepping for Philbrick, and days would blur by like calendar cards on a Rolodex.

Peter set his sweatshirt back on his desk. "And now for the second gift." He handed it to me, a book-shaped rectangle. Assuming it must be a poetry collection, I tore through the paper, anticipating a title and the name of a poet. Instead, I found myself staring at a roughly-cut leather cover, no title, no author. I turned the book in my hands—he had given me a new journal. A new journal made of raw ivory paper, the binding hand-stitched, a thin leather cord looping the pages closed.

"I—" I could barely see Peter's eyes through my tears. "I love it." I smoothed my palm over the cover.

Peter drew me into him again, the journal pressed between us.

"I didn't get you anything to remember me by," I said.

"Thank goodness you're unforgettable then." His chin rested yet again on my head. I wanted us to be a living statue, flesh and blood and deemed to remain in that pose forever. "Your old journal is nearly full." His voice was a nudge that lifted my face to his. "Open this one," he said.

I held the journal out, untied the cord, and lifted the cover. Peter had made an inscription:

To Vivienne, mon buveur d'encre.

"Your drinker of ink."

The name was perfect—a more elegant version of *rat de biblio-thèque*—"library rat," or "bookworm."

But I knew that Peter meant the phrase for more than that.

Touching my fingers to his sharp-angled words on the milky-cream paper, I could see myself in my bed, at my desk, in the library, in class-rooms, on steps and in atriums, at Peter's house, and a few times, re-clined on his chest—writing, writing—ink on the callouses of my fin-gers, sometimes smeared like dark juice in the creases of my lips.

"Keep turning." Peter nodded at the journal.

At the top of every third or fourth page, he had written a poem. I paused on one at the beginning: *First, there is the question of distance—*

He'd taken the first line of one of the poems I had written about Maman in his class, and then made the rest of the poem his own—

> *First there is the question of distance—*
> *the length of her hair, the arc*
> *of her shoulder, her willow-thin arm*
> *from the elbow down.*
>
> *How many steps,*
> *how many days, how many*
> *words till I hold her?*

"That one's for the first time I saw you." Peter tried to tuck a stray wisp of hair behind my ear. "I hoped like hell that you'd be a good writer, because every time I looked at you, I'd see you in my arms."

I read another:

> *I know I taught class today,*
>   *said something*
> *about metaphor, but all*
> *I could think was*
>   *Why won't she look at me?*

My head shot up. "You thought that?"

"Every single day. You'd be writing up a magnetic storm in your notebook, and I'd be thinking you couldn't even identify my face in a police line-up." He tugged at a particularly unruly wave of my hair. "But at least your notetaking made me feel interesting."

Even with tears in my eyes, I laughed.

"But the poems in this journal, Vivienne—they're simple, plainspoken—"

I looked up. "I like plainspoken."

"They're not as sophisticated as your cookies," he smiled. "I didn't write everything I could have, or wanted to—"

I touched my fingers to his lips. "I love them."

I love you, I wanted to say, but sensed—I have always sensed—that for right now, in this one piercing sliver of time, just before we are parting, and even though we have written and said so much of language, there are some words we will not say yet.

I pressed his gift of a journal closed between my hands, held it to my chest and looked at him—this nomad, Peter Breznik, a man without home or anchor, who could stay in his family's country, but was choosing to come back to New York, to me.

I said, "Most beautiful thank you."

Friday, April 26, 1991

I think I'll be all alone till this evening. Hillary is with friends in Carmel till next week, and Peter defends his dissertation on Monday. I've been packing my room up one shirt, one skirt, one book at a time, and I think I'm nearly ready to fly home.

Fly home.

Just over a month ago, I would have written the phrase and envisioned little beyond the hushed yellow lamplight of our sitting room in Manhattan. Yet now I imagine Peter, too—sitting beside me on my bench in Central Park, autumn leaves twirling down—and I feel the lift in my bones that I always feel when he's with me.

I'm not sure I will even see him tomorrow—a fact that makes me want to cram my head inside my pillowcase, block all light from my brain, refuse food and water, and waste away. But one batch of perfected chocolate chip cookies, plus my final poems and craft essay are due on Tuesday, and I haven't even perfected my recipe or started writing my essay.

I keep thinking of things I've learned from Peter, about clarity, image, resonance, and metaphor.

I think of Maman and the woman in the Bible, who crawled through the multitude to touch the Lord's robe.

I keep thinking about the words we don't say, but the feelings we communicate anyway, through things. Longing, hope, heartache, love. Through stories, baked goods, sweatshirts, poetry.

I keep hearing, *For what I think will be long enough*—

I keep turning the gift of his journal in my hands.

I could start the essay with *We speak in degrees of metaphor.*

I think I might possibly stick with that. Stanzas are pretty hard to write about.

———

Monday, April 29, 1991
10:57 p.m., alone in my room, in my bed

Peter defended his dissertation today. Still in a white shirt and tie, he found me at the library afterward to tell me he'd passed with distinctions. We had planned to eat at a French restaurant he'd discovered last week called Poésie, but by the time we reached his car, he was spent, and I was soaking up almost-goodbye tears with my cardigan sleeve.

When I mentioned that Hillary was still in Carmel, Peter said, "Could we go to your place and talk?"

We held hands in the late-afternoon light, walking beneath syca-mores to my dorm.

By the time the door to my room shut behind us, we weren't tired anymore but were kicking our shoes off before falling to my bed in a tangle of limbs and kissing.

I glanced at the answering machine out of habit, relieved to see *0 Messages,* before Peter said, "Let me just take my tie off."

I yanked him back, begging, "Please, don't leave me."

And then the phone rang.

"Don't answer," Peter whispered at my ear as the caller began leaving a message.

"Vivi, it's Luc. Something's happened. If you're there, pick up."

Peter snapped from my bed to the phone, handing it to me as I inhaled a slow breath. "Luc?"

His voice through the handset felt like a hot match. "Maman's not dying, but you should come home. I know you would want to be here."

"What's happened?" Still dizzy and tingling from Peter's kisses, I teetered to standing, holding the phone out between me and Peter, just as he had done when he spoke to Tilen.

"I don't—I don't know exactly—" Luc never stammered. "She's bleeding—not a lot, but . . . like—well, I heard her say—it could be like the start of . . ."

"A miscarriage?" I flinched when my voice came out louder than I'd intended.

"Yes." Luc sounded like his much younger self, the one who couldn't sleep and needed his sister. "They left for the hospital about six hours ago. Maman called me twice from Emergency to say that doctors were still doing scans, but I haven't heard anything more for . . . well, it's been a few hours."

I double-checked my machine: *0 Messages.*

A patched fabric inside myself was re-tearing. In my head, I could hear one pop of a stitch, then another.

My mother.

The woman whose life I had saved my breaths for, would save all my breaths for—give my cells to if they would cancel out her faulty ones—give my heart—

She could not even dial—or ask my father to dial—eleven numbers on a phone to tell me that she was in peril, that her baby, my sister's, life was uncertain. Even after I thought her silence was over. Even after I thought we trusted each other.

"So why hasn't she called me, too?" I had to raise my voice even louder to clear the tears gathered to the size of a fist in my throat. "Did she tell you not to call me?" I turned in circles between my bed and Hillary's, as Peter stood with his arms bent slightly in front of him, as if ready to catch me if I lost balance.

"She hates worrying you, Vi—"

"Luc. Did she say: 'Do. Not. Call. Vivienne?'"

I could imagine Luc's panicked eyes rapid-blinking. "She said she had experienced this once before, with me, and there was no point in alarming—"

"So possibly . . . she is sitting in a hospital bed with a phone console one foot away from her fingers. She can call you twice, yet—"

"Vivi, why do you always expect—"

I was Papa's Theory of Escalation incarnate. "WHY ISN'T SHE CALLING ME, LUC?!!!"

"Whoa, Vivienne—" Stopping me mid-circle, Peter wrapped his arms around me. He had to work to turn me toward him. "Vivienne, it's okay. I'll help you call an airline."

"I'm not leaving." I spoke into the handset, looking at Peter. "We have four days." I resumed circling.

"Four days with who, Vivi?" Luc's voice sounded flimsy as it diffused into air. "Is that a guy? In your room?"

I pulled back my arm as if to hurl the phone through my window.

"Vivienne—" Peter took one cautious footstep toward me.

Jamming the phone to my ear, I varied my pacing from circular to linear. "It's *whom,* Luc. You meant four days with *whom.* The relative pro-noun is the object of a preposition, dammit! And I'll tell you who *whom* is. His name is Peter. He's a grown man who tells me what he means and what he's thinking. He's upfront and honest and treats me like an adult, and I'm not going to cut short my time with him for a crisis I'm not meant to know about! So you need to keep Maman alive for four days!"

I don't know what I expected when I turned toward Peter, but it was not to see him standing at the end of my bed paralyzed, the flush from our kisses washed from his face. "Are you sure you don't want to fly home?" His lips barely moved with the words.

Fly home.

Like a pigeon.

You be my home. My eyes stung from staring at him.

"Why in God's name is she not calling me, Luc?!" I lifted the phone again as if I might throw it, but Peter finally bid his legs walk and pried the phone from my hand. "What's wrong with Maman?" I cried at the handset.

Peter held it up to his ear. "Luc, this is Peter Breznik. I wish we were meeting in person under more pleasant circumstances, but until that occurs, please know that I care very much about your sister."

Is that all? I wanted to weep at him. *You care very much?*

Because I love you.

I love you, I love you, I love you.

"Do you know which hospital your parents went to? . . . And which airline does Vivienne typically fly? . . . And this would be to JFK, correct? . . . Who would be waiting for Vivienne there? . . . No—I would prefer that she not take the subway." Peter spoke to my brother like a teacher settling a meltdown at recess, and I didn't even care that I was a child storming across the room to my Keds and shoving my feet into them without untying the laces.

"Tell Luc that I'll see them on Thursday." I flung my bedroom door open.

Peter said something controlled and calming into the phone before returning it to the receiver and joining me under my doorframe. We looked like two people bracing for safety in an earthquake. "You know you could call your parents right now," he said like a spokesman for all composed persons everywhere. "She's at New York-Presbyterian." He'd pushed his hands into his pockets as he had on the morning he'd crossed a line in the library.

I felt like I barely knew him, or like he didn't know me, or like I didn't know myself. I felt like I didn't know anything—what to do, where to go—and like no one actually knew me, either, not even the people who conceived me.

Though I knew I was wrong in one respect: Peter knew me. He knew all my words, and he knew the deep hurting places that all the words came from.

He even knew what I was going to say next, because he said the words I was breathing in air to say to him. "How about we walk."

"Okay." My head pounded and my trachea hurt.

"Vivienne." Peter wrapped his arm around my shoulders.

We left my dorm to walk under a half-moon's light, sometimes holding hands, sometimes not, sometimes pausing beneath the silver-dark trees to hold one another. I told Peter that I wanted to stay with him until Thursday, that I was certain my mother would endure without me, as she had never expressed need of me in my life.

Peter kept asking, "Are you sure that's what you want? Are you sure you're okay?"

I kept answering yes to both questions, though the words I'd said to Luc kept repeating in my head. *Why in God's name is she not calling me?* The seams of the patched fabric inside me kept snapping like pockets of bubble wrap.

Finding ourselves at the west end of campus, Peter and I stopped beneath a lamppost. I looped one of my arms tight through his. "Were you hoping to talk in my room before my brother called?"

He looked up at the night sky's teacup of white moon. "We'll be together tomorrow."

Eventually, we ended up standing at the bottom of the steps to my dorm, facing each other, our hands linked together. "I'm meeting with Fletcher tomorrow morning at 8," Peter said. "Could you meet me at my office at 10?"

"Of course." I automatically pressed one side of my face to his heart—I've been thinking that his heart beats a rhythm in my life, too. "I'll drop my craft essay off in the English department, and then I'll walk over to you."

He smoothed a warm hand over the side of my face not pressed to his heart. "If you decide you want to fly home, I can help you finish packing and drive you to the airport. But we need to talk first."

My home. I breathed in the Dove-soap scent of him.

Maybe right then I should have told him I love him. Maybe it is the sorry excuse of a feminist in me that waits for him to say the words first. I wanted to say something close to *I love you,* though, even if I couldn't say those very words. I wanted to be precisely accurate. He had tipped his head over mine, so that I could feel his breath on the back of my head.

I said, "You are everything I ever hoped for."

He said, "You are that and more to me."

Should I have asked, *Peter, what does 'more' mean? Does it mean 'love' to you?* After which I could have said, *Because I feel more, too.*

Instead, I let him kiss me goodbye. Often with him, I feel out of my depth, like a girl playing grown-up in a dream. I don't know how all the parts should go—who should say *I love you* and when. I don't want to misstep, bring what we've made tumbling down.

For two hours now, I have been writing in my bed, not thinking about what is happening to Maman or why she hasn't called to tell me that I should be there, or that she would like me to be there, or that we will both be okay if I am not there till Thursday.

I am crying now, as I have countless times, for the painful things that might happen—that do happen to people every day—cancer or war or possibly, in my family's case, the loss of a baby.

My sister.

It is still baffling to me that the moment a life you never fathomed begins, its loss can be a blow to you—a sorrow.

I think I was born with a biological defect—I believe that heart-beating things should keep beating forever.

Tuesday, April 30, 1991
11:43 a.m., my desk

A taxi will arrive in one hour. A normal adult would not be sitting at her soon-to-be-former desk writing this. But I am not normal, nor am I an adult. I am more certain of this now than ever.

And I know who this journal is for now—it was never for my children.

I lay in my bed wide awake last night, hoping to receive a call from any member of my family, or even from Mr. Phillips, our doorman, but the phone never rang.

After dropping my craft essay on metaphor into Alene Bautista's box, I saw Julie gracefully clicking her heeled way toward me in the hall that connects the English and history departments.

"Vivienne, it's been weeks since I saw you!" Julie's silky-tanned arms flung around my neck. Stepping back, her eyes turned abruptly studious. "You look happy! Don't even say it—I know—you've gone out with Peter!"

My cheek muscles went powerless against my smile.

"Oh, my GOSH! You've gone out with PETER!!" She punched her fists in the air, twirled around until she stopped and smacked a palm to her mouth. "Oh, my gosh! Peter!!" She shook her head in pity and distress.

"What about him?" I glanced down at my watch to make sure I'd arrive at his office by 10.

Julie's hand fell from her mouth to her heart. "Well, I found out by accident—"

Found out? Found out . . . I wracked my brain for something anyone might find out about Peter.

Julie dove deep into details, explaining that she had decided to write her senior thesis on a few paintings done by Holocaust survivors, so this morning, she met with Fletcher Ahlstrom's assistant to discuss which history professors might be best qualified to sit on her committee.

"Peter told our poetry class that he'd accepted a position in New York"—her fluttering pink fingernails were giving me vertigo—"but I had to make sure this morning, because you know Peter would be perfect for my committee. When I asked Dr. Ahlstrom's assistant, though, she said she was pretty sure Peter had just told Dr. Ahlstrom that he accepted the position in Ljubljana." Gazing up at the heavens, Julie sighed before touching a hand to my shoulder. "At least you probably have plans to see him again." She widened her cornflower blue eyes at me. "Vivienne? Please say you already knew this."

I could feel tiny shocks sparking off in my face, as though my body had just been yanked from its energy source.

"Yes," I barely found breath to say. "Yes. I'm just on my way to meet him right now. Good luck with your project, Julie." I thought of squeezing her arm in goodbye, but all my brain could manage was convincing my legs to walk. Left foot, right. I stepped down the hall to the history department.

Two men stood embracing each other outside the chair's office. When they pulled back, one of them was wiping his eye. It was Peter. "Vivienne," he said when he saw me approaching.

I stopped, mouth open, vision blurring with tears, or maybe hysteria.

"Is she about to—" Professor Ahlstrom might have asked

something, but I couldn't hear. My brain was a racket of questions and refusal—a malfunctioning control panel. Only days ago, I wondered if I had crash-landed in another woman's charmed life, but then suddenly, today, I crash-landed for real in St. Brigid's history department. I stood bewildered as I always am, in front of a man I believed that I loved, and who behaved as though he loved me. But he'd lied to me. I wondered what else I didn't know about him. Had his affection been a lie, too?

Professor Ahlstrom retreated down the hall. My feet walked into Peter's office.

His electric tea kettle hummed on a bookshelf. For one stab of a second, I wondered if he had planned to offer me tea.

When the office door shut, I turned to find Peter standing before me. I had never felt anything remotely like anger when I'd looked at his face, but I stood in his office, inches away from him, feeling myself burn with fury.

He closed his eyes. "You heard that I accepted the job in Ljubljana."

I could only stand there, still burning, knowing helplessly in that moment exactly what Peter Breznik had been to me.

He had been my love. He had been love breathing outside my body.

"Dear God. Vivienne." His head fell into his hands. "How?" He looked at me. "How did you hear? I told Fletcher one hour ago—"

"Julie. Just now." My own voice reached my ears as if from the far end of a tunnel. "Ahlstrom's assistant overheard, and Julie was asking—"

Peter exhaled in bafflement. "I only decided two days ago." His fingers stabbed at his forehead. "I've been trying to tell you. I planned to explain last night, but your brother called, and your mother might be ill again, the baby coming too soon. You've been so wounded, so hurt. I couldn't—"

"You didn't tell me." I had the fleeting thought that the dead can talk. I couldn't feel my heart beat in my body. In my head, I was entering my family's Manhattan apartment, staring at my mother in a lavender snow hat. *We did not mean to deceive you.*

"For only two days, Vivienne—"

"But you didn't decide in one second." I blinked back to the present with a charge to my brain, a torrent of words assembling. "You've been thinking. You've been changing your mind as you kissed me, as you listened to me make plans for New York. You made me believe—" My voice didn't break, but I'd run out of air; I'd run out of life. I felt weightless.

"Please." He reached for my face, but I lurched away. My heart felt as though it had turned to sharp glass. Every time I breathed in, it shattered.

Peter, I kept trying not to say—I didn't want to hear the intimacy of his name, but it was echoing in my head in all the sweet ways I had said it. "You deceived me. Just like my parents. Only, this is much worse. At least my parents never lied to me in person. But you—you spoke words to my face—"

"No. Vivienne." He shook his head. "You know I've meant every word I've said to you. Every touch—"

"No. I don't." All our words in my mind were lifting away, as if plucked up by a typewriter in reverse.

"But you do. Please. Don't look at me like that."

"Like what?"

"Like you've died, for God's sake! Like you're not even in there. I have a family, too! I have parents who have spent barely half my life on the same continent as me—their son! I have a brother who will get himself shot, or worse, if I don't try to anchor him. I have a history, Vivienne, a country. California isn't my home. New York is not—"

Eyes closing, I flinched. "You said no place was your home. You were homeless. You let me dream of a home for you. I planned a home for you—for us"—I thumped a fist to my chest—"in New York."

His fingers found my wrist as he spoke. "We can still make a home, Vivienne. What I feel for you isn't in question. You are not an option—I mean—"

I tore my hand away. "You made me feel like an option—"

"That is not what I meant. If you'd simply listen. I meant that losing you was never an option—leaving you is not—"

"But you're going to leave me. You made the decision, and you know I won't go." I heard my voice rise as it had with Luc on the phone last night. "I can't go. I need to be in New York for my mother—for the baby—" I covered my face with my hands, frantic to call Luc, to ask what was happening, then hang up and dial an airline. "The baby—" I tried to quiet the words with my palms.

Peter stepped closer, as if soothing a wild thing, his voice strained and trembling. "You can't go with me to Slovenia right now, Vivienne. I would never ask you to come with me right now. But in time—after—"

"After what?" I was suddenly entirely present.

"I believed that you'd come." His hands flew out. "I *believe*—present tense—that after—"

I squinted at him till my brow hurt, our pause like the silence before a balloon pops.

"After what, Peter?" My voice turned as thin as a needle.

"After your mother's baby." He was trying but failing to speak calmly. "After time—if your mother were ill—after—"

"After my mother dies?" The question ended as a sharp cry. Razored white stars flickered in my peripheral vision.

"No! Of course not! I would never wish—"

"Then what, Peter?"

"I just think that with a little more time—"

"Time?! What does any of this have to do with time?"

"I mean that after, maybe then—we can—"

"After what, Peter?!" I stomped my foot so hard that books shook on his shelves.

Peter stared at my foot, tore a hand through his hair.

"After you grow up, dammit!" His eyes locked on mine.

The hum of his electric kettle stopped.

My head and his office—the whole world—went still. Light flared through the blinds as though clouds had passed, or a bomb had exploded. I waited for the floor beneath us to shake, but the tremors only happened inside me. I reached a hand to a shelf as mine and Peter's brief history splintered—

Peter pausing on my name the first day in Poetry.

Peter offering me his sweatshirt, then wearing it himself and breathing it in at the library.

Peter seeing me at Arugula, writing me a letter, opening his office door to me.

Kissing me, holding me, whispering my name.

Helping me plan for New York.

He had only been waiting for time to pass by, as though I weren't yet strong or brave or smart enough. He was waiting for me to grow up.

Hadn't I always known I was young—too young to attach myself to Peter, even as he had made me feel like his equal? I had played grown-up with a man who was a dream. He had earned three degrees, three job offers. I didn't have a job or a degree, and I didn't know where I'd earn one. I didn't even have Peter's adult consideration.

What I did have was a deluge of memories of myself telling Peter about the city we would inhabit together—bakeries, museums, Central Park, bookstores.

Right then in his office, I squeezed my eyes shut, unable for the first time, since the first time I saw him, to envision him and me together.

"Vivienne." He remained in front of me, blocking the door. "I'm not saying what I mean—that is . . . I'm not finding proper words. Right now, sometimes, six years between us feels large—"

"Exactly." I could never have imagined myself speaking so callously to him. "So you treated me like a child, keeping your plans to yourself so that my child heart wouldn't break. But you've behaved childishly, too—nodding along as I talked about you and me in New York, allowing me to believe that you were committed to working there—that you were committed to me. If you wanted me to act like an adult"—I hit a fist to my palm—"you shouldn't have treated me like a child. Did you hear what I said about you to my brother last night on the phone? That you treat me like a grown-up and tell me things? That you don't hide? I trusted you. I trusted you, while the people I should be able to trust most aren't trustworthy. You're just like them. Or no—it's me. I'm—" I stood shaking my head, wishing I wouldn't have to open my eyes again.

"Vivienne." He tried to cradle my head with one hand. "Stop. Vivienne. Look at me. Please."

I looked beyond his face at the door. "It's over," I barely whispered.

"There is no way in hell—"

I reached for his office doorknob.

"You'd do this," he said, trying to angle his face to where my eyes were staring. "You'd stand here in front of me, essentially holding a map to happiness in your hands and shred it like you'd never want to know the way back."

He braced when I burst out in mad laughter. "There are no metaphors here, Peter. It's just me. This is who I am. I thought I was direct, as an adult would be—I never said I'd go with you. I never said I'd be yours if you left. There are things I can't do, places I won't go. Not now, maybe not ever. This is who wrote a response to you in her journal. This is who you wrote back. This is who you kissed and walked with and wrote poems to and convinced to love you without even trying."

His blue eyes filled with tears.

I peered down at my Keds, my kid shoes. I thought, *I just told him I love him.*

He kept talking as though he hadn't heard. "I have always been trying, Vivienne. I'm not letting you go. Stay here and talk to me. Or no—let's go to my place—"

My head felt too heavy to lift. "I'm all out of words."

"Please. Let me hold you then."

I turned the doorknob behind him to go.

"No, wait—" He reached a hand back to the door.

"You're trapping me?" I asked.

"I'm explaining to you." He stood so close to me. Before that hour, I would have leaned my ear to his heartbeat. "In all my decision-making—as deceptive as it may seem to you—I never once imagined us not—"

I turned the doorknob more forcefully. "No more imagining. You're an adult. You know what you want. You should have it. Please don't come to my dorm."

"Don't open the door." His beautiful broad hand dropped away. He stepped aside.

I remembered him standing right there, holding my hands seven weeks ago, smiling. *I opened the door.*

This time, I opened the door and walked out.

He didn't follow me.

Returning to my room one hour ago, I saw that our resident assistant had slipped today's mail beneath my door. I picked up an envelope embossed with blue in the corner. *The Philbrick Program for Writers.* I tore open one end of the envelope.

Dear Vivienne, the letter began. *We are pleased to welcome you to our writing program.*

The paper is folded inside my backpack.

A taxi will arrive in ten minutes. I will ask the driver to stop at Peter's so I can leave my journal on his doorstep. My flight departs for New York in three hours.

I have already packed my two suitcases. I left my bedding and towels in a box in the laundry room, and Hillary can keep our computer.

Luc called again to say I should come. It's the baby. He said that he told Maman and Papa that he had called me and that they would phone me themselves this afternoon. I will be on my way by the time they call.

From the first breath of this journal, I have wanted to fly home, and now that I am, I don't feel as though I'm leaving a place I dislike as much as I'm leaving a person I don't want to be—a scared girl so frail, other humans do not dare speak the truth to her.

Peter, if you're reading, know that I wrote these words mostly for you. Over time—in your class, in my poems, in the library, in my arms— you became the reader in my head. Forgive me if leaving my words on your porch as I go seems manipulative or spiteful or juvenile, but they're yours—my words, all the care I took with them.

You think of me as a child, and maybe I am a child for wanting to return home so badly. But in my childish mind, I weep that you haven't found a home. I fear that once you are surrounded by the people you love most, in their native country, sharing their bread and other sweet things, you will look up at the stars and still feel adrift. I wonder if you will know what home feels like, if you will picture us that day as we wandered toward the coast, standing but at rest—*tranquille,* you said—as people passed by on the sidewalk.

The taxi is honking now. You might not reach this last page, these last sentences, but if you do, and if you ever feel lost—

Let these words be a home for you.

Read back and remember how, for one raindrop in earth-time, we found each other.

Vivienne

WANDERING SLOVENE

Wednesday, April 24, 1996
305 West 89th Street, New York

I dreamed that Vivienne and I made a baby again. It is always the same. I am holding her in some quiet brightness, spooned behind the slight curves of her body, as she tugs my hand, palm-down, to her belly. *Peter, it's ours,* she says in her sweet, urgent voice, and I am overwhelmed by the need to love her.

But always I wake—just as the sky is hinting at light outside the window.

For the past year, this has been the way of my dreams of her. She never makes an extravagant appearance, but simply touches my arm or my chin or the bare skin just above my waist, as if she has been long beside me. And then when we kiss or love each other entirely, there is always some reason for me to stay, some reason she is so happy. A baby, a bakery, an apartment. But then I wake, and she's gone, and the catch of her absence is so sharp in my chest that I have to stand and drink water.

Please, Vivienne, I never fail to think as I swallow. They were the words I spoke as she turned from me in a hallway five years ago, and the words I would speak to her now. *Please, Vivienne. Please don't go.*

I have been in New York for three days.

Her journal rests on my desk like a holy thing.

———

Saturday, April 27, 1996

For the past five years, I have documented how a country attempts to become itself, how borders are drawn and bled for. Every morning in the gray of a soon-ending night—whether just managing to survive along a road in Croatia, or sitting at home at the desk Ati built for me—I have opened a notebook to write, my brain desperate to fill its own tunnels with facts. I recorded atrocities that I could not speak out loud, that overwhelmed the stab of my own burning losses—Vivienne in New York, Tilen's body unburied in a village west of Zagreb.

For five years, I gave words to whatever was not happening to me and sent them off to Ati's editor at the *Times*, and now I am here in Manhattan with a book—my collected works of a nation's unthinkable, inevitable dismantling.

Now that I'm here, there are fewer words to hide behind.

Now I am wondering how many steps till I find her.

I miss Tilen with a gnashing that tears like a wolf at my chest.

I am unpracticed at saying what is happening to myself. It is taxing to construct the sentences.

Here are a few—

I will be a visiting scholar at Hadley College for the next year. Kieran invited me to apply for the position and is urging me now to consider a permanent post that the department announced last week.

Coniston Books has scheduled me to read from my essays at least two nights each week for the next three months at libraries and bookshops between New York and Baltimore.

My apartment near Riverside Park is small. All I can think is *Where is she? Is she writing? Is somebody smoothing her hair back?*

Reading her journal again isn't helping.

———

Sunday, April 28, 1996

A sentence for today—

The past is never where you think you left it.

This evening I read from my book on the third floor of the 67th Street Library, which I supposed must be near Vivienne's family's apartment. Though I knew that fact offered hope of nothing. Even if Vivienne was aware of my essays, why would she seek out a man whose actions five years ago conveyed the cruelest possible rejection?

Five minutes into my essay on Croatia's Battle of Vukovar, I was straining to keep my voice steady through description of a boy wandering alone down a shelled village street. Pausing at the end of a paragraph to breathe, I looked up. An olive skinned woman stood as still as a tree at the back of the library reading room.

In the breath that I saw her, I noted short-cropped raven hair and black-coffee eyes. I thought of a melancholy pixie-sprite.

Memory and recognition accumulated in seconds. The luminous dark eyes beneath a thick fringe of lashes. The long, slender nose turned so slightly and endearingly up at the end. The sharp curve of her chin. A dark freckle—more pronounced within the frame of short hair—a quarter-inch below her left eye.

And then there were her hollows and angles—the shadowed depressions beneath her dark eyes, her bare, razor-edged elbows. The thumbprint-sized well at the center of her collarbone, peeking out from the gauzy white of her blouse. I remembered pressing my lips there.

When I looked up from my book again, our eyes caught.

Vivienne.

Vivienne was in the same room I stood in.

A whisper like a breeze washed over my skin.

My lungs grew too full for my chest.

In all my memories, on each page of her journal, she speaks to me from a past left in California, but in that moment, my past appeared in a New York library. It merged with the present. Vivienne and I breathed the same air.

For the next twenty minutes, I simply vocalized sounds for each discrete block of letters on whatever page I was reading. Words signified nothing. Sentences unfolded blankly. I heard my voice as if from an overhead speaker. My pulse quickened with need and awareness of the presence at the back of the room, which was not, for once, a dream, but materially and entirely a woman.

I could hear myself reading. *Between 2,000 and 3,000 Croats died in the siege of Vukovar.*

Vivienne pressed the fingertips of one hand to her sternum.

Don't go, don't go.

The phrase chanted itself in my head until I thought I might speak it. I wanted to speak it, the way I always wanted, from the first moment I saw her five years ago, to say words that might draw her aside, keep her still, require her to look at me for even the span of one breath—

Vivienne, if you could just wait here a moment as I finish.

But somehow, I knew that she was not going to wait tonight, that she would not wait, even if I set the words free into the microphone to ask her. This older Vivienne appeared even sharper than the bird-quick form I had held in my arms at St. Brigid's. She looked as if any last cells of girl had all been carved out. Along with hope. And a significant portion of happiness. I could see tight knots of muscle in her wiry arms. This woman would do precisely what she wanted.

"Excuse me for one moment," I said to the audience as I finished the essay's last sentence. Already I could see that this new Vivienne was walking quickly, directly, gracefully toward an exit. Not escaping, exactly. It felt more like refusing.

Refusing me.

The ghost of a man who never told her he loved her. Who betrayed her trust, and in his own immaturity, called her a child. A man who permitted her, against the unspoken love in his heart and his own better judgment, to leave without a fight.

She made her way through the airless reading room's door just as a knobby, age-spotted hand wrapped around my wrist and a voice asked in Slovene, "You will sign our books?" The library's head of international collections leaned too close to the microphone behind us to say in a low, school-marmish tone, "Eh-hem, Professor Breznik?"

"Five minutes." Half-turning, I raised a palm at the librarian, gently extracting my other arm from the elderly Slovene woman's hand. As if on their own, my feet rushed toward the door. "I believe I saw an old friend of mine," I said over my shoulder.

Beyond rows of shelves outside the reading room, a dark-haired woman wearing a trim red blazer was determinedly striding forward, tugging the hand of a small dark-haired girl.

With the addition of the jacket and the child, I didn't immediately take the woman to be Vivienne. I slowed momentarily, pausing to look down the book-aisles, feeling transported to St. Brigid's library, when, even on unnecessary evenings, I would make my way to the Humanities stacks, eyes open wide and heart beating fast, searching for the young French woman who wrote searingly clear, devastatingly tender poetry.

But then, well ahead of me, turning with the red-jacketed woman to descend a staircase, the small girl yanked back and cried in immaculate French, "Wait! Wait! That's the writer who was reading!" When the girl's gaze locked on mine, my feet ceased walking.

Eyes like dark coffee, a bold sweep of eyebrows, even a freckle beneath her left eye.

The girl's face appeared a small copy of Vivienne's.

Who are you? was all I could think. I couldn't speak or move forward for wondering if the girl was Vivienne's child.

Vivienne's own voice jolted me from the question, as she unleashed a French tirade at the girl, the speed and fervor of which I have never even in France heard the like.

I lunged forward, but my book agent, Adèle, appeared from the blue, taking hold of my arm, insisting I return to my audience. Of the rapid-fire French echoing from the stairs, I only deciphered one exclamation: "Nicole! Papa is waiting!"

"I just need—" I turned to Adèle. What did I need? With my free hand, I rubbed at my eyes. "—that . . . woman."

As I write now, I believe that one sentence might embody all the need of the last five years of my life.

Adèle touched my sleeve. "She's your friend?" Her brow lowered skeptically.

Vivienne's voice had faded on the staircase.

"I need to catch her." I stepped back. "One minute, Adèle, I swear to you. Upon my parents' homeland. And their ancestors!"

Adèle stepped back, too, shooing me forward, clearly relinquishing her authority to the panic I could feel distorting my face.

I bolted down three flights of stairs, nearly leaping to the first floor.

Outside the library, Vivienne and the girl were already climbing into a black BMW at the curb, their doors locking shut behind them.

As if finally exceeding the capacity for pressure in my throat, her name burst forth—"Vivienne!"

She turned, alarmed, meeting my eyes through the front-passenger window. She touched the glass with what I knew to be soft fingertips.

As quickly as it had found me, her gaze shifted.

"Go," I watched her lips say, to me or the driver, who even from that poor angle, through dim windows, looked exactly like Robert Carson, the would-be medical student who clasped a string of beaded ladybugs around a neck I dream beneath my lips every night. In her journal, Vivienne had wondered if he might teach her about human intimacy.

Go.

She probably said it to both of us. For different reasons.

Is Robert Carson the little girl's papa?

Does Vivienne belong that intimately to him now?

The little girl was so small. She couldn't be Vivienne's sister, who would be almost five years old if Vivienne's mother hadn't miscarried. Besides, following Vivienne's departure from my office and St. Brigid's— after I had broken, no, shattered her trust and demeaned all sense of her adulthood—her roommate deigned to inform me that Vivienne's mother was indeed losing her baby.

I signed 107 books tonight.

I am tired of writing.

Monday, April 29, 1996

Is it comical or pathetic—how quickly I am able to turn from documenting the course of a war to charting the erratic pulse of my heart?

I suppose it is both—

Hilarious and pitiful.

I came home from the reading two nights ago resolved not to find her. To finally, cell by cell of my flesh, let her go, as she obviously has let go of me.

But then I woke before dawn yesterday, the tense weight of her in my arms and a sentence in my head—

She wished to see you.

I lay in bed, asking myself why else she would have come. Arriving and positioning herself in the library's third-floor reading room took effort.

But why had she wished to see me? I wondered throughout the day—as I spoke to Hana and then my mother on the telephone, as I walked along the Hudson afterward, as Kieran and I lunched at his place over a bright pesto pasta that his wife, Mary, had made. She kept whisking by, patting my cheek like a doting great aunt and telling me another good reason to live in New York. While the name of the primary reason was sounding in my head like a foghorn.

She wished to see you.

All day, I could picture her eyes at the reading. Dark as black treacle, observing. As open as they'd always been in the past, still questioning and taking me in, her chin tipped downward, shy. Directly in my line of vision.

In how many other spots or seats might she have tucked herself away and simply verified by sight that I was still living? How much easier might it have been for her to have slipped from the room, to have left the reading sooner, to have not met my gaze through her possible lover's or husband's tinted car window?

Why had she wished to see me?

I paused from writing for a moment to open her journal, as if she might whisper an answer. But all I could do was stare at her name penned inside the front cover, the ink smeared from the hours I have spent over the last five years just touching it before pressing the book closed and holding it to my chest or placing it beside my bed like precious light I would use through the dark next day, like a book of lost prayers.

She has been my talisman.

Dr. Etienne Lebrun is listed in the phonebook with an Upper East Side address.

On my bike, I could be there within 30 minutes.

If anything, I should return her journal.

Monday, April 29, cont.

I'm becoming Vivienne—making more than one entry in a single day. I read her entries and imagine writing her back—

My Dear Vivienne, I never looked at you and thought of finding a urinal or eating a sandwich, as you so dismally speculated at St. Brigid's. Even on that first night we met in the library, when that insufferable student had gone off to make copies, I wanted to pull you by the hand into bookshelves, smooth back your wild hair and kiss you.

But I'm digressing.

After journaling first thing upon waking this morning, I cycled through the park as though training for the Tour de France, arriving helmet-haired and flushed at Vivienne's family's apartment building by 7:38 a.m., morning sun barely cresting the East Side buildings.

A blue-capped doorman, whom I assumed to be Mr. Phillips, stood at the entrance of 301 E 78th Street, gray-haired, wrinkled, congenial. "Hello, lad," he said in what struck my ear as a Yorkshire accent. "Bit early to visit a resident."

I glanced at my watch for possibly the 60th time since leaving my apartment. "Yes," I agreed. And *Yes,* I wished to add, *I am obviously desperate. I hardly sleep anymore for the dreams in my head of a woman who once, or still, lives in this building. She spoke highly of you in her journal.*

"I wonder . . ." I looked down at the frayed hems of my jeans, a Rorschach-like sweat-print blazing down the front of my military-green t-shirt. "Could you tell me if Vivienne Lebrun still resides in this building?" *And,* I felt almost wretched enough to ask, *is she happily married? Or is she possibly only half-heartedly committed to the quarterback physician who collected her from the 67th Street Library last night?*

As if sensing the agonized bent of my thoughts, the doorman shook his head, offering a good-humored, sympathetic smile, even as he backed toward his building's glass doors, effectively blocking my entrance. "I don't report on residents, sir—past or present—but you seem a good sort, and I can't say I blame you for searching out our Vivi."

He startled when a little palm thumped one of the building's glass front doors from inside. I startled as well when I lifted my eyes and saw that attached to the hand was the dark-haired little girl from the library. She was grinning with a mischief unlike Vivienne, though the sharp-angled jaw and wide mouth were the same.

"Mornin', Miss Nicole!" The doorman stepped aside as the beat-up-on door flung open.

"Bon matin, Monsieur Phillips," the little girl declared. *"Ça va?"*

She was wearing a posh private-school uniform—a short, pleated navy skirt, with a white blouse beneath a sky-blue blazer. Strapped below her shoulders was an azalea-pink backpack. I thought to myself that only Vivienne would purchase such a tote—a bright block of color against duller hues.

I, too, carried a small pack on my back. Vivienne's journal rested inside it.

"Ça va bien!" Monsieur Phillips shook his salt-and-peppered head at the girl, chuckling. He patted her shoulder until she abruptly ceased her purposeful march out the building, stared at my bike and then up at me.

She was Vivienne in miniature. Incandescent dark eyes, slender nose almost upturned at the end. Lips pressed together in question.

How could this child be a sister? I thought. I felt blood drain from my face as I stared at what could only be parental DNA transmission.

"Regardez!" The little girl pointed at me and looked back toward the broad-shouldered man who walked through the glass doors behind her wearing a Philadelphia Eagles sweatshirt and green medical scrubs. *"C'est l'écrivain de l'autre soir!"*

"Nicole, please," Robert Carson said. "I'm not French."

"É-CRI-VAIN," Mr. Phillips enunciated, as if to a delinquent French-language student. "The WRI-TER."

"From the other night." Petite Vivienne switched to Anglais in a trice. "At the library."

"La bibliotheque." Mr. Phillips peered down at her, nodding in agreement and possibly pride at his knowledge of her family's first language.

"The writer from the library . . ." Robert took the small olive hand that the girl—his daughter?—reached up to him. His narrowed eyes may as well have been peering at me through a rifle scope.

"A visitor, Mr. Robert," the doorman said.

Muscled like a Heisman Trophy quarterback, Robert stood before me as a time-lapsed memory.

Resuming his post at the building's front doors, Mr. Phillips elaborated in a quieter voice, "A visitor for our Vivi."

"Comment vous-appelez vous?" Petite Vivienne asked my name.

"I believe we might have met once, a long time ago, at a restaurant." Robert claimed the silence awaiting my answer to the little girl's question.

But before I could tell the girl my name or ask if her mother, Vivienne, was at home, and thereby possibly learn Vivienne's marital status, Robert bent to lift Nicole to his hip, as though she weighed no more than a Shih Tzu. "We're late, baby girl. Am I jogging you to kindergarten or what?"

"Oui! Vite!" Nicole shrieked in laughter, giving Robert's brawny shoulder a horse-whippish smack.

"I know what that means!" Robert jostled Nicole onto his back. "Let's run like the wind!" He sprinted to the street corner like an Olympian—like Zeus, the foremost of Olympians—Nicole with her pink satchel bouncing merrily on his back.

"Au revoir, écrivain!" she called back, clearly more enamored of her sleek ride to school than of me.

And why should she not be? I asked myself. Father or friend, Robert Carson was unquestionably kind, if understandably wary of Vivienne's visitor. Moreover, he appeared to be committed to Nicole, as well as to Vivienne. Likely more committed than I had been.

But the girl is in kindergarten, my brain seemed to argue with itself. Nicole would have to be five years old. Was it even possible that Vivienne had given birth to her? Or was Nicole, somehow, Vivienne's sister?

Notwithstanding, relationships existed—Vivienne and Robert, Robert and Nicole, Robert and Vivienne's family.

I stood before Mr. Phillips with my eyes shut, having almost convinced myself to pedal away, to leave Vivienne and her ebullient miniature to live the life they had led before I arrived in their city. To allow them firm footing and happiness with a good sturdy man like Robert.

"Our Vivi works at *LA COC-I-NELLE.*" Mr. Phillips patted my shoulder. "On West 82nd and Amsterdam."

In the half-second required to open my eyes, any resolve I might have felt to depart from Vivienne's life vanished.

"Thank you." I swung my leg over my bike, forgetting the questions I might have asked him—*Is Miss Vivi married or single? Is that child her daughter or her sister?*

Mr. Phillips tipped his doorman hat to me. "Tell her Mr. Phillips liked the look of you."

La Cocinelle means "The Ladybug." I had to look it up in the tattered French dictionary I packed from my bookcase in Ljubljana on the off-chance I might speak French to someone. And the someone I envisioned was, of course, Vivienne. Vivienne, who was perhaps pouring tea as I walked for the tenth time past her shop window this morning. Or perhaps slicing warm bread she had kneaded and shaped with her nervous but certain hands. Vivienne, who made her way to me in the library two nights ago. And perhaps remembers in sudden, disjointed sound bites as I do—perhaps was remembering even as I paced the sidewalk in front of her café—threads of the words we spoke and wrote to each other, the tug and give of our lips, the sparks in our skin.

Vivienne, if only I could have left her a note, *I will stop by tomorrow to see you.*

In the time I've been writing, Hana has left three long messages.

———————

Tuesday, April 30, 1996

I opened the door to *La Coccinelle* at 7:23 this morning, remembering that I had forgotten Vivienne's journal, but immediately forgiving myself when I realized that the oversight offered me a practical reason to see her again.

A merry cluster of bells announced my entrance to the café. A gaunt hairy man, sitting beside the front window in running attire, looked up from a newspaper and a stemless wine glass filled with orange juice. Other customers sat scattered about, leaning elbows on roughly-hewn tables topped with squat vases of pale pink and rose-colored peonies.

"*Bonjour!*" a dark-haired woman sang from a mammoth glass-front-ed counter at the back of the shop. "You wish to sit or take something away?" she asked in the quick, firm syllables of a French accent.

"I—" I forgot her question entirely as she side-stepped behind the counter into clearer light. She looked vaguely like Vivienne—dark hair, angular features—but taller and aged forward about 20 years. Was she Vivienne's Aunt Evelyn? Or, I hardly dared wonder, her mother?

The light blue shop door jangled gleefully shut behind me, as if to purposely deride my speechlessness. In the momentary hush of the shop, I realized that even after visualizing Vivienne in her workplace for the last 24 hours—until by late afternoon I took an aspirin and pressed a warm cloth to my eyes—I had not actually planned what to say should I find Vivienne or any of her family staring with their soulful dark eyes at me.

"Perhaps you need time to decide." The woman swiped at the glass case with a tea towel before turning to whatever task waited behind her.

"Yes . . ." I walked slowly forward.

Variously-sized, vintage-looking cloth birds hung from the ceiling. The adjacent wall nearly hummed with a meticulously arranged cacoph-ony of whimsy—jewel-framed, vibrant, scientific-like paintings of wild birds, insects, and pastry—green finch, fuchsia ladybug, a daisy-sprout-ing chocolate cupcake.

And interspersed among all that, poems. Whole poems, brief ex-cerpts, on canvases of all sizes, the words lettered in what I knew as well as my own script to be Vivienne's sharp-and-then-abruptly-looped handwriting.

I approached the words, my head tilting back, mouth open, all chatter in the shop abating. My mind caught on one sequence of fragments—

Hope is the thing with feathers . . .

You are the body
of my world . . .

I am the blossom pressed in a book . . .

Dickinson, Hass, Kenyon. Poets she had loved. Poems we had read. I barely dared hope the lines read like a history of our time together.

"Do you read poems?" From behind me, a low female voice set my hair on end. My heart thumped in every atom of my body.

I turned and found Vivienne.

Only, I could tell just by looking that she was not precisely the Vivienne I had known at St. Brigid's. There was her wild raven hair, cut choppy and short, dark orchid-tendril wisps curling out from her neckline. Her eyes, always luminous, burned like a night sky over fire as she studied me. She seemed somehow fiercer, her chin slightly raised, her gaze more direct, perhaps more discerning. I felt myself smiling even as I feared she might have outgrown me.

I had found the woman Vivienne had become.

Standing beside a low open refrigerator case in the center of the café, she wore a tight pink sleeveless top tucked into a not-quite-too-short denim skirt, a ladybug-printed apron tied around her waist. She held a wooden tray of wrapped goods—sandwiches, sliced cake, and cookies—assembled like gifts for a gourmand's birthday.

When I managed to swallow and choke out, "Hello," her tray tipped slightly sideways, sending three wrapped cookies to the floor.

In one thud of a heartbeat, I stepped to her, the two of us kneeling down. "Forgive me," I said, inadvertently (or not so inadvertently) touching a fingertip to one of her knuckles as I reached for the fallen cookies. "I caught you off guard."

My finger burned.

She had beaten me to the cookies, one broken in half in her palms. With her tray beside her, she crouched on the fat wooden floorboards, peering at my hands.

I thought to say, *I remember exactly what you feel like,* but then my hands closed to fists, as though to advise me to keep the words in.

But I did—I do—remember what she feels like. Wiry and warm. Like the essence of bird. You hold your breath every second you touch her.

"I do read poems," I said, despite the increasing depletion of oxygen in my lungs. "I recognize the ones you've hung here." I glanced over my shoulder at the wall. When I turned back, Vivienne's dark eyes shot up to mine—infinite pools—two whispers of lines appearing between her brows.

"Do you recognize them from when we read them together? Or simply from the enormous number of hours you've spent reading in general?"

I wasn't prepared for her bluntness. "I . . . I read them with you, I believe, at—"

She was shaking her head, the two of us still kneeling. "You came," she said.

"Yes." I couldn't tell if her head-shaking was surprise or frustration. Regardless, I could not look away from her.

"I should—" She pressed her left hand to her cheek. My head, of its own volition, bent forward, my eyes refusing to so much as blink at the sliver of gold encircling her left ring finger.

She snatched her hand away, pushed the fallen cookies into her apron pockets.

There was no use pretending that I hadn't noticed the ring. Or that I didn't care, even after living almost halfway around the world from her. She was wearing a symbol of loyalty and affection for a man who, as sure as every bullet that had ever missed my heart or my head, wasn't me.

I asked, "Are you married?"

She attempted an awkward ascent to her feet with the tray, so I stood and took the load from her hands. And watched graceful divots in her shoulders contract as she lifted herself upright in front of me.

Thank God my own hands were encumbered by baked goods.

I wanted to wrap her in my arms, enfold her against my body, tuck her away.

I wanted to go back.

To somehow—through time, history, and distance—return to the night she left me.

Vivienne, I'm sorry for my decisions. I'm sorry for what I said. I take everything back. I promise, I'll stay.

Could I have said that to her? Could I have made the words true? Chosen us over my parents' need and my brother's peril?

Taking her tray from me, she balanced it on her hip, turning slightly away to stock the standing refrigerator case with the good things her hands had made. Her fluttery-tense hands, that were, for almost two brilliant months of my life, nearly always nestled in my own or shyly skimming some stretch of my body.

My arms singed at the memory.

Are you married? God knows it's dramatic, but I envisioned the question mark of that sentence dangling over my head upside-down like a noose.

I wanted her to save me. I wanted her to be the instructor this time, to teach me the blurry way back to her.

She was quite possibly about to tell me she was married, and I couldn't stop myself from stepping toward her.

"No." She glanced up at me, inching closer to the case, the supple curve of her upper arm stretching taut each time she set down a baked good. I wanted to take that curve in my mouth. I wanted to press my face to it.

"No," she repeated.

I couldn't tell right away if she was halting my advance or answering my question—untying the noose hanging over me.

"I'm not married."

The question mark in my mind faded away, relief flooding my nerves like the coolest water. I let go a suspended breath.

Vivienne rearranged her baked goods. "I just wear the band to ward off—" She squeezed her lips together.

My lungs expanded with the new air I'd breathed in. "To ward off assholes?"

I wondered if she would remember the reference.

"Yes." She allowed her lips a tight smile. "There always seem to be a few out there." I assumed she included myself in that category.

"And you?" She continued arranging her baked goods. "Are you married?" Her eyes dropped to my left hand.

"No. I am not married."

As she set down one last slice of dark cake in a clear plastic container, my hand reached her wrist. For a moment, I could feel curious eyes in the bakery watching. At the counter, the older French woman's body leaned in.

"Vivienne—" When my fingers wrapped around her petal-soft skin, she gasped. At the touch, no doubt, and my lack of propriety, but also, I knew, because I had spoken her name. She used to always, in the past, ask me to say it. *You say it correctly,* she'd whisper at the tingling curve of my ear. *Absolument correct.*

Her lips would touch mine before the soft *enne* of her name went quiet on my tongue.

But *Vivienne*—her name was a prayer in my throat—wasn't legally bound to Robert-the-quarterback-physician. The thought quickly followed—miniature-Vivienne must be adult-Vivienne's younger sister. But if that were the case, why was Robert accompanying the little girl to school? Say the girl wasn't quite four years old—could Robert and Vivienne have had a child together? Vivienne would have had to have suffered a complete disassembly of her passionate views on childrearing to have embraced marriage-less parenthood. But tragedy or trauma could induce such disassembling. Had she been unraveled by her mother's death, then? Or was her mother still alive?

Standing amid an internal ricochet of questions, the air I breathed turning thin again, I took Vivienne's hand in both of mine, feeling, absurdly, that as long as we touched, I could spare her from pain, past and present, and keep us from having to part again. "Could we walk for one hour?" I asked. "Right now?"

She glanced back at the counter. Was the alert French woman standing there Vivienne's and the little girl's mother?

I revised my question. "Or could we walk later?"

She bit her bottom lip.

A strange flash-vision scrolled past my eyes—the sunlit apartment she'd described in her journal. The one with two desks. The one I had mentally added notebooks, garden boxes, and bookshelves to. I could smell the warm bread, see the bedsheets. I could hear the three babies she imagined us making. I hadn't known that these images had taken such hold of my senses. I hadn't realized that the world she described in her journal was a world I had allowed myself, without hope or reason, to count on, and a world I might never live in.

Letting go her hand, I stepped back, deciding against all desire in my heart, to convey respect for her space and wishes. "Dinner then. Tonight. Let me take you to dinner."

She set her tray on top of the containers in the case, smoothing her palms down her ladybug apron. I wanted her palms to be mine on her abdomen. I wanted to be her apron.

"I think there are words—" I couldn't decide how to rationally say, *Vivienne, I need to tell you I love you. I want you. I have never not loved or wanted you. I thought I would give you what you thought was best for you, but it was not what was best. I am best for you. We are best together. Every day since we met, I have seen you in my mind in innumerable sweet ways—in my arms, beneath my lips, your fingers in my hair, your palms on my wounds, your belly swollen—*

"There are always words." She twisted the ring on her finger, her shoulders tensing almost to her ears.

"Vivi, you have cakes in the oven!" The French woman at the counter called to her.

Vivi, I stood thinking.

Vivi. From the Latin—*vivus.*

Alive or living.

Breath in the throat. Blood in the veins.

"Vivienne—" My eyes shut.

"Thursday."

When I opened my eyes, she was hugging her tray. "I have Thursday off," she almost whispered. "I could meet you at Central Park in the morning." She looked down at her bare wrist, as if there might be a watch there to guide her. "At ten?" Her eyes met my shoulder. She did not want to look at my face any longer. "We could meet at the East 79th Street entrance. Or, well, where are you coming from?"

I couldn't recall where I was coming from.

From a classroom devoid of all color but her.

From a library carrel wedged between shelves of poetry.

From a red-brick house and my desk she would write at.

From the heat of her lips and the hurt in her face—

"Ten," I found voice enough to say. "Don't start walking without me."

She pressed her lips tight before speaking. "I don't really like waiting."

As she stepped away, I caught her elbow with a jolt of desperation, but also of courage, the source of which I still can't explain. I ran my thumb over the curve of her bicep.

I motioned to the canvases she'd hung on the wall like a map of her mind. Her eyes, I could feel them, studied my profile. That wall was like reading her poems—the ordinary turned bright and magnified, flashes of light and image.

Where are her poems? A tight snap pricked my chest at the thought that she might not be putting her own words on paper.

"Could you tell me before I go—" I looked at her chin, then her hands, remembering how ink would be splotched there.

Her skin was a scrubbed-blank page. Except for a dusting of flour above one eyebrow that I would have loved very much to kiss away.

"Are you still writing?" I asked.

Pulling her arm from my grasp, she reached into the refrigerated case and ran a finger along a few wrapped items before tapping a cookie and picking it up. She set it in my hand without touching my skin.

"Not writing"—an oven-timer was buzzing—"but I perfected the chocolate chip cookie." She took another step away from me. "Among taking care of some other things."

I peered down at the cookie in my hand as though it were a gift of the most fragile blossoms.

"Thursday," I said, and she nodded.

On Thursday I will ask about her "other things." I will tell her about mine.

I will tell her that she is the one thing I will never again leave behind.

Postscript: I saved Vivienne's cookie until just after finishing this entry. It's true—hint of almond, tiny shower of salt. The thinnest crisp surface, then soft, thick, and sweet. Sophisticated but comforting.

She perfected the chocolate chip cookie.

Wednesday, May 1, 1996

I do sometimes think of Hana. But not as she would like me to, not in the way Tilen thought of her. She called this morning as the Manhattan sky glowed pale blue through my window shades.

After she whispered, *"Nasvidenje,"* and I clicked off the line, I remembered the night Tilen met her. I was 16 years old, home in Yugoslavia for the summer before entering my final year of private high school in California. I can't even recall why Tilen was at our parents' apartment in Ljubljana. Just visiting, I guess. He was good to come home and kick around the city with me, to do nothing but sit and talk.

We'd converse about everything—governments, culture, philosophy, books. Backpacking, journalism, girls (women, in his case—he was 25). He always conducted what felt like a background-check interview any time I confessed to kissing someone. He asked the subject-in-question's name, age, village, and country of origin. Her interests, perceived intelligence, hobbies. Her hair length and color, the exact shade of her eyes and shape of her lips. Her height and approximate bone structure. What did her kiss make me feel like, and what was the first thing she said or did after? Tilen would sit and envision the details, which I suppose might strike a stranger as slightly disturbing, but anyone who knew Tilen understood that that was how he lived in the world. He experienced everything.

On the night he met Hana, he crept into my bedroom well after midnight. I had awakened to the weary creak of our communist-built apartment's front door, and lay in bed waiting for him to come in and report on the night's adventures. He stopped to open the refrigerator as he always did—I can picture even now how he must have looked, ducking his head to reach for a square of Mati's *kremšnita,* the refrigerator bulb lighting his face like that of a renegade saint.

When he entered our bedroom, I could feel a current, as though he were an electrical-circuit box. His body was humming.

"Hey," I remember saying in a voice I would have used if he and I had crossed paths on the street. I was sharply awake.

"Hey!" he whispered, falling backward on the wobbly narrow bed next to mine. I waited for a sigh or a laugh but heard nothing. He, along with every chirping summer insect in Ljubljana, seemed to be holding a breath.

"I met someone," he finally said, still flat on his back, gazing up at our ceiling as though charting the stars. The moonlight filtering in through our shutters illuminated the crooked bridge of his nose.

"Name?" I adopted his method of interrogation.

I'll never forget. He pressed a palm to his heart. "Hana."

"Village of origin."

"Zagreb. She's a Croat. I'm going to marry her. We're going to travel the world and make beautiful Yugoslavian babies."

I was 16. I felt a stirring down low in my abdomen.

It is difficult, of course, for human beings besides Vivienne to remember past dialogue. But I can still hear myself ask if Hana of Zagreb had been apprised of this information, and I can still hear the echo of Tilen's laughter. "I told her as we were kissing in the stairwell of her apartment building, and she promised to think about it. She's only 18, so she wonders if there is more of life yet to live, but I assured her there is very little of interest outside of me."

"You should write her a poem about yourself." I barely finished the sentence before erupting in laughter. Our parents had to have been listening.

And then—this, too, is clear in my memory—Tilen said in his elegant journalist fashion, "No. Hana is a poem. Just looking at her captures all the feelings and the words and the lifetimes in my being. Anything I were to compose would only reveal my own banality."

Writing this now, I wonder that Tilen did not write poetry.

Writing this now, I realize that I know—that I knew immediately, almost the moment Vivienne stepped into my class at St. Brigid's—exactly what my brother felt.

His and Hana's story often unfolds in my mind. How in seven months, they were married. And how, in what seems this universe's fiercest of cruelties, their babies refused to stay long inside Hana's womb.

They lost six before little David arrived five years ago, three months before his *ati's*—his mother's first love—my parents' first son—my one brother's—murder.

When I allowed Hana to kiss me three years after Tilen was taken, my heart did manage to rest a moment. I let myself wonder for the first of many times if I could possibly accept what she was offering—a second-place for both of us. Hana's kisses were experienced and direct. They conveyed a degree of intent that for one or two heartbeats, I wished to believe in.

Until nerve-memory of Vivienne flooded my skin—the burn of her lips, shy and wondering, tugging at me with questions my own lips had been helpless to resist answering. Every kiss she bestowed bore unspeakable awe.

That night in Zagreb, Hana pulled away, pressed her hands to her mouth, abruptly weeping. I held her in the dark on the tiny balcony of the apartment she had shared with my brother, my tears falling into her hair. Tears for my brother, yes, but also—I felt the truth of it in his wife's damp face at my neck—tears for the raven-haired woman I would always imagine myself writing poems to. Wherever she was, four thousand miles away, I could feel her embodying all my feelings and words and lifetimes.

This morning on the phone, Hana asked me again to reconsider. To choose a life with her and with my brother's son—flesh of my flesh, though genetically removed by one step—in Slovenia. My brother's son, David, whose little hand always finds its way inside mine, who carries a satchel with a pen and a notebook, a photograph of his *ati* and me pasted inside the cover.

Again on the phone, I said to his mother, "*Prosim. Hana. Rad te imam . . .*"

I hear it in the heavier English now—*Please. Hana. I love you. But not as a man should love you, not as Tilen did.*

She did not cry this time. Her voice was nearly as quiet as air. "No one will love me again like that."

"Then why would you ask me to be second? Why should I not love a woman as you have been loved? Why should you not believe in being loved again in that way?"

Our words repeat in my head.

"Because we are here, Peter. We are alive at the same time. And we do love each other, if not in the way of odes or fireworks. I care for you. I could be happy with you. I could be . . . content. David loves you. We could be a family. People lose that gift every day."

I knelt beside my bed, the telephone like a stone against my ear.

Vivus. Alive or living.

I know that Hana makes a wise point. I do care for her. She is intelligent and warm and interesting. The boy she made with my brother is radiant. Hana says David has written me four letters but will not risk sending them on a plane, as they might drop into the ocean. I would call him my own tomorrow.

If Vivienne cannot see a way back to me—a way back to us—if I do not still signify any feelings or words or lifetimes for her, if she does not wake every morning as I do, with a hint of our kisses brushed over her lips—I will agree to Hana's offer. I could be almost happy, if not precisely content.

I am reading tonight at a bookshop in Hoboken. Spring term at Hadley begins Monday. Tomorrow, I remind myself, is Thursday.

Any unforeseen reader of these words should not be mistaken. Though I have managed to distract myself with this entry and have kept busy these two days preparing for classes, Vivienne is the rhythm underlying my thoughts, the pulse pressing each minute forward.

Thursday, May 2, 1996

I pedaled across town this morning and locked my bike to a rack along Fifth. I hadn't taken five steps before I saw Vivienne paused at the East 79th Street park entrance wearing a robin's-egg-blue cotton sundress. She held a small tote topped by a white tea towel, a scored baguette peeking out. I paused for a moment, watching her.

When she was younger—when I was her teacher—I never looked at her for long. If she dared raise her hand to offer a comment, I tried to appear as though strictly listening.

I saw her mainly in stolen glances—as she or I would enter or exit our classroom, as she'd read her poems aloud during workshop. When she came to my office after finding the letter I'd folded inside her journal, all I wanted was to look at her without blinking.

That's how I felt on the sidewalk along Fifth. Her eyes scanned the park, but I kept watching her for whole seconds, savoring the luxury.

Nothing about her appearance seemed older. Rather, she was . . . I can't decide on the word . . .

Purified.

Eyes and hair darker, the bones of her face more pronounced, faint curves of muscle in elegant new places—shoulders, arms, calves.

She is a baker now, apparently, and one might think she'd round out a bit, but she looks as though any excess of flesh and emotion has been stripped away. As though she exists only by what is essential.

Still, she looked beautiful—a cross between Audrey Hepburn meeting Gregory Peck for champagne, and a farmer's wife come to the fields with refreshment.

I imagined her in a meadow threaded with wildflowers. I wanted us to lie down together.

By the time she turned and noticed me, I had to think through the work of swallowing.

"Is that another thing you've perfected?" I nodded at the glossy-gold bread as I walked toward her.

Vivienne's head tilted upward the closer I stepped, a tremor of what struck me as sadness flitting over her face. I wondered how she'd imagined our walk playing out today. What words had she hoped to say to me? Did they end with *Goodbye,* or *When should we meet again?*

Heart pounding like a magistrate's gavel, I realized that neither one of us knew the other's desire. I had suddenly appeared in New York. She had come to my reading. I had sought out her apartment and appeared in her bakery. She had said we could meet at the park. As far as either of us knew, the other could be deep in a life brim with love and birdsong, nothing more than curious about where an old flame had landed.

But if Vivienne were content, why did her eyelids look heavy, the irises flat, her face unaccustomed to crinkling in laughter?

"This might not actually be perfect." She squeezed the bread between her thumb and fingers as if testing it, and then lifted the tea towel from the tote to reveal a small cream-colored crock full of butter. "This butter might be, though. I churned and salted it."

She glanced up at me, eyes earnest, as if to ask if I approved—if I'd like tasting that butter. If I'd like her as a churner and salter of butter. And I was suddenly aware, as cars blurred along Fifth, that although she wasn't writing poems at present, food was a kind of poetry for her. If I took time to taste it, I might know exactly the slant of her heart.

I couldn't help but smile dumbly at the sidewalk.

And remember that I had forgotten her journal again.

"What would you say constitutes perfection then?" Remembering I had arms, I reached for her tote.

"It's not heavy." She held onto it, crooking her elbow beneath the cloth handle.

We entered the park side by side, walking.

"I guess perfection is just . . ." Dropping the tote-strap to her hand, she began slowly swinging it. "Not thinking of what could be different."

We walked in the echo of her answer, gazing up, glancing down, crabapple blossoms falling nearly like snowflakes.

This was how conversation always went with her. We could be talking about apple trees or grasshoppers, and in the next breath, we'd be contemplating the origins of the concept of beauty. Or as was the case in this moment, after five years of silence—butter and bread and the requisites of perfection.

When Vivienne stepped from the path onto a shaded circle of lawn, I followed, heart in my throat. My hand reached up to press the small of her back before I caught myself and refrained, only to notice the delicate lift of her shoulder blades. She walked toward an empty park bench.

"Do you often wish things were different?" Out loud, my question sounded more pointed than it had in my head. While I wanted her to answer what it implied—*Do you often wish that what happened between us had been different?*—I inwardly cringed at my lack of subtlety.

Vivienne pressed her lips into a straight line. *A line of poetry void of words,* I thought.

She lowered herself to the bench, gazing off at a cluster of children gathered on the grass a stone's throw away. They were shrieking and tossing bread at what seemed to be, by the volume of wing-flaps and warbling, a ravenous swarm of pigeons.

I could imagine David in the mix, though he would not have been standing and tossing, but crouching down low, reaching out his hand and humming a quiet song to the birds.

Because we are here . . . We are alive at the same time, I heard his mother say.

I sat down at least two palms' width away from Vivienne's hip. She set her tote between us.

"I try not to spend a lot of time wishing," she said.

I peered with her into the distance, wishing simply to take her hand and stroke my thumb over the pulse of her wrist. "I am rarely not wishing."

A few au pairs or mothers stood chortling with each other at the periphery of the bird-feeding, lending the scene an air of distracted supervision. But before any of them might have cried, *Pigeons on the move!,* the birds had ascended in a Hallelujah Chorus of flapping wings.

In a whoosh, they landed around Vivienne—at the toes of her cloth-woven sandals and just behind her bare heels. On our seat bench and seat back. Warbling and bobbing their fat hungry heads, rushing for Vivienne's bread in a whir of beady eyes and blue feathers.

I leapt to my feet, brushing at the pigeons with one hand, lifting Vivienne from the bench with the other.

"They think your bread is perfection!" I cried, meaning to shield her against my chest and swipe all the birds away like an avian-battling knight. But she pulled away, snatching the bread from her tote and holding it aloft, transforming herself into a baguette-wielding bird magnet.

Inspiration for Hitchcock's *The Birds* could not have been more feather-flung or disturbing.

"Vivienne!" I called through the attack. "Drop the bread!"

But she swung at the birds as if her baguette were the baseball bat to a living piñata. I attempted reaching into the fray for the bread.

"No! It's my *bread!*" Vivienne shouted at the pigeons.

In my peripheral vision, the bird-abandoned children sprinted toward us, hollering in horror or elation, their au pairs or mothers hastening behind. I could see, too, that park walkers and cyclists had paused to rubberneck. A man in a cowboy hat peered through the scope of a video camera.

"For God's sake, Vivienne!" I yanked her from the flight path of a bird about to clip the side of her head. "It's not the Bread of Life!"

Still angling for a chance at a knightly rescue, I lunged for the bread and, finally grasping it, flung it across the lawn like a scorched iron brand. The birds and children all surged after it, leaving us blessedly behind.

Vivienne stood watching, shoulders shaking, hands pressed fast to her mouth.

Instinctively, I knelt at her feet, running my hands up her shins, searching for blood or scratches, until my fingers reached her knees, and I thought, *What the hell am I doing?* I jerked back on my heels, looking up at her.

Tears splotched her cheeks above her fingers. She could not catch her breath.

"Are you hurt?" I grabbed her tote as I sprang to my feet.

She inhaled long and deep, shoulders still shaking as she expelled air. Only then did I realize. She was silently laughing.

I handed her the bread-empty tote, sunk my hands into my pockets and smiled.

Smiling back, she erupted into what sounded like the poetry of all laughter—relentless, musical, clear as a stream tripping over sharp stones.

"Ohhhhhh . . ." She wiped tears from her eyes as she collapsed to the lawn. Setting aside her tote, she leaned back on her hands, dress resting mid-thigh, her legs stretched out straight. "I don't remember anything so funny." She turned in the direction of her bread, ravaged to a Hansel-and-Gretel trail of crumbs in the grass, pigeons pecking at the remains. Her head fell back as she laughed again. "I hope you weren't hungry."

"I'm good," I said. I thought, *You're enough.*

Lowering myself next to her, I positioned my limbs parallel to hers on the grass. I could have looped my pinky finger over hers if I'd dared.

"You don't love things by halves, do you?" I asked as she swept a white petal from her dress.

She laughed a buoyant cascade of syllables. "Did you really say 'Bread of Life' as I was swinging a baguette in the air like a light saber?"

I chuckled softly.

"And then," she had to pause to compose herself, "you catapulted my Bread of Life across the lawn? In Central Park? Like a prophet punishing the birds for their wickedness? 'Penitence, pigeons! Be gone!'" she cried to the heavens, and then bumped the length of her mostly exposed leg to mine, propelling a startled laugh from my chest.

Here we are, I thought. In the same pinprick of time, on the same continent, in the same park, with the same grass tickling beneath us.

The moment called for daytime fireworks or champagne or a strolling violinist bowing a tune brim with hope and melancholy.

We were facing east, sun cresting the trees. When she looked at me, I pictured a scene from her journal, from the ephemeral life we had lived together—her, crouched on a sidewalk, embracing a Golden Retriever with the same passion she'd summoned to hold onto her bread.

I wanted to clasp both her shoulders and say, *Let's not belabor this. If you don't love someone else, if you still sometimes think of me, let's decide right now to be together.* I would carry her to my bicycle, pump her to my apartment, slip that blue dress from her shoulders, and ravish her for the first of what would be, over the course of our lives, infinite, matchless encounters.

In the grass, I held my legs very still.

Vivienne brushed the tears of laughter from her cheeks. "I know your book agent, Adèle Boisson," she said, as if she understood that I had been wondering for five days how she founletd me.

"What?" I could feel disbelief contorting my face, along with an astonished smile. "How do you know Adèle?"

Vivienne shrugged. "Her husband helped treat my mother. And once Maman knew who Adèle was, she began loading her with essays I had written about poetry and food and Manhattan, and . . . Adèle was very kind to read them. She keeps encouraging me, but I know it's mainly out of—" Vivienne's soft voice trailed away. She flexed her sandaled feet in the grass, as if to halt her current line of thinking.

Was her mother alive and well then? I intended to ask as soon as our conversation permitted.

Vivienne continued. "Adèle mentioned in February that she'd sold a book of essays on war in Croatia, by a Slovene professor-journalist, and I realized very quickly that the author was you."

In the slow seconds she took to study my face, I wondered what that realization might have felt like for her. If she would have wanted to hear more about the man whom she believed had accepted the gift of her trusting heart only to cast that rare sweetness aside for other loved ones. Would she have wanted to read what that man had written, having no idea that her own words had served as balm through his book's darkest passages?

As if I had telepathed the questions, she answered, "I missed the essays when they came out in *The Times* a few years ago, but Adèle let me read your book early. I went to your reading to see if you were all right."

I couldn't move or say a single word to that. I was afraid to hear what she had seen. To learn that I had appeared a man too broken, too flawed, for her to risk trusting again, risk caring for. But weren't we both a little broken even before she lost faith in me? It was being together that felt like perfection, like we could never want for anything different.

Again I worked through the effort of swallowing. "And did you see that?" My words sounded like cotton balls brushed together. "Am I all right?"

Somehow, she managed to quickly and modestly shift herself to her knees at my side and without any warning motion or word, touch the fingertips of one hand to my cheek as I watched her. She pressed a thumb to my lips, both surprising me and not. I was, at that moment, living both in our past and a strangely unfolding present.

"Your essay the other night was staggering," she whispered. "But no." A tear appeared on a lower eyelash. Her whole palm pressed my skin. "You're not all right, are you, Peter." She said the sentence as a fact, not a question.

As I closed my eyes, her hand fell away.

When I opened them, everything in the park looked distorted, too large and too bold, too close to me.

Vivienne traced a fingertip across the back of my hand. "Your brother died."

I sat up straight in the grass. "Would you like to walk again?"

I do not rage anymore at the whole of Croatia and Serbia for Tilen's death. I no longer bargain for his life with higher powers that may not exist. I haven't wept in over a year. But I was uncertain, even with Vivienne's hand touching mine, as to whether or not I wished to risk unpicking my carefully stitched weave of emotion for Tilen.

I pulled my legs in and stood as Vivienne reached for her tote and allowed me to help her to her feet.

We walked along the path, the trees sweetly fragrant, the sky above us a delicate blue, trembling almost as I was with fragile relief from the gray of winter.

"Tell me what happened to you." Vivienne slowed beside me.

"I recorded it in my essays." I meant to relieve her of having to hear of my suffering, but I sounded more like a wounded child.

"Let's sit again." She pointed to a park bench, clear of birds and children, near a just-greening red plum tree.

We sat down vast inches apart.

She was patiently waiting, smoothing her dress over her thighs, perhaps wondering, as I was, how far this would go. In her case, how far my immediate silence. In my case, how far our new-found connection.

And how, I wondered on that park bench, staring off into trees— how could I hope to secure a full life with Vivienne if I didn't share my grief with her? If she didn't share hers with me?

I turned to her. "Tilen was killed in gunfire between Serbs and Croats in a village called Borovo Selo. It's a village in Croatia, but heavily populated by Serbs. It's on the Danube—directly across from Serbia."

"Tell me what happened." Vivienne touched my forearm. "Even if it's in the essays."

I leaned forward, clasping my hands between my knees.

Vivus beside me, alive and living.

"I bought a plane ticket to New York the day after you discovered I planned to teach in Ljubljana. I was going to fly to you that weekend and stay until we had made plans for a future that allowed us to be with our families for the time that they most needed us."

Vivienne's breathing seemed to have halted. I wanted to take her hand between both of mine to anchor my own ascending heartbeat and keep her on the bench beside me.

"But that evening—it was a Wednesday—my father called to say that

Tilen was missing. He and Hana had traveled to Zagreb to introduce Hana's ailing father to David. They had planned to stay for one week, because no one wished to stay for very long in Croatia. But Tilen convinced Hana to allow him to travel one last time to surrounding villages, to gather personal histories of a people who would, by all political indications, soon be former citizens of a forgotten country."

Still leaning forward, I glanced over my shoulder at Vivienne. She nodded slowly, as if to say, *It's okay. Continue.*

I nodded in return, peered straight ahead again. "Tilen had a vision for a book—he was writing essays, transcribing histories—but he was first and foremost a journalist. He had a way of gravitating toward hotbeds of breaking stories—dangerous events. That week, he had wandered to Borovo Selo, which had been barricaded due to escalating violence between Croats and ethnic Serbs. Croatia intended to declare independence from Yugoslavia, while Serbs living in Croatia were opposed to the effort and—" I straightened on the bench, throwing my hands. "You probably don't need this much detail. It's impossible to understand—"

"I had a general understanding at St. Brigid's. You taught me about Yugoslavia, remember?"

I sat up, almost smiling. "You never needed a teacher."

"And I've read your essays."

No doubt she had parsed out and memorized Yugoslavia's impossibilities with her first read of a book that took me three-and-a-half years to write.

I watched her for as long as I could before looking away again. I was re-living Tilen's loss as I do when I recount it, but I was also remembering the loss of Vivienne. I lost her and Tilen in the same strangled breath of time.

"The point is that Tilen ended up there—at Borovo Selo. I don't know how he got in. I don't know why he would try. He believed he was impervious to disaster, even though anyone who loved him could see he was courting it. Or tempting it. When he had a wife and a baby." I covered my face with my palms. I did not want to weigh Tilen's character.

Vivienne leaned the slightest bit closer.

My hands dropped to the bench. "After you left, my parents called, frantic to locate Tilen. No one could reach him by telephone. I was terrified. And you—"

A soft patter on fabric caught my attention, and I turned to find Vivienne crying, her tears plinking down on her dress.

I wanted to comfort her. One hears of the stalwart mourner, his reserves of empathy intact, capable of consoling those who grieve his own loss. *I'll be okay,* that mourner can say to the weeping other, who sits removed from the suffering. *I am still here. My life will keep going, the sun will still rise, etc.*

I have not been that kind of mourner.

Again I peered into the distance. "I was enraged at myself for betraying your trust, but I was also . . . upset . . . with you. I felt like you had made the wrong choice, though I knew that was unfair of me. I had not been transparent with you, and I had made you doubt yourself, your sense of our relationship. But my family was so far away. Their lives were splintering, and you wanted to be in New York with your mother. Our sorrows, yours and mine—the whole world's—seemed out of proportion."

Vivienne's breath was stuttering.

I breathed in to say what should have been said long before the day her heart broke in my office. "I loved you, Vivienne—your words and gentleness. Your face and your form. You were love to me, in one body, like I'd never known it."

"You never told me," she whispered.

"I should have." I stared at her hands in her lap, remembering how even touching them had felt like a declaration of love for me. "I was so afraid of hurting you. But we should have said *I love you* as the punctuation between sentences. It *was* the punctuation between sentences."

"Yes," her breath caught.

"But you'd gone, and you'd told me to leave, and my brother was lost, so two days after you left, I flew across the Atlantic. By the time I hitchhiked from Vienna to Ljubljana, my parents knew that my brother was dead."

"Peter." Vivienne's eyes opened to mine. "I was a child, as you said—"

"No. For so long, I have wanted—"

She touched my arm. "No. You were right to have thought that and said it. I *was* a child. An adult would have stayed to talk to you—to understand. And if I had stayed for even one day, I would have known about Tilen—"

"Vivienne, your mother was losing her baby. She was ill—"

"No," Vivienne said again. "I don't see how you can forgive me. How you can sit here beside me. I thought only of myself back then—" She looked at the grass, her voice tear-filled and rising. I shut my eyes to her words. "You deserve selfless, unwavering friends, Peter. Ones who remain at your side. I would do anything . . . but I didn't—" She leaned forward as if she might leave.

I pressed my hand almost to her leg. "Stay," I said, my fingers tensed on the park bench. She had to know I was pleading. "Don't go yet. Let me finish my story."

The words settled on her like a weight I recognized. One of time and loss and distance. Of regret. She rested stiffly against the park bench as though she were a patient submitting to a dismal prognosis.

"After I arrived in Slovenia, my father and I took a train to Croatia. We found Hana with her parents, but in her grief, she was empty of breast-milk. The baby slept so deeply. I wasn't always sure he was breathing."

Vivienne looked up to the sky. Feathers of white clouds stroked across the spring blue.

"My father and I found infant formula and made plans to travel back to Ljubljana with Hana and David. But near Slovenia's border, at a Zagreb train station, we encountered—" I paused at the look on Vivienne's face. It had appeared that stricken the first time she told me about her mother. Out of habit—or out of the ghost of a habit—I reached to tuck one short wisp of ink-black hair behind her ear.

She winced away, shivering. *Because my touch surprised her? Or because someone else smooths her hair now?* I wondered.

"What about Tilen? I know from the essays that you weren't able to bury him." She turned a marble-esque kind of still.

"No—" My lungs insisted on air. "We did not bury Tilen. We could not enter Borovo Selo. Croatian police buried Tilen. His grave is not marked."

Vivienne pressed her fingers to her lips. "And you?" Her voice broke. "What happened to you, Peter?"

I described more of what I detailed in my essays and have re-lived in my head uncountable times. How at the Zagreb train station, we ran into a younger journalist my father knew, the journalist who had been with Tilen at Plitivice—Mats Krušec. He intended to follow the war in Croatia and send news to the rest of Europe. He needed a second journalist but said he'd settle for a solid writer.

"It was a death wish of a venture." My eyes felt riveted to the grass. "Serbs were brutal to journalists, and both Croat and Serb media only sold propaganda."

But I explained to Vivienne that I had been out of my mind with grief, with loss. "And you . . . you were part of that loss, too." I finally shifted my gaze to her. "That is not in the essays."

She stared down at her hands as though praying, her cheeks paler than they'd been when I'd begun talking. Her shoulders rose and fell with her breath.

I told her what she had no doubt read. That I had the idea as we spoke to Krušec that words were what I could give my brother. If I wrote down what was happening to us—a divided people, who had tried under the delusions and fists of our leaders to live as one nation—if I could bring foreigners to know and feel the tremors of our country collapsing, I could attempt to make Tilen's death count for something. I might help wake a paralyzed world to unspeakable crimes and suffering.

"You went with Krušec." Her voice couldn't have stirred even a particle of air.

"Yes." Still studying the grass, I envisioned that goodbye at the Zagreb station, and still see it now as I write. Ati in a tentative, compassionate agreement with me, but wary, terrified of the effect my leaving would have on my mother, not to mention his worry for my life. Hana holding me with one arm and a fussing, baby-skeleton David in the other. She was almost unable to breathe through her weeping. Her skin looked like paper sinking into in a puddle.

Ati placed his hands on my shoulders. *In bocca al lupo,* he spoke the Italian good-luck wish he always saved for our gravest departures. *In the mouth of the wolf.*

"That's how you came to write the essays." Vivienne summoned me back from memory.

"Yes." I turned to her. "I am glad they are written. I think they do honor Tilen's work. But I also think . . . I think I could have drafted powerful work even if I had returned to Ljubljana. I felt angry and reckless and . . ." A butterfly batted past Vivienne's shoulder, drawn to her light just as I was. My arm reached along the back of our bench, my fingers stretching behind her.

"I felt desperate at the station in Zagreb. Forsaken, I think. By God, by my brother, by—"

I did at that time feel forsaken by Vivienne, but I knew even then that I had not been. I had in a sense, unintentionally and perhaps irreparably, forsaken her.

Yet I wanted her to know that I would not have gone with Krušec if I hadn't lost her. I would never have left her in New York to worry about my life in addition to her mother's.

"I wouldn't have left with Mats in Zagreb—" I tried to explain what I knew in my heart. "If I had been upfront with you—if you and I hadn't—"

Vivienne looked up from her hands at me. Her mournful eyes glittered with stars of a past that never was, one that we might have lived together. If I hadn't delayed telling her of my change of life plans, if I had given words earlier to what I was feeling.

Sitting with present-tense Vivienne on a park bench, I felt more powerless than ever to revise our past.

I moved on. "Mats and I traveled in Croatia for one year—recording from as up-close as possible its secession from Yugoslavia and subsequent war for independence. We barely escaped the joint Yugoslav-Serb attack on Vukovar in northeast Croatia, and witnessed too close the Yugoslav army's siege of Dubrovnik."

I reported on the facts of my past like the unaffected journalist I've never been. Vivienne peered into the blossoming trees, hands folded tight in her lap.

I simply named main events, omitting one life-saving fact that felt too intimate to disclose yet—

I had traveled to Croatia with her journal in my pack.

I would read her entries at night, sometimes only for seconds, by the light of Mats's stolen cigarette lighters. I would lift the cover as if opening sacred text. Before the end of one sentence—one phrase—I'd fall into the hush of the past. I would smile, even laugh, until I was too spent to read, and then I would lie on my back and, most nights, silently weep.

To Vivienne, I relayed much of what she likely already knew from my essays. How Mats and I interviewed Croat refugees escaping Serb violence, sheltered in Adriatic resort hotels. How by Christmas of 1991, Mats and I watched citizens of Zagreb celebrate Germany's recognition of Croatian independence.

Finally, I told her how, a few weeks after Christmas, the UN assisted Croatia in negotiating a ceasefire with the ethnic Serb army, and Mats and I returned to Ljubljana, even though conflict had barely begun in the Republic of Bosnia. What had been Yugoslavia would continue unraveling, but I would no longer be chasing its threads. Neither my brain nor my body could witness or document more suffering.

"For one year after that," I told Vivienne, "I carried my own grief on my shoulders like a boulder of lead. I wrote very little and could not compose myself to find work. But then my father arranged for me to teach a class at the University of Ljubljana, and the more I spoke of what I'd witnessed, the more I could write. For two years following that, I taught at the university, writing and sending essays to my father's friend Richard Haskins at the *Times*. He published them there and eventually passed them on to Adèle, who sold them to Coniston, the publisher of my book."

Turning her gaze from the trees, Vivienne met my eyes. The clear light of the spring day illumined her irises to the melancholy amber of a medicine bottle. Or the shade of vanilla extract. A mix of both sad and sweet.

Why had I reported so much to her? I had just as well set my elephant burden between us on the park bench. How could she ever reply?

As was always her way with responding, in writing or speaking, she did not try to account for the world's larger woes. Instead, she held to the personal. "I wanted to write you. After you left, and last year, as I began reading your essays. I didn't have an address, but Adèle would have given me one." She touched a hand to her neck, where petals of red had formed, as they did when she would speak in my class so long ago, and I would want to touch my lips to the blooms, rest a hand on her heart and whisper, *It's just me, Vivienne*—as I wished to right then. "I wished I would have known about the essays when *The Times* printed them. I would have—"

What? What would you have done? I silently asked her.

"I would have liked that." I wanted to fold my outstretched arm around her. "I would have liked receiving your letter."

Vivienne peered down at her hands in her lap. "How is Hana?" she asked. "Is she recovering? Where are she and David now?"

"Hana is somewhat improved, but fragile," I said, and then, before I could think of implications—and because in my mind, Hana and I were not, will never be, a remote possibility—and also because, Good God, I'm an idiot—I said, "She thinks I could make her almost happy."

Vivienne consulted her watch.

I couldn't tell where we were headed. I couldn't tell before, but now Vivienne shivered, and my chest stung in the way it used to in Croatia at the first sound of gunfire.

"And David?" she asked before I could clarify about Hana, assure Vivienne that I did not intend to attempt to make Hana almost happy.

I decided to answer her question. "David is like a balm of honey and puppies, Vivienne. He is five now, but tall enough to be seven. He is just like my brother, curious about the smallest details of the world, and good-humored and brave and playful. Except he is quieter than Tilen was, I think. More contemplative. In that way, I suppose he is more like—"

"Like you." Vivienne's opposite hand wrapped tensely around her watch.

"Possibly," I nodded. "But what about—"

"Adèle said you might be teaching here?" Vivienne lifted her tote from the bench. Clearly, she intended to go.

"Yes. A friend—well—" I sat up, bracing to catch her arm in case she suddenly fluttered away. "You remember my father's friend at Hadley. The chair of the history department?"

"Yes." Vivienne inched farther away on the park bench. "I remember him."

Of course she did.

"Kieran O'Connor. He asked me to interview for a one-year visiting-professorship of history at Hadley. I'll start teaching on Monday, but there might be opportunity for—that is, I could possibly—"

Vivienne rolled her lips between her teeth, her brows lowering as if I had just announced that I abhorred her family, her baked goods, and her salted butter.

I remembered that day in my office—before she'd read my response to the one she had written to me in her journal, when I was trying to make clear that I cared for her, and she wasn't having any of it. "Vivienne—" I became an echo of our past.

And she turned to echo as well. "Peter, I'm so sorry—" She glanced at her watch again. "I have to go. Right now. I have to pick up Nicole at her school."

"I'll go with you," I said, so intent on not losing her bodily presence that I did not even have the presence of mind to ask, *Your daughter? Your younger sister?* I simply jumped from the bench, like a mirror of herself.

She looked over her shoulder as if someone else might be meeting her, and maybe someone else was—Robert-the-muscular-physician, probably.

"That wouldn't work," Vivienne said. "But I don't want to end this way. I want to hear everything—"

Let's not end at all, my inner voice countered.

She rummaged through an outside compartment of her tote and snapped out a pair of sunglasses. Slipping the stems over her ears, she began walking, so that I had to rush to keep pace with her.

"Sunday." Her head turned my way, but I couldn't tell if her shade-covered eyes even looked at me. "We could finish on Sunday at my place—"

I felt like she wanted to run, away from me or toward her destination. Odds were in favor of both. I had burdened her with a cumbersome story, and I hadn't even apologized for the decision I had made five years ago. The decision that had served as the catalyst to the separate paths we now traveled. I hadn't apologized for the words I'd said, either—for saying I was waiting for her to grow up. I hadn't even asked about her.

But she hadn't let me.

"Over dinner," she said. How she sprint-walked in those heeled sandals boggled my mind and my feet. "Could you meet me at *La Coccinelle?*
At 5? We close early."

We could finish on Sunday. We could finish—

Did I really wish to say yes to that?

I am rarely not wishing.

"Yes, I can be there," I slowed on the path, worried that I might be
like a stray tom to her. Like she might feel obligated to procure a saucer
of milk for me from her tote. Or simply melt her untouched churned
butter.

Abruptly she stopped, looking up at me through her sunglasses. We
had contemplated perfection, survived hostile birds, suffered the theft
of fresh bread, covered the losses of my personal life, as well as a few of
the former country of Yugoslavia, and we were ending on a Central Park
path with Vivienne staring speechlessly up at me through a pair of tor-
toise-shell cat-eyed Ralph-Lauren sunglasses. Despite loss and heartache
and tragedy, the corners of my lips trembled against a smile.

Vivienne removed her shades, her sad-and-sweet eyes watering.
"Peter," she touched a hand to my heart, "I am sorry for everything you
have lost."

For possibly two seconds—for as long as she would allow—I covered her hand with mine. A shower of blossoms shed forth in my heart.
"*Najlepša hvala,*" I said. Her skin was memory turned warm and tangible.

She nodded. "Most beautiful thank you."

And then she turned and continued walking.

Before writing on the run for one year in the midst of war in Croatia,
I would read the detail of Vivienne's journal entries incredulously, chuckling from time to time at the dialogue and detail. But after surviving
that year and writing about it, and now, even as I write about this one
uncertain, shimmering-brief day, I know—to write is to allow pain and
love and memory and time to exist outside yourself. You breathe when
the words are out.

You can live until tomorrow.

Or in this case, possibly, until Sunday.

Friday, May 3, 1996

I woke before dawn again this morning as Vivienne left my dream, and I could not rest for one moment in the ache of her vanishing.

Consequently, I rose and walked from my apartment on West 89th past Vivienne's West 76th Street bakery, where stark yellow light blared from the tucked-away kitchen into the hushed empty shop (no glimpse of Vivienne). I trudged beyond Lincoln Center, to a just-waking Times Square that looked more like an abandoned stage set than the heart of a city. Its billboard lights cast a sad glow on down-gazing workers, who might have easily been actors, tired of their roles, but contracted to keep a great drama playing. The human narrative that waking up matters, that commerce, love, industry, and art ensure that our planet keeps spinning.

That thought makes me sound like a skeptic.

Of course, I believe that waking up matters. I believe in commerce, industry, and art. I believe in love. If I didn't, I wouldn't be in New York, blocks away from a woman whose heart I broke five years ago. I'd be staring at a cinderblock wall in a post-Communist apartment, somewhere in the former Federal Republic of Yugoslavia.

But I'm here, in this numbered grid of an American city, blue puddles along curbs, blossoms breaking open on branches and in pots and curb strips outside brownstones, as well as inside my heart—God help me—every time I even think the name *Vivienne*.

Since leaving Central Park yesterday, my mind has been a film screen flashing scenes I imagine for how Sunday night might go. How will she greet me—wearing her ladybug-printed apron? (*Here*, I could say, *I can help you untie that.*) Would she touch my arm, or my shirt over my heart again, as she flushed to the tip of her nose?

Would she allow me to cut to the core of my questions—*Are you with someone else now?* And if the answer were no, could we swing our tired hands together as we made our way home? To her home in a literal sense, but also to the home I feel when we are together—the home she has written about in her journal. The home I can't un-imagine us making.

On the sidewalk before we arrived there, I would ask, *Vivienne, can you forgive me for leaving? Can you forgive me for what I said?*

Walking back to my apartment this morning, busses and cars humming but not honking yet, a few shops opening their doors (still no Vivienne through the bakery window), I couldn't stop myself from remembering.

Vivienne with ink on the outside edge of her right hand, scrawling across the clean blank pages of her journal. Vivienne watching me from her classroom desk as if, inside her head, she was teaching me something essential to life and poetry—how to care for the one person you love more than everything, when to say and when to show what you mean. She was twenty years old. She had lived her life within the equivalent of a lemon-sized radius of three prosperous cities, surrounded by love and privilege, and somehow, she understood how to speak and offer love more honestly than anyone I'll ever know.

Likely she understands even better now, but yesterday, she seemed less certain. About me. About how much and in what way she cares. About how many and which words she wishes to say to me.

What was I expecting? My own actions five years ago—withholding information that impacted her future, leaving her to doubt her adulthood—relayed a lack of love so vast and tangible, it might have filled entire collapsing galaxies.

Once showered and dressed for the day, I sat at the squat fold-out tray of my kitchen nook, listing tasks in the palm-sized diary Hana gave me in a sack of going-away things.

I felt like a man in a world turned miniature—arms, legs, desires all too big for the space the current world has allotted him.

I filled today's hours with every chore I could think of. Review teaching plans for next week. Buy groceries at the West 81st Street Dutch market. Collect copies of all my course syllabi at Hadley. Work on several poems I've begun about time, death, and distance.

And love.

And home.

I can't keep those last two subjects out of it.

Nor can I deter thoughts of Vivienne. Even my body remembers her. I type, and my hands long to touch the shadowed skin at her neckline. When I walk out for tea, my legs anticipate her brisk pace beside them.

I pause between the sentences I write tonight and become lost in the reasons why two people see one another. Why—out of all the people seen in an hour, in a day, in the world—two human beings wish to see more of only each other. To find out where the other came from—their sidewalks, their people, their country. The words they say to describe the other as fascinating or beautiful. The intricate specific ways they speak metaphor.

If Vivienne has moved on, I—

I don't know that I will stay here.

I am heading out to walk again. It is midnight.

Saturday, May 4, 1996

Today Kieran's wife, Mary, a motherly sort with coarse salt-and-pepper bobbed hair and round horn-rimmed glasses that emphasize her psychiatrist curiosity, asked, "Why do you love this French girl, Peter? How do you know you're not in love with an idea or a memory?"

I had just stepped out of a dressing room at a J. Crew near her and Kieran's Upper East Side apartment, wearing new khaki pants and the softest gray sweater I had ever pulled onto my body. After walking the city again this morning, I had opened a stuck drawer in my one aged dresser and realized I own nothing respectable to wear—for teaching on Monday, or for meeting Vivienne tomorrow.

Panicked, I telephoned Mary, who told me exactly where to meet her and Kieran at 10:00 this morning.

As I stood for examination outside a dressing stall, it was Kieran, leaning against a wooden table piled with a rainbow of pastel crewneck t-shirts, who lowered his glasses at me. "The French girl is yours." He looked down at his watch. "Just wear that."

Mary was less easily convinced. She began folding rumpled t-shirts into crisp squares on the table. "But Kieran, love, what would the girl be choosing? An image whose surface she cannot, after so much time, see beneath? Our Peter needs a woman who sees to his center." She smoothed one shirt on top of another and walked over to me to pull the sweater's soft sleeves down to my wrist bones. "Though if you do need money, Peter"—she always pronounces my name with a short initial *e*, as one does in Slovene—"you could make a killing off modeling this stuff. But no," she raised her voice so that both Kieran and I might hear clearly, "I hold forth. Peter needs to articulate why he still loves this woman. Loves her right now, in this shop, in fact. And why he thinks she might still love him. People change, my darlings."

Tossing his head back, Kieran exhaled as if suffering heartburn. "Mary . . ."

"Can you say why you love me, Professor O'Connor?" Mary stood between her scowling husband and me, hands on her rounded hips. I took a backward step toward my dressing room.

"Oh, you stay right here, you lovestruck wandering Slovene." Mary reached out to tug me forward by my elbow, her Irish accent growing more pronounced by the syllable.

Still leaning against the merchandise table, Kieran folded his arms like a boy prepared to say something enraging. "I love you because you're still here, Dr. O'Connor."

Mary huffed, seemingly unsurprised by his nerve. But my heart might have stopped in my chest, as if shocked by a cardiac defibrillator.

Because we're alive. We are here.

The words shook me.

I wondered—was I missing what could be at least sustainable with Hana by pursuing an unattainable idea of Vivienne that still filled me to overflowing? Was Vivienne as I loved her only abstract? Could she be solely a memory now?

Could "almost enough" with Hana be almost as good as what Kieran and Mary had?

Vivus, I thought for the thousandth time, *alive or living.*

"You're unsettling the Slovene, Mary." Kieran stood from the clothes table as I breathed in and remembered to pull my jaw closed.

"You two are hopeless." Mary pushed against my chest until I stepped again toward the dressing rooms. "You're buying everything," she said. "I'll lend you an iron."

I heard Kieran approach Mary behind me and say in a deep Irish lilt I've never heard before in his speech, "I know I love you, Mary Anna O'Brien O'Connor, because even ten millennia with you would not be even almost long enough."

Sparks lit like a fuse in my veins.

The image in my head was akin to a children's fantasy film—notebook pages turning, myself falling inside a wildly-inked page, landing atop Vivienne's own line—

No time is long enough.

Of course, Kieran and Mary invited me to lunch at their place, but I could see in the wanting, intimate manner they looped arms around each other's backs as we walked in that direction, that they might live a more memorable afternoon without me.

So, four bags on my handlebars—two of which held contents Mary had purchased after she sent Kieran and me out the shop doors, claiming she needed to select a dress for their daughter (whom, Mary suggested, I might like meeting for coffee)—I cycled through the park for the fourth time since Thursday. Only this time, I wasn't meeting or leaving Vivienne. I was numbering in my head the reasons I know I still love her.

1. Words. You look at her and know that elaborate lexical nova are bursting in her cerebrum. As when, last week, I glanced up to find her watching me at my library reading. *You,* her eyes said, along with un-shaped words about loss and love so devastating I had to look down. Not because I needed to see my own words on the page, but because the words she wasn't speaking blinded me with their eloquence and grief.

I know these words from her journal by heart—

> *If I slept till tomorrow, you*
> *would lie down beside me. When enough days*
> *had passed, you would pull me to shore*

Her words have become my own now—

You, Vivienne. Lie down beside me. Enough days have passed. Pull me to shore.

2. Quiet. Not in the way of subservience or docility, but more in the way of a field sprung with wildflowers. Just after rain, the sky glowing violet at its edges. You want to walk to the very center.

3. Laughter. Vivienne didn't write much of laughter in her journal. But she laughs, and the cadence is . . . as it was in the park on Thursday, after the birds had swarmed.

   From the first moment I heard her laugh at St. Brigid's—when I kept teaching her things she already knew at that library workshop—I felt as though a song had been wound up in my heart my whole life, but was waiting for the notes of her laughter.

4. Sadness. I don't wish for her to be sad, but her sadness matches mine—the precise shade of light, a quarter-moon's amber glow. The last purple of day on the horizon. Dear God, I could sleep in it, my nightmares abated, just knowing her ache runs as deep as my own.

5. Vision. The world she sees and the world she saw in me. The notion that even as she stared her mother's possible death in the face at St. Brigid's, she could see me as anchor and axis. She could envision us—despite inevitable facts of human suffering and dying—making a fruitful life together.

   She could imagine the two of us expanding—our cells dividing to make brand-new human beings, my eyes, her smile—our words mingling on paper, describing the pang and joy of it.

   Even as she feared pending losses, she saw life. She might take me to task on that, but it's true. In words and bread and sweet things like chocolate, she saw potential to fill human need, to spark love and sustain it.

   Her bakery is proof. Poems and birds and ladybugs and nourishment—any small thing in this world might fill you.

6. Goodness.
   You're not all right, are you.
   Her palm on the side of my face.
   Your brother died.
   Were you able to bury him?
   I don't want to end this way. I want to hear everything.

7. She loves everything—
   Her parents, her childhood, button daisies in pots.
   Garden tomatoes, olive oil, French flaky salt.
   Warm bread and chocolate chip cookies.
   Words shaped on lines, words conjuring images, words speaking
   one shining idea.
   The shadowed skin just below her earlobe.
   Me.
   Once, many years ago, she loved me.

I will copy my list out and mail it to Mary.
I keep thinking, *I don't want Vivienne and me to end this way.*

Hana called as I finished that last sentence. She asked if somehow—
if she and I and my parents and her parents could gather up enough
money for plane tickets—she and David might come to New York.
"David is writing you a . . . *pesem*—a poem?—everyday." She insists on
speaking English with me now. Because she wants to be here. She wants
to be with me.

"He can show you his notebook. And . . . you—you and I—we could
. . . be."

I told her I had met with the woman who wrote the journal that
Hana had seen me guarding for the past five years. I told her I planned
to see that woman again.

"Vivienne," Hana said in a voice that reminded me of rain—sad, but
not angry, not even resentful—simply full of gray and quiet. "I do not
forget. But if she does not want you, have me."

Monday, May 6, 1996

I will not fit yesterday into one entry. I can try to start here—

I entered Vivienne's bakery at 4:45 p.m., not wishing to rush her, but physically incapable of waiting another fifteen minutes outside the sun-strength beam of her presence.

Vivienne's journal was tucked in my backpack again, this time wrapped in brown paper and twine that my mother had somehow convinced me to transport across the Atlantic. *Because you do not know when you might want to mail a gift home to your mother, my love. A bracelet, perhaps, from New York.*

Which reminds me—I need to find my mother a good bracelet. She rarely asks for anything, particularly since Tilen was killed, as she feels— as Ati and I have often felt, too—that any good thing might distract us from mourning Tilen properly.

Tilen, however, would wish beautiful things for all of us, even from an unmarked grave in Croatia. Had he been with me as I stepped through the bakery door, he would have vicariously felt the sudden drop in my chest. I knew instantly that Vivienne was not there—the little bell on the doorknob rang hollow. Customers slouched, their faces pale over color-less pastry. A tangible current of light was missing.

Tilen would have said, *Go! Find her!*

I approached the shop's front counter, where the French woman from the other day already counted the till. A wiry, dark-haired young man stood next to her, eating a torn chunk of baguette slathered in butter.

"Bonjour." The woman looked up as I halted on the other side of the counter. The young man, I noticed, stopped chewing. With a glance, I placed him as a seasoned, or possibly graduated, college student.

"Bonjour." I looked beyond the shop counter, feeling increasingly gloomy and chilled, certain that Vivienne wasn't there, yet unwilling to believe that she truly hadn't come. "Vivienne had asked me to meet her at 5?" I consulted Ati's watch on my wrist, feigning ignorance of each minute's passing. "I'm slightly early."

The young man set his bread down on parchment paper laid atop the counter's glass case.

"Ah, *oui.*" A sharp bell dinged as the woman smacked the till-drawer closed. "Vivienne has a headache. She said she will see you another day."

Clearing his throat, the young man stepped closer to the woman at the till. "But it's not just any headache." He was wearing a soft-as-tissue red Millenium Falcon t-shirt, arching a surprisingly delicate eyebrow that set my mind prickling with recognition.

"*La soupe pour laquelle tu es venu est sur la cuisinière.*" The woman glared at the young man and pointed to a soup pot on a stove behind glass windows that separated the café from the kitchen. And then—I'm sure I wasn't meant to see—she pinched the young man on the back of his arm, hard, just above his elbow.

"What!" He yanked his arm away. "He's Vivienne's friend, Evelyn. I know him. I'm Luc." He offered a quick nod to me, reaching an arm over the counter's glass case.

I lifted my hand to shake his.

"You're Peter," he said when words eluded me. "We met on the phone a long time ago."

"Yes." I envisioned that night, the last Vivienne and I were together. She'd been frantic, in a rage, telling her brother that the man in her room was always direct, always told her what he thought, treated her like a grown-up. The words I meant to say to her that night—the words I should have said in the park days before—returned to my tongue. *Vivienne, I need to talk to you, and I need you to know that above anything else, I want us to be together.*

From behind the shop counter, Luc blatantly studied me. "Nice sweater," he said. "It looks soft."

"Yes. Thanks." I ran a hand down the *dove-gray summer-weight cashmere*—as Mary had called it—that covered my chest. I stared at Luc, attaching his dark eyes to Vivienne's, along with the sharp, broad sweep of his cheeks, the subtle upturn of his nose. He had an easier smile than hers, though, less guarded, more wry, seemingly practiced in both sincerity and mischief.

From the kitchen, a metallic clatter of what sounded like metal pans pierced the Vivienne-less lull of the bakery. "Evelyn!" a high-pitched female voice shrieked.

"Evelyn!" Luc grinned at the woman beside him, tossing a thumb over his shoulder, toward the kitchen. The woman was not Luc and Vivienne's mother, then. She was their aunt. Their Aunt Evelyn. Relief and worry flooded my veins simultaneously.

"Deux minutes." Evelyn jabbed a finger into Luc's chest.

"I should have connected—you and Vivienne," I said once Evelyn had vanished, thinking to myself that all I knew of Vivienne's brother was that he had been, prior to myself, the catalyst of her near emotional unraveling five years ago. I felt wary of him and desperate for his help at the same time.

He leaned his palms against the wood countertop beside the register. "I just took a lucky guess." He smiled before lowering his voice. "I think I'm the only one Vivi's told about you. She said you were back. For a book or something?" He glanced over his shoulder, possibly gauging the whereabouts of his aunt.

"Evelyn and Vivienne own this shop," he whispered as though we were under surveillance. "Evelyn will kill me—well, both of us—if I send you to Vivienne." He lowered his eyes to a cake knife resting within the glass case beside what appeared to be a many-layered, chocolate, chocolate, and more chocolate cake.

Looking to my left, I noticed for the first time a framed photograph on the poetry wall—of three figures outside a French café. A grinning, brace-toothed Vivienne stood between her loyal and apparently-willing-to-murder-you aunt and another woman, as angular and lovely as Vivienne now, smiling but reserved, the fingers of one hand threaded through Vivienne's.

Her mother. *Is she alive today as she was in that picture?* I wondered. I wanted her to be. I wanted, as I gazed at that picture, for Vivienne not to have suffered her mother's loss. I wanted her to have left me five years ago and to have simply decided that she was happier without me. That I was untrustworthy, unworthy, that she could find better, that she could forget me and bake pastry or cookies, write poems, hang paper-mâché birds from ceilings. I wanted the sadness that permeates her now like mist in the winter to be only a predisposed temperament. I stood in her bakery wanting all of that so much that I could not even bring myself to ask her brother, rosy-cheeked and curious before me, how his mother was doing. I could not risk hearing, *Oh, has Vivi not told you? Our mother passed away.*

Behind the counter, Luc cleared his throat. "If Vivi's not meeting you here"—he waited for my eyes to meet his—"she probably wants . . . Well, let's be honest." He rubbed at a subtle dent in his chin. "She probably wants to push you away. She's sad and dramatic. She does that."

"Does what?" I asked, though simply to fill the air with two syllables. I knew what he meant, though he had been brash in sharing the information.

I skipped to a more important question. "Do you know that Vivienne is okay right now—with her headache, of course, but also—" I wanted to say, *in her heart?*

I tried to sound the smallest bit less emotional. "Is she hurting inside as well?"

I could see her in my mind as she was on our last day together in my office. As unyielding as concrete, one hand clasped over the opposite elbow, eyes turned to twin blank pools, as though her soul had gone numb in her body.

Yet I knew then—I could feel it—that inside herself, she was holding a sharp, bright wound.

And I couldn't even compel her to blink.

Luc watched me from behind the counter with the same evaluating gaze with which his sister observed me during the early days of our poetry class, when she was trying to ascertain if I was as smart as she was.

I wasn't.

But in the bakery, I felt like I might be on at least equal footing with her brother.

He leaned into his palms on the countertop again, speaking quickly. "She gets migraines when she's stressed, or . . ." His eyes narrowed. "Afraid." He swept a wave of hair, lighter than Vivienne's, from his eyes. "It's a real thing. Sometimes she can't stand up—it hurts her that bad. I don't think she'd lie to you. If she's not here, she's in pain—" He paused, peering into some distance, as if aware, as I was, that she was probably in more than one kind of pain.

We stood for a moment, considering one another, but also, I believe, considering Vivienne.

The words she had selected from poems and hand-lettered on canvases seemed to thrum on the wall behind me. The colors and chaos of her fractured interior self pressed in on me and her brother.

We both had wrongs to make right. For me, the course to that end stretched clear in my mind, a paved narrow path through dense woods toward light. But Luc had to decide if I comprised another wrong or a new right for his sister, before his aunt reappeared from the kitchen with a longer and sharper cake knife.

We spoke at the same time.

"Does she still live with your family?"

"I think you should take that soup to her."

Vivienne no longer lives with her family. Nor does she live in Brooklyn, a fact that continues to bat at my mind like a moth. A harried flutter that taps out one sentence. *She's not where she wants to be yet.*

She still lives on the Upper East Side, four blocks north of her family, in a fifth-floor walkup that, in one final, rushed deluge of information, Luc said that their father owns, though Vivienne insists on paying some rent.

As I walked my bike on the sidewalk toward the stoplight across from Vivienne's building, a navy-blue-suited Robert Carson appeared. Rather than simply mounting my bike and cycling back to my apartment, as any underqualified, underdressed foreign suitor might have done, I slowed my steps and imagined how the scene might look in a documentary. From a bird's eye perspective. The crisscross of American city streets, yellow cabs whirring by, one American and one formerly Yugoslavian male entering one another's proximity. The American is as poised as a prince, gliding away from a perhaps intimate encounter with the same woman that the former Yugoslavian hopes to find unattached and forgiving and willing to spend the rest of her life with him.

The American blazes forward, free of all care, confident in the glow of both his past and his future. The former Yugoslavian steps hesitantly, weighed down by all he has lived and seen and lost and knows he doesn't know for certain. No music accompanies him.

In the actual world, Robert Carson and I stepped close enough to truly recognize one another, and, improvising in a way that I never could have thought to script for him, Robert Carson looked directly into my eyes with all the foreboding of a thundercloud. And then snapped his gaze away and kept walking.

I stood at the intersection, deliberating which way to step—soup, bread, journal all resting inside my backpack.

But if she does not want you—

If Vivienne wished to be with Robert Carson, if he had stepped into her life to quiet and keep her heart when I could not—when I did not—then I would not suggest to her, even simply by finding ways to be near her, that she might contemplate a life with me. To attempt to imply that she turn from someone who might have cared for her so selflessly felt like the most egregious of sins.

Yet Robert Carson had been walking away from Vivienne, and not, I deduced by his glare, too happily.

And her brother had assigned me to deliver a carton of vegetable soup that he claimed she loved and needed.

And I still had a journal full of her words in my possession—her history, musing, heartbreak—that should not remain mine if she and I could not be together. I could not keep it and in clear conscience ever commit—albeit only in almost-happiness—to cleave to another woman.

After watching the traffic light blink from red to green four times, I eased my tires off the curb and walked toward Vivienne's.

Without a doorman to question me, I locked my bike to a rack outside Vivienne's building before opening the glass door and stepping inside. Upon finding the stairwell, I leaped the polished steps three at a time at first, but slowed to one-by-one as the fifth floor grew nearer and my confidence dwindled until it felt the size and consistency of a puddle that Vivienne might stomp in.

Just because I had found her did not guarantee that she'd allow me into her apartment or wish to engage again in our previous conversation. It did not even guarantee that she'd answer her door. Nothing I was attempting guaranteed remotely anything. And in realizing that, I felt within myself the gap I had so foolishly begun chiseling the moment I hung up the phone with Tilen five years ago, contemplating a life in Europe—a gap between that past and this present. Between Vivienne when she loved me, and Vivienne after five years of living without me.

Who was I to reappear and ask to be loved again?

Against the weight of misgiving, my feet kept ascending until I found myself facing her deep-paneled door. A cherry-blossom branch had been looped in a wreath and hung sweetly but slightly off-center. I wondered absurdly if that would be the sort of wreath Vivienne would hang from a door we lived behind together. The only way I'd ever know was to knock.

After doing so politely three separate times without answer or even the faintest suggestion of life inside the apartment, I gave the heavy wood one final thump before forcing my body to turn for the stairwell.

The moment I pivoted, the door's chain lock rattled.

"I told you to take your damn helmet," a tired voice ordered, as a supple arm quickly reached from the cracked-open door to thrust a miniature football helmet into my hands. When I instinctively turned it over for inspection, small white printed words appeared in a dark plastic window secured over the helmet's opening—*Cut your losses and run, bro.*

In the split second I stood regarding the psychic helmet, I wondered if the words were intended by the universe for me or for Carson. Even now, a day later, I'm not entirely certain.

"Do I need a helmet?" I winced at what was probably failed humor, unable to shift my gaze from the morose chestnut eyes that widened upon seeing me through the hefty door's thin wedge of an opening.

"How did you—" She glanced down at the helmet, retreating into shadow, grasping at the neck of her sweatshirt as if she felt trapped or exposed.

I set the fortune-telling helmet on the floor, slowly lowering my pack from my shoulders. "Am I interrupting anything?" I asked before venturing further.

Through the open slit of the door, Vivienne waved a dismissive hand at the helmet. "That was interrupted a long time ago." Her voice sounded dry and exhausted. She did not take the helmet back.

But her words nudged me forward. "Your brother sent me with soup and bread." Balancing my pack on my thigh, I pulled at the zipper.

"I could have made soup and bread for myself." She wasn't opening the door any wider.

I held the rolled-tight paper bag up in one hand. "Except your brother worried about your headache."

"And he sent you because . . .?" Three days ago at the park, Vivienne hadn't flung her arms wide at the sight of me, but she had been relatively open and warm. Her withdrawal behind her doorway suggested a certain slant of decision. A slant farther from me, not closer.

"Because . . ." Lowering the bakery sack, I returned my pack to my shoulder, Vivienne's journal still mine, wrapped neatly inside. "Because I wanted to make sure you were all right."

Stepping back, she eased her grip on the door, allowing it to creak open at least another inch. She still fidgeted with the neck of her sweatshirt. "I really do have a headache." She lifted a hand from her shirt to the center of her forehead, eyes slowly closing. "It helps to lie down in the dark. My dad likes to knock me out with a drug, but I can't think the next day, or follow recipes. Or read poems. So I opt for aspirin and turning out the lights." She lowered her hand to her eyes. "I'm sorry I couldn't meet you today."

I extended the bakery sack to her, abruptly aware that I stood in what could be a last moment of decision. Choose to speak, or choose to accept that I did not have courage or desire or strength sufficient to try to stem the predetermined forward-flow of history.

Nothing has been decided, I thought, *nothing guaranteed.* No success, sadly, but no failure, either.

I could allow Vivienne to determine our course—leave the requisite courage, desire, and strength to her. If she didn't feel it, I would have to move on.

Tilen's voice spoke to me then. *She embodies all my lifetimes.*

I touched my free hand to the door. "We could still talk if you wanted. I don't have to stay for long. I could heat up your soup, salt some oil for the bread." I felt the tension of her hand on the other side of the door.

I braved saying exactly what I wished for—

"Let me take care of you."

Vivienne reached for the sack, holding herself back in a way that made me think she planned on taking her food and slamming her door shut. Instead, with her shoulder, she pushed it open wide enough to turn around and walk into her apartment.

Along with the sweatshirt, she was wearing tie-dyed sweatpants and crocheted purple slippers, the entire ensemble—I can't say how it's possible—looking just as endearing and attractive as her Audrey Hepburn blue sundress. I wanted to bear-hug her in her sweatpants, however, while her dress had made me want to kiss her at the hollow of her collarbone.

"You can come in," she said, still walking.

Vivienne's apartment was not *like* a Victorian parlor; it appeared to truly be a Victorian parlor—a room out of time. An overstuffed, mauve velvet sofa amid two beige linen armchairs supported by delicately carved wooden legs, all framed by intricately molded side tables topped with jewel-framed photographs.

Books, stacked upright and sideways, lined dark built-in shelves behind the sofa, while still more books sat stacked on the floor beneath the tables and at one end of the sofa, almost as high as its rolled arm. The walls were papered with brushed, sepia-toned birds in flight.

It was not modern-whimsical like the bakery, but still whimsical—still Vivienne—a carefully-constructed collage of chaos, intelligence, and art.

Once inside, Vivienne headed straight for the overstuffed sofa. Lying back on a clutch of floral-stitched pillows, she covered her eyes with one arm, holding the bakery sack up with the other. "You can just set this in the fridge. I can't eat it right now."

I took the sack from her hand, sad not to have so much as brushed her soft skin, and walked perhaps six whole steps to a tiny refrigerator humming beneath a marble countertop that offered three feet of baking space at most. When I turned around, Vivienne had raised her arm to her forehead.

Through the dark slits of her eyes, she watched me.

I set my backpack beside a square kitchen table, certain my minutes were numbered.

"Do you remember that first night at St. Brigid's?" Eyes closed, Vivienne pointed blindly toward one of the tufted beige armchairs, about a foot or so away from her feet. "You can sit down," she said.

"Thanks." Tugging at the thighs of my slacks, I sat. I wanted to reach out and pull Vivienne's slippers off, hold her delicately tendoned feet in my hands.

I looked up to find her still watching me.

Her question hummed in the air.

Which first night? I wondered. *That night at the library workshop, when I sat beside you for the first time and wanted to cover your doodling fingers with my hand?*

Or that first night I ran into you at the library, wearing the sweatshirt I'd lent you and hadn't washed since you'd worn it?

I studied her sweatshirt—blue, flecked with gray, unraveling at the neck.

Vivienne's question, along with my sense of our ticking seconds, sparked an unexpected bluntness in me. "Is that mine?" I nodded at the fading-blue fabric. Had she feared I would recognize it in her doorway?

Turning to her side on the sofa, she crossed her arms over her chest, her hands swallowed up in the wrists of the sweatshirt. "Have you missed it?" she asked.

"I thought you probably tossed it from a cab window in California." I blinked my eyes against an image of myself removing my shirt from her person right then. "I didn't realize I had the option of missing it."

"But do you remember?" she spoke softly, covering her eyes again. "That first night, I mean?"

At some space between her words, I had committed to absolute directness. "The first night I kissed you?"

"Yes, but after that—" She winced, her head clearly hurting. "When we sat in your car and renamed constellations. We named one The Ladybug." She squinted toward the evening sky outside her thick, blurred-glass window pane. "It's in the sky again. Some nights I can almost see it, even in the city."

When I merely sat quietly in response, connecting overlooked figurative stars in my mind—her mother's necklace, our renamed constellations, her present bakery—Vivienne continued, "What kind of portent is that, do you think?"

I leaned my elbows on my knees, laced my fingers in between. "Do you believe in portents and signs, Vivienne?"

Opening her eyes, she peered down the span of her body at me. "No. But I wish I could see things coming."

I followed her gaze to a small, round walnut table next to the couch, just beyond her feet. A single photograph sat on top in a rose-colored crystal frame. The head of the woman I now recognized as Vivienne's mother was bent over a sleeping baby.

Let her mother be living four blocks away, I prayed to a lesser power than God, because I am not sure God entertains that kind of petition.

Before I could broach the question of Vivienne's mother, however, I needed to know if I had the right to sit at her feet with the hope of possibly holding her, or if I should prepare to exit her apartment without expecting to return. "Are you seeing the man who was interviewing at Stanford five years ago? Robert Carson? I passed him outside, and he appeared as though he might have been leaving your apartment. Possibly he left his football helmet?"

Vivienne's hold on her own arms seemed to tighten. "He did go to Stanford." She switched her heavy gaze between my face and the window. "And then last year he came to New York for a fellowship. We dated for a few months. He made me some version of happy. But not the real version. He keeps stopping by for things like his Sixers toothbrush."

I sat razor-straight in my chair as she tucked her chin into the neck of my sweatshirt.

I remembered kissing her in her dorm of all places, on that last night at St. Brigid's. She had been laughing and drawing me close to her. The phone had rung—

Robert Carson had obviously kissed Vivienne without interruption.

No matter how kind he might have been to her, I disliked Robert Carson.

"Evelyn and Luc never liked him very much," Vivienne echoed my own inclination. "He's had the week off, so he insisted on picking me up at the library last Sunday and taking Nicole to school that morning you stopped by Papa's apartment. Nicole was set on show-and-telling a doctor, and Papa had scheduled surgeries. Robert, of course, loves to be on display." Vivienne drew her knees to her chest, curling into them.

"And Nicole is . . .?" I asked for absolute clarity.

Living four blocks away with Papa and Maman, I willed Vivienne to say.

Her brow creased as she opened her eyes. "It's not obvious? She's my sister."

I couldn't decide if the way she eluded talk of her mother should give me hope that there was nothing significant to say, or if it should discourage me from nursing any hope at all.

I might have asked her that directly instead of saying, "I thought Nicole might be yours and Robert's."

I think the English expression for how her eyes stared at me has something to do with daggers.

"Your first assumption would be that I married him . . . or—" She buried her face in her knees again.

I wanted to lift her into my arms, encircle the sweet, cocooned shape of her, press her forehead to my lips. *I'm an idiot,* I'd say. *Just close your eyes.*

Instead, I behaved as a more typical male and verified. "So, you're not married, and you're not in a relationship?"

I watched her on the couch until her eyes met mine.

"No. I haven't been with Robert in a long time. And I'm not sad anymore, either." She swiped at an eye. "Not about that."

I could have asked what she was still sad about, but I felt certain we'd arrive at that eventually. In the meantime, her body was too far away and had been for too many years, across an ocean, on a far continent. I pressed my palms to my thighs and stood up. "Well, then," I glanced around for any sign of a door to her bedroom, just so that, I told myself, I could situate her more comfortably.

"Well, then what?" Her face looked suddenly stricken, appalled that I might have the audacity to leave so abruptly, but also terrified of what I might hope to do if I stayed.

"I'm holding you," I said, stepping toward the sofa, scooping her self-cradled form into my arms.

I had held her like that for countless times in the seven weeks I had spent as the man she loved, but just then, in her sitting room, we felt both familiar and new. Like two people reunited, but instead of bearing gifts from our journeys, we both bore scars to unwrap and show each other. If she could ever allow that.

"For how long?" Vivienne let her cheek rest lightly at my chest, not in the crook of my neck where it used to go. As if realizing the figurative timeline her question implied—*For how long in our mortal lives will you hold me?*—she shook her head cautiously. "I mean, standing like this could grow painful for both of us."

I stepped toward a door just left of the bookshelves. She closed her eyes, her head sinking heavier against me. "You can rest in your bed," I said into the short waves of her hair.

Her bedroom was simpler than her sitting room. It was quieter and light, a white eyelet comforter neatly tucked over the corners of a high bed situated beneath a wide, curtainless window. "That's where I try to see the stars," she said as I pulled back the bed covers, lowering her to the mattress. "Even in Manhattan."

"You need a curtain." I switched out the fat pillow under her head for a thinner one that let her neck curve more gently.

Before I'd carried her to her bed, I thought I'd have confidence to simply lie down beside her, rest a hand at her waist, or even pull her gently against me. But standing above her in her room, I knew I hadn't earned enough trust for that. "You can sleep." I reached a finger to the fine line of her jaw. "I'll wait in the other room."

Her eyes drooped closed as if she approved, but as my finger left her skin, her hand clasped my wrist. "Do you want to be with your brother's wife?"

I couldn't stop myself from revising her question. "Do I want to be with the woman who was married to my brother who was killed in Croatia?"

Vivienne opened her eyes, gauging, it seemed, the emotion behind my reaction. She didn't apologize, though, and she didn't back down. She wanted an honest answer, just as I had expected her honesty earlier. Both of us had tested each other. I hoped that by ascertaining the presence of another romantic entanglement, she was working to clear a path she could travel toward me.

"No," I answered her question. *Because you are alive. You are living.*

Dropping my wrist, she scooted over on her bed, resting her hand on the space she had lain in. "You could wait here. If you wanted."

I slipped off my shoes.

I slid under her covers and pulled her, as I had imagined, to my chest.

"You're warm," she sighed, turning into me, the tip of her nose grazing my neck. I had wondered for years—if any miracle might be wrought to grant me such a moment—exactly what touching her body again might feel like. Like hang-gliding from Everest? Like lying strapped to a torpedo as the fuse lit?

It felt like returning home. Not that I had ever before experienced that feeling. Not that I have called any place I lived home.

It was the first time I had felt it. Weightless and grounding, a warmth in my chest. Purpose, relief, and stillness.

Hope.

Vivienne's breath at my chest deepened and slowed, as if she had found a place to rest, too.

We slept for the next three hours.

I stirred to a finger tracing my face. Upward from my jaw to my temple, across my brow, down my nose, a circle around my lips, soft as light.

I could not bear to dream of Vivienne again.

But when I opened my eyes, she was there, wild-haired and awake in the window's pale light. The breath she inhaled sounded like paper snatched away. She tucked her hand beneath the bedcovers.

"I didn't mean to wake you," she said.

The sequence of events preceding that moment lined up in my mind like fallen dominoes set suddenly upright. "Hello." My voice sounded groggy in my ears, as though I'd been sleeping for years, or as though I hadn't slept deeply until I'd held Vivienne again. Perhaps I hadn't.

"How's your headache?" I asked. Unintentionally, my fingers brushed over the skin of her hip. She drew back shivering, even under her covers.

"It's lifted," she said, just above a whisper. She rolled away to step out of her bed as I fought an ache to pull her back in, wishing for things she could not be prepared for, like combing my fingers through a tousled shock of her hair, or nuzzling my nose to her cheek.

Or pressing my lips to her belly until she whispered my name.

I was sleep-drunk and love-struck and hungry. My veins were a flickering circuit board.

And she was still wearing my sweatshirt. She was the same degree of adorable as baby pandas and bunnies.

A silvery light thrummed through her window, turning everything distinct but colorless.

"I'll heat the soup," she said to the ceiling, before darting like a finch from her room.

I wondered what she'd say if I asked her to wait, but I'd lost my zeal for directness. My heart seemed to beat, *Tread lightly.*

At the stove, Vivienne stirred the soup, humming as though to avoid conversation.

"I've never heard you humming," I said from an elaborately carved kitchen chair.

"It's because of Nicole." She pulled a serrated knife from a block, roughly sliced the scored round of bread. "She won't fall asleep without humming or singing. My mother was really the best at that."

Was. The first time she had mentioned her mother. In the past tense, and not as *Maman.* Vivienne hung her head over the soup on the stovetop. It smelled of history and tears. Of longing.

I rose from my chair to stand silently behind her, touching my hand to her waist. She gasped.

"Vivienne. Tell me about your mother."

She ladled the soup into deep white porcelain bowls, switched off the burners, but then, exhaling a sob, thrust both bowls aside, broth droplets splattering.

She pressed her fists to the edge of the stovetop. "I keep feeling so damn angry!" she cried, turning into my chest to beat her fists at my sternum.

"Do you know what I want?" she nearly shouted as I absorbed the surprising force of her blows. "Do you?!"

"No," I shook my head. "Vivienne, I don't know what you want, but I want you to stop hurting."

"Ha!" She threw back her head, not like a mad woman in the way of insanity, but like a woman mad at the very weave of the universe. Exhausted by all its relentless givens—love, birth, struggle, death, and distance.

"Peter!" she shouted. "Peter!" She beat at my arms. "I want to go back. I want to go back before everything! Before you left, before she died—" Pausing abruptly, she steadied her breath, her hand resting over my heart as it had the other day in the park. "I want—" Her eyes were pleading, holding mine, as if begging me to name the object of her sentence, the salve that would take her pain away.

"I can't tell you what you want, Vivienne."

"I want—" She framed my face in her quivering hands. "I think I want—" She pulled my face down. "I just—"

Like a fire lit over dry brush, she was kissing me. As though we had never kissed before, more desperately than she had kissed me when we were together. She was gasping and crying, one moment her fingers pulling my hair, the next clutching the back of my sweater. I racked my brain for a soft word to soothe her. But words had vanished. I stood as if struck—by a wrench, by a meteor, by time in a freefall. Each catch of her lips turned to fractures of light, memories blinking out of darkness. Her lashes on my cheek, her spine beneath my palm, the scent of chamomile and apples. The pulse on her neck as my hand brushed over it.

I bent and pressed my lips to the thrumming.

After that, we were tripping toward the couch, falling onto the cushions. I rested my weight on an elbow to keep from crushing her. "Peter," she whispered through tears, racing her hands from my ears to my waist as if affirming that I was still tangible. In one schism of thought, I wondered how her kisses had become more certain—my heart panged for the days we had lost, for every touch that hadn't been mine. But then I only wanted more of her.

I was losing my breath, her body rising to mine, her mouth at my throat and then at my lips, my hand at the skin of her waist. I was an absence of thought, a capsule of feeling. Until she cried, "No!" and I dropped to my knees on the floor.

She was already weeping, curled into herself again, facing the sofa cushions, trembling.

"Vivienne—" I reached an arm around her middle to turn her toward me. "Vivienne." My pulse skipped from euphoric to terrified. "I'd never take what you didn't want to give me."

She held onto my arm at her abdomen. "I hate—"

Before she could say "you," I leaned my face over hers. "I'm sorry, Vivienne." My tears fell on her hair. "I'm sorry I didn't tell you I'd decided to teach in Ljubljana. I'm sorry for every word I said that hurt you. I'm sorry I left you. I'm sorry for every hour that you've been alone, every hour that you haven't been with me. I'm sorry for the walks we never took, the apartment we never shared, the books you haven't written. I'm sorry for myself. You should hate me, but—"

Vivienne drew a breath, her eyes flashing open. "I don't hate you." She pushed herself up on the sofa, turning so that she sat upright, her tie-dye-covered thighs beneath my hands as I knelt before her.

"How can you not?" I could barely summon courage to look at her.

Clasping the back of my neck, she lowered her forehead to mine, breath stuttering. "I hate that I can choose you now because she is gone."

I could taste the salt of her tears on my lips. "I don't understand."

She lifted her head, studying my face in what seemed like both sorrow and surprise. "Your eyes are so blue." She touched a tear as it brimmed to my cheek. "Even in a dark room."

"Tell me what you meant." I leaned back on my heels.

As I raised my palms to the sides of her face, she winced. No doubt we were refueling her headache. Her voice was so quiet. "You were dishonest with me in a way when you agreed to teach in Ljubljana, but I had always been dishonest with you—I could never have chosen you. You would have always been pulled to your country, and my mother was alive and living here in New York."

Alive and living. The words again. *Vivus.* Vivienne and I were alive when others were not.

I waited.

"You apologize for what you said back then," she spoke slowly, "but I *was* too young—"

"No. Stop. Vivienne—"

"Shhhhh . . ." She touched her forehead to mine again. "I was, Peter.

I was too young to see the truth. But I see it now. I could not have chosen you. No matter what you would have done, I would have chosen my mother. If she had been well, I would have chosen to help make her life easier. When she fell ill, I chose before anything else to nurse her. I would have chosen that path over you even if you had been here."

"But you wouldn't have had to choose." I smoothed her lip with the pad of my thumb. "Your mother would not have been one track to take and I another. I should have—and I swear, Vivienne, I would have—I would have walked with you—right beside you—if I'd stayed. I could have helped—"

The sad smile quivering on her lips conjured a sudden image in my head. The ghost of an injured bird wing. "Peter," she said, "Yugoslavia was in turmoil. Your brother was already missing."

I slipped my hands into her hair behind her ears, as if merely touching her head could change all the thoughts inside it.

Her fingers stroked the back of my neck. "I would not have allowed you to walk with me, Peter. I would have pared everything and everyone away. Not because I didn't love you, but because there was a catch—a misconception in my head from my childhood. My parents always worried that I couldn't survive without my mother, but as time passed, I came to believe that I was the one who could keep her alive. If I loved her—if I cared for her thoroughly enough. If I anticipated her pain before she or her doctors did. If I simply stayed in the room she breathed in, I could remind her to keep breathing. I was determined to thwart God's own power."

Lifting her hands away from me, she circled her fingertips on her scalp, as if to quiet a migraine, and certainly other deeper pain.

"Now she's gone, and I could choose you," she spoke in a hollow, one-note sort of voice, no sweetness or feeling behind it. "But how can I choose you now? It would seem like I approved of her dying, like I believed something good could come of it. It would appear as though I had been waiting."

An unshaped sound escaped my throat—one syllable of anguish. I had been the one, unintentionally, to give Vivienne that thought at St. Brigid's. Before I had said I was waiting for her to grow up.

I wished as I watched her try to ease her own aching, that I could erase our echoing words from her mind. Pass my hand over her eyes and speak all the ways I have thought to say, *I love you*, since we parted.

I pulled her face back down to mine gently, almost touching her lips, speaking as seriously as Ati had spoken to me on the afternoon I departed with Krušec. "Have you ever considered that I, too, chose my family before you and me? Choosing you is easier now because my family has changed. My only brother was killed. Do you think I should live in the pain of his dying forever? Do you think he would want me to? One reason I am here with you is because he is gone. But you—you and I—we're alive. Tilen's death taught me to never let the things I love go. Call that a lesson to come of his dying. I would never choose for him to be dead, but as I cannot bring him back, I would take that lesson a thousand times."

Vivienne tugged herself from my hands. Sitting straight, she peered over my head.

Sensing it was futile to try to alter her thinking, I cast back to her original longing. "Why do you want to go back to the past? If nothing could change, what would be the point of returning?"

She dropped her face into her hands, released a tremulous breath. "Just to stay there. To feel what it was like to have both you and my mother."

Her words were like a scythe in my chest. Or perhaps her words enabled me to feel the scythe in her chest, a blade that had scraped away everything but sorrow. I had to physically move if I wished to breathe.

So I turned on the hardwoods, leaned my back against the sofa. I was barely able to hear my own voice. "I have wished to go back, too, but now—" I could feel Vivienne lower herself to the floor beside me. "Now I want to do what I should have done five years ago. Time rolls forward. Two paths can merge. Sometimes you're handed a second go at things. And maybe this isn't even a second go—maybe it's a brand-new road. We could turn from the past, choose right now to walk our own path, together—"

Of all the sad, miraculous things she could do, Vivienne laid her head on my shoulder.

"Could you tell me about your mother?" I asked. "How did you come to be here, at this moment, speaking these words to me?"

She lifted her head, bent her knees to her chest, wrapped her arms around them.

"Why don't you call her Maman?" I asked.

"That was a name from my childhood."

I felt that blade in my chest again.

Vivienne spoke in a careful voice. "Two days before I left for New York, my mother thought she would miscarry. But she didn't. She delivered my sister on July eighth."

I did not breathe or speak in her pause. I tried holding my body as still as hers.

"In November, she was diagnosed with cancer in her ovaries, and she died 14 months later. She was 43 years old. I know the world is much crueler than that"—Her voice wavered. "I should be grateful for the time that God let us have her. People suffer much worse. You document proof in your book."

I shook my head. "All death is a sharp stab of heartbreak."

Vivienne propped her elbows on her knees, laid her forehead in her palms. "It's a sharp stab to me, obviously." I wished she would come back to my shoulder. "I don't want to be mad anymore. In fact, what I really want is to know if there's a heaven, because I want God to explain to me. Not just about my mother, but everything. It could be a big meeting, all of us souls raising our hands. You could ask about Tilen and the terrors of Yugoslavia."

"If we were there"—I reached out to run my fingers through the dark wisps at her neck—"then your mother and Tilen would be there. And all the people we ever lost."

"Even the dogs." Vivienne dipped her head lower, as if to say, *Keep touching me.* "My Hugo," she whispered.

I thought of my own words written down in her journal, spoken after she'd embraced a Golden Retriever on the sidewalk. *You're so full of love for things.* "Maybe we'd be too busy with happiness to sit at God's meeting," I said. "Maybe we'd be appeased, just knowing love lasts."

Vivienne's voice turned splintered and watery. "My skin burns when I think of Nicole never knowing our mother."

"Have you been Nicole's mother then?" I circled my fingers along the back of her neck, slowly, softly, tensing for her to move back to the couch or escape to her room so that I could no longer touch her.

"I've been Nicole's mother in a way," she shrugged. "I mean, she's smarter than that. She knows I don't wield ultimate authority. When I correct her, she likes to say, 'Where's my mother?' and then sometimes I cry, and she says, 'Oh, you poor baby.' Except usually she says it in French."

My chest shook with silent laughter.

"Isn't that something?" Sitting up, Vivienne turned, touched a hand to my sternum, her fingers shaky. "A person can be mired in sorrow, and laughter still finds you." Her skin looked sallow in the glow of old lamps.

"Come here." I reached an arm around her shoulder. Clearly, we'd lived a near lifetime apart. We had so many words left to speak. But night was growing late—or night had almost become morning. I had three classes to teach, and Vivienne needed more sleep.

Yet I wanted to touch on essentials. "So you mothered Nicole and opened a bakery."

"Yes. Three months after my mother died, her sister Evelyn moved here from Paris as she always said she would. Except she planned that my mother would be here. Like a lunatic crossed with a Mother Teresa, Evelyn took me on as a partner, and Papa supplied my collateral. I've promised to one day pay him back, but in the meantime, I am living in an apartment he owns and paying half-rent. My debt to him accrues by the millisecond."

"Though what you've provided Nicole is invaluable."

She was curling into herself against me, the way she had curled up on the couch. She hardly breathed.

"Vivienne, can I carry you to your bed again? Do you need pills or water?"

"I think I didn't kick my headache." She paused for so long, I thought she'd fallen asleep. "But yes." Her head jolted up. "I hope I've been a good mother. To Nicole, I mean. I hope my mother would be happy. I still stay sometimes at Papa's, but it's nice to have my own place when I want it."

I wrapped my arm tight around her. I knew I should let her rest. She was making pained sounds in her throat like a puppy. But I had so many questions. "What happened with St. Brigid's? Did you graduate? Or go to Philbrick?"

"I still have twelve credits to finish for my English degree at St. Brigid's, and I withdrew from Philbrick when my mother was diagnosed. I don't think much about the culinary arts degree, but the writing—" Her shoulders tightened beneath my arm.

"You should apply at Hadley." I wrapped my other arm around her. "You could finish the credits and begin work on a masters."

"More time," she groaned. "More money." She began slowly rocking, even as I held her close. "Peter?"

"Yes?" I lifted my head from hers.

"I'm going to need some of my father's medication."

Once I'd tucked her beneath her comforter, fetched water and pills under her direction, I sat at the edge of her disheveled bed, stroking her arm, not knowing if she was aware of it.

But then she burrowed down deep in her covers. "Maman used to tickle my arm like that." She pulled her elbows in tight to her chest, comprising a soft narrow lump in the darkness—darkness tinged by a wash of pale blue. I would be teaching in approximately four hours. Night had opened to a pocket out of time.

"You should call her Maman," I said in the quiet. "She'd want you to."

"Peut-être," Vivienne sighed. *Perhaps.*

"And maybe she'd want you to choose what you want." I dared say it, because I doubted Vivienne could hear me. "That is, if she saw you as the woman you are now—if she knew what you wanted."

I wanted to be what Vivienne wanted, and I wanted her to want everything she deserved—love, happiness, bread, poetry. I wanted her to want me with it. But she was asleep, and she was afraid, and I have learned that she is not easily dissuaded.

I leaned down to kiss the shadowed skin below her earlobe. "I love you, Vivienne," I whispered. And then, mainly to myself at that point, and the solitary, unblinking lights outside her window, "Even if we don't choose each other, they will still be gone. Please," I said just above her forehead. "Please let us choose a new path together."

Sitting at her small secretary desk in her sitting-room, I switched on a faux oil-lamp and opened the desk's hutch, searching for a scrap of paper. Of course, Vivienne would never keep scraps. She did, though, have a tin box filled with a color wheel of square-cut heavy paper. I extracted a white square and picked up a fine-point black pen.

The note I wrote was so simple.

My Dear Vivienne—

In a way, this journal is just what you want.
To go back,
before everything happened.

You can choose again
and be happy.

Every word you wrote
helped me forward.

Please let me know
you've recovered.

I am reading at The Argo
on Friday at 8. Will you come?
I'll walk you home after.

Yours—

Peter
212-555-6877

Once I had tucked the note behind the twine I had wrapped around her journal, I left it in the center of her desk.

Friday, May 10, 1996

Still no call from Vivienne. I'm a man stranded in a desert without her journal. My heart feels as parched as my tongue would be.

My reading at the Argo begins in three hours.

I cycled to Central Park after class today. The air smells of almonds and cinnamon from where I sit near the Pond with my notebook.

The entire city appears to be out—men, women, adolescents, and babies. A handful of mime artists twisting perfectly good balloons into poodles.

A strolling accordionist keeps circling by, and so far, I've counted six violinists. Each time I look up from writing, I'm convinced I'm about to see Vivienne.

I wish I had typed out her journal for myself. But that would have felt like a theft, a violation of her intellectual privacy, even though she gave her words to me to keep. She welcomed me into the glinting chamber of her mind with *This journal is the only thing I ever talk to.*

I wonder, though. Can an act violate if the one who is violated has no knowledge of the violation? Vivienne's journal was mine, her words written, in large part, for me. The young woman who wrote the words, until the penultimate page, was mine. I have a ridiculous dream of binding our journals together—hers from St. Brigid's and mine from these weeks in New York. The two of us talking, in a way, across the chasm we chiseled between us. We could possibly give a copy to our children.

I sound like Vivienne now. Or I sound like she used to, when she wanted few things more than a life with her graduate instructor of poetry. Few things more than our children. And why, I would like to ask her now, had she only wanted three of them?

She wanted her mother, her family, more than everything.

Perhaps she always will.

But the thought of not hearing Vivienne's voice in her written words again—

I have lived without her physical voice. But I have not lived, for five years now, without the rhythm and pitch of her voice in her writing.

I keep thinking of Ljubljana. The clear water, the trees, the stone bridges. The red-tiled roofs of the center city. I do not feel any great pull to go back, but I envision those familiarities and tell myself that I could return. There are details that anchor me. As well as people.

I spoke to David on the telephone yesterday. Hana had taken him to a male friend's farm in Maribor, two hours away from Ljubljana. I can't imagine Hana feeling attraction for a farmer, but I am guessing the farmer feels attraction for her. She is racing toward a life of contentment.

After describing the ears, the noses, the eyes, and the hooves of the milk cow, the pigs, and the shaggy-maned work horses called Ira and Jona, David asked, "How is the woman in New York? Do you think you could love me and Mama?"

"I love you already," I said. "But that does not mean I will be your *ati* or marry your mama. I am your uncle."

I squeezed my eyes shut, anticipating his sorrow, but he only said, "Jakob Fidler taught me to do a somersault."

"Don't hurt your neck." I pictured my little-boy self flopping onto my backside in front of my elder brother. "Tuck your chin to your chest. Keep your weight on your hands."

That is what David's *ati* taught me.

I wonder if Adèle would permit me to cancel one reading.

———

Saturday, May 11, 1996

"*Non,*" Adèle said when I called her from my apartment one hour before the reading. "*Absolument pas.*" In French because she knows I understand, and she was irritated. As soon as she breathed, she returned to English. "Peter, Coniston has invested so much in you, and you have without question delivered to this point, but please, remember that you are not just a writer in the case of this book. You are a country and a witness, and you are Coniston. When you succeed, Coniston succeeds. But when you fail your readers, so, too, does Coniston. And Coniston will not fail, Peter. Readers deserve steady brilliance!"

I felt so despondent, I couldn't respond. I jumped to a prevailing personal topic. "You never told me you're acquainted with Vivienne Lebrun."

"*Ah, oui,*" Adéle switched to French again. She reminded me of Vivienne's descriptions of her mother. "*J'adore Vivienne. Elle est exquise.*"

She is exquisite, I mouthed the words to myself.

I stood from my armchair—there's no room for a couch—to choose which of Mary's clothing contributions to wear. "I quite agree," I said to Adèle. "I'll see you at 8:00."

"At 7:30, Peter! And for God's sake, for tonight at least, wear something purchased in this or the last decade. And possibly in this country."

I considered buttoning up the dungarees I saved from a bin in Zagreb in 1992, just to assert my writerly independence, but reaching for them in my dresser drawer, I realized that I had become too self-respecting, or possibly too vain, to wear them. I selected the indigo straight-leg jeans (yes, I might very well refer to all clothing by its catalog-worthy name from now on) Mary picked out for me, then unrolled the corresponding braided cherry-leather belt from a small box in my nightstand. Finally, I tugged a crisp-white Oxford from one of five clothes-bearing hangers in my closet.

I slapped my cheeks in the bathroom mirror to stimulate blood-flow, grabbed my writing portfolio, and left my apartment.

Vivienne was not present as the reading began. When Adèle took the podium on a small platform stage in front of a full, though intimate, reading auditorium at The Argo—a bookstore known for its patronship of discerning readers—I stopped even looking for Vivienne. I merely sat in my metal folding chair behind Adèle on the stage, staring at my hands pressed down on the worn leather of my portfolio. Tilen's portfolio, actually—the one he saved his published articles in. I kept the last one he'd published tucked inside—a short piece entitled, "Yugoslavia, You Can't Have Everything."

It was not so much a news article as it was a personal essay about what Yugoslavians—or its individual peoples—should work to keep, no matter the end-state they arrived at. Of course, according to Tilen, love was what Yugoslavians, or whomever they turned out to be, should work to cultivate and hold onto over everything. Tilen mentioned Hana, their unborn baby, Hana's parents, our parents, and finally, me. *Come home, little brother,* he wrote at the end. *Come love your dismantling country.*

Sitting on that small stage of the dimly lit auditorium, I heard a bout of clapping, and then, "Peter?"

Adèle had stepped back from the mic, apparently finished with introducing me.

"Oh. Yes!" I bolted to my feet.

"Good evening," I said at the podium.

Usually, I give some background of the essay I'll be reading. I thank the audience, tell them how a story accomplishes nothing until it is heard or read and a reader decides to act, even if that act is as small as changing his or her perspective, sharing an essay title with a friend, or just passing along true information. And then I always thank Adèle and Coniston. I praise Coniston as a liberator of human voice.

But I couldn't say any of that tonight. My throat was tight, my head buzzing—*Is she coming? Are she and I finished? How could she not even be here?*

"I'm going to read an essay called 'A Dog, A Bra, A Barbie—The Road We Took out of Dubrovnik.'"

Adèle cleared her throat behind me, but I launched into my text with perfect monotone, reading about the literal, as well as the political and emotional roads out of a city destroyed by warring armies comprised of its own people. I did not look up. I barely paused between sentences. The topic, even the mere words, deserved better of me, but I had reached the end of a different road. I had reached the end of my hope for my personal future. Did I believe countries could rebuild? Yes. Did I believe families could heal after displacement and death? Eventually. Did I believe I could pack up my New York apartment and forget the woman who embodied all my envisioned lifetimes?

No.

When Adèle cleared her throat for possibly the eighth time—I was more aware of the phlegm in her mouth than I was of enunciating my own sentences—I glanced up from my essay.

And saw Vivienne.

Pale and purse-lipped, her eyes red-rimmed and watery.

Leaning forward a bit on the second row.

I'd been searching too far back. Or she'd entered late. Or she'd simply sat as her observant, unassuming self, watching me.

Her crow-black hair—I noticed in my lengthening pauses between sentences—was combed slightly down, the short wispy sides tucked behind her ears. She was wearing what J. Crew might have called a smart, crushed-velvet button-up vest, in violet, over a tight white t-shirt. Even as I pronounced the words of my essay, I disjointedly considered how each of her outfits made me want to approach her body differently. This ensemble, for instance, left me wanting to leave the podium mid-sentence to slow dance with her, one hand at the small of her back, the other at the nape of her neck.

The mere sight of her touched off a feeling of home, as well as hope—the difference between the two words just one letter—as if the English language's linguistic ancestors understood that the words meant so much the same thing. Both are what the people of nations live for, the forces that sustain us on the roads we travel.

Vivienne was in the audience. She had come to the reading. She had survived her migraine and her father's medication and our middle-of-the-night conversation, not to mention half-truths and heartbreak, death and disappointment, the passage of years and loneliness. She had survived. She had discovered my poem-note and her journal and traveled nearly the length of Manhattan to sit fifteen feet away from me.

I skipped two information-light paragraphs, read the essay's conclusion in one single breath, did not express thanks, and sat down.

The audience clapped as they always do, while Adèle sat beside me a few moments longer than usual, skewering me—I think the expression is (there are so many ways to say *looking* in English)—with her eyes.

"She's here," I said amid the applause. "Your friend. Vivienne. The exquisite. She came."

"You should exercise slightly more faith, Professor Breznik." Adèle raised herself elegantly from her seat, peering down at me. "But you did dress appropriately."

And then, in an instant, Vivienne rose, excusing herself over shocked people's feet, walking toward the back of the small auditorium. "W—" I couldn't even cry, *Wait!* before Adèle, at the podium, thrust a silencing finger at me.

She turned to speak regally into the microphone, "Ladies and gentleman"—She pointed at Vivienne rushing away. "You might notice the brilliant young writer currently attempting to make her way to the podium?" Her voice rose at the end in a bright but questioning optimism.

All audience heads swiveled toward Vivienne frozen against a wall, perhaps three feet from a door, eyes so wide, an alarm obviously ringing in her head. She had not been making her way to the podium.

I wanted to replace Adéle at the microphone and ask, *Why? Why, Vivienne, before all these curious witnesses, would you appear at this venue after I have ached for your voice for five days, not to mention the five years preceding, only to leave before saying hello, before allowing me to ask how you feel, what you think, and if I might ever see you again?*

She peered longingly up at an exit sign before turning, as if her body bore the weight of a small planet, toward the stage. Her heeled sandals clipped a lonely beat against the wood floors. I glanced at the audience, all eyes darting between Adèle and Vivienne, who had clearly devised some sort of plan together.

"Friends," Adèle began, "please welcome Miss Vivienne Lebrun, who was absolutely not making her way toward an exit in a moment of stage fright."

The auditorium hummed with a genial laughter. Adèle fidgeted with the stitching of her plate-sized lace collar, as though even she, Queen of Bookdom, were nervous.

The silence between Vivienne's heeled steps grew gradually longer.

"Vivienne is a devoted friend of The Argo. And a personal friend of mine." Adèle's eyes narrowed on Vivienne. "We agreed that she would give a brief reading tonight. An excerpt, I believe, of a love story." No one in the room could have missed how Adèle's head turned from watching Vivienne to glancing back at me.

Vivienne stood at the base of the three steps up to the stage, face ashen, a roughly cut leather-bound journal shaking in one of her hands as though her body were host to its own earthquake.

I stood to make my way to the steps. "Hey," I said, reaching my hand out.

"Hey," she more or less mouthed at me. The hush that had fallen over the audience was deafening.

"Do you want me to walk you out of here?" I asked.

For a second, Vivienne's shoulders relaxed, as if that might be what she wanted. She lifted her hand for mine, but instead of pulling it toward her and resuming a path to the exit, she squeezed my fingers, climbing the first step. "No," she said, "I think I'll read this."

I gave her a light upward tug, her eyes shifting from mine to the podium before resting on mine again. "Okay," she breathed out before walking on her own to the microphone.

Adèle embraced her. *"Ma gentille fille,"* she whispered, perhaps too near the microphone. "Your mother would be wetting her pants right now."

"Somewhere, she probably is," Vivienne said just loud enough for the audience to hear.

A low rumble of chuckling swept through the seats, people gazing at Vivienne with parted lips and half smiles.

Sitting down as straight as a pole in my seat, I felt clammy and stiff, as though cast in plaster, almost unable to breathe. Angling forward a little, I rested my palms on my knees. Many pairs of eyes zig-zagged between Vivienne and me.

"Thank you for permitting me to read tonight." Vivienne opened her journal on the stand at the microphone—the journal, I recognized in that moment, that I had filled with my own brief poems and given to her at St. Brigid's.

"I would like to read from my greatest work." She lifted her face to the audience. "Which, I confess, is not any manuscript, but a personal record"—she pressed one hand to the journal, slightly turning her head as though to look back at me—"a poem that demonstrates the continual broadening of my own vision." Every listener appeared rapt by the warmth and cadence of her voice. By the unexpected gift of her presence. She was endearing and shy and intelligent—entirely herself—a quiet woman who sought to escape all attention but could nonetheless command a smart audience.

She peered down at the journal I had assumed she'd never write in.

"The Last Time I Saw You, Re-Written."

A shocked breath—almost a cry—escaped someone's throat, and when Adèle touched my back, I understood that the throat was mine.

"The last night you kissed me," Vivienne began reading, all business now, maintaining tight rein on her voice, "we kissed until morning."

I could hear the lines in her words—

> The last night you kissed me, we kissed
> until morning. The sun through the curtains
> speckled my skin. You laughed
> that it tasted like lemon drops.
>
> You told me you weren't coming back
> to my country.
>
> I said I was leaving, too—going home
> to a woman I loved, who was dying.
>
> Your family's country was dying, too.
>
> For a long time, we would not
> be together. You dressed me
> in a blue sweatshirt, braided my hair, packed
> my two bags and kissed me.
>
> We said, Do all the things
> that need doing. We said,
> Write and call. Be safe.
>
> We said, Of all the creatures on earth
> I choose you.
>
> I love you filled the space
> between sentences.
>
> Time passed as a sea.
> We suffered our losses. The bones
> sank beneath us. When you returned,
> cherry blossoms were snowing.

I said,

     My love,

             here

are branches. Let's build
another place
to hold us.

When Vivienne finished, the silence in the room felt heavy—a suspended weight of anticipation, of wanting to hear more, of resonance— every heart having suffered some parting, some loss and some hope to start new again.

A collective breath rushed as a breeze through the rows of the reading room.

"Brava!" an elderly man at the back cranked up to his feet. *"Brava! Bellissima!"*

"Say you'll accept her revision!" a young man's voice called out from the front. When I looked for his face, I saw that it was Luc, standing with a miniature Vivienne in his arms. She clapped her hands, grinning.

A distinguished, gray-haired gentleman stood smiling affectionately beside them, watching Vivienne, his hands in the pockets of his black suit pants. He nodded at me with Vivienne's dark eyes.

Her father. Reassuring me, after all our great losses.

Some of the audience began filing out. The majority remained, watching the stage.

"Peter, *mon cher,* why are you sitting?" Adèle gripped my arm, tears dotting her cheeks.

"Thank you." My arms broke through my paralysis, flying around Adèle's shoulders. "Thank you for insisting I come tonight. Thank you for insisting she stay. *Merci,* Adèle."

Adèle held my cheeks, her lips twitching. "Catherine would have liked you. Eventually."

Vivienne watched me from the podium, the journal I had given her closed in her hands.

In two steps, I stood cradling her face. "You kept it." I glanced down at the journal.

"I only started writing in it this week. But I think it could be my best one yet."

Our life, I thought. *The beginning.*

I said, "You were very brave."

She bit her bottom lip, searching my face, a tincture of sadness and uncertainty, but also—it came to her eyes as a fleck of amber light—

Hope.

Hope was in her.

Her lips pressed together in a smile. "I could probably use some feedback."

I smoothed stray wisps of hair behind her ears. "I like giving you feedback."

As she lifted a hand to my elbow, I guided her to a door just down from the stage steps, what was left of New York City's most discerning readers suddenly applauding, as though they understood that two people, against all rational odds, had chosen one another at last.

Through the auditorium door, the shelf-crammed bookstore rested in silence. Green-shaded wall lamps offered dim pools of illumination. I led Vivienne to an aisle of books I had absent-mindedly perused just before the reading. The poetry aisle. Two high shelves facing one another like gaunt broody sentinels, squat cases of classical essays and nineteenth-century fiction nearly blocking either end.

Patrons exited the reading room, exclaiming in delight, their forms blurring past our shadowed nook between bookshelves. A small card on one shelf read *The Romantics.* Vivienne set her journal beside it. "A secret alcove." She looked left and right. "Books no one's touched in years."

As she lifted the fingertips of one hand to my lips, I caught sight of black smudging along the edge of her thumb. *"Mon buveur d'encre,"* I said, my throat turning tight.

"Always yours." She touched her other hand to my cheek, angling her melancholy-sweet eyes up at me. "I'm glad you understood who the 'you' in my poem was."

My head tossed back before I could think. I heard my own voice, bright and automatic, echoing a sudden memory of my laughter on the night Tilen told me about Hana.

I smiled at Vivienne, feeling at once both young and grown, broken and healing, fatigued and renewed, with the pulse of the sun in a desert.

Her own smile washed over me like water.

I held her face in my hands.

"You." She looped her arms above my waist, pulling me closer with a fierce, hopeful tension. "Peter. I love you."

In the minutes, the hours, the days I had spent with her, both past and present, she had enacted that sentence in infinite ways. Yet there it was in a bookstore, spoken. A sequence of discrete sounds, each its own shape and weight in my brain.

I wanted to speak like sunlight, the way it conveys what it means in an instant, without the slightest thought of arrangement of parts or eloquence.

Vivus, Vivienne. Let's be alive at the same time, together.

But words would have been inefficient.

Bending to her lips, I kissed her like the definition of love depended on it.

With my hands in her hair and her laughter in my mouth, a low little-girl voice called in English from a gap between bookshelves, with the barest hint of a French accent, "Luc! Papa! I found Vivienne and the writer!"

Vivienne is asleep in her bed now. I am writing, sleepless, amazed, at her desk.

We kissed, as she wrote, almost until morning.

As I attempted to step from her room without waking her, she stirred, whispering in the voice that has wakened me from dreams on so many mornings, "Peter. My love."

And then on a sigh, in perfect stresses, *"Najlepša hvala.* We're home."

MILK GIVER

Tuesday, June 17, 2004
at my desk at my window, in the dark, after my sixth professional reading

Bonjour, ma famille!

I assume you are *ma famille* if you're reading. From the first word—no, the first breath—of this journal, I imagined you. Your incredulous brown eyes (I would pass on my brown eyes to you, wouldn't I?), the little *o* your mouth would make in surprise. I imagined you.

Peter asked me to make this last entry. He's compiling two past journals and has begged me to write a stirring conclusion. A summary, an update, a nod to the future. I suppose he accepts that the task is beyond him.

I say life is short. The old words—let them rest. They had their day in the light.

And who would we let read what we wrote all those years ago, anyhow? I know I set out to document my life for you, Progeny, but that was before I had progeny. Would I really want Petit Luc or Catie or whomever else comes along—though darling and gifted and compassionate they'll be—to read how I wanted to—and do, in fact—kiss the tender blue vein that runs like a poppy stem down their dad's neck?

No. No, I wouldn't. Not really.

And I won't attempt to even briefly summarize Peter's contributions to this narrative. How he somehow manages to keep writing critically acclaimed tomes on European history instead of making millions at Harlequin is yet further evidence that a person does not always pursue their soul-matched profession.

I kid. Sort of.

Peter says that I become a tiny bit more sarcastic each day. He says I'm becoming a skeptic.

But that could never be entirely true, O Posterity.

Because, if you've read me, you know this: I believe too wholeheartedly in loving things. Today, sitting beside Peter on a blanket in Prospect Park, just two blocks east of our apartment, I loved the light brush of his hand on my knee (I'm as guilty as he is; I can't omit sordid details), the sunlit scruff on his cheeks, and him—I loved him—as he kept turning his head from the kids back to me. I was thinking how I love the depth of his heart and his conversation, his calm-breathing body mere inches away.

I loved the kids, too—our Petit Luc, almost four, crying, *"Tantie!"* after my sister, Nicole, who walked beneath the wide-branching green trees with David, our nephew, whom we bring to New York for a month every summer. He kept crouching down to examine seed pods and leaves, sometimes pressing one into Luc's little hands, other times extending one to my sister. She'd tuck them into the pouch of her sweatshirt.

And all the while, I loved baby Catie, asleep on her back between Peter's legs, her rolly arms flung up, framing her face, the dark tendrils of her hair shifting in the breeze, her already-round cheeks flushed new-apple pink.

I want hours like that to last for eternity, and sometimes, I believe they can. And isn't that decidedly un-skeptic?

But hours pass, Heaven help us, and almost before I could blink this afternoon, our rag-tag brood was sauntering from the park toward home, Catie tight in a pack against Peter's chest, Luc tugging his hand from mine in efforts to hold Nicole's, though he was continually shaken off with reprimands, in French, along the lines of, *"Cheri,* I am talking to *David."*

And then, as fast as I am writing the words now, Peter and I had laid the kitchen table with plasticware, shaved parmesan over noodles, and kissed each other goodbye as I left for my reading. He attended the first with a two-week-old Catie asleep in his arms, but in the three months that have passed, she has grown too noisy and wiggly, and neither Peter nor I have the courage to leave her with *Oncle* Luc or Papa or an au pair yet. Peter's parents will arrive in a week, though, and then Peter can join me at readings.

Adèle didn't schedule many readings initially, knowing I'd be attached to the baby, but New Yorkers, and even people from as far away as Denver (Adèle received an email yesterday) seem to be reading my book—*A Poet Bakes in Brooklyn*. It's made of essays and recipes, a kind of food memoir with photographs and snippets of poetry.

Libraries and bookstores—and we should have guessed: bakeries!—have been interested in the book, so Adèle has assembled a respectable docket of readings.

When I arrived home after ten from tonight's gathering at Amanuensis, Peter was asleep on the couch with Catie, her little body swaddled tummy-down on his chest, their breaths a whispery lullaby.

I bent to kiss both their heads.

After I'd changed into sweats, filled a small bowl with raspberries, and taken my old journal from Peter's nightstand so that I could write this last entry, I passed by the couch to find Peter sitting up, patting a wide-eyed Catie's back, tears dotting his cheeks like raindrops.

"What on earth?" I sounded like Maman, sharp but sympathetic, a little wry, disbelieving. I set the berries and the journal on my desk before walking back to sit down beside Peter.

He rubbed a fist at his eyes. "I never imagined. How much. I mean, this. It's so hard, but so happy. I wouldn't want anything to be different—"

"I imagined it," I couldn't help interrupting. "I imagined it every day." Taking Catie from him, I sank into his side.

He wrapped us both in his arms. "I know you did. I read those sentences you wrote so many times"—he nodded toward my journal on my desk—"about us. About the life you imagined. Some days I'd wake up believing it had happened."

I lifted my face to kiss the point of his chin. "I wish it could have happened less painfully." I kissed Catie's nose, her eyebrows, her forehead. She watched me with Peter's Adriatic-blue eyes. I know they're that color, because I have visited Peter's sea, at the narrow, southwest shore of Slovenia.

"It happened the way life happens, don't you think?" He leaned forward to lift a copy of my book from the coffee table. "It happened unexpectedly." I heard a catch in his throat as he sat back on the sofa.

Nestled into him again, I thought of that day we had allowed ourselves to be separated—my unbalanced steps down the long hall of St. Brigid's history department, Peter calling, *Vivienne!* from his office door. I pictured Maman in her red-checked robe in her bed on the last day she heard me say, *I love you,* and I envisioned Tilen clapping Peter on the back as he says Tilen did the last time they said goodbye at an airport.

A string tugged across a map in my mind, the ends pinned to New York and Ljubljana. I imagined tying those ends together. It didn't matter anymore where you pinned the knot; the knot was the home. The places simply contained it.

"Yes," I said in agreement to life's way of happening. "And do you know what I expected the least?"

"Tell me," Peter said.

I grinned a wide open smile at Catie, trying to coax her to do the same, this second bright life that Peter and I made, despite distance and desires that had pulled us in different directions. Despite death.

"I never expected that you'd really come back." I touched a finger to the center of Catie's palm, and just like that, her silky-warm hand wrapped around it. "But every day I imagined you coming."

"You never told me how you imagined that." Peter opened my book in his lap with the hand that wasn't wrapped around me and Catie. Together, he and I peered down at my acknowledgements page—

> *To Maman—*
> *Catherine Abrielle Olivier Lebrun—*
> *who was not here long enough,*
> *but loved enough, and taught me*
> *almost everything*
>
> *And to Peter, my love, my axis*

"I imagined finding you at a reading," I said.

Peter thumbed through pages in his lap. "And then you ran away, and I found you at a bakery?"

Catie was opening and closing her mouth like a frantic banked fish in my arms. Her impatient cry made me smile just a little as I lifted my blouse to nurse her. "I imagined I'd be the one reading, and you'd think I was brilliant, and you'd know all my words were for you, and then, I don't know—I thought we'd go make some babies."

When Peter laughed, Catie startled, letting go my breast to simply gaze milky mouthed up at her dad, as though she understood how many miles and sorrows had been traversed to give her the chance of living right now, a blend of cells of the two people gazing smitten and exhausted at her face.

"I'd say your vision was almost accurate." Shifting his focus from Catie to my book, Peter flipped through more pages until he arrived at my bio. He laughed again, silently reading. "You're the only person I know who hears a love story in a bio."

"Bios are epic love stories," I said as Catie breathed deep, nursing again. "Read it out loud. You know you love it."

"I love you, Vivienne." He kissed from the crown of my head to my temple, down my cheek, till he caught the edge of my lip, his breath ragged and wanting. "Do you want to go make another baby?"

Catie pulled back again, studying us, as if waiting to hear how I'd answer. "Maybe next year." I giggled like I always have, trying to help Catie re-latch. "In the meantime, you can read me my bio."

Peter's attention had been diverted by Catie. "I could have never imagined this part." His arm around my shoulder fiddled with Catie's blanket until the soft tiny pearls of her toes peeked out. "Just think, if the first day I saw you, someone had said, 'You're going to be sitting next to that woman in thirteen years, your second baby in her arms drinking her milk.' I never could have fathomed that sweetness—the quiet life events in a home."

"Peter." I covered Catie's feet with the blanket. "Please read my bio."

I wanted to hear his voice say the words. I wanted to relive everything they implied and embodied—that two people, amid war, death, birth, and wandering, found each other, and, as I wrote in this journal and hoped for a long time ago, made a loving life together.

Peter cleared his throat—

Vivienne Breznik moved with her family from Paris to New York City when she was six years old. She attended St. Brigid's College in California and earned a Master of Fine Arts in Creative Writing from the Philbrick Program for Writers in Brooklyn.

In 1993, with her aunt Evelyn Olivier, Breznik opened La Cocinelle, *a New-York-Times-heralded bakery and café in Manhattan's Upper West Side. Just last year, the pair opened a second shop in Park Slope, Brooklyn.*

Breznik is married to the Slovene-American essayist and Hadley College Professor of History, Peter Breznik, with whom she has two children. They currently divide their time between Brooklyn, New York and Ljubljana, Slovenia.

Breznik's mother passed away in 1992. She taught Breznik to write in both French and English at age three and cut butter into flour for croissants at age four. She taught her that life is short and love is strong and no amount of time is long enough.

Which is one reason why food and books should be delicious.

In the silence that followed the story, Peter and I re-read the sentences, my free hand over his at the bottom of the page, Catie's eyes fluttering closed as she nursed.

A sequence of memories played in my head: Peter, Maman, Nicole. Peter, Petit Luc, and Catie.

California, Manhattan, Slovenia, Brooklyn.

Peter and me.

Our story embedded in the words of my bio.

The thought occurred that for my whole life, I have feared what might happen; but in that moment next to Peter, reading a skeletal map of my life, I feared for what might not have happened. What chances, what risks, what words, what love might not have been notched into my life's constellation. If hard hadn't come with good. If sorrow hadn't precipitated longing. If loss hadn't intensified love.

"It's a good bio," I whispered.

"A good life," Peter nodded, though when I glanced up at his face,

I noticed that his brow was furrowed. He circled his finger around the Garamond font of my name.

"What?" I nudged my leg against his.

He shook his head slowly, a smile upturning his lips. "I was just thinking of Adèle coming unhinged when you said you'd be publishing under your married name."

With a tiny *pop,* Catie's mouth unsealed from my breast, her head lolling back in my arms. I tugged my blouse down and cuddled her. "Adèle says it's writers like me who set back womankind."

"I guess she was warned." Peter clapped the book closed with one hand, chuckling. "You always said you were a miserable feminist."

Rising from the couch, he lifted our baby girl from my arms. "Write that last entry." He turned for our bedroom, where Petit Luc was already sprawled on our bed like a cartoon character smacked into a brick wall.

The night deepens.

We sleep in our nest, hearts broken and mending. We are torn and re-woven, day after day.

And so I have written.

POETRY COLLECTIONS CITED AND BELOVED
BY VIVIENNE AND PETER

Dickinson, Emily. Excerpt from "'Hope' is the thing with feathers," as Peter and Vivienne would have known it—originally published in *Poems by Emily Dickinson*, second series, 1891—is in the public domain.

Hass, Robert. Excerpt from "Letter" ("You are the body / of my world ..." page 245 in the novel) from *Field Guide*. Yale University Press, 1973. Reprinted with permission of the author.

Kenyon, Jane. Excerpt from "Briefly It Enters, and Briefly Speaks" ("I am the blossom pressed in a book," page 245 in the novel) from *Otherwise*. The Estate of Jane Kenyon, 1996 (poem originally published in 1986).

Milosz, Czeslaw. Excerpt from "Introduction," ("Question: What is the central theme of these poems?" page 34 in the novel) from *Talking to My Body*. Copper Canyon Press, 1996 (essay originally published in 1985).

Rexroth, Kenneth. "What is the Matter with Me?" (page 133 in the novel) from *One Hundred Poems from the Chinese*. New Directions Publishing Corp., 1970.

Šalamun, Tomaž. Excerpt from "I Have a Horse" ("I have a body. With my body I do the most beautiful things that I do," page 107 in the novel) translated by Christopher Merrill, from *The Four Questions of Melancholy: New and Selected Poems*. White Pine Press, 2007 (poem originally published in 1971).

Swir, Anna. "I Am Filled with Love" (page 34 in the novel) and excerpt from "I Sleep in Blue Pajamas" (page 49 in the novel) from *Talking to My Body*, translated by Czeslaw Milosz and Leonard Nathan. Copper Canyon Press, 1996. (Swir's poems and Milosz's introduction first appeared in Swir's out-of-print collection *Happy as a Dog's Tail*, published in 1985, a year that would allow for Peter and Vivienne to read them in 1991. Because of this, I have referenced that title in the story.)

Szymborska, Wisława, et al. Excerpt from "True Love" ("True love. Is it normal . . ." page 201 in the novel) from *View with a Grain of Sand: Selected Poems*. Harcourt Brace, 1995 (poem originally published in 1972).

AND A FEW POETS VIVIENNE MENTIONS, ALONG WITH COLLECTIONS YOU SHOULD CHECK OUT

Lucille Clifton, *Blessing the Boats*

Louis Glück, *Averno* and *Meadowlands*

Jorie Graham, *Hybrids of Plants and of Ghosts*

Lisel Mueller, *Alive Together: New and Selected Poems*

George Oppen, *New Collected Poems.*

Tomas Tranströmer, *New and Selected Poems, 1954-1986*

ACKNOWLEDGEMENTS

A thousand thanks.

To you, gracious reader, for reading.

To my writing teachers: Deb Allbery, Matthew Olzmann, Daniel Tobin, Alan Shapiro, Lance Larsen, Susan Elizabeth Howe, and the late James Longenbach. I don't think I can write one sentence without hearing at least one of them guide or challenge me.

To Stephen Dobyns, a supervisor in my writing program, with whom I never worked, but whose ideas about poetry and metaphor run through my own (and Peter Breznik's) as inextricably as light falls through branches. If you liked what Peter had to say about metaphor, resonance, and the poet as a cartographer, please read Dobyns's masterful essays on the topics in his books *Best Words, Best Order* and *Next Word, Better Word: The Craft of Writing Poetry*.

And more thanks—

To every ARC reader and Bookstagrammer who worked to spread positive news of my book in the world, and to my friends and family who read early drafts of this story: Sue, Meg, and Marielle Nielsen, Cassie and Izzi Castleton, Kirsten Slaugh, Leslie Hansen, Brenda Hymas, and Norma Hendrickson. And my parents, Craig and Jerrie Nielsen, whose love story is the first I ever heard and aspired to.

To my brother David, who responded patiently to every revised sentence I pasted from my story into a text for his approval.

And to my daughters: Amy, who made Vivienne a baker. Mara, who advised me in all things Slovene and still throws her hands up at my pronunciation of that language. Samantha, who launched my author IG account and did not let me quit writing when I announced I was quitting. And Brynna, who kept Luka, our big mountain dog, too busy to nose-smack my fingers from my keyboard.

To Mary Lou Hassall, cancer warrior and mom extraordinaire. The most generous reader and most beloved neighbor. Thank you for giving precious time to me.

To Erin Rodabough, who suggested the most challenging revision I attempted, and made Maman a real person.

To Nichole Van. My friend. Your books, your unbending, your genius. Your writing-buddy proposal. That long drive in Scotland. This story you midwifed. The book cover. You've changed my life forever.

And to Steve. The body of my world. Each root and flower. I think Robert Hass wrote that poem for us. But you—you've walked the world with me. Green hills, quilted valleys, city lights, salty bread. You give me everything.

As for other sources that inspired this book . . . In the history of hard subjects to write about, Yugoslavia might rank almost first. And I didn't even write much about it. What I did do is begin to learn about a region whose people have suffered and endured much, and who continue to redefine themselves with great strength. Thank you to the Slovenes who embraced my daughter while she lived among them, and who helped make their country her home away from ours. While I have tried my most conscientious best to present events of their history accurately, I ask them to forgive me for mistakes I have made.

Finally, thank you to the authors whose books guided me and shaped my characters—

Benjamin Curtis, *A Traveller's History of Croatia*

Slavenka Drakulić, *The Balkan Express,* and *How We Survived Communism and Even Laughed*

Brian Hall, *The Impossible Country: A Journey through the Last Days of Yugoslavia* (Tilen Breznik's efforts to gather narratives throughout Yugoslavia is loosely based on Hall's work)

Erica Johnson Debeljak, *Forbidden Bread*

And to the God of this earth, the God of words and love and family. Thank You.

READING GROUP QUESTIONS

1. *Drinker of Ink* is a celebration of the love between two people, but it is also a celebration of their love for words—language, poems, essays, stories. What aspects of Vivienne's and Peter's lives might have made them particularly attune to the nuances, power, and beauty of language? Can you relate to their love of all things written? What words, poems, and stories illuminate and anchor your life? Do you think words take on even greater weight and meaning in times of uncertainty and suffering?

2. Poetry is a driving force in the novel. How would you define a poem? Did you learn anything new about poetry from Vivienne and Peter? Are you familiar with any of the poets Vivienne names in the novel? Robert Hass, Jorie Graham, Louise Glück? Wisława Szymborska, Czesław Miłosz, Tomaž Šalamun? If you have time during your conversation, consider looking up one of these poets on the Poetry Foundation website and reading one or two of their poems. Do they "resonate" with you? Did you feel a connection to any of the excerpted poems in the novel?

3. Metaphor is another theme in *Drinker of Ink*. Do you feel like you understand the mechanism better after reading the novel? What metaphors in the story stick with you? What would your "happiness" or "grief" poem be?

4. Vivienne's parents chose to withhold life-altering information from her that destabilized her young adulthood. How do you feel about their decision, particularly since Vivienne struggled with anxiety and independence from her childhood? Was her parents' choice ultimately a loving one? Knowing Vivienne through her journal, do you feel that she would have taken the news any better if her parents had shared it right away? Can you identify even a small way that her parents' approach might have benefitted her, even though Vivienne could not see it? Was her summer in Paris a crucial formative experience?

5. Vivienne and Peter initially connect through the words they write for and to each other. Have you ever connected to another person through a tangible note or letter? What do you think a letter might convey more powerfully than spoken words, if anything? Has a loved one ever written you a letter that you plan to keep forever?

6. *Drinker of Ink* is told in journal entries. How did this work for you as a story-telling device? Was the detail of Vivienne's and Peter's journals believable? Why or why not? Did you hear Vivienne's and Peter's journal voices as distinct from one another? What differences do you notice in their writing styles?

7. How do you feel about Peter's decision not to tell Vivienne right away about his plans to return to Ljubljana? How do you feel about Vivienne's decision to end their relationship?

8. What do you think of Vivienne's and Peter's older selves? Did they become the people you expected they would? Were you satisfied by their reunion? Do you feel that Vivienne's final poem captured their heartbreak, as well as their past and present love for each other? Had she believably grown up?

9. Finally: the question we're all waiting for! What actors would you choose to play Vivienne and Peter on stage or screen? Who would play Maman, Papa, Luc, Nicole, etc.? Do you think the novel could be adapted for stage or screen? Why or why not?

10. What songs would comprise the novel's soundtrack? Message the author on IG, @shannon.castleton, if you would like to hear her playlist! And please send her yours!

About the Author

Shannon Castleton has been telling stories in her head for as long as she can remember. But she always wrote them down as poems. And then she studied poems, for years, and published some. But she always wanted to write a *long* story. A love story. *Drinker of Ink* is her first attempt, inspired by her love of words, poems, books, French, baking, kissing, obsessive-compulsive people, and long walks in Europe. She and her husband, Steve, fell in love in a university Physical Science class. He first kissed her in a stairwell. In no time, they had four daughters.

Shannon is a graduate of the MFA Program for Writers at Warren Wilson College. She lives with her family in a town called Bountiful.

Made in the USA
Monee, IL
09 October 2024

67587810R00194